Danny Fog ... stood a head ... the legendar ... Hondo. Des ... and a low-slung gun belt showed him as a man to be reckoned with.

Danny Fog had a mission – to break up the cow-thieving outfit that was terrorising Caspar County, Texas. Ahead of him lay danger – gun-crazy outlaws and cut-throat Mexicans who would kill a man for his boots.

But when Danny learned that the boss of the cow thieves was a woman, he needed help bad. And what better help could a man ask for than that of Martha Jane Canary – or, as folks called her, Calamity Jane.

Revised list of **J.T. EDSON** *titles in chronological and categorical sequence:*

Ole Devil Hardin series

YOUNG OLE DEVIL
OLE DEVIL AND THE CAPLOCKS
OLE DEVIL AND THE MULE TRAIN
OLE DEVIL AT SAN JACINTO
GET URREA

The Civil War series

COMANCHE
THE START OF THE LEGEND
How Belle Boyd Became The Rebel Spy }*
YOU'RE IN COMMAND NOW, MR.
  FOG
THE BIG GUN
UNDER THE STARS AND BARS
THE FASTEST GUN IN TEXAS
A MATTER OF HONOUR
KILL DUSTY FOG!
THE DEVIL GUN
THE COLT AND THE SABRE
THE REBEL SPY
THE BLOODY BORDER
BACK TO THE BLOODY BORDER

The Floating Outfit series

THE YSABEL KID
.44 CALIBRE MAN
A HORSE CALLED MOGOLLON
GOODNIGHT'S DREAM
FROM HIDE AND HORN
SET TEXAS BACK ON HER FEET
THE HIDE AND TALLOW MEN
THE HOODED RIDERS
QUIET TOWN
TRAIL BOSS
WAGONS TO BACKSIGHT
TROUBLED RANGE
SIDEWINDER

RANGELAND HERCULES
McGRAW'S INHERITANCE
THE HALF BREED
WHITE INDIANS
THE WILDCATS
THE BAD BUNCH
THE FAST GUN
CUCHILO
A TOWN CALLED YELLOWDOG
TRIGGER FAST
THE MAKING OF A LAWMAN
THE TROUBLE BUSTERS
DECISION FOR DUSTY FOG
DIAMONDS, EMERALDS, CARDS
  AND COLTS
THE CODE OF DUSTY FOG
THE GENTLE GIANT
SET A-FOOT
THE LAW OF THE GUN
THE PEACEMAKERS
TO ARMS! TO ARMS! IN DIXIE
HELL IN THE PALO DURO
GO BACK TO HELL
THE SOUTH WILL RISE AGAIN
THE QUEST FOR BOWIE'S BLADE
BEGUINAGE
BEGUINAGE IS DEAD
MASTER OF TRIGGERNOMETRY
THE RUSHERS
BUFFALO ARE COMING
THE FORTUNE HUNTERS
RIO GUNS
GUN WIZARD
THE TEXAN
OLD MOCCASINS ON THE TRAIL
MARK COUNTER'S KIN
THE RIO HONDO KID
OLE DEVIL'S HANDS AND FEET
WACO'S DEBT

*Title awaiting publication

J.T. EDSON OMNIBUS
Volume 7

THE BULL WHIP BREED
TROUBLE TRAIL
THE COW THIEVES

CORGI BOOKS

J.T. EDSON OMNIBUS VOLUME 7
A CORGI BOOK 0 552 13608 5

THE BULL WHIP BREED, TROUBLE TRAIL and THE
COW THIEVES originally published in Great Britain by
Brown Watson Ltd.

PRINTING HISTORY – THE BULLWHIP BREED
Corgi edition published 1968
Corgi edition reprinted 1971
Corgi edition reprinted 1975

PRINTING HISTORY – TROUBLE TRAIL
Brown Watson edition published 1968
Corgi edition published 1968
Corgi edition reprinted 1969
Corgi edition reprinted 1972
Corgi edition reprinted 1976
Corgi edition reprinted 1982

PRINTING HISTORY – THE COW THIEVES
Brown Watson edition published 1965
Corgi edition published 1968
Corgi edition reprinted 1969
Corgi edition reprinted 1972
Corgi edition reprinted 1976
Corgi edition reprinted 1982

Corgi Omnibus edition published 1991

Corgi Books are published by Transworld Publishers
Ltd., 61–63 Uxbridge Road, Ealing, London W5 5SA, in
Australia by Transworld Publishers (Australia) Pty. Ltd.,
15–23 Helles Avenue, Moorebank, NSW 2170, and in New
Zealand by Transworld Publishers (N.Z.) Ltd., Cnr. Moselle
and Waipareira Avenues, Henderson, Auckland.

Printed and bound in Great Britain by
Cox & Wyman Ltd., Reading, Berks.

The Bull Whip Breed

CHAPTER ONE

Lieutenant St Andre Meets An Unusual Lady

PHILIPPE St. Andre was said to be the youngest and most hand-some man ever to reach the rank of lieutenant on the New Orleans police force. Only he did not seem likely to remain the most hand-some for much longer. The four bulky, burly men who came from the shadows of the dark, narrow street intended to alter the shape of his face, or St. Andre missed his guess. While a bright moon shone in the sky, very little of its light filtered down into the area between the houses; which might be ideal for lovers, or even people who merely wished to act in the manner of lovers, but was surely hell for a handsome young detective lieutenant faced with the possibility of a savage beating. He could neither see their faces nor enough of their clothing to be able to recognise them at a later date—should they leave him alive to do so.

"Are you St. Andre?" asked the biggest man in a muffled, dis-guised voice.

"I am."

"Then you get after Vivian Vanderlyne and don't go poking your nose into things that don't concern you."

Instantly St. Andre clenched his fists and prepared to fight for his life.

While St. Andre had been born into one of the oldest, richest and proudest New Orleans families, and dressed, now he was a member of the newly-formed detective bureau of the police de-partment, to the height of fashion, he was also a trained and very smart peace officer who knew his way around.

Following a lead in his current case brought him to the dark side-street and he knew the four hard-cases had not stopped him merely to pass the time of day. Ever since starting his investigation into the murder of Vance Cornwall, a prominently rising young lawyer, St. Andre's lawman instincts told him that the affair cut much deeper than a lovers' quarrel which went too far. Cornwall had been a married man, with a very rich, if much older, woman for his wife; an ill-tempered shrew, if all rumours be true, so Cornwall sought solace by taking an *amie*. Most of the evidence pointed to Cornwall's *amie* having done the killing, but the blonde, beautiful and talented young actress, Vivian Vanderlyne, appeared to have done the opposite, disappeared, for no trace of her could be found.*

The murder appeared to be an open-and-shut case, a trifle sordid maybe, but ordinary. Yet St. Andre felt that certain facts did not fit into the picture of a lovers' quarrel ending in violent death. Why had the murdered man's rooms been thoroughly searched? From whence came the faint smell of expensive perfume which mingled and clashed with a slightly cheaper brand used by Vivian Vanderlyne?

Being a conscientious lawman, St. Andre tried to find the answers to his questions. While following up the most obvious suspect, he also went to visit the dead man's wife and brother, asking questions and finding both to have perfect alibis for the time of the killing. So St. Andre looked elsewhere and a tip from an informer brought him to the side road and the waiting quartet. Somebody clearly did not want too close an investigation into the young lawyer's private life. It would seem that St. Andre's lawman instincts were correct—only he did not appear to be likely to stay alive long enough to solve the mystery.

"And if I don't?" he asked, measuring his distances.

The first blow hissed over his head as he ducked. Coming up inside the striker's guard, St. Andre threw his well-manicured, but rock-hard fist under a bristle-covered, bandana-masked jaw with enough power to send the first attacker staggering backwards. In almost the same movement, as the man he hit went away spluttering curses, St. Andre pivoted around and delivered a stamping kick to the pit of the second man's belly. Continuing his turn with the fluid grace of a ballet dancer, St. Andre shifted his weight to his rear foot, drew his raised right leg up and in front of the left and lifted his body slightly on the ball of the left foot. The crossing of the right leg gave it greater distance to move and provide extra momentum and kicking power. How effective the *chasse croise*, or front lateral kick of *savate*, proved showed in the way the second man went down as St. Andre lashed up and sideways with his right foot, leaning his body away from the recipient and delivering a slashing, stabbing kick at the jaw.

After which the ball ended and the piper requested payment. The third man's fist came driving into St. Andre's cheek as the detective returned to his fighting stance and before he could take any further action. Caught by the blow, St. Andre shot across the

*For further details of the Vanderlyne case read THE MAN FROM TEXAS by J. T. Edson.

8

street and collided with the left side wall. Before he could recover, the fourth man sank a fist into his stomach and jack-knifed him over. Bringing up his left knee, the man smashed it into St. Andre's face, jerking the detective erect again with blood gushing from his nostrils.

"Fix him!" roared a voice.

Through the roaring pain-mists which engulfed him, St. Andre saw the four men coming at him and his fighting instincts reacted to the situation faster than could his spinning brain. Like a flash St. Andre brought up his right foot in a kick which sent the toe to catch the closest of the quartet *real* low and in a manner which would have caused the detective's instant disqualification if used in a sporting contest at Duval's *Savate* Academy. However St. Andre was not indulging in a sporting contest, but fighting for his life. So he drove his toe into his nearest attacker's stomach and sent the man stumbling from the fray in moaning, doubled-over agony.

Fists thudded into St. Andre's face and body, savage blows that drove pain through him. While he hit and kicked back— *savate* permitted the use of the hands as well as the feet—St. Andre knew it to be merely a matter of time before the remaining trio reduced him to a bloody, battered, broken wreck. Fighting on through the beating, St. Andre tried to so mark his attackers that identifying them would be comparatively easy. Not that he was likely to be in any condition mentally or physically to do any identifying unless he received help quickly.

It may be that at that moment St. Andre became the first man to think, "There is never a policeman around when you need one," for mister, he needed not one but a good dozen big, brawny policemen's aid just about as badly as anybody in the whole United States at that moment—or five minutes earlier if it came to a point.

A passer-by walked along the street which intersected the one down which the trio of hard-cases practiced playing in the percussion section of an orchestra, using St. Andre's body instead of a drum. While most people in a city like New Orleans might have glanced at the disturbance, they knew sufficient about the facts of life to show their interest in the welfare of others by walking away hurriedly. Not so the slim, somewhat boyish shape, for it came to a halt, then started heading along the street towards the struggling group of men.

Turning from St. Andre, one of the attacking trio let out a bellow of rage calculated to scare off even the most nosey citizen.

"Get the hell out of here!" he bellowed. "Shift it, or you'll get some of the same."

At that moment one of the men was landing a kick into St. Andre's ribs, while the second gripped the detective's hair, held his head back and smashed the other hand into a bloody face; St. Andre being on his knees and, although just about conscious, too far gone to defend himself. It was a sight, taken with the third hard-case's warning, liable to scare off anybody with an interest in their own well-being, no matter how much they might wish to help the sufferer.

Only neither the warning nor the sight appeared to frighten and drive off the slim intruder. Taking in the boyish build of the new-comer, the tough who gave the warning started forward, intending to carry out his threat. Skidding to a halt, the newcomer shot a right hand under the left side of an open jacket and brought something, most likely a weapon thought the burly tough out from beneath the coat's flap. Not a gun or a knife, the tough saw to his relief, but what at first glance appeared to be a two foot long police baton. Matched against a burly, six foot tall, one hundred and ninety pound rough-neck, that boyish shape, at the most five foot seven in height and not heavily built with it, did not appear to be showing good sense in relying on such a puny weapon.

Which only went to show how wrong appearances sometimes are.

Even before the tough came within arm's length, in fact while he was still several feet away, the newcomer's arm raised and swung down again. For a moment the tough thought that the newcomer had panicked and tried to throw the club at him. It proved to be his last coherent thought for some time. Something hissed through the air towards the tough and cracked like a pistol shot. Instantly the burly man's face felt as if it had burst into flames. Bright lights seemed to be exploding before the tough's eyes and he reeled backwards, hands clawing at the blood which oozed from a mysterious gash that had suddenly appeared across his face, running from his right temple down to the lobe of his left ear.

Hearing their pard's screech of agony, the other two men swung away from St. Andre and prepared to take retaliatory measures against the brash intruder who dared come between them and their prey. Being experts in their particular line of work, if complete and utter failures at any task requiring brains or finesse, the hard-cases liked to give good service when sent on a mission. So they figured working over an inquisitive interloper would give them just a little more of the practice all men know makes perfect.

Unfortunately for the men, that slim newcomer did not intend to take a brutal beating in the interests of helping them perfect their technique. Again and again the intruder's right arm swung up and down, each time being followed by a hissing crack and a yell or howl of pain from one of the trio of attackers. All the time a flow of hide-blistering invective, in a voice raised by either fear or excitement to what sounded almost like a woman's tones, flowed from the intruder.

Nor did St. Andre's saviour remain content to stand back and use whatever weapon caused such consternation among the detective's attackers, but moved forward step by step in an attempt to drive the hard-cases away. St. Andre tried to force himself to his feet so as to lend his rescuer a helping hand. However the pain and exhaustion spawned by his beating prevented him from rising, nor could his spinning senses give the order to draw out his police whistle and summon aid. While the newcomer seemed to be handling things quite satisfactorily, St. Andre wanted to capture his attackers if possible. A good peace officer always liked to know who sent men to attack and beat him up; and not entirely for personal reasons.

"Agh!" howled the biggest man, following one of the cracking noises. "Do something, Max!"

His words appeared to be directed at the man St. Andre put out of the fight with a low kick. Holding his injured region with one hand, the man crawled painfully to his feet. However, on hearing his friend's shout, the man dipped his free hand into a pocket and brought out a squat, heavy calibred Derringer Pocket Pistol. Before he could bring his weapon into line, the man saw the newcomer look, then swing the right arm in his direction. Something leathery-feeling curled around the man's wrist, gripping it in a sudden, frightening, vice-like hold that crushed the bones and snapped them like rotten twigs. A scream burst from the man's lips as a fresh pain almost made him forget his previous injury, and the Derringer clattered unfired to the ground.

"Let's get out of here!" one of the quartet yelled.

Panic had always been infectious and so it proved in this case. Shaken by the inexplicable pain caused by whatever kind of weapon the intruder held, knowing that at any moment St. Andre might recover enough to start blowing his whistle to summon help, and having a fair idea of their fate if captured by the police after attacking and brutally beating a popular member of the legion of the blue, the four hard-cases decided enough to be sufficient for the day. Having reached that conclusion, they decided to chance their employer's wrath at failing to do a *real* good job on St. Andre. So they turned and took to their heels, racing away down the street, leaving a sick and sorry police lieutenant and a slim boyish-looking shape in possession of the field.

After the sound of the quartet's footsteps died away, the intruder turned and walked towards St. Andre. Coiling the lash of the long bull-whip handled with such deadly precision, the newcomer thrust it back under the jacket and bent to help a groaning St. Andre to rise.

At first the detective thought of asking his rescuer to take out his whistle and blow on it to summon aid. Then he realised that there would be little chance of catching the four men. If he knew their kind, and he reckoned he did, they would have a good escape route planned and be away before the police managed to surround the area.

Taking St. Andre by the arm, the newcomer started to lift as he struggled to get to his feet. Weakly he reached towards the other, wanting to get support for a pair of legs which hardly seemed capable of supporting his weight.

"Th—Thank you, young man," he gasped as his rescuer eased him upwards.

"Mister," replied a most unmasculine voice, "happen you think I'm a young *man*, they either damaged you real bad, or you've not been around very much."

Even before the lack of masculinity in the voice registered on St. Andre's pain-slowed mind, he rested his hand for support under the jacket and on the shirt below. He jerked the hand away much quicker than he placed it on, for, slowed by the beating or not, St. Andre's faculties told him that what he touched, or what lay beneath the shirt he rested his hand on, most certainly did not belong to a young *man*.

"I should think so too," said the voice, showing no embarassment. "You're too stove up and feeble right now to get ideas like *that*."

"I—I—assure you, young lady—," St. Andre began, feeling the girl brace herself as his weight leaned against her. "I—had—no intention—."

"If you had, you're a tougher cuss than I expected to find in New Orleans," the girl answered calmly. "Soon's I've found that feller's gun, we'll get you some place where I can see how much face they've left you. Only I'd sure as hell hate to leave a loaded gun lying where some darned city kid could find it and likely blow his head off, not knowing any better than fool with it."

Gently the girl leaned St. Andre against the wall. Then she turned and walked across the narrow street, scuffling her feet along. One of them struck something which moved and struck the wall with a metallic click. Taking out a match, the girl rasped it on the seat of her pants—for she appeared to be wearing trousers and not a skirt. Bending, her back to St. Andre so he could see little of her features in the faint glow of the burning match, the girl picked up the discarded Derringer. She lowered its hammer before dropping the deadly little single-shot pistol into her jacket pocket. Blowing out the match, the girl turned and walked back to where St. Andre leaned against the other wall.

"Derringer hide-out," she said. "Don't reckon he could've hit me with it. Only I sure as hell didn't aim to stand around and wait to find out. How're you feeling now? Any pain in your side when you breath?"

While watching the girl, St. Andre was feeling at his ribs and wondering just how much damage had been done. His face felt raw and his throat burned with the taste of swallowed blood. A sick fear crept through him as he realised he could not see through his left eye. Weakly he raised a hand to touch it, feeling something wet and sticky. Over the eye lay what felt like a two inch wide, one inch deep cut which trickled blood down. St. Andre hoped that blood from the cut and nothing more caused his left eye's lack of sight. From the way his nose felt, swollen and blocked up, he guessed that it still ran blood and his jaw seemed to be enlarged to twice its normal size. However, while his ribs ached badly, he found he could breath without any of the pain which could spell a broken rib or two.

"I—don't think so," he replied to the girl's question.

Taking the detective's right arm, the girl eased it across her shoulders and braced herself under his weight. The street seemed to be spinning around before St. Andre's eyes and his legs felt as if they had lost their bones. For a moment he thought he would fall, but the girl's strength supported his weight and kept him on his feet.

Born to a society which expected its female side to be fragile, gentle and pampered creatures, St. Andre had seen sufficient of the rest of the world to know that some women had to be strong enough to handle a hard day's work. For all that, the strength of the girl whose timely appearance saved him from serious injury, if not

13

death, took the detective by surprise. If the way she stood up under him be anything to go by, St. Andre figured she must be about as strong a woman as he had ever met.

"How is it?" she asked, making no attempt to move or go down under his weight.

"A—A little better," replied St. Andre as the dizzy feeling left him.

"Happen you're up to it, we'd best get you off the street. Who was they, angry husbands?"

"I—I—."

"Now don't you pay me no mind, nor bothering answering, feller," interrupted the girl. "I'm only doing it to take your mind offen your hurts. I've got me a room around here someplace. Leastways, I reckon it should be around here. Trouble being I didn't blaze no trail and these city streets all look mighty alike to a half-smart lil country gal like me. Where-at's the *Rue de la Paix*?"

While talking, the girl started to walk, assisting St. Andre's still feeble legs to support and carry him. By the time she asked her question about the direction to her temporary home, they had reached the intersection. Although the girl pronounced her street 'Roo dee lah Packs', St. Andre understood. Weakly he nodded in the direction the girl had been walking before she came to his aid.

"Next street—left," he told her.

"Hell, I wasn't so far wrong after all," she said and stiffened him as he stumbled slightly. "Just keep your legs moving, friend, and lean on me. You can rest up a mite when we get to my room."

Gritting his teeth, and promising himself that he would not throw any more strain than necessary on the girl, St. Andre forced his legs to move. His superb physical condition aided him and the dizziness began to wear off. They walked along the side of a slightly wider street, keeping to the shadows. This latter was the girl's idea although one which St. Andre agreed with in principle.

"Them four riled-up husbands, or fathers, or whatever they was, might come back," she said, steering him into the shadows instead of crossing to where the moon illuminated the other side of the street. "It'd be best if we saw them afore they saw us, I reckon."

After walking for a time, coherent thoughts began to flow into St. Andre's head. While he did not feel like throwing somersaults with joy, or even trying to walk without the girl's aid, he could now think. Being a policeman who had just taken one hell of a beating, his first thoughts turned to his attackers.

The name 'Max' yelled by one of the quartet might possibly

help in locating them, although St. Andre could not even try to guess how many hard-cases in New Orleans went under that name. It would be several decades before any police department maintained more than the most fragmentary records and in the early 1870's the useful idea of keeping a 'monicker' file, which listed criminals by their nicknames had not been thought of, so St. Andre had no such aid to assist his search.

St. Andrew wanted those four men badly and ought to blow his whistle, bringing patrolmen to help him begin his search. Yet in his weakened condition the prospect of being able to get off his feet for a time and have his injuries treated prevented him from doing so. The four attackers would be well clear of the area and St. Andre did not feel up to the task of starting at that moment.

All four men bore marks from his fists and feet, of that he felt sure. From the way they yelled and howled as his rescuer tackled them, the quartet might carry other identifiable injuries too. St. Andre suddenly realised that he did not know just how the girl managed to drive off four burly rough-necks. If it came to a point he knew very little about his saviour. Who she might be; what she looked like; how she came to be on hand; where she came from; all those questions remained unasked as she helped him towards the *Rue de la Paix*.

"This's it," remarked the girl, steering him towards the door of a cheap brownstone apartment building. "We'll have you fit as frog's hair afore you know what it's about."

Opening the door, the girl helped St. Andrew through the dimly-lit hall to a room on the ground floor. She let them into the room and assisted St. Andre across to a bed, sitting him on it then easing him deftly on to his back. Even now St. Andre had seen little of his rescuer for the room was in darkness.

"Just lie easy there, friend," she ordered. "I'll light the lamp and then see to fixing your hurts."

With a sigh, St. Andre relaxed and waited for the lamp to be lit and allow him to take a good look at the girl whose opportune arrival and prompt actions saved him from serious injury.

CHAPTER TWO

So You're The Famous Calamity Jane

ALTHOUGH St. Andre did not feel like acting the part of an observant detective, he looked around him as well as he could with only one eye working properly, when the lamp's light illuminated the room. He found himself in a small, clean room furnished with a wash-stand on which stood a pitcher of water and a towel, a small table bearing the lamp, a couple of chairs, a wardrobe and a comfortable bed.

From his rapid study of the room, St. Andrew took his first clear look at his rescuer. Remembering the robust language she used when driving off the quartet, St. Andre half-expected to see a harsh-faced, middle-aged harridan of some kind. He received a very pleasant surprise. Maybe his rescuer could not be termed ravingly beautiful, but she was good looking and well below middle-age.

Most ladies of St. Andre's acquaintance, and there were several, went in for blonde hair that season, whether born blonde or not, wore it long and taken up in elaborate styles; while their faces retained a pallor aided by powder and make-up. His rescuer had a mop of short, curly red hair on which perched a battered U.S. cavalry kepi at a jaunty angle, and her face bore a healthy tan sprinkled with a few attractive freckles. The eyes of most women St. Andre knew were languorous, inviting; yet a man never knew when he accepted the invitation if the girl would submit in blissful delight as he took hold, or scream for her papa to bring on a shotgun and a preacher. That red haired girl's eyes held no hidden deceit. Meeting St. Andre's scrutiny calmly, they seemed to say, "All right, son, hurt or not, you figure you're the world's greatest; but I'm from Missouri, I've got to be shown."

Showing her might prove mighty interesting.

After his study of the girl's face, St. Andre watched her walk across the room. Removing the fringed buckskin jacket she wore, the girl hung it on a wardrobe peg then bent and opened a battered box standing against the wall. A tight-rolled scarlet bandana, knotted at her throat, trailed long ends over an open-necked man's shirt that, like the levis pants she wore, looked to have been bought a size too small and shrunk in the washing. The shirt's neck was open low enough, and clung tight enough to her rich, full bosom, to dispel any doubts that might possibly have remained in St. Andre's French-Creole mind as to her sex. From the bosom, she tapered down to a slim waist, without the use of corsets or other artificial aids, then swelled out to plump, curving and eye-catching hips and shapely legs that the levis tended to reveal rather than conceal, and ended in feet clad in Indian moccasins unless St. Andrew missed his guess.

Lifting his gaze from her feet, St. Andre studied the broad leather belt which slanted down at an angle from her left hip to her right thigh. Surely she did not wear a gun? Yes, it showed as she turned from the box. An ivory-handled 1861 Navy Colt, butt forward in a contoured fast-draw holster such as members of the Texas Light Cavalry wore during the War Between the States, or St. Andre missed his guess; the holster bottom fastened down by a thong around the girl's thigh. An affectation if ever he saw one, probably the girl had been on her way to a masquerade ball when she found him in need of her aid. A long lashed bull-whip hung thrust into the left side of her waist belt. More affectation—at that moment St. Andre remembered the pistol-like cracks and the pain-filled howls of his attackers as the girl drove them off. That whip was no affectation, no matter what the gunbelt and Navy Colt might be.

"Damned if everything you want's allus at the bottom," she remarked and swung back to root in the box again, a few muttered curses leaving her lips.

St. Andrew found himself wondering what kind of girl he had come across. She was refreshingly different from his aristocratic and socialite friends, or the actresses and other entertainers he knew or met in his duty. Some of the young ladies of St. Andre's social set, profound admirers of the intellectual writer Browne Crossman used bad language to express their progressiveness; but they did it self-consciously, showing only that they tried to prove a non-existent point. The red head cursed naturally, in the manner of a man out fishing when he caught his thumb with a hook point. St. Andre grinned as he thought of the vitriolic flow of invective the girl poured upon his attackers while her savage whip-attack drove them off.

"You should tote a gun, friend, happen those were your neighbours," the girl said, coming to the bed with a buckskin bag in her hands. "Sit up and let's take a look at you."

Gently, yet showing that she had handled injured men before, she helped him sit up and remove his jacket. Her eyes studied him and formed their conclusions. While he did not look much right at the moment, mussed up and all bloody, she decided he would be a handsome cuss most times. Black curly hair, regular features, a neat, thin moustache; wearing expensive clothing and looking like he was used to doing so, but with a good spread to his shoulders, a lean, fighting man's waist and, if the way he fought those four jaspers be anything to go on, hard muscles that he knew how to use. In fact, he looked a tolerable hunk of man to her way of thinking.

"I—have—a—gun." St. Andre replied.

"Then why in hell didn't you start to using it?" she sniffed, swinging the jacket on to the bed rail.

Something hard clinked against the rail and the girl turned, dipping a hand into his inside pocket to lift out a fancy, pearl-handled Smith & Wesson No. 1 Pocket revolver which she eyed with distaste. Yet she did not shriek in simulated horror and drop the gun, or wave it around with a finger on the trigger to the danger of life and limb. Handling the gun with obvious knowledge of such things, she turned smiling eyes to him.

"See now why you didn't use it," she said and laid the revolver aside. "Reckon you didn't want to knock the dust off their jackets."

Despite his injuries, St. Andre was still a Frenchman in the presence of a pretty girl and as such figured it to be time he asserted some of his masculine superiority over that calm, competent young female.

"It would have done more than just dust a jacket, *cherie*," he told her, sniffing the dripping blood up his nostrils.

"Maybe," she answered, sounding doubtful. "The name's not 'Sherry', it's Martha Jane Canary, though I'd not thank you for calling me 'Martha'."

"Then what do I call you?"

"My friends call me Calam, or worse. Which, afore you ask me, is short for Calamity."

While speaking, the girl had opened her bag and taken out what looked like a powderhorn, tipping some snuff-like grains of dust on to the palm of her hand. Turning, she approached St. Andre and held the hand towards him.

"Here, sniff some of this up your nose."

"Huh?"

"Could allus call in one of them fancy city doctors and he'd look

18

you over then tell you what we both already know, that somebody handed you a helluva licking, and charge you five dollars. Only I like to do it more gentle and cheaper."

So saying, the girl brought the palm of her hand up under his nose and stabbed her other forefinger hard into his stomach. Taken by surprise, St. Andre breathed in, sucking a quantity of the powder up into his nostrils. For a moment his nose felt clogged up, but the bleeding stopped.

"What was that?" he asked, watching the girl put away the powder and open a large snuff box.

"Powdered witch hazel leaves. And this here's gum from a balsam fir. I reckon it's better for stopping open bleeding like this on your face. This might hurt a mite, friend."

She went to the washstand and poured water from the jug into a bowl. Returning with the bowl and towel, she gently washed the blood from his injured eye. For a moment St. Andre felt scared as he saw the concern show on her face, then relief replaced the expression of anxiety.

"Calamity you said your name was," the detective said, trying to ignore the stinging pain the bathing caused. "Well, it nearly was a calamity. The life of New Orleans' best detective might have been cut off in his prime had you not come along when you did."

"Was there two of you in the alley?" asked the girl with a smile. She spread something cool and sticky on the gash over his eye.

"Only one. I, myself."

"And you'd be who?"

"Philippe St. Andre, Detective Lieutenant, at your service."

"Right pleased to know you. Might not be seeing too good out of that eye for a spell, but at least you've got an eye left and the cut over it don't need any stitching."

"I suppose you could have done that too?"

"I've had to afore now," the girl admitted. "Stop the pain by making 'em chew on the bark of a pepperwood tree, if there's one handy. If not, I've got a couple of other real good pain-killers. One of 'em's make the hurt feller drink whisky until he goes to sleep—."

"I'd imagine that would cause him to cut himself again when he woke, to get the same treatment," St. Andre interrupted.

"If it does, I use the other pain-killer next time."

"And what might that be?"

"Hit him over the head with the empty bottle," she answered calmly, then eyed him with interest. "Ain't never been a gal for being nosey and asking questions about things, so I'm not going to ask you if them four *was* riled-up fathers after your hide."

"*Mon Dieu!* I forgot them, *cherie*."

"Likely they'll not forget *you* for a spell. Shouldn't be hard to cut from the herd, happen you look for the marks that old whip of mine put on 'em. One'll have a busted wrist most likely and the others'll all carry marks."

"You're quite a girl to have around in a calamity, Jane," smiled St. Andre, then he stiffened and stared at the girl, realising how the last two words came out. "Calamity—Jane—You can't be!"

"Want to bet?" she grinned back.

"*Sacre bleu!*" St. Andre ejaculated. "So you're the famous Calamity Jane!"

"Yep," replied the girl, clearly just a mite proud that her name and fame had reached as far as New Orleans. "I'm the famous Calamity Jane. Only I didn't know I was famous down here in New Orleans."

St. Andre stared in fascination at the girl he previously believed to be no more than a legend created by Westerners for the purpose of joshing dudes. Many highly sensational tales of her adventures, prowess and capabilities had appeared over the last year in such magazines as the *Police Gazette* and *New York Ledger*; in fact even the sedate *New Orleans Picayune* occasionally carried stories concerning the life and times of Calamity Jane.

In the highly coloured stories St. Andre read, Calamity had been portrayed as either a fire-breathing middle-aged dragoness, or a ravingly beautiful woman of high birth who fled to the West to forget a lost lover. Calamity was neither, but merely a rather unusual product of the times. Before disappearing into the West, Charlotte Canary left Calamity and the rest of her children in the care of a St. Louis convent. However, there had been too much of Charlotte's spirit in Calamity for the girl to accept the nuns' rigid discipline. On her sixteenth birthday, Calamity—then plain Martha Jane—hid in one of Dobe Killem's wagons and was not discovered until that evening at the end of a day's trip. She might have been returned to the convent had Killem's cook not been too drunk to make a meal for the men. One of the few things the nuns managed to teach Calamity had been cooking and the meal she threw together for the hungry men ensured that she could stay with the outfit.

That trip raiding Sioux wiped out two other outfits, but missed Killem's wagons. On reaching their destination, Killem made a good profit and his men began to regard the girl as a good luck charm. So they kept her with them. At first Calamity helped the cook, did chores around the camp, then graduated to driving. From the men she learned to handle a six-horse Conestoga wagon, use a bull-whip as tool and weapon, shoot well with rifle, revolver or shotgun, and generally take care of herself on the plains country of the West. Due to a licking at the hands of a saloon girl, Calamity learned to fight. More than that, she developed a liking for fighting which led her to enter saloons and toss down a challenge to take on the best gal in the house, all-in hand-scalping with no holds barred. Her outfit picked up a fair amount of cash betting on her, for so far Calamity had never been beaten in a fight.

St. Andre knew none of this. All he saw was a merry-faced, competent and capable girl, unconventional perhaps and well outside his considerable knowledge of the opposite sex. She reminded him of the fresh-faced, buxom country girls one saw around the poorer section of the city; wholesome, naive, innocent —only he doubted if Calamity would prove all that innocent if things came to a head.

"How about your ribs?" she asked.

"I think they'll be all right," he replied, feeling suddenly shy and not doubting she would want to examine his torso should he claim different. So he changed the subject. "What brought you to New Orleans?"

"Somebody in the Army bought up a big bunch of horses cheap down here and wanted 'em shipping up the Big Muddy to St. Jo. So they sent for Dobe Killem, he's my boss, to handle the collection and delivery. We come down by steamboat and here we are. I went out to see the sights just afore dark and got lost coming back. Reckon the boys've gone off to that Madam Darcel's place and want me to meet 'em there."

"Madam Darcel's—," gasped St. Andre. "You mean the *Cheval D'Or*?"

"Yep. Though what the hell a 'Shovel Door' is, I ain't figured out."

"*Cheval D'Or*," corrected the detective. "It means Golden Horse. But it's no place for a young lady."

"Happen I see any going in," grinned Calamity, "I'll warn 'em."

Knowing something of Madam Darcel's saloon, St. Andre felt he ought to give a further warning.

"I owe you my gratitude for saving me, Miss—,"

"Happen you want to show that gratitude," she interrupted,

21

"stop calling me 'Miss' and start saying 'Calam', or Jane, or even that there 'Sherry'. And don't go to fretting. The boys protect me—and I protect them."

"Is any of the boys your—," began St. Andre, then tapered off, not knowing how to finish his question.

"Nope. None of 'em's my 'your—'. They're like a bunch of big brothers to me. Reckon I'll go on out and find em."

'Unless you have other ideas,' her manner hinted.

St. Andre, as has been said, was a Frenchman, a lusty healthy young man with an eye for the ladies and a heart that took kindly to romance. Unfortunately he was also a policeman responsible for keeping the peace and investigating crimes. The peace had been broken and a crime committed, which meant he must put duty before what he felt sure would be a pleasure.

"I must also go out and try to find somebody, *cherie*," he said regretfully, and waited for an explosion. No girl liked having *that* kind of offer tossed aside.

"Them four?" she asked calmly; perhaps the calm before a breaking storm.

"Those four," he agreed. "There are questions I must ask them."

"I figured there might be," Calamity stated showing neither disappointment nor annoyance, only complete understanding. "A good lawman can't let anybody get away with working him over. It gives other folks wrong ideas and puts bad medicine in 'em."

"Who told you that?" asked the detective in surprise.

"The best danged man who ever wore a law-badge—west of the Mississippi that is."

"And who would that be, Wyatt Earp?"

"That fighting pimp?" scoffed Calamity. "I'm talking about a real man. You maybe heard of him. Dusty Fog."

"You *know* Captain Fog?" asked the impressed St. Andre, for the man named had been one of the most talked-about soldiers in the Confederate States cavalry and much in the news since the meeting at the Appomattox Court-House brought an end to military hostilities.[*]

"Met him a couple of times," Calamity admitted. "Know his pard, Mark Counter a whole heap better."[†]

"I also met Captain Fog, during the War when I rode with the

[*]Dusty Fog's adventures are told in J. T. Edson's Floating Outfit novels.
[†]Calamity's meetings with Mark Counter are recorded in THE WILDCATS and TROUBLED RANGE.

Greyson Daredevils. He was a fine soldier and correct about a lawman's duty."

"Old Dusty gets right about more things than any two fellas I know," answered Calamity. "Say, did you ever see the fancy way he fist-fights? That's sure something to see."

"You are right," agreed St. Andre. "He uses a unique method. I wish I knew half as much. Of course I know *savate*—."

"What the hell's that?" asked the girl, packing away her medicines in the buckskin bag.

"*Savate?* French foot-fighting. It was brought to perfection by a man called Michel in Paris, France. I learned at Duval's academy and he studied in Paris under Charles Lecour, Michel's star pupil."

"Must be real fancy, taking all that learning," Calamity said dryly. "I can kick real good and never took a lesson in my sinful young life."

"Ah, *cherie*, there is kicking and—*la savate*. Perhaps during your stay in our fair city I might be permitted to take you to Duval's and show you how *savate* is learned."

"Allus willing to learn something," the girl replied and took the bag to her small trunk.

Although she did not know it, Calamity was due for a lesson in the noble art of *savate* a whole heap sooner than she expected. Her main thought-line at the moment of stowing away the medicine bag was that she would be seeing that fancy-talking, handsome young feller again. Now that might be *real* interesting.

Reaching up his hand, St. Andre touched the cut over his left eye. The blood, assisted by the gum, had congealed and the groove felt much smaller than when he previously examined it. One thing brought relief to the detective. Although the vision was blurred, he could still see and the damage to the eye appeared to be only to the lids and surrounding area. He wondered if a doctor could have handled his injuries any more efficiently than had the girl.

"How'd you like me to see if I can raise a cup of coffee?" Calamity asked as she returned from the box.

It was a tempting prospect for St. Andre, as he had not yet thrown off all the effects of the beating. However he wished to make a start on the hunt for his attackers before his injuries began to stiffen up. He knew that the longer it took him to start, the harder commencing would be. So, although his body craved to stay relaxed on the comfortable bed, he declined the offer.

23

"Perhaps another time, *cherie*," he replied, rising from the bed and reaching for his coat. "Now I must go down town and start work."

"Reckon I'd rather have a snort of red-eye myself," Calamity admitted. "How do I find the 'Shovel Door'?"

"It is on Latour Street. As a matter of fact, I intend to start my inquiries from the Latour Street station house. If you wish, I'll ride over there with you. We can hire a carriage."

"You know the range and I don't. Hey, aren't you forgetting something?"

Having put on his jacket, St. Andre started to walk towards the door of the room, but the girl's last words brought him to a halt. He turned and looked at her, but her eyes were not on him. Following Calamity's gaze, he saw his gun lying where the girl laid it aside.

"Oh that," he said. "I suppose I'd better take it with me."

A frown creased Calamity's face as she watched St. Andre drop the Smith & Wesson into his jacket pocket. No Western lawman would have left his weapon behind. One might forget his hat, or possibly his pants, but never his gun. Come to that, no Western peace officer would straddle himself with such a puny, feeble revolver as a .22 calibre Smith & Wesson. While that handsome young cuss might be real smart in some ways, it was Calamity's considered opinion that he had a lot to learn about being a lawman.

Not wishing to create dissension, Calamity did not mention her thoughts. She drew on her buckskin jacket, decided that she would not need her bull whip again that night and went to blow out the lamp. Then she left the room on St. Andre's arm, acting for all the world like a for-real New Orleans' lady. Or as near one as wearing man's clothing and with a Navy Colt hung at her right hip would allow.

CHAPTER THREE

Miss Canary Walks In The Park

WHILE Calamity never felt really comfortable riding in a vehicle with somebody else at the ribbons, she found the one-horse carriage they hired to take them to Latour Street had its advantages. Sitting inside, without the worry of keeping the horse going, Calamity relaxed and St. Andre pointed out various places of interest as they rode. At last they came alongside the large, open space known as the City Park, and the detective waved his hand towards it.

"Latour Street is on the other side of the Park. But we will have to go around it to reach the *Cheval D'Or*."

A saloon girl who Calamity once fought with, beat, then befriended, had come from New Orleans and in the course of a conversation mentioned taking walks in City Park. From what the girl said, walking there had a special appeal and Calamity decided she might as well give it a whirl while so close.

"Reckon I'll save the horses some sweat," she remarked, "Tell the feller up there to stop and I'll walk across."

"You mean you wish to walk through the Park alone, and at night?" asked St. Andre, staring at the girl.

"Won't be going to the 'Shovel Door' in the morning, so it'll have to be tonight. Only I don't reckon you're feeling like walking, so I'll be alone."

"*Mon Dieu!* Haven't you heard of the Strangler?"

"Nope. Who's he?"

"I wish we knew. All we know is that he has killed seven girls in the Park."

If St. Andre hoped to frighten or shock Calamity, he appeared to fail badly. Not by a flicker of her face did she show any fear or concern. However, her right hand dropped under the side of her jacket and touched the butt of the Navy Colt.

"I'm dressed," she said quietly. "Stop the carriage, Sherry, and I'll take me a walk."

St. Andre did not understand the connotation behind a Westerner's statement about being dressed. It had nothing to do with the fact that the speaker wore all his, or her, clothing, but implied that the one who made the statement carried the most important article of West-country property, a gun.

One thing St. Andre did not know, even after a short acquaintance; once Calamity made up her mind, very little under the sun would cause her to change it. However he could not allow a girl, even one so competent as Calamity, to chance walking alone in the park after dark, even on a bright moon-light night.

"If you are determined," he said, "I'll walk with you. And a lady does not call a gentleman '*cherie*'."

"So who's a lady?" grinned Calamity. "Reckon you can stand up to the walk?"

"I'll try my best," St. Andre answered and tapped on the roof of the cab.

Dismounting and helping Calamity down, St. Andre paid off the driver. Then he took Calamity's arm and they walked through the big, wrought iron gates into City Park. Even in the early 1870's New Orleans possessed a really fine park, although under the present conditions various senior police officials wished that the area had been built over instead of used as a recreation spot.

The Park might have been designed with the needs of the Strangler in mind, St. Andre decided, not for the first time, as he and Calamity strolled along. Winding paths ran through clumps of bushes which effectively hid one from the next. Scattered little wooden shelters offered places where courting couples could rest and do the kind of things they had done since men threw away clubs in favour of more gentle and pleasant methods of snaring a pretty young maiden. In that tangle, a man-made jungle-like maze, the Strangler could stalk his prey, slip his killing cord around a slim, delicate female throat and silently add another victim to his growing list, then be gone before the body was found.

So thought Philippe St. Andre, detective lieutenant, as he walked along keeping to the grass verge alongside the path. He hated to make a noise as he walked and so always tried to stay somewhere that muffled his footsteps. At his side, Calamity's moccasins fell silently on the path. Neither spoke as they walked, each busy on his or her line of thought.

In Calamity's case, the thoughts ran to the fun she would soon be having with the boys and wondering what a big city saloon offered in comparison with a similar place out West. She also wondered if the city detective meant his invitation to visit the *savate* academy. If so, how much further would their friendship develop? Calamity had no objections to the friendship blossoming, for, from what she heard, those French-Creole fellers were sure something at handing out the things a girl dreamed about on the long, dark, cold and lonely winter nights.

While passing across a joining with another páth, Calamity saw something from the corner of her eye. Even at such a moment, the girl's instincts were to keep alert, so she turned her head to look more carefully at what attracted her. What she saw brought her to a halt and made her tighten her grip on the detective's sleeve.

"Don't make a sound!" she hissed. "Down there!"

The very intensity with which Calamity spoke forced St. Andre to obey in silence. Turning to look in the direction Calamity pointed, St. Andre felt as if his eyes would pop out of his head at the sight before him. If the sight meant what he believed it did, St. Andre figured himself to be having more luck than even the youngest and most handsome lieutenant of the New Orleans Police Department rated.

In pre-Strangler days the sight of a man standing behind a girl in the City Park would have attracted no attention. Yet seeing such a sight now aroused any right-thinking policeman's suspicions. The man stood with his back to Calamity and St. Andre, was medium sized, portly, wearing a top hat, stylishly-cut broadcloth coat, white trousers, the new-fangled spats that had become all the rage, and shiny shoes. Ahead of him, also with her back to the watching couple, stood a buxom, blonde, flashily-dressed girl who most probably was not his lady wife, and likely could not even claim to be a lady. Such a sight had never been so rare in the Park as to attract more than a glance, a cynical grin and some conjecture about how much the girl would make—until the Strangler started operations. Since the killings began however, the sight of a man standing behind a girl and dropping something over her head demanded not only a second glance, but instant action.

Despite his injuries, St. Andre found that he could still think fast. Even as the portly man's hands came level with the girl's throat, the detective let out a yell.

"Police here! Let go and stand still!"

Jerking his head around, the portly man gave a startled squawk. Thrusting the girl aside, he started to run away as fast as his legs would carry him. Ahead lay a corner and once round it he could disappear in any of a dozen directions, or hide in the bushes.

St Andre knew that as did the fleeing man, so sprang forward in pursuit, ignoring the screeching blonde who had landed on hands and knees at the side of the path.

Even as St. Andre leapt forward, Calamity also acted and showed a classic example of the difference between Eastern and Western thought on how to deal with such a problem. St. Andre hoped to run the man down in a foot-race, or at least keep him in sight until reinforcements arrived and cut off his escape. Although the detective carried a fully loaded revolver—even if only a tiny .22 Smith & Wesson—he did not give the weapon a thought, regarding it only as a means of extreme self-defence.

Not so Calamity. Raised on the Western plains, friend of numerous fast and handy gun-fighting gentlemen, she knew the value of a revolver in the present situation. Once around that corner, the man might escape and, if he should be the Strangler, stay free to kill again.

Twisting the palm of her right hand outwards, Calamity curled her fingers around the butt of the Navy Colt and brought it out fairly fast. By Western standards 'fast' meant to be able to draw a gun and shoot in at most three-quarters of a second and Calamity took a quarter of a second longer than that to bring her Colt into action. However, to draw and shoot in a second still licked the 'be-jeesus' out of running when it came to halting a fleeing criminal. Taking careful aim, for she had heard that these civilised areas did not take kindly to having dead owlhoots scattered about the scenery, Calamity fired. On the crack of the shot, the man's tophat somersaulted from his head and bounced on the path ahead of him, although it must be stated that Calamity did not intend to come that close.

Never one to look a gift horse—or a real lucky shot—in the mouth, Calamity acted just like she always hit her mark in so spectacular fashion.

"Hold it!" she yelled. "Stop, or the next one goes clear through you."

Which, with a touch of dramàtics—Calamity could never resist a chance to play the grandstand a mite, even though she had never heard of the term—brought about the desired result. However, for a moment Calamity thought a second shot, this time for effect, might be needed. Then the man skidded to a halt, turned and jerked his hands into the air.

"D—Don't shoot!" he quavered. "I—I—only have a few dollars and my watch on me.'

"Well dog—my—cats!" Calamity growled, thumb-cocking

28

her Colt. "He's trying to make out like he thinks we're fixing to rob him."

"Or he really thinks so," St. Andre answered, for he could not see the Strangler, with only the gallows waiting, surrendering so easily. "Holster your gun, Calam, we won't need it any more."

Figuring that a man who forgot to put his weapon into a pocket before leaving a room could hardly set himself up as an authority on when a gun would be needed, Calamity retained hold of the Colt and kept it from leather.

"I'll believe that when I'm sure of it," she answered.

"Hey!" yelped the gaudily-dressed girl, struggling to her feet and clapping a hand to her throat. "You fellers wouldn't ta—My pearls!" The last two words came in a wild screech. "They must have bust when he pushed me. You lousy bastards made me lose my pearls!"

At the same moment the portly man came forward on shaking legs. He reached under his jacket, causing Calamity to prepare to shoot. However, she held her hand for something told her the man was harmless. In fact from the front he showed what would normally be a florid, pompous face, yet which now held a pale, terrified expression as befitted a very respectable member of society believing himself to be under a threat to his life and well-being. Nothing more dangerous than a well-filled wallet came from his jacket front and he held it forward timidly.

"H—Here!" he squeaked. "T—Take my wallet—."

"You yeller crumb!" screeched the girl. "Do something! They made me lose the pearls you just gave me."

"All right!" snapped St. Andre, walking by Calamity. "I'm a police lieutenant. Let's be quiet and talk this out."

While the detective's cold, authoritative voice chopped off the girl's indignation, it brought a change of attitude in the portly man. The fear went and he thrust away his wallet with an angry gesture. Righteous anger came to his pompous features as he pointed at St. Andre and Calamity.

"Police!" he snorted. "Then why did you shoot at me?" Without giving either the detective or Calamity a chance to answer, he went on, "I'll have you know that I'm a personal friend of the Mayor and the Chief of Police—."

"Your sort allus are," sniffed Calamity, setting the Colt's hammer on a safety notch between two cap-nipples and twirling the gun into leather with a fancy flourish.

"What did you say?" boomed the now fully indignant citizen. "I'll have you know, my good man—."

"I ain't good, I for certain ain't your'n, and I sure as hell ain't no man, mister!" growled Calamity, listening to the sound of heavy, official feet pounding along a path towards them. "We saw you stood behind that gal and tossing something over her head—."

"It was a string of pearls!" howled the blonde, down on her hands and knees and scrabbling around with her fingers. "Light a match, one of you and get down to help me find 'em. They cost him a hundred bucks and he gave them to me instead of paying."

Which cleared in a most satisfactory manner the matter of why the man stood behind the girl and acted as he did; although St. Andre knew enough about tax-paying citizens of the portly man's type to doubt if the pompous one would be pleased to hear somebody took him for the Strangler. There would be stormy times ahead unless St. Andre handled the business just right, and the blonde's words offered him a reasonably good way of dealing with the pompous man.

"Hum!" said St. Andre, nudging Calamity in the ribs gently as a warning for her to let him handle the matter. "A hundred dollar pearl necklace lost. That's a serious affair, sir. I'll have to ask you to come along to the nearest station house and make a full statement."

At that moment a couple of burly policemen came into sight, skidding to a halt and studying the group before them. Then one of the patrolmen recognised St. Andre and threw up a salute.

"Heard a shot down here, lootenant," he said.

"Er—Lieutenant," the portly man put in, his voice no longer pompous or indignant as he considered his position in the light of St. Andre's words. "Do we have to go on with this?"

"With the loss of a hundred dollar necklace, on top of your being shot at?" answered St. Andre. "I think we must."

Gulping down something which seemed to be blocking his throat, the portly man held out a hand. "I—I understand that you and this—this—you misjudged my intentions. The whole affair was no more than a regrettable error and should be forgotten, don't you think?"

"And the pearls, sir?"

"The—They were not that valuable, lieutenant. You look like a man of the world—."

"What was their true value?" interrupted St. Andre coldly.

"A—Two dollars fifty. They were freshwater pearls."

"*What!*" screeched the girl, coming to her feet with fury showing on her face. "Why, you cheap, mealy-mouthed—."

"Now you just quieten it down, Sally," put in one of the patrolmen.

"Me?" yelped the girl. "And what about him? He gave me them to—."

"Likely," said the patrolman. "You'd—."

"That's it!" the blonde screamed. "Side him! It's like Browne Crossman is always saying, you lousy police are just tools of the rich and—."

At which point Miss Martha Jane Canary decided it was time she took a hand. Not having received the benefit of a college education, Calamity felt respect and admiration for most lawmen, knowing the thankless job they did. So she disliked seeing folks call down a peace officer without having a damned good reason.

Shooting out a hand, Calamity gripped the other girl's dress, sliding fingers between the valley of the girl's breasts and taking a firm hold of the material. With a sudden jerk, she hauled the blonde up close and thrust an angry face within inches of the other girl's startled features.

"Now shut your god-damned mouth and listen to me, you cat-house cull!" yelled Calamity and when that girl raised her voice, man you could hear it for a good country mile. "We saw you in what we reckoned looked like danger of winding up wolf-bait, so we jumped in and saved you. Only it come out you didn't need saving after all. And if you're so damned dumb that you fall for an old-as-the-hills trick like the pearl game, you've got no cause, nor right, to complain."

While Calamity never followed the other girl's profession, she possessed a number of good friends who did, so knew enough about it to talk to the blonde in terms they both could understand. Her angry tirade stopped the blonde's speech describing Browne Crossman's views on the position of law officers as tools of the idle rich and oppressors of the poor.

Anger glowed in the blonde's eyes at first, then died again. The two patrolmen knew something of the girl's temper and expected her to tie into the red-head in a hair-yanking, nail-clawing brawl. In this expectation they did the blonde an injustice. Full of righteous indignation she might be; a rough girl in a tough trade she most certainly was; but she had enough sense to think before acting. Taking note of Calamity's free hand and seeing it folded into a useful-looking fist, remembering the strength behind the other girl's pull, and figuring that anybody who knew enough about her work to mention the 'pearl game' must also know other basic essentials like self-defence, the blonde decided not to take

31

the matter further. If she tangled with that girl in men's clothing, her every instinct warned her she might regret the decision. There was too much competition for customers without operating under the added disadvantage of sporting a fight-battered face. So the girl relapsed into sullen silence, contenting herself with throwing a malevolent glare at the portly man.

Watching Calamity release the blonde, St. Andre fought to hold down a grin. It seemed the young lady from the West had good answers to most of the world's problems. However, there was the matter on hand to be attended to before he could compliment Calamity on her numerous talents.

"Do you want to take the matter further, sir?" asked St. Andre, eyeing the portly man in his most chilling and authoritative manner.

Under other conditions the man might have liked to show his tax-paying superiority over the three public-servants whose salary he helped pay. But not when he could be taken to the police station house and maybe word of his escapade get out. Unfortunately for him, 'making an investigation for social reasons' had not yet been invented as an excuse for his proposed conduct—and anyhow his wife would never have believed it—so he decided to keep quiet and get away while the getting be good and still open.

"No. I realise it was all a simple mistake," he said magnanimously. "If you don't mind, gentlemen, I think I'll be on my way."

Turning, the man scuttled off at a fair speed, ignoring his bullet-holed tophat which still lay where it fell. The blonde watched him go, then gave an explosive and angry snort.

"Why that—!" she began.

"Call it one of the hazards of your trade, my pet," St. Andre interrupted. They stood listening to the rapidly departing patter of the man's feet for a moment, then the detective went on, "But I wouldn't advise you to go into the Park with strange men in future."

Strange as it may seem, the blonde had never thought about the Strangler when she accepted the portly man's invitation to take a walk in the Park prior to visiting her room and getting down to business. Nor could she think of a single good reason why she should not take advantage of the civic amenities to put her clients in a romantic mood which tended to make them open their pocket-books all the wider when paying for her services.

"Why not?" she asked.

Before any answer could be made, a horror-filled male scream rang out from the direction in which the portly man took his hurried departure. It rang out loud, drowning the faint, but ever-present noise of merry-making from Latour Street. So hideous and shocking was the sound that it froze the three men and two girls for an instant. Calamity recovered first, or maybe the drawing of the Navy Colt was no more than reflex action. All three policemen stared in the direction of the sound and the blonde's face lost its colour as her mouth dropped open.

"What was that?" she finally gasped.

Her words bounced off departing backs as Calamity and the three men went racing away in the direction of the scream.

"It could be the answer to your question," Calamity called back over her shoulder as she ran.

For a moment the blonde stood staring. Then she remembered the Strangler and realised why St. Andre and Calamity acted as they did on seeing her standing before her prospective client as he slipped the string of freshwater pearls around her neck. Suddenly she saw that the departure of the police left her alone and a feeling of terror hit her.

"Wait for me!" she screeched and fled after the others as fast as she could run.

CHAPTER FOUR

Miss Canary Sees A Strangler Victim

CROUCHING hidden among the bushes at the side of the track the Strangler let out a low hiss of annoyance as he watched the blonde's hurried departure on the heels of the rest of the running group.

While making his way out of City Park after killing his eighth victim, the Strangler had come on the sight of the portly man and the blonde. Deciding it would be both interesting and amusing to watch what happened, the Strangler crouched in the bushes and awaited developments. The developments came swiftly with the arrival of that damned aristocratic St. Andre and the girl wearing men's clothing of an outlandish cut and style such as one saw Westerners clad in. Much to the Strangler's amusement, St. Andre took the portly man's actions as being an attempt to strangle the blonde.

Then the Strangler's amusement died as the girl with St. Andre swiftly—the move looked amazingly fast to the Strangler's untutored eyes—drew a revolver from under her coat and shot the fleeing man's hat from his head. The Strangler had often heard of Westerners drawing and shooting their weapons in lightning fast moves but as *he* could not do so, doubted if any less intelligent person would be able to perform the feat. Having seen the girl with St. Andre draw and shoot, the Strangler began to wonder if he might possibly have been wrong. If her clothes be anything to go by, the red haired girl came from the Western plains country, and the Strangler had never seen anything so fast as the way she moved.

Thinking of the girl's speed made the Strangler freeze in his hiding place instead of sneaking off and escaping. If he tried to flee and made a noise, that girl might start shooting at him. To the Strangler's way of thinking, his life's work was too important for him to risk capture and hanging because he killed a few worthless girls with so little to offer the community. So he remained crouching in the bushes and watched the smooth manner in which St. Andre handled the righteous indignation of the portly citizen. Being born to riches, St. Andre ought not have shown such efficiency, but he invariably did as the Strangler well knew; and the Strangler hated the thought of his preconceived ideas of aristocratic behaviour being shattered.

The Strangler thought the affair must be over when the portly man departed, and that he would soon be able to leave the area in safety. On hearing the man's scream, the Strangler knew his latest victim's body had been found. As the Strangler watched the rapid departure of the three policemen and the Western girl, he had an idea. Why not kill that gaudily-dressed blonde? If word came out that he took a second victim in such a manner, St. Andre would be dismissed and the people's faith in the police further diminish.

Even as he slid the cord from his pocket, the Strangler savoured the thought of what to do. Maybe the girl would hear him, but her kind never mistrusted *him*. She would think nothing of his presence; they never did. Then the cord would be around her throat from behind, tightening, driving the three knots into flesh and cutting off her voice, turning, he would carry the cord up over his shoulder until they stood back to back and he could use the extra leverage to speed her death.

Only before he could step from the bushes, the girl fled after the departing party. Giving a sigh, the Strangler coiled the length of cord and dropped it into the large pocket of his jacket. He threw a disappointed glance after the fleeing blonde, then walked on to the path and away. His route would take him out of City Park in the direction of the old French Quarter, the upper-crust section of the city.

Not knowing how close they had been to the Strangler, Calamity and the three policemen ran swiftly along the tracks. Despite his earlier beating, St. Andre made good time and he alone kept pace with Calamity as she sped along. The girl did not run with the exaggerated hip-wagglings and arm wavings of most of her sex, but strode out like a man and covered ground fast in her moccasined feet. Behind Calamity and St. Andre came the patrolmen, their uniforms and heavy boots not making for speed of foot; and in the rear staggered a scared, gasping blonde street-walker, the least used to running of them all.

Rounding a corner, Calamity and St. Andre came face to face with the portly, though no longer pompous man. Instead he looked almost on the verge of collapse, face white and drawn in an expression of extreme horror, eyes staring and mouth open, muttering incoherently as he pointed behind him.

"B—b—b—ba—there!" he gasped. "Its'—I—She—I—."

Which told Calamity and the detective little or nothing, but all they needed to know. Thrusting by the portly man, Calamity started to move towards that crumpled heaped-up thing lying in the centre of the path. St. Andre also passed the portly man, who had never been more pleased to see human faces and police uniforms in all his life. Catching Calamity by the arm, St. Andre stopped her. Once again St. Andre tried to assert his inborn French superiority over a member of the weaker sex. After all, and despite her smooth efficiency in practical matters, Calamity *was* a woman—and St. Andre knew just how terrible a Strangler's victim looked.

"Let me," he said.

He went by Calamity and walked towards the shape on the path, fighting to keep his stomach from heaving at the thought of what he would see. Even as he dropped to one knee by the body, St. Andre heard a soft foot-fall beside him and a low feminine gasp. He realised that Calamity had ignored his advice.

In the course of her life as a freighter on the Great Plains, Calamity had seen a fair amount of death: from Indian arrow, war lance or scalping knife; by bullets; through illness and accident. She reckoned to have a stout stomach which no sight could trouble any more. Yet for all that Calamity felt sick as she looked down on the moon-light illuminated features of the Strangler's eighth victim. She sucked in a deep breath and let it out in a slow hiss of revulsion and anger.

The cord which ended the victim's life no longer coiled around her neck, but a livid mark on the pallid skin and indented deeply into the flesh showed where it passed around and tightened, choking off life-giving air and killing far more silently yet just as efficiently as any bullet. Maybe in life the victim had been a beautiful girl, there was no way of knowing from her hideously distorted features now purplish-black, the tongue protruding through open lips and the eyes bulging out of the head. The body, clad in the cheap finery of a street girl, looked good, rich, full and inviting—unless one also looked at the face.

Even the two patrolmen, not sensitive, highly strung or easily moved by scenes of violence, showed nausea at the sight. One of them let out a low curse and the other, slightly younger, turned his head to look away from the hideous thing which had so recently been a living, breathing, happy and maybe good-looking girl.

"Is this the Strangler's work?" asked Calamity, her voice hoarse and strained and her tanned face pale.

"His eighth victim," answered St. Andre bitterly, looking at the three deeper indentations in the flesh, signs of the special type of cord the Strangler always used.

"Maybe he's still around!" snarled the younger patrolman and started moving towards the bushes.

"Hold it, friend!" snapped Calamity, an idea coming to her.

The urgency in Calamity's voice brought the man to a halt and he looked at her. So far nobody had got around to explaining who that girl in men's clothing might be, but she appeared to be on amiable terms with St. Andre, and it did not pay a young patrolman to ignore or give offence to the friends, especially lady friends, of a lieutenant; particularly a lieutenant tipped to wind up as Chief of Police one day in the future.

"What's up, ma'am?" asked the patrolman, sounding more polite than usual.

"He's long gone and you couldn't find him in the bushes at night, so don't go tramping all over the sign. Comes morning I can get a feller here as can track a bird through the air—."

"If you mean follow the Strangler's tracks, Calam, it won't work," St. Andre interrupted. "We tried it with bloodhounds and got nowhere."

"Which same don't surprise me none," the girl answered. "I bet every time a gal's been found, your fellers started chasing around in the bushes looking for the jasper who done it, going every damned which-ways and getting no place 'cept all over the Strangler's tracks. Then there's the folks who use the Park each day, they walk about in hell's chance of laying nose to a trail and holding to it—more so when you wouldn't know what tracks to lay 'em to."

"You sound as if you know what you're talking about," smiled St. Andre, thinking of how accurate Calamity's description had been of what went on after the finding of other Strangler victims, and seeing why the bloodhounds failed to assist the police's search for the killer.

"Dobe and the boys are hound-running fools when they're not on the trail," Calamity explained. "They taught me some about it."

"Is there any chance of your friend following the Strangler's tracks?"

"As long as they haven't been trampled under-foot and the feller stays off the paths, ole Tophet'll follow him. I don't want you to expect Tophet to trail the Strangler to his home, but he'll point you the direction that bastard went off after killing

37

the gal, and maybe tell you a mite more that could help."

For a moment St. Andre did not reply. As an avid student of the flood of Western fiction currently appearing in the popular press, he had read of Indians and a few white men who possessed the ability to follow a human trail by using their eyes. St. Andre had discounted the idea as being no more than another joke foisted on the stories' authors by Westerners. Knowing Calamity would not joke at such a moment, St. Andre wondered if her friend could help the police by following the Strangler's tracks.

There was one small detail to be remembered by St. Andre. The Strangler case had been assigned to Lieutenant Caiman, an older man, shrewd, tough and capable, but sadly lacking in imagination. Maybe Caiman would not care to have outsiders interfering in the investigation. Somehow St. Andre could not see Caiman taking to a newfangled notion like using a visual tracker.

"Why not bring on your tracker tonight?" he asked, deciding that what the eye did not see caused no worry to the heart of Lieutenant Caiman.

"Tophet's good," Calamity replied, "but he can't track at night, even in moonlight this good, or when he's all likkered up. Which same he's likely to be by this time. Leave it until daylight and he'll read you some sign."

"We've nothing to lose. However, it's Lieutenant Caiman's case and it will have to be his decision."

"Reckon Lou Caiman's about ready to try anything, Lootenant," put in one of the patrolmen. "The *Intelligencer*'s been roasting his hide over the killings."

"What's that?" asked Calamity.

"A newspaper," St. Andre replied in a tone that suggested he did not care for the *New Orleans Intelligencer*. "We'll leave it to Caiman to decide. One of you stay here and don't let anybody touch the body, the other one take care of that man and the girl. Take them to the station house until Lieutenant Caiman's seen them."

Giving a distasteful grunt and a shrug, the older patrolman said he would stay on the spot and allow his partner to escort the witness to the station house. Long service had its privileges, but it also bore responsibilities. So the older man took the more unpleasant of the two assignments.

"Say, do either of you boys know her?" Calamity asked, not looking at the body again.

"It's hard to say, ma'am," the older patrolman answered. "From her clothes she worked the streets, but that covers a

38

helluva an area. From Latour Street down to the river-front you'd find hundreds like her."

"We've never managed to identify one of the victims yet, *cherie*," St. Andre went on. "The girls don't often live with their parents. In many cases only their mac would miss them. That's their—."

"I know. We call 'em the same, or say they're blacksmithing, out West," Calamity interrupted.

"No mac would come near the police, he'd merely figure his girl ran out on him and go looking for another. Let's get going, Calam, we can do no more here."

Already the younger patrolman had joined the blonde and was helping a very pale, portly man rise. Calamity looked at the blonde for a long moment, then walked towards her.

"Look, blondie," Calamity said. "Reckon you could face up to taking a peek at that gal."

An expression of shock and fear came to the blonde's face. While she had never seen one of the Strangler's victims, her instinct told her the sight must be real unpleasant.

"N—No!" she gasped. "Why should I?"

"Because that gal's the eighth to be killed. The man who killed her's got to be stopped."

"Then let the police stop him!" croaked the blonde, backing away a couple of steps and staring with horror at what she could see of the body.

"They want to," answered Calamity. "Only they've no place to start looking. Maybe if they knew who the girl was, they could make a start at finding the Strangler. Only they don't know who she is. You might."

St. Andre looked first at Calamity, then turned his eyes to the blonde. While the Strangler was not his case, the detective wanted to see it solved. Yet he knew that girls like blonde would never volunteer to help the police once clear of the crime. If she did not try to identify the body right then, the blonde would most likely be nowhere to be found the following day, unless held as a prisoner which would not make her feel in a co-operative mood on her release.

"It's possible you could help us a great deal, my pet," he said gently.

Shaking her head, the blonde tried to turn away. "I don't want to look!" she gasped, the fear of death strong on her.

"I could tell you that it's not too bad," Calamity said gently, "but I won't. That gal there looks bad." She laid her hand on the blonde's arm, stopping the other girl backing away. "It'll not be easy. Only she might be somebody you know. A pard, a kid you like."

"I don—!" began the blonde.

"Listen to me, gal," Calamity interrupted, still quietly. "The man who killed her has to be stopped. The law don't know him. Maybe if they know who the girl is they could find out who she's been with tonight, and that'll take 'em to the man who killed her."

While Calamity had no idea of how a detective worked, she figured the method she outlined might be as good a way as any of finding the Strangler. Something in Calamity's voice and touch reached the blonde, sank through her fear of what she would see and give her courage.

"I—I'll take a look."

"Good gal!" Calamity answered.

"You—You come with me," the blonde went on.

There were many things Calamity would rather have done than taking another look at that hideous body, but she kept her hand on the girl's arm and led her to the side of the corpse. The elder patrolman had covered the face with his bandana handkerchief and the sight did not look too bad. While it still retained the slightly awe-inspiring look that death always gives a human frame, the main horror stayed concealed.

"I don't know the clothes," the blonde stated, after sucking in a deep breath and looking down. "They're the sort of thing a whole heap of us girls wear."

"Try the face, Sherry," Calamity said.

Throwing a look at Calamity, St. Andre bent down. His hand touched the bandana, then he looked at the pallid-faced blonde.

"Go ahead, Sherry," Calamity ordered. "She'll take it."

With a pull, St. Andre exposed the face. He saw the blonde girl stagger and Calamity support her. For a moment St. Andre thought the blonde would faint, but a street-walker's life made her tough and hard. She mastered her emotions and looked at the face.

"N—No!" she ejaculated in a strangled voice. "I—I don't know her."

St. Andre covered the face again and came to his feet. "You're sure, my pet, that you don't know her?"

"Can't tell, the way her face is, not for sure. But I don't think I know her," answered the blonde, turning away.

"You've done well," said St. Andre. "Go with the patrolman to the station house."

Suspicion sprang to the blonde's face. "Are you arresting me?"

"No. You'll be given a cup of coffee, and sent home. See she goes by a hack and charge it to me."

"Sure, lieutenant," replied the younger patrolman. "Come on, Sally. And you, mister."

Watching the patrolman assist the portly man and blonde away, Calamity gave a shrug. "It might've worked."

"Certainly, *cherie*," replied St. Andre. "Now I must take you to your friends and then go to make my report."

"Does that feller allus jump gals?" asked Calamity as she and St. Andre walked along the path and away from the body.

"He does, if it is the same man," the detective answered. "And the same method is used, so we believe it to be the work of one man."

"I sure wish he'd try it on me," remarked Calamity, her right hand stroking the butt of her Navy Colt.

Following the direction of the girl's gesture, St. Andre remembered his duty as a policeman bound by the rules, ordinances and laws of the city.

"You'd best let me keep your gunbelt, *cherié*," he said.

"Why?"

"It's against the law to wear a gun in New Orleans—and it will give me an excuse to come and see you in the morning."

"Land-sakes, do you need an excuse for that?" grinned Calamity, but she unbuckled the gunbelt and freed the pigging thong at the bottom of the holster. "See you get it back early in the morning, mind. I want to clean the gun."

"How early is early?"

"Come as early as you like—as long as it's not too early. Say by seven, I ought to be wake by then."

"*Seven?* And you say that's not too early!"

"Sure ain't, back west of the Big Muddy. Ain't it here?"

"I mostly get into my office by nine o'clock," smiled St. Andre, not bothering to mention the numberless occasions he had worked for eighteen to fortyeight hours at a stretch without going home, when involved in a difficult case.

"Shuckens," Calamity gasped. "You city folks sure have an easy life."

Then she thought of the girl lying back on the path and decided that not all city folks had an easy life.

However, Calamity had never been one to brood on or mope about the past. Knowing there to be no chance of nailing the Strangler's hide to the wall that night she forced the memory of the dead girl from her mind and prepared to buckle down to helping her friends enjoy their first evening in New Orleans.

On leaving the Park, Calamity found herself on Latour Street, an area apparently given over almost entirely to entertainment. Saloons, a theatre, a couple of cafés, billiard halls, a dancehall and gambling houses flanked a wide street, each giving out with its own blare of noise. In many ways the street made Calamity feel at home for the first time since reaching New Orleans. This was her part of town, tough, boisterous, rowdy, like the main drag of a trail end or mining city back in the West. Maybe the buildings looked a mite more permanent, being built of brownstone instead of adobe or timber, but the noises and sights reminded Calamity of the kind of places she knew and loved.

A couple of bouncers heaved a drunk from one saloon, sending him flying across the pavement to narrowly miss landing in one of the large horse-troughs that lined the street. Calamity ignored the drunk and studied the water-filled troughs.

"You sure have some thirsty hosses down here," she remarked.

"Not really," St. Andre answered. "We use them in case of fire. There's the *Cheval D'Or* now."

Coming to a halt before the largest, noisiest and most garish place on the street, Calamity looked it over with critical gaze. "Sure looks fancy. Say, are you coming in for a drink?"

"I have work to do, *cherie*," the detective replied, taking her hand in his, carrying to it his lips and kissing it.

"First time anybody ever kissed my *hand*," Calamity stated. "I sure hope that ain't the only place you fellers kiss."

"That," St. Andre told her with a grin. "Is something you will have to wait to discover. *Au revoir, cherie*."

"I don't know what it means," replied Calamity, "but the same to you, and many of them."

With that Miss Martha Jane Canary turned and entered the *Cheval D'Or*.

CHAPTER FIVE

Miss Canary At The Cheval D'Or.

DESPITE its fancy-sounding name, the bar-room of the *Cheval D'Or* appeared to be little or no different from the kind of place Calamity had looked upon in a whole heap of top-grade saloons throughout the West—with one exception. A small but rowdy band played music at the left side of the room and instead of performing on the stage, the saloon's show girls whirled and kicked their legs in the centre of the open space mostly left free for public dancing. The crowd lining the long bar, or seated at the various tables, lacked cowhands, buckskin-clad plainsmen, yet seemed to be little different from a Western saloon's customers in class or social standing; except for the folk at a couple of the tables on a small raised section close to the band. From the expensive clothing of the people on the dais, the fact that a couple of waiters showered attention on them full-time, and that champagne appeared to be the popular tipple served, Calamity figured them to belong to the richer class, the women of the party included.

Out West the 'good' women only very rarely entered a saloon, and ladies of the upper classes more than most stayed out of the places of entertainment. However, in New Orleans, and other Eastern cities, the desire to see how the other half relaxed and played became fashionable and brought parties of socialites to better class saloons to do so. Or course the socialites did not wish for too close contact with the revelling *hoi polloi*, so the obliging saloon-owners—always eager to satisfy the whims of well-paying customers—erected little segregated areas, often with their own private entrances, on which those who had the right background, and could afford it, might sit in comfort and see the fun. From their little raised sanctums, the ladies looked down on the herd enjoying its pleasures, watched shows which they regarded as being thrillingly naughty, and left with a sense of having improved their knowledge of life.

After a tolerant glance at the champagne-sipping upper-crust, Calamity forgot them and scanned the room for her friends. Sure enough the boys sat right where she figured they would be, at a table slap-bang on the edge of the dance floor and from where they could have an uninterrupted view of all that went on. Big, burly, white-haired Dobe Killem, her boss; lean, dark and tough looking Tophet Tombes, who acted as scout for the outfit; Chan Sing, the Chinese cook whose lapse from grace first gave Calamity acceptance to the outfit, and the other boys sat at ease, or as near at ease as their shop-bought, city-style clothes allowed, drinking whisky, squiring half-a-dozen or so saloongirls and ogling the waving black-stockings and exposed white thighs of the dancers.

Calamity gave the dancing girls a casual glance as she walked across the room to join her friends. With one exception, the girls dancing looked nor performed no better than she had seen in Western saloons. Mind you, that exception danced a heap more fancy than Calamity could ever remember seeing anywhere. The exception was a girl Calamity's size, with a slim, but shapely figure in an abbreviated white outfit that left her arms and legs bare and who wore—although Calamity did not know them as such—ballet slippers on her feet. Showing far greater grace, agility and style, the girl whirled, spun and kicked her well-muscled legs in a manner that made the others look heavy-footed as a bunch of miners at a hoe-down. Her red hair was taken back and pinned up at the rear in a severe fashion, and her rather pale but pretty face held an expression of rapture as if she enjoyed every minute of her dance.

A man, engrossed in watching the red-haired dancer's gyrations on the points of her ballet slippers, felt Calamity bump into him as she crossed the room, glanced at her, turned back to observe the dancer, then swivelled his head hurriedly to Calamity's departing figure. For a moment he stared after Calamity and rubbed his eyes. Deciding that he had better stop drinking, for he could not possibly have just seen a pretty girl dressed in men's clothes pass him—although, if it came to a point, the feller who bumped into him sure walked fancy —the man emptied his glass and left the room.

"Hey, Calam gal!" whooped Dobe Killem, eyeing his protege. "Come and get sat down, gal. Damn it, where've you been to?"

Suspicion gleamed in the saloon-girls' eyes as Calamity took the offered seat. Unlike the man Calamity bumped into, they knew for certain the newcomer was a woman and did not care for the idea of an outsider moving in on what showed signs of developing into a real humdinger of a party.

"They're my brothers, all of 'em," Calamity remarked, reading the signs as if the other girls bore them painted on their bosoms.

She reached for the drink Killem poured and went on in explanation. "My mother had a fast hoss."

Then she grinned at the men of the outfit, wondering if any of them would have dared walk into a Western saloon dressed in those derby hats, white shirts, fancy neck-ties and town suits. Dared might not be the correct word, for those freight-hauling sons feared nothing but their boss.

"Where've you been to, Calam gal?" asked Tophet Tombes, who looked about as at home in his new clothes as a skunk would in a church hall. "We waited, but you didn't show."

"I got lost," admitted Calamity. "Then I ran into a young feller as needed some help from four jaspers who was walking all over his face."

"Trust you!" said Killem dryly. "There's time I reckon we should ought to call you 'Trouble', not Calamity,"

"Calamity!" giggled one of the girls. "That's a funny name."

"Likely," answered Calamity, eyeing the girl with a warning stare. "Only don't push it, sister, or you'll wind up with a set of ingrowing buck-teeth."

Anger glowed in the other girl's eyes as she glanced towards her friends for moral and actual support. Slapping a big hand on the table top, Killem glared around at the girls, his bland face filled with innocent-featured malevolence.

"Now hold it there, all of you!" he ordered. "Just listen good to me, 'cause I don't aim to say it twice. Calam here's part of my outfit. You mean-mouth her and she'll whup the whole boiling of you, which same'll spoil all our evenings. So you be nice and friendly with her. You hear me?"

Within certain bounds the girls were taught to regard the customer as always being right. So far they had been treated royally by the free-spending freighters and did not wish to slaughter a goose which laid such frequent golden eggs. Several of their fellow workers eyed the party with calculating gaze and would not hesitate to move in should any of the men give a hint of displeasure. Anyway, that girl in pants did not look as if she aimed to give them any competition.

Although quite willing to take on the saloon-girls individually or as a bunch, Calamity felt no desire to spoil her friends' evening so early on. Catching the attention of a passing waiter, she ordered drinks for the table and it was taken as a peace-offering by the other girls.

After a few more leg kicks, the dancers came to a halt in a bent forward posture that flipped up their skirts, exposed frilly-edged, short-legged panties to view and caused Killem to make a hurried grab which hauled one of the over-stimulated freighters back into his seat. With a bound, the red-haired solo performer sailed into the air and landed on the floor in a split which brought a gasp from Calamity. However, the girl bounced to her feet without any sign of injury, dropped a graceful curtsy in reply to the applause which rose high, and skipped off the dancing space, between the tables and out through a door at the side of the bar.

"Where at's the gambling?" asked Calamity as the applause died down.

"Upstairs," answered one of the girls, hoping Calamity would go, for she did not feel entirely happy at having the red-head at the table.

"Hah!" grunted Tombes. "You don't want no gambling, Calam gal. It air plumb sinful—and awful chancy too."

Listening to Tombes' sombre tones, Calamity might have taken the warning seriously had she not known him so well. On the way down river a well-dressed stranger inveigled Tombes and Killem into a game of poker. While neither gave any sign of their wisdom, both possessed a very thorough knowledge of all branches of the gambling business. On the fourth deal Killem objected to the dealer extracting for the improvement of a hand the seven of clubs from the bottom of the deck. Killem was 'dressed' at the time, and possessed a fair amount of skill in the speedy production of a weapon—leaning to his sheathed bowie knife on that occasion—and so was in a good position to make his point. A series of gambling scandals had recently rocked the Mississippi, causing the riverboat captains to be less tolerant of crooked gamblers than had formerly been the case. So the errant well-dressed stranger found himself penniless and standing on a sand bar, leaving Killem's outfit to share out eighteen hundred dollars of his money. In addition to their pay from a freighting trip to Fort Sherrard in the Dakota Territory, an advance of wages and expense money donated by the Army, the gambler's contribution ensured that the Killem bunch were well fixed to enjoy their visit to New Orleans.

Calamity decided to forego her investigation of the *Cheval D'Or's* games of chance and sat back in her chair to see how the saloon compared with a Western place in the matter of entertainment. After a brief rest, the band struck up with a lively tune and the saloon-girls led most of the men out on to the open space. Never one for dancing, except when toting more 'Old Whipping

46

Post' whisky than at present, Tombes remained at the table with Calamity. Taking her opportunity, Calamity told the leathery-faced scout of the incident in the Park, also about the suggestion she made utilising his knowledge of the ancient and honourable art of reading sign Western style.

"We'll take us a look whether he likes it or not, comes morning," Tombes stated when Calamity remarked that the final decision must come from one Lieutenant Caiman who she had not yet met. "Damn it, gal, I'd sure like to lay hands on that there Strangler."

"And me," Calamity answered, then her eyes swung from Tombes to gaze across the room with all the intent eagerness of a starving Cheyenne seeing a herd of prime Great Plains buffalo. "Say, who's that big gal there?"

Following the direction of Calamity's gaze and jerked thumb, Tombes studied the woman who so aroused his companion's interest. Big was no exaggeration when describing the woman. She stood nearly six foot tall and weighed at least two hundred pounds. Blonde hair piled high on the woman's head and her fat, jovial face carried stage make-up. Expensive-looking jewellery glinted around her neck, wrists and fingers and she wore a trailing, stylish, though tight-fitting blue dress.

"That's Madam Darcel, gal, the owner," Tombes explained and gave a warning for he knew Calamity. "And you forget it. She'd call the great siezer in and have you jailed happen you tried to start a brawl with her."

A grin creased Calamity's face at Tombes' insight of her character. "She'd be a mite too heavy anyways."

"Likely," the scout replied. "Just look at ole Dobe dance."

"He's about as graceful as a salmon-fed grizzly just afore winter," the girl answered. "Happen that black-haired gal ain't lively on her feet, she'll sure wind up with tired toes comes the end of the dance."

Although Killem's partner limped slightly as she returned to the table, her face held a smile. A saloon-girl learned to look happy under most conditions, even after having her toes stepped on by a partner who stood six foot two and carried a fair amount of weight. A round of drinks, bought this time by Chan Sing, who had a plump, dark-haired girl hanging to his arm, made Killem's partner feel happier.

For a time the party went on, drinks flowed, jokes bounced around the table and most of the girls appeared to be overlooking Calamity's sex, regarding her more as a paying customer rather than a rival.

Turning to the girl at her side, Calamity asked, "Hey, where'd a gal go, happen she wants to go?"

"Huh?" asked the puzzled saloon-girl, then the light glowed. "Oh! I'll show you where we go."

Watching Calamity and the saloon-girl walk away from the table, Killem thought over what Calamity had told him about her rescue of St. Andre. A grin came to the big freighter's face. Dang that Calamity, never happy unless she was mixed up in some fuss or ruckus; but life would sure be dull without her around.

The dark-haired girl seated on Chan Sing's knee had only recently come to work at the *Cheval D'Or* after being employed in a rather lower-class establishment further along Latour Street. In her previous post, the management expected her to augment her salary by collecting donations from the customers—without their being aware, of the removal of their wealth—and reckoned the same rule applied at the *Cheval D'Or*. Deciding the Chinaman would offer her the best possibilities, she latched on to him and had been on the point of extracting his wallet when Calamity arrived. Since then, the girl had not found an opportunity to take the wallet, for Calamity had none of the distractions offered to her male friends. Naturally when augmenting her salary without the owner of the wallet's permission, one required privacy. So the girl left Chang Sing's wallet where it rightfully belonged. When Calamity left, the girl thought she might find a chance. Seconds ticked by with nothing to take the attention of the other occupants of the table. Then a couple of jugglers made their appearance and the men gave the performers their attention.

Still keeping one arm around Sing's neck, the girl slipped her other hand into his jacket and slid out the wallet. Being skilled at her trade, Sing did not feel his loss and the girl believed her action went unnoticed. So it did among the occupants of the table—however, somebody had seen the move, a person well capable of dealing with the matter.

The dark-haired girl's first warning that things had gone wrong came as she prepared to slip the wallet into the front of her dress. Suddenly a strong hand dug fingers deep into her hair, twisted hard, and hauled her from Sing's knee.

With a screech of pain, the girl twisted around, though still held by the hair, and faced her assailant. The wallet fell from the girl's fingers as she prepared to defend herself against Calamity who, having seen the attempted theft, came to the rescue of her unsuspecting friend. Before the girl could make a hostile move, Calamity swung her hand in a slap which caught the other across

48

the cheek. Showing superb timing, Calamity released the girl's hair and the force of the slap sent the pickpocket staggering backwards. After taking several steps to the rear, the girl tripped and landed hard, rump-first on the floor at the centre of the open area.

Spitting curses, the girl started to rise. She was slightly taller and heavier than Calamity and noted for being a tough dame when riled, which same she appeared to be at the moment. An air of eager anticipation ran through the room. On the upper-class dais all chatter stopped and every eye turned to the dance floor. Predatory interest crept on to the men's faces—although the upper-crust males were not alone in that—and the women pretended to be shocked at the sight, while waiting eagerly to see the next drama of raw, lower-strata life being played before them.

Even as the dark-haired girl prepared to throw herself at Calamity and take revenge for the slap, a deep voice boomed out a warning.

"All right, my children! Enough of this folly."

Calamity took her eyes from the other girl for long enough to glance quickly at the speaker. From the authoritative tones, she could have guessed it to be the mountainous Madam Darcel who spoke. The big woman bore down on the girls like a battleship in full sail. While in the girl's toilet Calamity had removed her jacket and carried it back. The tight fitting shirt and levis left no doubt as to her sex. She did not relax, but kept her attention on the other girl after her quick glance in Madam Darcel's direction.

Instead of throwing herself at Calamity, the dark-haired girl prepared to bluff her way out. Still crouched ready to spring, the girl turned a sullen, defiant face, that bore just a hint of fear, to her employer.

"What is all this about?" Madam Darcel went on.

"That dame grabbed me—!" began the saloon-girl.

"Sure I did," agreed Calamity and pointed to the wallet lying on the floor. "Do you let your gals lift wallets from the customers?"

Throwing a scared glance at the big shape of Madam Darcel, the saloon-girl gave a screech of, "It's a lie!" and threw herself at Calamity, hoping the ensuing fracas might silence the red-head and evade the issue of whether she stole the wallet. Only she did not reach Calamity with her talon-like, grabbing hands.

With a surge of her shoulder, Madam Darcel propelled her big right fist forward so it crashed on to the saloon-girl's jaw. The force of the blow sent the girl shooting off course even before Calamity could take steps to meet the attack and the pickpocket

49

landed on the dance floor, sliding almost to the bar before coming to a stop in a limp heap.

Calamity studied the blow with the air of a connoisseur. While it looked just a touch slow, that right hand packed such weight and power behind it that on landing would cause the recipient to think the roof had fallen in on her—when she found herself capable of thinking again, that is.

Glancing at Chan Sing as the Chinaman stood feeling in his jacket's breast pocket, Madam Darcel knew she must prove that she had no knowledge of the theft and did not condone stealing. Nothing could lose the carriage-trade for a saloon quicker than letting thieves rob the customers, or by the place gaining a reputation for dishonesty. The feeling of the girl had been the first stage, now Madam Darcel aimed to cement the knowledge of her innocence more firmly in the minds of her customers.

"Is that your wallet, John?" she asked, pointing to the floor.

"By clacky, it is!" Sing yelped, bending and picking the wallet up.

"I don't allow pickpockets in here," the saloonkeeper went on in a loud and carrying voice, then looked towards the silent bar. "Eddy, see this gent gets anything he orders for the rest of the evening, on the house."

"Sure will, Madam," answered the head bartender, catching his cue and following it up like a professional actor.

A low rumble of approval ran through the room which had fallen silent and expectant at the start of the trouble. Madam Darcel knew her actions had cleared her and figured the money it would cost to keep the Chinaman supplied for the rest of the evening to be a cheap price when her house's reputation had been at stake.

Then Madam turned her attention to Calamity. The saloonkeeper's first thought was that Calamity followed the profession of street-walker and dressed in men's clothing to gain entrance to the *Cheval D'Or* in search of customers. On studying the girl more closely, Madam Darcel revised her opinion. No streetwalker, working at night and following an unhealthy trade, ever carried such a tan as did the red head. Possibly the girl was a camp-follower of the Killem outfit, brought down to New Orleans to save hiring local talent. Whoever the red-head might be, Madam Darcel did not intend to let her stay in the saloon.

"All right, girlie," the saloonkeeper said. I don't like trouble-makers in here—."

"So who's making trouble?" Calamity replied. "I've got good

money in my pocket, I'm sober, white and old enough to do a hard day's work—and I'm staying right here."

Madam Darcel read the challenge in Calamity's eyes and an idea crept into the saloonkeeper's head, showing her a chance of some added entertainment to spice up her customers. With a clientele that liked its fun gamey, unrefined and fullblooded, a fight between two girls had a salutary effect on the spirits and also the sales over the bar. Unless Madam missed her guess, that red-headed girl could handle her end in such an affair. So there only remained the problem of selecting a suitable opponent and that was easily arranged.

Not that Madam Darcel intended to be the one who took on Calamity. The days had long passed when the saloon-keeper could trim down a tough young girl who knew the art of female self defence. While Madam did not doubt that she could lay Calamity low with one blow, there remained the problem of making contact with her fist. From the look of her, the red-head would not be fool enough to stand still to be hit, nor unprepared as the pickpocket had been.

"Are you going quietly?" Madam asked.

Throwing back her head and standing with hands on her hips, but ready to dodge a blow and attack, Calamity roared with laughter and replied, "I never go anyplace quietly."

"And what if I have you thrown out?" said the saloon-keeper.

"Are you fixing to do it yourself?" Calamity countered.

"Not I. But one of my girls will."

"Happen you got a gal who reckons she can do it, bring her on and let her get to throwing."

In her untrained way Calamity was every bit as much a show-man as Madam Darcel. Both spoke loudly and their words carried around the silent room. Calamity glanced around her, studying the girls. While some of them looked hefty, rough and capable, none struck Calamity as being anything special. Anyways, it ought to be right interesting to see how a big-city girl stacked up in comparison with some of the tough dames Calamity tangled with out West.

Madam Darcel hid her delight as Calamity accepted the challenge. Turning, the saloonkeeper called, "Hey one of you, ask Jacqueline to come in here."

Grinning broadly, Calamity walked towards her friends' table and wondered who Jacqueline might be.

CHAPTER SIX

Miss Canary Studies Savate

"Good ole Calam!" Tophet said as he listened to the girl accept Madam Darcel's challenge. "Trust her to fix it so to we could win us some money."

"She'll take that city gal like Grant took Richmond," another of the outfit went on, remembering other times when Calamity tied into a saloongirl in a brawl.

Despite his men's words of confidence, Killem did not feel so sure. Not that he lacked faith in Calamity, but he knew Madam Darcel of old. If Madam aimed to start a brawl between Calamity and one of the saloon's girls, the big woman figured to have a better than fair chance of her representative winning.

"Hold hard there, Madam," he called. "Reckon you don't know who my gal is."

"I don't care if she is Calamity Jane—," Madam began.

"That's just who she is."

Talk welled up at Killem's words, eager and excited chatter, for the name of Calamity Jane had come down river ahead of her. Yet few of the occupants of the room really believed the girl to be *the* Calamity Jane. Certainly Madam Darcel did not believe Killem and thought the freighter merely wanted to save his girl from a thrashing. Madam did not intend to state her doubts. One glance around—taken with her considerable knowledge of human nature—told her the crowd wanted the red-head to be Calamity Jane; much as hold-up victims always wanted to believe some famous outlaw band robbed them. So Madam went along with the suggestion as if she took Killem to be speaking the gospel truth.

"I have heard of her, Dobe. But I also believe Jacqueline can throw even the famous Calamity Jane out."

"I've got fifty dollars that says she can't!" whooped Tombes.

"You-all wanting to bet your gal can do it, Madam?" went on another man.

"If you wish," Madam replied.

"We wish!" whooped the freighters. "Lordy lord, how we wish."

With that the Killem outfit produced its money and Madam signalled one of her men to accept the wagers. Apart from the freighters, there was little betting so far, the other customers wanting to compare the fighters before risking wealth on one or the other.

Calamity ignored the betting as she walked to Killem's table. The girl who had escorted Calamity to the toilets handed back the jacket she took on observing the attempted theft of Sing's wallet.

"Thanks, Maisie," grinned Calamity. "Say, who is this Jacqueline."

"You've seen her once tonight," replied the girl.

While waiting for the mysterious Jacqueline to put in an appearance, Calamity prepared for the fight. Taking off her kepi, she laid it on her jacket. Next she removed her bandana, rolling it into a ball and dropping it into the crown of her kepi. Calamity always removed her bandana, given time to do so, since a girl almost choked her insensible in an early fight by grabbing hold and twisting at the neck cloth.

"What's eating you, Dobe?" she asked, glancing at Killem's face and reading his concern where most folks could have seen nothing at all.

"Was just wondering what sort of gal Madam's got in mind," the freighter answered. "Maybe this Jacqueline's one of them gal prize-fighters like was with that wagon train that went to Fort Sherrard with us last trip."

"Shucks," grinned Calamity. "I whipped that one, and she claimed to be the champeen gal fist-fighter of the world. Don't reckon this Jacqueline gal'll be any tougher'n that one." *

"Here she comes now," said one of the saloon-girls, pointing across the room.

Turning from the table, Calamity glanced in the direction indicated by the other girl. Killem and his men also looked and the big freighter felt puzzled by what he saw. However, Killem's men, possibly because they did not share his ability to carry a load of liquor, nudged each other and exchanged knowing nods or winks. The men, with the exception of Killem, agreed that if the girl who approached was *the* Jacqueline, Calamity should lick her so easy that the bets would be as safe as finding money in the street.

For a moment Calamity studied her proposed opponent, then swung to face Madam Darcel, wondering if the other woman made a joke.

*Told in TROUBLE TRAIL by J. T. Edson. Wagon Wheel Western.

"Is this *her*?" asked Calamity.

"It is."

"Hell, you can't expect her to tangle with me."

"Why should she not?" inquired Madam Darcel.

"That skinny kid won't have a chance," replied Calamity.

Yet she was no fool and, like Killem, knew that Madam Darcel would be most unlikely to act as a philanthropist by taking bets when, on the face of it, the saloon's representative had no hope of winning. With that thought in mind Calamity had been expecting to find herself matched by a big, buxom, tough girl. Instead she found herself faced by the slim, red-headed girl who performed as a solo dancer. The red-head still wore the same outfit as when dancing, including her ballet slippers—a point Calamity overlooked.

Annoyance glowed in Jacqueline's eyes at Calamity's words. In an age when the ideal female tended to be buxom, Jacqueline was conscious of her slim though shapely build and did not care for Calamity's reference to her as 'that skinny kid'.

"Are you afraid?" hissed Jacqueline.

"I sure am," agreed Calamity. "Afraid I'll hurt you real bad."

"Let *me* worry about that!"

Frowning a little, Calamity gave the other girl a close study. One thing was for sure, that scanty costume prevented any chance of Jacqueline being a young man dressed as a girl, a possibility that had occured to Calamity. Nor did it allow Jacqueline to carry concealed weapons; not that Calamity figured Madam would chance such a thing. While slim, Jacqueline's hips were well developed, her long legs showed a good set of thigh and calf muscles. Yet she did not have the weight to take on a girl Calamity's build. Calamity enjoyed a fight, but she had never been a bully or wished to take an unfair advantage of anybody.

"Hell, Madam!" Calamity objected. "This's not fair on your gal."

"She seems content to take her chances," Madam answered. "I'll tell you what I'll do. I'll give the winner five dollars for every minute the fight lasts."

Calamity shrugged, the financial side of the affair meant little or nothing to her. Having leaned over backwards to save Jacqueline from a licking, Calamity reckoned she had done enough. However, even with the prospect of earning five dollars for every minute she kept the other girl standing, Calamity decided to make a rapid end to the affair. Once she sent Jacqueline tearfully on her way, Calamity reckoned she would see how tough Madam Darcel could act and teach the big blonde not to send her employees to take a licking when they did not have a chance.

"It's her that gets the lumps," Calamity remarked.

"Start as soon as you like," replied Madam Darcel and went to join Killem.

Calamity threw a glance at the slim girl, then grinned at Dobe Killem.

"This won't take long, Dobe," she said. "I'll be right back."

And Calamity spoke truer words than she imagined.

With fists clenched ready, she moved towards the Creole girl and wondered how the other aimed to make her fight. Calamity found out soon enough. Watching Jacqueline's eyes and hands, Calamity overlooked the other girl's feet. Suddenly and without any warning Jacqueline kicked upwards her long right leg driving into the air to catch Calamity under the jaw. Taken by surprise both by the unexpected tactic and the power of the kick, Calamity sprawled backwards and landed on her rump at Killem's feet.

"That fat old bitch!" Killem growled, looking at the smiling saloonkeeper. "She's thrown Calam against a *savate* fighter."

Calamity did not hear the words. Forcing herself to her feet, she charged into the attack once more. Much to Calamity's surprise, Jacqueline moved forward to meet her as if ready for a hair-yanking tangle. Only at the last moment the slim girl side-stepped, leaned out of Calamity's reach and delivered a horizontal sidekick, her toe catching Calamity in the stomach. Giving a croaking gasp, Calamity grabbed at her middle and doubled over as she staggered by Jacqueline. Pivoting gracefully, the slim girl placed her foot against Calamity's tight-stretched pants seat and shoved hard. Calamity shot forward to crash into the bar. Grabbing hold of the polished mahogany, she hung there while she tried to catch her wind and clear the fog from her head.

Just as Calamity regained control of herself and turned, Jacqueline came gliding in. Halting before Calamity, the dancer rose on to the point of her right slipper and executed an almost perfect *fouette en tournant* by whipping her raised left leg from bent at the knee to extended waist high so as to spin her entire body around. Four times she spun in a circle, gaining momentum. Then the toe of her left foot crashed into the side of Calamity's jaw. The impact sprawled Calamity sideways even as she prepared to make an attack of her own.

While Jacqueline did not particularly care for fighting, she meant to keep the brawl going for a time. Nor did Calamity's insulting references to the dancer's slim build entirely account for the decision.

Ever since the day Jacqueline sneaked into a theatre and saw a ballet dancer perform, she longed to learn the secrets of the graceful art. Being from a very poor family, she had no chance of taking formal lessons. She took every opportunity to see other dancers and practiced the steps she saw, learning the various positions and manoeuvres even without knowing their names. Two years back Madam Darcel had seen the girl dancing on a street corner and recognised her talent, so hired Jacqueline to perform at the *Cheval D'Or*. From then Jacqueline improved tremendously, yet lacked formal instruction to bring out her talented greatness.

Learning *savate* came as a precaution against the petty jealousies of the saloongirls and Jacqueline found it a useful way of augmenting her earnings. On the dozen or so occasions when she fought another before the customers, Madam Darcel gave her a bonus and when the money went to swell her slowly-growing savings ready for the day when she could afford to take lessons at a ballet school.

So while another kick might have finished Calamity off, the slim girl did not land it. Instead she slapped Calamity's face with each hand, rocking the red-head from side to side. Pain partially cleared Calamity's spinning head and she thrust herself from the bar, throwing a punch which ought to have flattened her at Jacqueline's head. The blow missed as Jacqueline whirled aside and Calamity stumbled forward. Twisting around, Jacqueline delivered a slap to Calamity's rump as the red-head went by.

Then began the most humiliating five minutes of Calamity's life. Laughter and jeers rang out from the watching crowd as Calamity tried to catch up with, or lay hands on the other girl. Gracefully, and demonstrating her dancing skill to perfection, Jacqueline avoided Calamity's rushes and wild blows. Sometimes she would whirl around Calamity so fast that the other girl did not know whether she came or went, then stop in front and slap her face, or halt behind and either push her, deliver a whack to her rump or push her. No matter which way Calamity turned, she could not catch the other girl. It seemed that Jacqueline could deliver a kick from any angle, and when one landed, whether with toe, ball, heel, outside or inside edge of the foot, it hurt.

Blood trickled from Calamity's mouth, mingling with the sweat and tears on her face. Pain, rage and humiliation filled the Western girl at the thought of taking such a licking from a city dweller. It forced Calamity to stay up and take more of those wicked horizontal and vertical kicks while trying to lay hands on Jacqueline and fight barroom style.

Only once did Calamity try to take Jacqueline by the slim girl's own method of fighting. Jerking back her leg, Calamity launched it in a kick. Jacqueline watched the other girl's right foot lash at her legs and countered the kick by coming into the *chasse croise* position so Calamity missed her. Then as Calamity's leg went by, Jacqueline brought the side of her right foot in a circular kick against the Western girl's calf. Caught off balance, Calamity staggered and Jacqueline followed up with a kick to the pants seat which sprawled her on to the floor. Skipping forward Jacqueline gripped Calamity by the hair and waist belt, hauling her up. Before Calamity recovered enough to defend herself, Jacqueline delivered a high kick to her face and started her nose bleeding.

"Damn it hell, Madam!" Killem growled, watching Jacqueline spin away from Calamity. "She's making a fool of my gal."

"I thought your girl feared hurting Jacqueline," replied the saloonkeeper. "If your friends are willing to concede their bets, I will signal Jacqueline to make an end of this farce."

"You'd best do that afore these boys of mine get riled and take your place apart at the seams."

Before Madam could decide whether to make the signal, Jacqueline prepared to bring the affair to an end. Never had she seen a girl take so much punishment. On other occasions, her opponent took at the most half-a-dozen kicks then either collapsed and refused to rise, or ran sobbing from the room. Yet the Western girl kept coming back for more, trying to lay hands on her tormentor. Jacqueline guessed that even now it would go rough on her if Calamity did once get to grips. So she decided to make an end to the affair. The kick to the face had sent Calamity stumbling into the bar where she hung on for support, her legs looking like heat-buckled candles. From her opponent's general appearance, Jacqueline decided that honour had been satisfied and it would be a long time before the red-headed Westerner insulted another slimly-built girl,

Once more Jacqueline went into her *fouette en tournant*, building up her momentum to deliver a *coup de grace*. In this she made a bad error in judgement. No other girl Jacqueline had tangled with, even those trained in *savate*—after seeing the interest Jacqueline attracted for the *Cheval D'Or*, other saloonkeepers sought out challengers to meet her—faced her with such determination. So Jacqueline reckoned that one more kick ought to stretch Calamity out on the floor, limp and unable to prevent the slim girl gripping her by the feet and hauling her from the room. Once outside, Madam's bouncers would take over, carrying the beaten Western girl to the rear of the saloon, call in a doctor if needed, and revive her. Then Madam Darcel would most likely give the beaten girl a few dollars to recompense her.

Jacqueline's thoughts came to an abrupt and painful end right then. Even as the slim girl spun around on her right slipper's point, Calamity forced herself from the bar and swung a fist around in a looping blow. Taken by surprise, unable to stop her spinning body, Jacqueline swung straight into the punch which stopped her dead in her tracks. Like a flash Calamity struck again, ripping her other hand up as Killem taught her, catching Jacqueline under the jaw and sending her reeling backwards to crash on to the floor.

Turning to the bar, Calamity caught its top and steadied herself, looking at the bartender. "Gi—Gimme—a—drink!" she gasped.

Obligingly the man poured out four fingers of whisky and passed the glass to Calamity. Tilting the liquor down her throat in a single gulp, Calamity glanced into the bar mirror. Much to her surprise, Calamity saw the other girl struggling to rise. Setting down her glass, Calamity turned and crossed the floor. She bent down and dug her fingers into Jacqueline's hair, ruining its coiffure for the first time in the fight. With a heave Calamity raised the other girl to her feet, swung her and sent her reeling across the room into the bar.

At that moment Jacqueline forgot *savate*. Dazed and hurt by the blows, the slim girl became a woman pure and simple. Suddenly she thrust herself from the bar and met Calamity's advance, her fingers digging into the other's red curls. Calamity replied in a like manner and the girls spun around in a tight circle, clinging to hair, lashing out wild kicks at each other's legs and forgetting more scientific fighting. More by accident than design, Jacqueline hooked a leg behind Calamity and brought them both crashing to the floor.

Despite her earlier rough handling, Calamity buckled down to a real old-fashioned, roll-around, hand-scalping bar-room brawl with all her usual gusto. Nor did Jacqueline fail to do her share. Out-weighed by Calamity, not as strong as the Western girl, Jacqueline's wiry body had strength to spare and she gave almost as good as she took. Over and over the girls rolled, fists and legs flying, gasps, squeaks, squeals and yelps rising from them.

During the earlier stages of the fight, the crowd, though rowdy, stayed either seated or standing well clear and watched the girls. However, once Calamity and Jacqueline went to the floor, those of the audience at the rear found they could no longer see the sport. So they moved forward and in doing so impeded the view of other customers, causing those impeded to also leave their seats until the dance floor and fighting girls were surrounded by an almost solid wall of wildly excited, yelling people.

At that point of the proceedings, Madame Darcel began to feel like the man who caught a tiger by the tail and could not let go. Without ever having heard of or understanding the words, Madam Darcel possessed a very thorough knowledge of crowd psychology; and knew that when excitement reached a certain pitch any slight thing might start a full-scale riot. Yet she knew that if she attempted to separate the wildly fighting girls, the crowd would object violently; not only because their fun was being spoiled, but because quite a number of the customers had bet heavily on the result of the fight. So she stayed out of the affair, leaving the girls to settle their dispute and keeping a weather eye open for potential spreaders of the conflict.

Coming to their feet, the girls stood facing each other, panting and glaring.

"H—Had enough?" asked Calamity.

Jacqueline did not answer in words. Instead she flung herself at Calamity again. Normally she would have used *savate*, just as Calamity's self defence ought to have been with her fists, but exhaustion caused the girls to forget such tactics and fight on woman-style. Reeling across the room, clinging one-handed to hair, the other slapping, punching and grabbing, the girls caused a hurried scattering among the crowd, all of whom knew better than come between a pair of furiously fighting females. Still locked with each other, the girls hit against the upper-classes dais. Pinned against the raised stand, Calamity wriggled back upon it. Jacqueline followed her under the protective rail and the girls came to their feet. One of the waiters, outraged at the invasion of the carriage-trade's privacy, moved forward to either request or force the girls to leave. In this the man showed mighty poor judgement and sense. Coming between a pair of bobcats scrapping over a mate would have been on a par with getting between Calamity and Jacqueline at such a moment. The girls turned on the waiter—a man chosen more for his knowledge of upper-class requirements than those qualities necessary when dealing with the rougher elements of the saloon's clientele—and worked him over. To the accompaniment of yells and laughter from the onlookers, fingers tore at the waiter's hair and clothes, feet hacked at his shins and a set of teeth at one point clamped on his ear, giving him a painful nip. Then the girls shoved the waiter aside and sent him sprawling over the protective railing into the crowd beyond.

Having dealt with the interruption, Calamity and Jacqueline turned their attention to each other. The occupants of the dais, three men and two young women at one table and a couple of young bloods squiring a beautiful girl at another, all came to their feet and looked on. None of them knew if the fight be merely something arranged by Madam Darcel for their entertainment, or cared. All showed the same excited stimulation as did the *hoi polloi* beyond the barrier at the wild fight they were seeing.

A shove from Jacqueline sent Calamity reeling to fall on the table of the larger party. One of the women, a beautiful, if rather sullen-looking blonde in an expensive satin dress, did something she thought to be wildly amusing. Stepping forward, she took an open champagne bottle from its ice bucket and emptied its contents over Calamity's head, shrieking with laughter as the fizzing liquid ran over the red-head's face.

Across the room Dobe Killem watched and gave a groan, for he knew his Calamity very well. That upper-crust girl was due very shortly to learn the error of her ways, or Killem would be most surprised.

CHAPTER SEVEN

Miss Canary's Soothing Syrup

WHILE Calamity had tasted champagne on a couple of occasions, and decided that as a drink it would never replace whisky, she objected to having it poured over her head even as a joke. Although she felt no resentment or antipathy towards folks more fortunate than herself in the possession of the world's goods, Calamity failed to subscribe to Madam Darcel's view that the upper-class customers must be treated as sacred and permitted to take liberties.

Shooting out a hand as she forced herself from the table, Calamity caught the blonde in the same manner that she grabbed the pickpocket earlier. With a heave, Calamity plucked the blonde from the bosom of her friends and jerked her forward. Letting out a startled squeal, the blonde dropped the champagne bottle as Calamity swung her around and gave her a push which sent her staggering. Striking the protective rail, the blonde's weight broke it and she fell into the arms of the laughing, jeering crowd. Set on her feet, the blonde swung around. A female face came before the blonde, so wild with rage and mortification, she swung a resounding slap at it. Already over-excited by the fight she had seen, the blonde's victim forgot that the carriage-trade was to be treated as sacrosant, and grabbed hair. With a screech of pain, the blonde dropped lady-like dignity and a second hand-scalping battle began. Not a bad one either, considering that blonde's upbringing and education sadly lacked in such matters.

On the dais, the blonde's female friend gave a yell as she saw the assault. Excitement and stimulation at watching the pagan sight of two girls fighting led the second into folly. Grabbing up a bottle by its neck, the girl, a brunette of some charm and attraction, started around the table, meaning to attack Calamity and avenge her friend.

Also moving in to the attack, Jacqueline caught a movement from the corner of her eye. Turning her head to check more thoroughly on what attracted her attention, she saw the bottle-armed brunette approaching. The sight recalled Jacqueline's *savate* training once more. Like a flash Jacqueline rotated her

61

body half a turn to the left, leant forward from the waist, drew up her right leg under her, pointed its toe at the charging brunette and kicked upwards. She caught the brunette under the jaw with the bottom of her foot, landing an almost classic *savate* horizontal high-kick. The force of the impact shot the brunette to one side. Dropping the bottle, she staggered full into the female member of the other party. The two girls had long been social rivals, which did not help towards a peaceful settlement when the brunette collided with the other and grabbed wildly, tearing the left shoulder of a new, latest style dress. Giving an angry squeal, the third girl, a beautiful and shapely red-head, let fly with a slap to the jaw already sore from Jacqueline's kick, setting the brunette back on her heels, and following it up with a grab for the hair which started yet a third battle.

Like the ripples stirred up by a stone thrown into a pond, the fight spread across the room. Excitement had reached the pitch Madam Darcel feared it might as the blonde socialite's fight with the saloongirl started other battles. On the dais one of the brunette's escorts sprang forward meaning to grab hold of the redhead. That brought the second party's male members into the fray and a rousing battle began upon the upper-crust's country.

"Looks like you've got trouble on your hands, Madam," drawled Killem, shoving aside Tophet Tombes as the scout tied into a burly city man who had earlier made some insulting remarks about Calamity's fighting prowess.

"Help me, Dobe!" replied the big woman, swinging a blow which felled a riverboat man before he could tangle with Chan Sing. "Head across that way and make for the door. You'll see a policeman on the street. Yell and tell him there's a riot in here. He'll know what to do. I'll try to make it the other way."

"You're on," grinned the freighter, taking up Calamity's clothing and slouching off on his rescue mission, felling anyone who tried to block his path.

Madam Darcel paused long enough to order her employees, such as were not already involved in the fighting, to protect the merchandise and more expensive fixtures. All around her fights broke out, a wild brawl where one tied into the nearest person and, other than showing a desire to join the fun, meant nothing by doing so. Cursing as tables overturned, chairs shattered and glassware broke, Madam Darcel tried to force her way through to the door. The fighting blonde and saloongirl blocked her way and she threw aside her rules for the correct treatment of the carriagetrade. Shooting out her hands, Madam grabbed each dishevelled girl by the neck, cracked their heads together hard and dropped their limp bodies to the floor. Then she backhanded a man aside and tried to get through the crush so as to be able to summon aid in ending the riot that threatened to wreck her room.

On the dais Calamity and Jacqueline joined battle again after dealing with the socialite interference. Diving forward, Calamity tackled Jacqueline around the waist and rammed the girl backwards. Locked together they crashed into the protective rail, shattered it and fell to the floor. However, Jacqueline was tiring, for she had performed her speciality act twice that evening. On the other hand Calamity's champagne-dousing had partially revived her and her extra weight wore on her opponent. For all that, the fight went on until they reached the wall by the main entrance. Shoving Jacqueline back to the wall, Calamity uncorked a round-house swing as the slim girl bounced off. Even as Jacqueline drew back a foot for a kick, she walked full into the punch. Give Calamity her due, she knew how to throw a fist. The blow carried Calamity's weight behind it and Jacqueline helped by walking into it. Back snapped the slim girl's head, her body crashed into the wall, her eyes glazed over and she sank slowly to the floor.

A chair whizzed by Calamity's head and crashed into the wall. Whirling, she stood as well as she could and stared at the brawl taking place before her. More, she saw Madam Darcel emerge from the crowd and formed the wrong idea of the saloonkeeper's motives.

To be fair, Madam Darcel's only intention was to reach the door and summon assistance before the riot went too far. However, she had neither the time nor the inclination to explain such things to Calamity at that moment. Instead she clenched her right hand, throwing it at Calamity's head. Happen Calamity had been her usual self instead of all tuckered out from as rough a brawl as she could remember, she could have easily avoided the blow. In her present exhausted state, Calamity moved too slowly and the fist crashed into the side of the girl's jaw, depositing her in a heap on top of Jacqueline. As blackness came down on her, Calamity wondered if the roof *had* caved in upon her head.

Pain throbbed through Calamity as consciousness returned to her. The roots of her hair felt as if on fire; her left eye throbbed and she reckoned it would have a marvellous mouse under it come morning; while her nose felt twice its usual size, she knew that to be a normal reaction under the circumstances; for the rest, her bruised, grazed body seemed to send stabs of agony from different points in rotation. Slowly she raised a hand to her jaw and groaned. Then she realised that her clothing appeared to be soaking wet.

Making an effort, Calamity opened her eyes. The first thing to meet her gaze was the sight of Killem and that fancy city lawman, St. Andre looking down in some concern at her.

"Are you all right, *cherie?*" asked St. Andre worriedly.

"Only time I felt better was when a hoss throwed me, walked over me, then tossed me into a bobcat's nest with its hooves," Calamity answered, after manipulating her jaw gently to make sure it still worked. "Where was you when I needed you, Sherry?"

"I came as soon as I heard, my pet. But I found you sleeping like a babe."

Before Calamity could think up a suitable reply, she glanced at the room and what she saw drove the thought from her mind. Everybody and everything appeared to be soaking and no longer showed any inclination to fight. Firemen coiled a couple of hoses nearby and Calamity saw why Latour Street maintained the extra large horse-troughs.

"That's how we end trouble down here, *cherie,*" St. Andre went on, following her line of thought. "When this kind of trouble starts, the police bring a fire engine along to damp the fighters' ardour."

"Then why in hell didn't they come in sooner and damp that skinny gal's ardour, whatever it might be. That gal'd got ardour to spare and sure needed it damping down a mite—Hey, where is she?"

Trying to rise, Calamity looked around her. She found Jacqueline to be still out cold, but a couple of saloongirls tended to the slim dancer. Across the room Madam Darcel went among the crowd, holding out a derby hat into which men dropped cash donations to help pay for the damage caused by their fighting. Forcing herself to her feet, Calamity shook off Killem and St. Andre's restraining hands, then walked slowly across the room towards the saloonkeeper.

"Come on boys!" Madam called, offering the hat to the redheaded socialite's friends as they escorted the girl towards the door. "You've had your fun and I've got damage to pay for."

"Talking about money, Madam," Calamity put in.

Slowly Madam Darcel turned and looked Calamity over. "Were we talking about money?"

"If we weren't, we sure as hell soon will be. I figure me 'n' and the gal went at it for ten minutes. At five dollars a minute, according to a half-smart lil Western gal like me, that's fifty dollars you owe me."

Before any more could be said, the red-haired socialite whispered to her escort and took some money which he removed from his billfold. All the trio bore marks of the battle, the men in soaking, rumpled suits, minus neck-ties and with shirts torn; the girl sporting a black eye, swollen lip and a couple of scratches, while her cloak did not entirely cover the fact that her dress had taken some hard pulling and needed holding up with one hand. However, despite all that the girl gave a friendly smile as she came towards Calamity and held out the money.

"I hope you won't be offended at this gift," she told Calamity. "For years I wished to get my fingers into that cat Celestine's hair, and you did what I have long wished to do to Paulette."

"Thanks," answered Calamity, accepting the five ten dollar bills. "You did all right yourself once you got started."

"I must admit it was fun while it lasted, though I don't know what Papa will say when he hears."

With that the red-head joined her two male friends and after each man slipped a donation into Madam's hat, they left the room. Calamity watched them go, a grin on her face. It looked like those fancy-dress dude Frenchmen were some hecats when a fuss started; but she already knew that from her earlier meeting with St. Andre. Anyways, business came first and Madame Darcel still had not made good her promise of remuneration.

"Hey, Madam," Calamity said, turning her attention to the saloonkeeper once more. "How's about the money? I'd hate like hell to have to come in tomorrow night and ask for it again."

"I believe you would come again tomorrow," said Madam Darcel. "Just as I now believe you *are* Calamity Jane."

"I never doubted *that* for a teensey minute," grinned Calamity and held out her right hand. "Fifty dollars, I'll take it in tens."

With a broad smile, Madam Darcel counted off fifty dollars and handed it to Calamity. "I'm almost tempted not to pay. Your fight was a good attraction. But I don't believe the police would go for two riots in a week at my place."

"I'll mind that, if I come tonight. Anyways, you couldn't get another gal as tough as that skinny kid. See you up the trail, Madam."

Crossing the floor. Calamity made straight for where Jacqueline had been helped to her feet by the other girls. Seeing her opponent approaching, Jacqueline shook the other girls' hands from her and prepared to defend herself. St. Andre also

65

expected trouble and started to move forward. A huge hand closed on his arm and held him back despite the fact that the detective was no weakling himself.

"Don't bother, friend," said Killem's gentle voice. "Calam's not fixing to cause fuss."

"Hey there, easy," Calamity stated, holding her hands hip high and spread with open palms towards Jacqueline in the Indian peace sign. "We raised enough lumps on each other for one night. How'd you feel, sk—gal. Which same, I reckon you feel just about as sick and sore as I do."

"I'm all right."

"Yeah, I tell lies too," grinned Calamity and counted out fifty dollars.

"What's that for?" Jacqueline asked, staring at the money.

"Your cut. I sure as hell couldn't have won it without you."

"But—but—."

Letting out a mock serious sigh, Calamity said, "Don't tell me I've got to lick you again afore you'll take it."

"Are you serious?" gasped Jacqueline.

"I'm allus serious where money's concerned, sk—gal."

Wondering what kind of girl she had met, Jacqueline accepted the money. She tried to express her thanks, but Calamity laughed them off. At that moment Madam Darcel arrived and gave her girls orders to take Jacqueline to their quarters so a doctor could examine her injuries.

"And you, Calamity, he'll examine you also," the saloon-keeper went on.

"Shucks no. I've broken nothing," Calamity scoffed. "I'll just rub on some of my soothing syrup and I'll be fit as frog's hair comes morning." Then, knowing something of saloonkeepers' ways when dealing with their employees, she decided to hand out a warning. "I shared the money with sk—Jacqueline here. It's for *her*, Madam, understand?"

Madam Darcel understood all too well. Strangely she felt no resentment at Calamity's words or what they implied, but took them as the girl meant, as an interest in seeing Jacqueline received fair dealing.

"You'd best be getting home, Calam," Killem remarked. "Don't want you all stove up with a chill comes morning."

"Or me," agreed Calamity, then studied her employer closely. "Hey, how come you aren't wet?"

"When the fuss started, I got out and yelled for help."

"Spoilsport!" sniffed Calamity.

"Anyways, I saved your coat, hat and bandana from a wetting."

"Thanks too much! Why didn't you leave them and save me?"

"Shucks, gal, I saw you enjoying yourself with that Jacqueline gal and didn't want to bill in."

"One of these days, Dobe Killem," Calamity began, "I'm going to tell everybody your name's—well what we both know it is."

Killem suffered under the given name of Cecil, a fact Calamity alone of his outfit knew. When her boss grew obstreperous, she used the knowledge to bring him back into line.

"And what is Dobe's name?" asked an interested Madam Darcel.

Thrusting the coat, hat and bandana into Calamity's hands, Killem gave a warning growl. "You tell her and I'll peel your hide. Get off home and leave me to round up the rest of the boys."

"May I escort Calamity home, sir?" asked St. Andre stepping forward and remembering the girl's statement that her boss and fellow workers treated her like their sister.

However, he need not have taken the trouble. With a grin, Killem nodded to the girl. "Try asking her, friend. She'll damned soon say 'yes' or 'no'."

"Let's go, Sherry," Calamity said.

"Tuck your shirt in first and put on your coat, preferably with the buttons fastened," replied St. Andre.

For the first time Calamity realised that at some point in the fight every button had been torn from the front of her shirt and its flap hung outside her pants. Showing no embarrassment, she made the necessary adjustments to her dress and finally pulled on her coat. Having worn a man's vest under the shirt, Calamity knew she showed little that might raise eyebrows in polite society. Winking at Killem, she accepted St. Andre's arm and walked from the *Cheval D'Or*.

At the end of Latour Street, St. Andre hailed a passing cab. He helped Calamity inside, then gave the driver instructions and swung up to sit by the girl. On the ride to the local station house, where they collected Calamity's gunbelt and Navy Colt, St. Andre learned the cause of the fight.

"Madam Darcel's honest, Calamity," he told the girl. "She wouldn't allow a pickpocket in her place—not for long anyway."

"That one sure didn't stop," agreed Calamity. "Say, that Jacqueline was one tough kid. Was them kicks she gave me that *sa—savate*, or whatever you call it?"

"It was. I've seen Jacqueline at Duval's and at the *Cheval D'Or*, she's good, very good."

Putting a hand to her nose, Calamity winced slightly. "I'll take your word for it."

Not until the cab circled the edge of City Park did either Calamity or St. Andre mention the murder. However, while listening to Calamity's discourse on the subject of Jacqueline's fighting prowess, an idea began to form in St. Andre's head. No matter how hard he tried to force the thoughts down, they kept recurring, nagging at him, yet he did not put them into words.

"What happened about the gal who got killed?" Calamity asked, glancing out of the cab's window.

"I'm on the case now. Caiman has gone down with a convenient bout of fever and the Chief of Police put me in charge."

"You're a real lucky feller."

"I wouldn't say so. Both the *Picayune* and the *Intelligencer* are after somebody's blood over the failure to trap the Strangler. Unless he is caught soon, I fear my head will roll."

"Which same'd be a right shame," remarked Calamity. "We'd best start to think how we'll lay hands on him."

Although he relapsed into silence, St. Andre thought only indirectly about trapping the Strangler. On a visit to the *Cheval D'Or*, he had seen Jacqueline meet and defeat another skilled *savate* fighter. Knowing more than a little about foot-boxing himself, St. Andre could figure how rough tangling with Jacqueline was likely to be. Yet Calamity did tangle and defeated the slim girl. St. Andre already knew how tough and capable Calamity could act. Such a girl might—he let the rest of the thought trail off unused. Such a thing had never been done before, the risks were too great for him even to suggest his idea.

St. Andre moved restlessly and gave a low grunt of pain as his sore body protested.

"Aching a mite?" asked Calamity turning to look at him.

"I'll be as stiff as a plank in the morning."

"Got me a real good cure for that, happened you'd like to try it."

"*Cherie*, I would try anything. It is not good for a lawman to be stiff."

"You can say that again," grinned Calamity.

So St. Andre found himself once more in Calamity's room, seated on her bed and watching her bring a small bottle full of an oily-looking liquid from her medicine bag. Drawing the cork with her teeth and spitting it aside, she walked towards the detective.

"This's something an old Pawnee witch-woman whomped up for me," she said. "Take off your jacket, vest, shirt and that fancy undershirt I bet you wear."

While St. Andre did not lead the life of a Trappist monk, he felt slightly embarrassed by the girl's calm request that he stripped to the waist.

"You mean now?" he gasped.

"Naw, in a week, after I've gone back up-river. You don't drink this stuff. It gets rubbed on the hurt part and I can't do that with your clothes on. And don't get all modest, I've seen a feller's hairy chest afore today."

Deciding he may as well give in, St. Andre stripped to the waist. Without any blushing, simpering, or showing any more than casual interest in the muscular exposed torso, Calamity sat him on the bed. Pouring some of the liquid into the palm of her hand, she carefully applied it to the bruised skin. Whatever the liquid might be—and St. Andre feared to ask—it worked fast, soothing and cooling the ache from his bones and flesh.

"You're a wonder, Calam," he said when she finished.

"Why sure," she agreed, then flexing her arms. "Whooee, I'm sore."

Was there a hint of challenge in her voice, St. Andre wondered.

"Miss Canary's soothing syrup did me good," he remarked.

"It's sure hell to put on yourself," she answered. "Hell, my clothes are wet. I've got to get out of them."

Rising, she peeled off the shirt and vest, standing with her back to him. Even so, a mottling of bruises showed on her ribs as she dropped the clothes on to a chair.

"Calam—," St. Andre began. "Can we talk?"

"Know for sure I can, and I've heard you doing it all fancy and nice."

"Then sit by me, I'll put some of that stuff on for you and we'll talk."

CHAPTER EIGHT

Miss Canary's Suggestion

DAYLIGHT streamed through the window as St. Andre drew the curtains. Stepping to one side, he flexed his arms and marvelled at the ease with which he could move. By all fair means he ought to be so stiff and sore that even the smallest movement caused agony, yet he felt relaxed and almost his normal self. Behind him the bed creaked and he turned to study Calamity's sleep twisted face showing over the blankets.

"How are your injuries, *cherie?*" he asked, crossing to sit by her.

Hooking a hand behind his neck, Calamity drew his face down and kissed him. "Shucks, don't feel a thing," she answered when they parted. "What'd you want to talk about last night?"

Looking down at the girl as she lay so innocently on the bed, St. Andre did not answer for several seconds. Last night while applying Miss Canary's soothing syrup to Calamity's injuries he had thought of making use of the girl's undoubted courage and unusual talents to trap the Strangler. Now in the cold light of dawn, and after a night which proved beyond any doubt that Calamity *was* all woman, the idea no longer seemed possible. His plan would be too dangerous for any woman to risk her life trying it out.

Seeing the girl's lips tighten in a way he guessed meant she aimed to have the question answered, St. Andre forced himself to think fast.

"I was thinking about your suggestion that your friend tries to track the Strangler," he answered, using the first lie to come into his head.

His attempt at a bluff missed by a good country mile. Looking the detective over with calculating eyes, Calamity grinned and said, "What'd you do if I called you a liar?"

"Why not try it and see?" he challenged.

Calamity tried it; and saw.

Half an hour later, as he finished dressing, St. Andre felt even more certain that he could never put his plan into operation and risk Calamity's life. Hoping to evade the issue, he felt at the stubble on his cheeks and remarked that he needed a shave.

"Go down and get some breakfast," Calamity told him. "The boys'll be in the dining-room by now and one of 'em'll loan you his razor."

Although he did not feel sure of what kind of reception he would receive from the members of Killem's freight outfit, St. Andre followed the girl's advice and headed for the dining-room. Inside he found the members of the outfit sat around the clean, well-stocked table. All eyes turned towards him as he entered the room; but, much to his surprise, he found grins, not indignation or fury on the freighters' faces.

The way Killem and his men looked at the present situation was that none of them had the right to censure Calamity's morals. Even the married members of the outfit took female company when away from home on a trip, so none of them expected Calamity to sit alone and nun-like while they whooped things up. She did not throw herself at every man who came along, and the old Pawnee medicine woman had fixed up something which enabled Calamity to make sure that nothing permanent happened as a result of her friendship. In the final reckoning, the freighters allowed any man who became *that* friendly with their Calamity-gal must be all he-cat and well worth knowing—even if he be a town-dwelling, fancy-dressing and talking French-Creole aristocrat and a lawman to boot.

"Bring on another breakfast, maw!" called Dobe Killem as the owner of the apartment house looked in. "This young feller done stayed the night with us and he looks a mite hungry."

While St. Andre was not used to having four eggs and a pile of ham placed before him at breakfast, he tucked in and demolished the lot; which brought broad grins and friendly chaff from the freighters.

"Never did see a feller as could eat so much," remarked Killem.

"They do say *it* makes a man real hungry," Tombes went on.

"I missed dinner last night," St. Andre explained.

At that moment Calamity entered and St. Andre thrust back his chair to come to his feet. Much to his surprise none of the other men broke into ill-mannered comment on his show of etiquette. While they might be a mite long on the social graces themselves, Killem's outfit never mocked anybody whose early training gave him polite manners and habits.

"Morning, boys, hi Sherry," greeted Calamity innocently. "Say, did you come back here last night?"

"Reckon he must have," grinned the owner of the house

71

guessing the girl's words had been aimed in her direction. "You ready for breakfast?"

"Ready, willing and all set to eat it, maw," agreed Calamity, then turned to Tombes. "Hey, Tophet, happen you can see two inch afore your nose, Sherry here wants you to help trail that Strangler cuss."

"And we got them hosses to tend to," Killem went on. "I'll loan you my razor when you're through, Sherry."

By the time he had washed, shaved and tidied up his appearance as well as possible, St. Andre found he possessed a new name. It stuck and for the rest of his life St. Andre's friends called him 'Sherry'.

Calamity made no reference to the question she knew hovered around in St. Andre's head and which he fought down each time before speaking. Figuring the detective would get around to asking in his own good time, Calamity shared a cab with St. Andre and a silent, morose-looking Tombes, and rode to City Park. After St. Andre paid off the cab, the trio strolled through the Park. In daylight it looked different; innocent, friendly, not the kind of area one would associate with a brutal murder.

A couple of policemen stood guard on the place where the body had lain. Both of them exchanged glances as they watched St. Andre's party approaching.

"There's a feller whose job I'd hate to have," remarked one of the officers.

"And me," replied the other. "Anyway, he's got plenty of money and don't need this lot to live on."

Saluting St. Andre, the two policemen fell back, wondering why he had brought that mean-looking cuss and a gal wearing men's clothing along to the scene of the crime. Not that they objected in Calamity's case, she sure filled out that pair of blue jeans a treat. Neither officer wasted any time in asking questions, but stood back and awaited orders.

"What do we do now?" the detective asked.

"Just stand right back and don't get under-foot," grunted Tombes, never too amiable first thing in a morning, and less so when recovering from the previous night's celebration. "I sure hope your fellers haven't been tromping every damned which ways down here."

"I left orders for them to stay on the path."

After making a check on the ground at the left of the track, Tombes returned to the detective and nodded. "They done what you telled 'em. Ain't nothing aged right on that side. I'll look on the other."

St. Andre had never seen a human tracker in action and looked on with mingled interest and disbelief as the lean Westerner advanced towards the right side of the track and bent forward so as to study the grass. Possibly they would learn nothing through the scout's efforts, but St. Andre knew Calamity had not been joking when she made the suggestion.

A low grunt left Tombes' lips as he came to a halt, bent closer to the ground and examined something which caught his eye. Then he stood erect and turned to face Calamity and St. Andre.

"Feller come along the path with the gal."

"Could you tell me how you know, so I can write it in my report," St. Andre answered.

"Easy enough," grunted the scout. "There's a set of tracks that's the right age comes off the path here. Just the one set. Happen she'd come along the path alone, he'd've left sign in the bushes where he waited for her and walked out to stop her. After he'd killed her, he walked off into the bushes over there."

"Couldn't both the Strangler and the girl have come from the bushes?" St. Andre inquired.

"Nope. There's only the one set of tracks, going on to the grass and through the bushes."

"And you say he walked away?"

"Sure, Sherry. It's easy enough to tell the difference. Come here and take a look at his sign."

Bending forward, the scout pointed to the grass. Only by careful study could St. Andre see anything different from the spot at which Tombes pointed and the surrounding area. Even when seeing that a small oval-shaped patch of grass had been crushed down, he could not decide how Tombes knew the Strangler made the indentation when walking away from his victim. Seeing the detective's puzzled expression, and knowing how little chance the average city-dweller had of watching a visual tracker at work, Tombes explained his findings.

"Look at the shape of the mark," he said. "When a man walks, he puts his heel down first, brings the rest of his foot down. But when he runs, he lands on the toe. With walking you get a bigger mark than when he's running. The amount the crushed grass's come up tells me how long ago the sign was made."

"I'll take your word for that," St. Andre answered admiringly.

"You can sure do that," Calamity put in, conscious of the two patrolmen studying her shape with anything but official interest.

73

"Ole Tophet can track a man across rock by the marks his shadow left on it. Mind though, it has to be fairly soft rock—and a *real* sunny day"

"What would you do if I called you a liar, *cherie?*" smiled St. Andre.

"Nothing right now. I reckon you've got all kinds of laws against doing *that* in the open. Let's leave it until later and get after ole Tophet."

"What the hell's all this about, Mike?" one of the patrolmen asked in a low voice as they watched Tombes, then Calamity and St. Andre move away.

"Don't ask me," grunted the other. "Say, I wonder who worked St. Andre over?"

"That girl's got a mouse under her eye. Maybe it was her."

"Naw. St. Andre charms 'em, he don't beat 'em until they're ready for it. I reckon we'd best tag along and see what happens."

"Be as well. If we stay here we'll be in the wrong, and if we follow it'll be the same, but at least we might learn something."

Moving slowly, his eyes scanning the ground ahead of him, Tombes led the others through the bushes. Calamity kept her attention on the route they took, noticing that the Strangler's direction was such that it never came into plain view of a path but made a looping half-circle in cover. Just as she was about to remark on the matter, Tombes halted and looked back at St. Andre.

"Feller's around five foot ten tall, slim build, wears city shoes," the scout stated.

"How do you know?" asked the detective.

"Easy enough. Length of his stride, amount he crushed down the grass, shape of a couple of real clear tracks he left. Which same don't help you much, I reckon."

"At least it eliminates a lot of people. Where did he go from here?"

All the time they walked St. Andre had been studying the direction they took and noting it in his memory. If they ever caught the Strangler after a killing, it might be possible to shock a confession from him by describing the route he took from one of his victims.

After following the tracks for another fifty yards, Tombes came to a halt. He stood at the edge of a clump of bushes, looking around him. On joining the scout, Calamity and St. Andre found themselves overlooking a piece of track and the girl particularly

74

developed an uneasy feeling she knew the place which lay before them.

"What is it?" asked St. Andre, now convinced that Tombes had done all Calamity promised.

"Feller stood here for a fair spell, looking towards the path," Tombes answered. "I'll cross over and see what's on the other side. He went this ways, come on to the path here." However, after crossing the path and searching around, the scout returned to the others. "That's as far as we go. Feller didn't cross the track on to the other side and I can't trail him on this hard ground."

Interested though they had been up to that point, Calamity and St. Andre hardly heard a word Tombes said. Both stood staring at the bullet-holed top hat which lay on the ground ahead of them. Then they turned and their eyes met.

"He must've been stood here last night, watching us," Calamity breathed.

"If the newspapers hear of this," replied St. Andre. "I'm finished as a policeman."

"Can't see why," the girl answered. "Hell, who'd've expected the Strangler to come here and stand watching us? You couldn't have known about him."

"My dear child," said St. Andre gently. "The *Intelligencer* has never approved of the police, or my rise through its ranks. They will be only too pleased to make capital of this incident."

"Why don't you go along to their office, ask the boss to walk out into the alley and talk some sense to him with that there *savate*?" asked the practical Miss Canary.

"It is not as easy as that, *cherie*," the detective answered a touch regretfully. "You see the *Intelligencer* is a protector of the rights of the down-trodden, under-privileged mankind, and its owners have a very stout idea of how to gain full protection from the law for their actions."

Before St. Andre could enlarge on the working of a newspaper like the *Intelligencer*, Tombes returned to them and jerked his thumb towards the track.

"I've been down both sides and he didn't go off again near at hand. Reckon from the way he come off the grass, he was headed down that ways."

"Towards the better part of town," answered St. Andre. "Of course he would hardly, come the other way. We'd just gone along there. Well, that's all we can do for now."

"Hope I helped some," Tombes replied.

"You've given us a little more than we already knew," St.

Andre said. "I'm grateful for your help. Let's go back to town."

"What's your next move?" Calamity inquired, after collecting the discarded top hat.

"We wait," St. Andre told her.

"Just wait?"

"That's all we can do."

"Hell!" spat the girl. "He might kill again."

"He might," admitted St. Andre, "but until we have something to go on, we can't think of catching him."

"Do you know who the girl was?" asked Calamity.

"Not even that. People in her way of business avoid the law as I told you last night—."

"That feller acts like a stock-killing cougar," Tombes interrupted. "Ain't but two ways of hunting down one of them. Run him down with a pack of hounds, or stake out a bait and lure him to your gun."

"Now there's a right smart idea, Sherry." Calamity put in. "Get a gal to act as bait for you."

For a few seconds St. Andre did not reply. He walked along between Tombes and Calamity, the patrolmen following on his heels, his head sunk forward and thoughts racing through his mind. At last he shrugged and looked at the girl.

"We have three police matrons at Headquarters, but I doubt if they would be of any use as bait. All the Strangler's victims were shapely and good-looking girls, at least we assume they were good looking, their distorted faces give little clue of that. Our matrons are all bigger, and not so handsome as Dobe Killem."

"Shucks," answered Calamity, not looking at the detective. "I'm a mite smaller and a whole heap prettier than ole Dobe. Why not let me be your bait?"

"You?" asked St. Andre, trying to sound as if the idea had not been beating around in his head for the past few hours.

"G'wan!" grinned Calamity. "You've been fixing to ask me to do it ever since last night."

St. Andre slammed to a halt, turning and staring at the girl with dismay on his face. Seeing the grin on her face, a smile fought its way to his features, then died off once more.

"It could be very dangerous, *cherie*," he warned.

"Did you ever drive a six-hoss Conestoga wagon through hostile Injun country, Sherry?" she countered. "You might say that's dangerous too—I've done it."

Resuming walking again, St. Andre watched the girl's face. His thoughts turned over the idea which had played back and forth since the previous night, trying to decide how justified he was in endangering Calamity's life.

"We could have men following you," he finally said, then shook his head. "No! It's too much of a chance!"

"Reckon I'm the best judge of that," she answered.

"Reckon you just might as well give up and let her do it, Sherry," warned Tombes. "Ole Calam's done made her mind to be the bait, so she'll do with or without your help."

"Which same it'll be safer with your help," the girl pointed out. "Look, Sherry, I know how dangerous it'll be and I'm still game to give it a whirl if you are."

"It might work," admitted St. Andre. "But you would have to dress for the part. One sees few street-walkers dressed in men's clothing."

"You mean I'd have to put on a dress and all?" gasped Calamity.

"And all," agreed the detective.

Calamity let out a long, suffering sigh. Here was an aspect of the affair her impetuous nature failed to notice when forming the plan. Such an important decision might have taken some girls a long time to settle, but not Calamity. She stiffened her shoulders and looked at St. Andre.

"All right," she said in the tone of a martyr agreeing to be tossed to the lions. "I'll even wear a dress, happen it'll nail the Strangler."

"Let's go somewhere and make our arrangements," St. Andre suggested.

"How about those four jaspers who worked you over?" Calamity inquired.

"I have feelers out for them, but the Strangler case is of more importance right now."

Finding a cab, St. Andre took his party across town to Police Headquarters, a large old stone building which did not resemble any lawman's office Calamity or Tombes had ever seen. The Detective Bureau occupied the second floor and St. Andre's small room faced the Captain of Detectives' quarters. After seeing his superior and explaining his idea, then being granted permission to try it out, St. Andre took Calamity and Tombes into his office where they started to plan their campaign.

First St. Andre called in four men to act as escort when Calamity went out as bait. They would work in plain clothes instead of uniform and were not known in the Latour Street area. Supplying Calamity with the correct clothing for the part offered no difficulties. However, there were snags.

77

"How well does Calamity know the area?" asked Redon, the shortest of the escort and its senior member.

"I don't," Calamity admitted.

"That may be difficult." Redon stated. "We can't be too close to her—."

"Hey!" interrupted Calamity. "I know somebody who might be able to help."

"Who?" asked St. Andre.

"That skinny gal I fought last night, Jacqueline. I bet she'd jump at the chance of helping."

St. Andre shook his head. "I don't know about that."

"Then let's go ask her," Calamity suggested. "She can only say 'no'."

Rising, St. Andre prepared to leave the room. He told his men to collect their clothing and meet him at his office after lunch. Then he started for the door with Calamity and Tombes at his side. Suddenly the detective came to a halt.

"I've just thought of something, Calam!"

"Such as?"

"The Strangler saw you last night, and with me. He might recognise you."

"He might at that," agreed the girl. "It's something else we'll have to think about."

CHAPTER NINE

Miss Canary Acts As Bait

DOBE Killem saw the flashily-dressed blonde girl standing before the open door of Maw Packer's apartment house and felt surprised. While the *Rue de la Paix* could not be classed on the same social level as Bourbon or Toulouse Streets, it was not an area frequented by young ladies of that type.

While walking towards the blonde, Killem studied her, deciding she looked vaguely familiar. She had a nice figure that a cheap, gaudy blue dress revealed rather than concealed, sported the usual parasol and reticule of her kind and wore a large-brimmed hat on her blonde hair. Figuring she might be one of the girls his party entertained at the *Cheval D'Or* the previous evening, Killem nodded as he went by her. Killem decided he would find out which of the outfit invited her over and request that the one involved refrained from bringing calico cats to the house.

"You getting too rich and high-toned to talk with the hired help, Cecil?" asked Calamity's voice.

Although Killem had a well-deserved reputation for being a real good poker player who rarely showed his emotions, he came to a halt as if running into an invisible wall. His mouth dropped open as he turned to stare at the flashily-dressed blonde. For a moment he thought his ears had played a trick on him, then slowly Calamity's face formed out of the blonde curls and make-up.

"What—!" he croaked. "How—."

"Shut your mouth afore you get flies in it," grinned the delighted Calamity and looked towards the door of the building. "I'd say it works, Sherry."

Seeing a couple of thin, pinched, sanctimonious faces peeking from behind the curtains of a house across the street, Killem gave a low angry grunt. His eyes took in the girl's appearance again, noting that the heavy make-up she wore all but hid the mouse she carried under her left eye. However, standing in front of a house on the respectable *Rue de la Paix* was hardly the place to start asking questions about his employee's appearance.

"Let's get off the street!" he growled.

"Scared I'll ruin you socially, Cecil?" inquired Calamity with a mischievous and merry grin.

"I'll ruin you!" the freighter spat out.

Bobbing a curtsy to the watching women, and causing a hurried disappearance behind the curtains, Calamity grabbed hold of Killem's arm. Giving an annoyed grunt, Killem tried to pull himself free of the girl's grip, but she hung on all the more as they headed towards the door of the Packer house.

"What's wrong, Cecil?" she grinned. "Ashamed of being seen with me?"

"Damn your ornery, fool hide, Calam!" Killem snarled back. "I'll take a switch to your butt!"

"Which same I wouldn't feel it through this bustle," answered the girl, hauling him into the hall of the house. "I bet old Nosey and her pard over yonder are getting some right smart ideas of what's going to happen now."

"And me!" snapped Killem.

While Killem enjoyed a piece of rough-and-tumble good fun as much as the next man, he felt that Calamity had gone a whole heap too far this time. To his way of thinking, a practical joke should only cause discomfort to the participants and not bring embarrasment on innocent heads. New Orleans, even this poorer section of the old city, had advanced beyond the rough-and-ready Western town Calamity knew. Calamity's joke might bring down repercussions on Maw Packer's head when the two watchers across the street spread word that she allowed street-walkers to make use of her premises.

On entering the hall, Killem found not only St. Andre but Maw Packer standing facing the door. Instead of being furious at Calamity's behaviour, the woman grinned broadly.

"How'd it go?" Maw asked.

"He walked right by me," answered Calamity proudly. "Acted all honourable and up-right like a deacon going down a cat-house street. Never gave me more than a look-but-don't-touch look."

"Just what the hell's all this about?" demanded Killem in a hoarse bellow. "Damned if I don't—."

Then he stopped, staring at Calamity, and began to roar with laughter. On entering the house Calamity had stepped clear of her boss and removed the hat and blonde wig which so altered her appearance. For a moment Calamity stared at her employer, then swung towards Maw and St. Andre who both joined in the merriment.

"What's so funny? she yelled.

"L—Look in the mirror, *cherie!*" St. Andre managed to get out through his laughter.

Calamity followed his advice and looked into the hat-stand mirror. A reflected vision greeted her and she saw the cause of her friend's laughter. While the heavy make-up and long, glistening pendant earrings had been in keeping with the picture-hat and blonde curls, they looked incongruous framed by her mop of short natural red hair.

"Land-sakes!" she gasped, after joining in the laughter. "I'll sure have to keep my shop-bought white scalp on all the time. Say, Maw. those two old pills across the way were like to swallow their teeth when they saw me haul Dobe in here."

"It'll give 'em something to talk about," Maw answered calmly. "I can allus quieten them down by threatening to give the Reverend Postle all their sassafrass tea."

"Now me," Calamity remarked. "I'd be more likely to keep quiet happen you told me you'd make me *drink* sassafrass tea."

"So would they, only they flavour their tea with maybe seven-eighths gin."

"How's about somebody telling me what this's all about," suggested Killem.

"Let's go into the dining-room and I'll explain," St. Andre replied.

In the dining-room, seated at the table with cups of coffee before them, St. Andre started to explain the reason for Calamity's disguise.

On their arrival at the *Cheval D'Or*, Calamity and St. Andre interviewed Jacqueline and the *savate*-fighting ballet dancer agreed to help all she could on hearing they planned to try to trap the Strangler. However, she stated that she felt Calamity would not be able to pass herself off as a street-girl with the little aid possible between then and night-fall, there was too much Calamity needed to know for that. Quite calmly Jacqueline offered to go along with Calamity and act as a second piece of bait. In vain St. Andre tried to point out the dangers involved. Jacqueline claimed she could chance anything Calamity risked and the Western girl added her weight to the argument.

The question of clothing came up next, but found an easy solution. Having to obtain permission from Madam Darcel for Jacqueline's absence, St. Andre took the saloonkeeper into his confidence. Immediately Madam Darcel offered every assistance and, without telling the real reason for the request, obtained the

81

loan of clothing which fitted Calamity for her part as a street-walker. Madam also came up with the idea of a blonde wig, without knowing that the Strangler had seen Calamity and St. Andre together, saying the girl would look more in character without that mop of short hair.

Calamity, dressed in her new outfit, returned to Maw Packer's place and had been explaining her actions to a sceptical and suspicious owner when they saw Killem returning from the river-front where he spent the day. Deciding to try out her disguise, Calamity slipped out of the house and awaited her employer's arrival. If Killem's reaction be anything to go on, Calamity doubted whether the Strangler, who only saw her by moonlight and from a distance, would recognise her.

"So you're aiming to use Calam and that Jacqueline gal for bait," said Killem when St. Andre finished his explanation.

"I am," agreed the detective. "But I'll give them every protection."

"You see you do!" warned Killem. "Happen anything goes wrong and that gal is hurt—."

"Dobe honey!" whooped Calamity, throwing her arms around her boss and gave him a kiss. "I didn't think you cared."

"Who says I care?" grunted the freighter, gently standing the girl at arms' length and ruffling her hair. "Only the Army done give me an advance on your pay; and anyways you're such an ornery cuss that happen you got killed you'd come back and haunt me. Danged if you aren't trouble enough alive, without having you around as a haunt."

"Who're you trying to convince?" asked Calamity. "Us—or you?"

Ignoring the question, and not wanting his concern for Calamity's welfare to be too obvious, Killem released the girl and turned to St. Andre. "You want a few of my boys around?"

"I'd rather use my own men," the detective replied. "They know what to do. After all, you wouldn't expect policemen to be able to handle your big wagons."

"Reckon you're right," admitted the freighter. "Say, Calam gal, do you have a gun?"

"I thought of it," replied the girl. "But I don't want to spook the Strangler happen I meet him."

"I doubt if he would chance his games with an armed girl," St. Andre pointed out. "Some of the girls do carry a Derringer in their reticule, but none of the Strangler's victims have had one with her."

Killem frowned. While he knew Calamity to be a girl who knew how to take care of herself, mostly she had either her Navy Colt or bull-whip handy. Dressed in such a manner, she could hardly carry either. The big freighter did not care for the idea of his Calamity tangling with the Strangler unless adequately protected. However, he knew that St. Andre would not endanger Calamity's life if he could find any other way of catching the Strangler, and in making use of the girl as a decoy meant to take every possible precaution to ensure her safety.

"All right, play it your way," he said. "I know you'll do right by our lil gal, Sherry.

"That I'll promise you, Dobe," answered St. Andre. "But you'll not let any of your men butt in."

"I'll see they don't," Killem promised.

That evening, dressed in the cheap finery sported by the type of girl from which the Strangler selected his victims, Calamity and Jacqueline went out into the city as living decoys. Calamity had hoped to see something of New Orleans during her visit and that evening partially got her wish. Not that she saw the stately buildings, coffee-houses, cafes and theatres of the better part of the old French city. If it comes to a point, such places did not interest Calamity. Such an area was not the Strangler's hunting grounds. He picked his victims from the Latour Street district, selecting girls whose disappearance would arouse little comment. So the two girls went from place to place, visiting the gathering spots of the street-walking sisterhood. While Jacqueline had never worked the streets in such a capacity she had many friends who did and learned enough from them to locate their haunts and carry off the impersonation.

Hovering always in the background came Redon and his three men. They never bunched together and dressed in different fashions, but all in a style which blended into the background. Redon looked like a cheap gambler, the others could pass as riverboat hands, water-front workers, or general town dwellers of the lower-income bracket. Under St. Andre's instructions, the four men were not to interfere should a possible suspect attempt to pick up one of the girls. Instead they must trail the man and girl, stay far enough away so as not to scare him off, but close enough to save her should the man be the Strangler looking for another victim. Only by catching the Strangler in the act could they be sure of a conviction; and the girls willingly accepted the danger to their lives to bring this about.

One useful thing had been learned from Tombes' display of

the art of reading signs that morning. Now the hunters knew they could discard all but men of around the five foot ten mark and with slim builds. With that in mind, Calamity and Jacqueline steered clear of such offers as came from men who did not fit into the general area of Tombes' estimation of the Strangler's size and heft.

At about eleven o'clock, two foot-sore girls found themselves in a small but busy saloon at the lower end of Latour Street. Jacqueline wore her hair down, so nobody recognised her as the graceful star performer of the *Cheval D'Or*. Flopping down at a table, the girls looked around the room. So far nobody of the right height and build had propositioned either girl and they were beginning to realise the enormity of the task ahead of them.

"Whooee!" groaned Calamity, working her toes in the borrowed shoes. "My feet hurts like hell."

"And mine," Jacqueline replied and glanced at a coloured waiter who came up. "Two specials, Sam."

"Yes'm. Does you-all work around here regular?"

"Our men've fixed it for us," Jacqueline answered.

"That's all right then. Only there was a big fight along the street last night and the law has passed the word that they don't want no mo' trouble down here for a spell. I'll git you-all's drinks."

"I wonder who was fighting," grinned Calamity as the waiter departed.

"They do say it was a beautiful, slim girl and a fat red-head," Jacqueline replied.

"Easy there, Skinny," warned a smiling Calamity. "You heard what the man said, the law don't want no trouble down here, so I'd hate to lick you again."

"It's lucky the police passed out that order," Jacqueline remarked. "Some of the real girls might have objected to us coming around otherwise."

"Old Sherry thought of everything," commented Calamity.

Knowing that the street-girls were apt to be jealous of intrusion by new girls into their territory, St. Andre caused the official warning to be passed out that the law would not countenance any more brawls down the Latour Street district after the fight in the *Cheval D'Or*. Such a warning carried weight and the regular girls, while watching the newcomers with suspicious eyes, did not try to assert their prior right to trade when Calamity and Jacqueline entered a place of business.

"Let's hope the plan works," Jacqueline said.

"And quick," augmented Calamity. "I hate that coloured water they serve the gals instead of whisky."

During her tour of the seamier side of the city, Calamity had discovered that the street-girls, while expected to drink something as they sat in a saloon waiting for trade, did not consume real intoxicating liquor. Instead, if they so requested, the girls were served with coloured water masquerading as real drinks, but costing much less than the genuine article. That way a girl could appear to be drinking steadily, had an excuse to be in the place, and still stay sober enough to handle the financial side of the business. In return for the service, they were expected to persuade any customer to buy at least one round of drinks before taking him to their business premises.

The waiter returned, placing the glasses before the girls. Dropping his voice confidentially, he said, "If you ladies wants any introductions—."

"We'll keep it in mind," Calamity answered.

Turning, the waiter walked away and the girls exchanged glances. Then Jacqueline stiffened slightly in her seat, staring at the door.

"Just coming in, Calam!" she whispered, although the new arrival could not possibly have heard her at that distance.

Calamity turned her head in a casual manner to look towards the door and at the man who just entered. For his dress, he appeared to be a seaman of some kind—ocean-going vessels used the New Orleans waterfront to discharge their cargoes—and he stood around five foot ten, a slim, wiry young man with a sallow complexion. For a moment he stood at the door, his eyes roaming around the room and studying the various customers at the tables. Finally his gaze came to rest on Calamity and he started to walk across the room.

Coming to her feet, a buxom brunette caught the man's arm and she made the usual suggestion. With an almost angry gesture, he jerked his arm free and continued his way towards Calamity's table. The brunette scowled, but her companion snapped out a reminder about the police's no-trouble order, so she took her seat again.

On reaching Calamity's table, for a moment he did not speak, his eyes on her face. Not by as much as a glance did he even show he knew of Jacqueline's presence. There was something unnerving about his fixed gaze and blank expression.

"Hi," Calamity greeted, looking up as if suddenly aware of the man's presence. You look lonely."

Calamity reckoned to be a better than fair poker player and capable of reading facial emotions. Never had she seen such a look

85

of hatred as passed briefly over the seaman's face, then was replaced by a smile which stopped long clear of his eyes.

"Reckon I could offer you a drink?" he replied.

"I thought you'd never ask. Pull up a chair and take the weight off your feet."

Even as the slim man sat down, the coloured waiter came gliding over to the table and grinned knowingly at Calamity.

"Is you-all wanting wine for the ladies, sah?"

For a moment the sailor did not reply. Instead he sat staring at Calamity with a fixed, unwinking gaze. Jerking his eyes from the girl, the sailor looked at the waiter and answered, "Bring me a beer."

"And the ladies, sah?"

"Go to hell, coon!" the sailor spat out.

"Take it easy, friend," Calamity put in gently. "He's only doing his job."

"Who asked you—!" the sailor began.

"If that's how you feel!" Calamity interrupted. "I'm going."

Shoving back her chair, she started to rise. The angry, hostile eyes followed her, then various emotions warred on the sailor's face. At last he forced a smile to his lips again.

"I'm sorry, M—. I'm real sorry. Only the mate gave me a bad time afore I left the ship and I've been looking to take it out on somebody. Bring wine for the ladies, feller, and buy yourself something."

Yet after the waiter left, the sailor dropped into a moody silence once more. He answered Calamity's comments on the saloon and its crowd with grunts of silence.

"I reckon we'd best be going, Jackie," Calamity remarked.

Once again the threat of departure brought a change to the man. "I'm sorry, Mavis," he said. "I was thinking."

"I like a thinking man," Calamity replied. "Only the name's not Mavis."

The sailor jerked his eyes to Calamity's face, scowling at her. Then a sly grin twisted his lips. "No, it wouldn't be. Where's that feller with the drinks?"

On his return, the waiter put the drinks on the table and in doing so bent so his mouth was close to Calamity's ear. In a low tone, the waiter issued a warning.

"You-all watch that feller, he's got meanness in him."

"I'll mind it," Calamity replied.

While finishing his drink, the sailor managed to sound more friendly. He laughed at a joke Calamity made and she decided

86

that she might as well get down to business. Finishing her drink, she looked at Jacqueline.

"Reckon we'd better be going," she said, then glanced at the sailor. "Unless you've anything in mind."

"How'd you like to take a walk?"

"I never walk with fellers I don't know," Calamity countered. "'Course, if you told me your name, I'd know you."

"Ben Cope."

From the way the sailor spoke, he thought Calamity should know his name. It meant nothing to her and she smiled.

"Hi, Ben. I'm Jane. Let's take our walk now I know you."

"I've got something to do myself," Jacqueline put in. "See you around, Ben."

Cope did not reply, his cold eyes never left Calamity's face as he rose and took her offered arm. Together they left the saloon and Jacqueline looked around for her escort, wanting to tell them that Calamity had a possible taker.

Outside the saloon, Calamity and Cope turned down Latour Street. Cope said little as they walked, but at last they reached the edge of City Park.

"Let's go in here." he said.

"I'd rather go back for a drink," she answered.

Gripping Calamity's arm tighter, Cope growled, "We're going in there, and if you make a squeak, I'll bust your arm."

From the strength in the slim man's fingers, Calamity decided he could make good his threat. So she allowed herself to be steered into the Park and hoped that St. Andre's men were on hand to come to her rescue.

CHAPTER TEN

An Attempt On Miss Canary's Life

COLD fear gripped Jacqueline as she watched Calamity leave the room with Cope. Despite the hectic and violent nature of their first meeting, a strong liking had developed between the girls during the afternoon and evening, and the dancer did not want anything to happen to her new friend. Something about Cope scared Jacqueline. It might have been Cope's moody manner, the way he stared at Calamity, or how his smile never reached his eyes. Jacqueline's every instinct warned her that Cope did not go with Calamity for the usual reasons.

Glancing around the room, Jacqueline suddenly became aware that, due to the coming and going of the customers, none of the escort had seen Calamity and Cope leave and did not know that they should be following the couple.

In later years such decoy work would be organised and mistakes avoided by careful planning. But this was probably the first time any police department employed such tactics to trap a criminal, so, having no precedent to guide them, they made mistakes. If the man with Calamity should be the Strangler, the poor positioning of the escort might cost her dearly.

Rising, Jacqueline started across the room in the direction of Redon who stood at the bar. The stocky detective glanced at Jacqueline, then towards Calamity's empty chair. A look of shocked concern came to his face, and he moved forward meaning to contact Jacqueline in the manner of a customer meeting one of the street-girls. From their places around the room, the other members of the escort read the signs and headed for the door.

A hand caught Jacqueline's arm as she walked towards Redon. Swinging around, and trying to pull herself free, she found herself facing a tall, burly riverboat man.

"Hey there, honey-chile," greeted the man. "How's about you 'n' me having a few lil drinks, then going to your place?"

"I—I've already got a man," she replied.

"Forget him—," the man began.

"She doesn't want to forget him," a voice cut in from the side, "so just take your cotton-picking hands offen her."

Redon did not want trouble, but he could not leave Jacqueline in such a position and the girl might know where Calamity and the sailor were headed. So the detective cut in and one glance told him the riverboat man did not like the interruption one little bit.

A grin creased the burly man's face as he studied Redon's clothes and appearance. All the man saw was a typical tinhorn gambler and not a big one at that. He certainly did not intend to surrender the girl to such a man without the other put up a right convincing argument. Reaching out, the riverboat man laid the palm of his big hand on Redon's fancy vest, meaning to thrust the detective aside.

There was no time to argue with the man. Every second wasted put Calamity's life into greater danger. So Redon knew he must act and act fast. Also that he must finish the burly man first go; and he knew how tough a riverboat worker could be. Such a man needed firm handling and stern measures if he was to be stopped without a hell of a fight.

Fortunately, despite his comparative lack of inches, Redon was a very tough lawman and knew a thing or three about the noble art hand-to-hand combat.

Up came Redon's hands, the left securing the man's wrist from the underside, the right slapping on to the man's fingers and pressing them against the fancy gambler's vest. When Redon bent forward at the hips, pain and the danger of broken bones brought the other man to his knees. Releasing his hold, Redon stepped back fast and lashed up his left foot, the toe catching the man full under his jaw. Back snapped the man's head and he sprawled to the floor, limp and unmoving.

"Some folks just don't know when to get tough!" Redon growled, looking around him and waiting for the unconscious man's friends to make a move.

However, the entire business happened so quickly that few if any of the crowd, appeared to realise what had been done. Redon did not give them a chance to find out, but took Jacqueline's arm and headed across the room.

"Calam's gone out with a man!" Jacqueline gasped as they hurried between the tables. "Raoul, I think he's the Stran—."

"Keep your voice down, Jackie!" the detective interrupted. "We don't want everybody to know."

Normally the owner of the saloon would have objected to a stranger mishandling a good customer, especially when the stranger only bought a couple of beers at the bar. However, the police warning about no trouble caused the man to hold his hand especially as the stranger was leaving, and looked like he might take violent objection to any attempt at showing him the error of his ways.

On the street Jacqueline and Redon came to a halt and looked around them. They could see no sign of Calamity and Cope among the crowd using the sidewalk. The remainder of the escort loomed up around Redon and the girl, all showing concern at their failure to adequately cover Calamity.

"He's killed the others in the Park," one man whispered, trying to avoid attracting attention to them.

"Could get to the Park several ways from here," Redon replied. "Split up, take a different way each. Jackie and I'll go down the street. I hope to God we're in time."

"Hurry, Raoul!" Jacqueline gasped, trying to increase her speed as they left the other members of the party. "We must run—."

"No, Jackie!" Redon answered.

For all the urgency of the situation, Redon knew he dare not run along the street. He had no wish to draw attention to himself and running would cause folks to take notice, might even invite pursuit. If the man with Calamity should be the Strangler, and they captured him, Redon did not want the people of the Latour Street district to know of it. Some of the folk in that area either knew or suspected that a missing friend must be a Strangler victim, even if they would not help the police by identifying the bodies, and would have no mercy on the killer. Should word get out that the Strangler had been captured, Redon doubted if he and his men would take in a living prisoner.

Explaining his reasons for not running, Redon held Jacqueline to a steady walk until they left Latour Street and came towards the entrance to City Park. Sick with worry for her friend's safety, Jacqueline stared ahead along the shadowy paths and wondered if they would be in time to prevent Calamity's death.

Calamity allowed the man to steer her along a path through the Park, trying to catch the sound of her escort's footsteps. Nothing but the normal night noises came to her ears, however, as yet she did not worry for she knew the men would not chance coming too close in case they scared off Cope before he made a move.

"Look, friend," she said, realising she ought to do something. "If you're after a free—."

"I'm only after one thing, Mavis," Cope answered.

"Mavis?" Calamity gasped. "Who is she?"

The grip on her arm tightened and Cope's breath came heavier as he snarled, "Don't try to fool me, Mavis. I recognised you as soon as I came into that place. That big hat, the blonde hair."

Suddenly the man swung Calamity around before him. Hatred and worse glowed on his face, and his hands rose towards her throat. Calamity hesitated a vital instant too long. Nothing had ever frightened her so much as did the sight of the man's face. Before she could take positive action, or even scream, the man's fingers clamped on her throat, the thumbs digging into the sides of her adam's apple and cutting off her breath. Panic hit Calamity for a moment as her hands grabbed instinctively at the man's wrists. Her head seemed to be filled with a roaring and throbbing and all she could see was that hideous, twisted, hate-filled mask of a face before her eyes.

Then Calamity regained control of herself. Something screamed a warning to her senses and she knew she must break the hold on her throat. She wasted no time in wondering where the escort might be. All her life Calamity had been self-reliant and that factor saved her life.

Discarding the futile pulling at the man's wrists, for his arms were too strong for her to drag them off by brute force, Calamity prepared to defend herself with a trick Killem taught her.

"You cheap whore, Mavis!" Cope was yelling and Calamity realised he must have been shouting all the time. "You led my wife astray. Now you're going to——."

At which point Calamity acted in her defence. Simultaneously she launched a kick against his shin and placed the palms of her hands on his elbows. For the first time in her life Calamity blessed wearing women's shoes instead of her comfortable moccasins. All that evening she had cursed the shoes which made her unaccustomed feet ache, but at that moment the shoes saved her. A kick delivered when wearing her moccasins would not have hurt anywhere near as much as did those reviled city shoes.

Pain caused Cope to relax his hold slightly, but it proved to be enough. Desperation added strength to Calamity's naturally strong arms. The sudden, unexpected attack on his shin caused Cope to loosen his grip on Calamity's throat and before he could tighten the fingers again, the girl's hands shoved inwards on his elbows. Cope's hands slipped from Calamity's throat and she thrust him backwards a couple of steps. Sucking in air, Calamity stumbled away from Cope. Before she could start to scream for help, as St. Andre warned her to do, Calamity saw Cope leaping at her, his hands reaching towards her throat, that same mad glare in his eyes.

Footsteps pounded on the path behind Cope. Even in his crazy rage, the sound rang a warning note in the man's head. Glancing over his shoulder, Cope saw a man in gambler's clothes and a slim, flashily-dressed girl running towards him. Gasping for breath, Calamity caught her balance and came forward, whipping around her right fist. Cope turned full into the blow, it caught him on the side of the jaw, coming with Calamity's weight behind it.

Staggering backwards under the impact of the blow, Cope clawed up a hand towards his jacket pocket. Redon sprang forward, the short leather-wrapped, lead-weighted police billie he had drawn on entering the park rose in his right hand and came down. Having seen the man reaching for a pocket and possibly a weapon, Redon took no chances. The billie landed on Cope's head and the sailor's hat gave him no protection. With a low moan, Cope crumpled and went down in a limp pile.

Hurdling the fallen body, Redon caught Calamity by the arms as the girl stood swaying.

"Are you all right, Calam?" he asked.

"Sure," replied Calamity—and fainted for the first time in her life.

Redon lowered the girl to the ground. Jacqueline arrived and shoved by the detective to drop at Calamity's side. Gently the dancer raised Calamity's head and rested it on her knees.

"Is she—!" Jacqueline gasped.

"Just a swoon," Redon replied. "She'll be all right in a couple of minutes."

Leaving Jacqueline to tend to Calamity, Redon drew the Bean Giant handcuffs from the inside pocket of his jacket. Even as he bent down to clip the irons on the unconscious sailor's wrists, he heard feet thudding on a path, coming towards him. Looking up, he saw a burly shape approaching and relief hit him as he recognised the newcomer as another member of the escort.

"Heard him yelling," the newcomer announced. "See you— God! He hasn't—."

"No. She's just fainted."

Voices swirled through the mists which clouded Calamity's head, distant yet clear although she could not make any sense of the words.

"Is she all right?" asked one.

"She'd best be," came another. "If anything happened to her, St. Andre'd have my badge at the least."

Shaking her head to clear it, Calamity tried to force herself into a sitting position. Hands gripped her shoulders and held her down. For a moment panic hit her as memory flooded back. Grabbing up, she gripped the wrists of the hands which held her. Then she saw a face above her. A pale, scared face, but not the hate-crazed features of the sailor.

"You—You're hurting, Calam!" Jacqueline gasped.

Only with an effort could Calamity open her fingers. She realised that she lay on her back, her head resting on Jacqueline's knees. Beyond Jacqueline stood Redon and another of the policemen—and to one side, stretched out upon the ground with his wrists secured by handcuffs, even though he would not be going anywhere for a spell, lay Cope.

Calamity stiffened, then fought down a momentary panic and hint of hysteria as she looked at the man and remembered his hate-filled face with the mad eyes glaring at her. Determined not to go 'woman', have hysterics in front of her friends, Calamity fought for and gained control of herself.

"I'm sorry, Jackie," she said and raised a hand to touch her throat.

Stepping forward, Redon helped Calamity to her feet, keeping a hand on her arm and steadying her. Something of the old Calamity grin came to her face as she watched Jacqueline rise and saw the worried expressions on the two policemen's faces.

"Danged if that coloured water we've been drinking wasn't stronger'n I thought," she said. "It's sure rough on a lil country gal like me, that's not used to drinking it."

"It sure is," grinned the second policeman. "Why, anybody'd think you'd fainted had they seen you."

More feet approached, but again it proved to be friends who arrived. Redon nodded to the remainder of the escort as they came up.

"You got him!" one said.

"Yeah. Did the noise attract any attention?"

"None as we noticed, Raoul," the other policeman replied and glanced at the groaning man on the ground. "Did he say anything, Calam?"

"Let us not stand discussing it," Redon put in before Calamity could reply. "Let's get this feller to the station house. If folks hear we've nailed the Strangler, we'll have bad trouble on our hands. Feelings are high about him."

"You're right about that," Calamity agreed. "I saw a lynch mob one time in Butte. It grew from nothing to—well, I don't never want to see another."

93

She did not mention that the lynching was prevented by prompt action taken by a bunch of really efficient lawmen, but doubted if the New Orleans police would have the equipment or ability to halt a mob. Sure St. Andre and his boys were tough and real handy in their own way, but it took gun-skill to handle a mob filled with hate and the desire to shed the blood of a killer.

"Are you sure he didn't hurt you, Calam?" asked Jacqueline gently.

"Not as much as you did last night, gal."

"You didn't give him enough time," remarked Redon dryly. "Get him on his feet. The Chief of Police'll be pleased to see the Strangler."

"If it's the Strangler we caught," said Calamity.

All eyes turned first to Calamity, then swung in the direction of the groaning man on the ground. One of the escort swung back to face Calamity and nodded to her as she reached up to touch her throat with delicate fingers.

"How'd you mean, Calamity?" the man asked. "This feller tried to strangle you, didn't he?"

"Sure he did. With his bare hands," she answered. "Way I heard it, the others were all killed with a rope."

"Maybe he didn't have the cord with him tonight," Redon suggested.

"Could b—," began Calamity, then stopped talking as her range-trained ears caught some sounds the others missed. "Quick, somebody's coming. Get him on his feet and hid among you. Then make like you're all drunk."

Without arguing or wasting time, two of Redon's men grabbed the groaning Cope and hoisted him to his feet. Calamity, Jacqueline and the remaining pair of detectives bunched around Cope, hiding him from view. Two men and two street-girls came into sight, walking arm in arm along the path.

"Poor ole Charlie," Calamity said, in a fair impersonation of a whisky-loaded voice. "Reckon that last drink was too much for him."

"We'd best get him home," Redon answered, sounding just as convincing. "He sure sounds awful."

Suddenly Cope recovered enough to stop groaning and begin struggling, letting out a mouthful of curses and trying to free himself from the handcuffs. The detectives gripped his arms, but could do little or nothing about his voice. However, they did not need to worry about the passing party interfering. Taking a look at the apparently drunken group, one of the street-girls gave a warning.

"The law'll be here soon. Let's get going."

Having no wish to be involved with the police, the girls' escorts hurried them by the swaying, rowdy group and along a path. Not one of the quartet realised they passed a group of law enforcement officers and a prisoner—perhaps even the Strangler himself—but took the others as being drunks liable to attract the attention of the police. Without a backward glance, the party hurried off and Redon stepped clear of his men, letting out a sigh and wiping his brow.

"All right," he said. "Let's get out of here. This'll make me old afore my time."

Keeping around Cope so as to prevent the fact that he wore handcuffs showing, the policemen started to walk him along the path towards the Latour Street entrance to City Park. Calamity and Jacqueline went along, adding their voices to the drunken song raised by the men to drown the struggling, raving Cope's tones.

"If he keeps this up, he'll bring the patrolman on the beat down on us," Redon remarked. "I'll have to quieten him."

"Do it easy," Calamity replied. "I'm still not sure we got the right man."

"Know something, Calam," Redon answered. "Neither am I."

On reaching the edge of the Park, Cope quietened down. Sending one of the men to find a couple of cabs, Redon kept the others in a group around their prisoner. Rowdy parties had never been so rare around the Latour Street district that they attracted any attention. Even the passing beat patrolmen gave the group no more than a glance before continuing on his way.

"We'll go straight to Headquarters," Redon decided when the cabs arrived. "You girls go in the second cab with Pete, the rest of us'll take Cope in the first. I won't be sorry to get him clear of here."

"What was it like, Calam?" Jacqueline asked as they sat in the cab and were carried towards the Police Headquarters.

"Bad, real bad!" Calamity answered and reached for the dancer's hands. "Let me handle it alone, Jackie gal."

"No!"

"Know something, you awkward little cuss. That's just what I thought you'd say. Only we'll have to make sure the boys get there quicker next time."

"Next time?" Jackie gasped. "But I thought—."

"I don't. This whole thing sits wrong with me," Calamity interrupted. "If he *is* the Strangler, why'd he change the way he killed? And why'd he chance making so much noise?"

On arrival at Headquarters, St. Andre expressed the same sentiments. Cope had sunk into sullen silence and steadfastly refused to answer any questions.

"Take him downstairs and keep him by himself," St. Andre ordered. "Then go to the riverfront and ask around the ocean-going ships, see if you can find where he came from."

The interview had been held in the Captain of Detective's office and St. Andre returned to his own room where Calamity and Jacqueline sat waiting for him.

"I think you're right, Calam," he said, his voice showing disappointment. "He's not the Strangler."

"Do you want us to try again tonight?" Calamity asked.

"No."

"We'll be out tomorrow then. And don't trying arguing, me 'n' Jackie here've made up our minds."

"All right. Tomorrow night then. Only this time I'll make sure the escort—."

"The boys did their best," Calamity interrupted. "Let's go, Jackie."

St. Andre escorted the girls to the front entrance of the building. After handing Jacqueline into the waiting cab, he turned to Calamity and took her hands in his.

"You took a risk. I don't know how I can ever thank you, *cherie.*"

"Just come 'round to my place some time and we'll call each other liars," Calamity replied. "Goodnight, Sherry. Maybe we'll have better luck next time."

CHAPTER ELEVEN

Miss Canary Learns How It Is Done

CALAMITY attracted some considerable interest when she strolled into the Police Headquarters building on the morning after the attempt on her life. The usual bunch of loungers in the main hall cast glances in her direction, for none of them were used to seeing a young woman dressed in trousers—especially tight-fitting pants such as Calamity wore. One of the girl's escort from the previous night came from where he had been sitting and nodded a greeting to her, then led her upstairs.

"Who's that?" asked one of the men to the desk sergeant.

"One of St. Andre's," the sergeant answered. "Not as fancy as some who've come to see him, but I bet she'd be a whole heap more woman."

Even had he wished to, the desk sergeant could not have given out the true reason for Calamity's visit. St. Andre insisted that only the people directly involved with the decoy job knew about it, for he did not wish word of his plan to leak out. Luckily for the scheme, young ladies visiting the handsome detective lieutenant had become common enough a sight not to attract any attention around Headquarters.

From the expression on her escort's face, Calamity guessed that their work of the previous night had not been entirely crowned with success. However, there were too many people on the stairs for a detailed discussion of the matter and Calamity reached the door of St. Andre's office knowing no more than when she entered the building. She knocked on the door, opened it and entered, coming to a halt as she saw St. Andre had a visitor.

"Sorry, Sh—Lootenant," she said. "They didn't say you had company."

"That's all right, Calam," St. Andre answered. "Come on in. This's Captain Holgate of the *China Star*. Captain, this is Miss Canary, the young woman who helped capture Cope last night."

Calamity looked at Holgate. A peaked hat sat on the man's head, his face had a weather-beaten look about it and bore an air of command. He wore a blue broadcloth uniform jacket of a kind

97

Calamity had never seen before, white trousers and well-polished boots. In height Holgate would almost equal Dobe Killem, though not quite so heavily built. Calamity took a liking to the man on sight, figuring he would be a good friend, but a real bad enemy.

"Howdy, Cap'n," she greeted, then looked at St. Andre. "Is Cope the Strangler, Sherry?"

"No," replied St. Andre, his voice bitter.

"Got to figuring that after he grabbed me," the girl admitted, walking forward and perching herself on the edge of St. Andre's desk. "He made too much noise and didn't use that cord."

"He also only docked late yesterday afternoon after a two year trip on the *China Star*," St. Andre went on, accepting a cigar from the case Holgate held out. "I wish it had been Cope. At least we would have the Strangler under lock and key now. But Cope hasn't been in this country for two years."

"Which same couldn't've been him that killed the other girls then," Calamity remarked. "But why in hell did he jump me last night?"

"I can answer that, Miss—," Holgate said.

"Make it Calam, like everybody does," the girl told him, eyeing the cigar case as its owner extracted a weed and hoping he would offer her one.

Captain Holgate proved irresponsive to thought suggestions, for he did not catch Calamity's mental message and hand over his case for her to accept a cigar. Taking his seat, from which he rose when Calamity entered, the captain lit his cigar and looked at the girl through the smoke. Suddenly recalling his manners, he gave a guilty start and looked down at the smoking cigar between his fingers.

"I'm sorry, Miss—Calam—," he said. "Does the smoke bother you?"

"Only when I'm the only one not doing it," she answered.

With a grin, and a knowing wink at St. Andre, Holgate passed his cigar-case to the girl. His entire attitude was one of male superiority as he prepared to call Calamity's bluff. Knowing her better, St. Andre could have warned Holgate that any bluff Calamity put out was likely to be forced through to the end. Much to Holgate's surprise, Calamity took a cigar from the case, bit off its tip in a professional manner, accepted the light the detective offered her and proceeded to draw smoke from the rolled tobacco with evident enjoyment.

"What was you saying about that feller Cope, Cap'n?" she

asked calmly, ignoring St. Andre's broad grin and Holgate's bug-eyed stare.

"Who—Oh yes. Cope!" The words bounced out of the captain in disjointed flow as he wondered what kind of a woman sat before him. "He's one of my hands. A good worker until the trouble. You see, he married in New York and while he was away on a ship his wife became friendly with a girl called Mavis. Apparently this Mavis was a bad one and she steered Cope's wife astray. When Cope came in from the voyage, he found he no longer had a home and his wife had gone. He met her later, working in a waterfront hell cn the New York docks. When he got the story out of her, he went hunting for Mavis. New York's a big city and he never found her. After a time he went back to sea. The trouble was that when he came to port and took a few drinks, he went looking for Mavis. No matter where the ship happened to be, he looked for her. Twice he was jailed for attacking blonde girls, but was fined and released."

"And you kept him on, knowing that?" Calamity said.

"He was a good sailor and they're hard to find. I thought it was just a drunken brawl and never troubled to go too deeply into the matter. On board he never made any trouble. Then last night, when the police came asking about him, I found two of his ship-mates and got the full story out of them. Apparently he had been brooding about his wife for days and gave them the slip when he went ashore. He must have gone looking for that girl Mavis and picked on you—but why you I don't know. Mavis was a blonde."

"So was I last night," Calamity replied. "I feel sorta sorry for him. What'll happen to him, Sherry?"

"We'll have to take him to trial," the detective answered.

"But if the Cap'n here takes him—."

"No, cherie. The next time he gets ashore and looks for Mavis, the girl he finds won't have a police escort—or be Calamity Jane."

"I'm afraid Lieutenant St. Andre is right, Calam," Holgate went on.

"By the way, Calam, the captain had seen the Strangler's last victim and thinks he knows how the killing is done."

"It's hardly a thing to tell a lady," Holgate objected.

"Ain't no ladies here that I know of," Calamity remarked, sucking appreciatively at the cigar. "This's a right good smoke, cap'n. How'd he do the killing?"

Holgate did not answer immediately. Looking at the girl, he suddenly became aware that she did not try to prove anything, but really enjoyed the cigar. Here was a girl completely beyond

99

his knowledge of women, one who lived by her own rules and neither accepted favours because of her sex, nor tried to out-do men despite it. He decided he could talk to Calamity with the same freedom that he discussed matters with his ship's officers.

"It's an old Indian trick," he explained. "One of my crew was killed in Bombay by the *thuggi*, they're a religious cult who dabble in murder and robbery. The way the *thuggi* kill is with a cord slipped around the victim's throat in a special manner. It is silent, quick and gives the victim little or no chance of escape or countering the hold. From the marks on the dead girl's neck, I'd say the Strangler either knows about the *thuggi*, or has come up with a mighty close imitation of their methods."

"What the hell's tribe do these *thuggi* belong to?" asked Calamity. "It don't sound Cheyenne, Sioux or Comanche to me, nor any of the tamed tribes neither. And I never heard of no place called Bombay on the Great Plains."

"That's not surprising," smiled Holgate. "Bombay is in India, and the *thuggi* are real Indians, not the kind you're used to meeting."

"Cap'n," grunted Calamity. "Happen you saw a bunch of them red varmints on the warpath, you'd reckon they was real enough."

"The captain offered to show us how *thuggi* works, Calam," St. Andre remarked with a smile, wondering if he would ever cease to be amused by the girl's unique female outlook on life.

"Yeah," replied Calamity suspiciously, putting a hand to her throat. "And who's he going to do the showing on?"

"On me, of course," the detective answered. "Who else?"

"Just thought you might want to see it done on me, just so's you'd know how it was done. Seeing it's you who gets it, Sherry, let's take us a whirl."

Reaching into his jacket pocket, Holgate took out a length of stout whipcord. Doubling the cord to find its centre, Holgate tied a knot in the middle, then one more on either side and about three inches from the first. With the knots tied, Holgate gripped the cord at each end, allowing it to hang in a long loop before him.

"Ready, lieutenant?" he asked.

Standing up with his back to Holgate, St. Andre nodded. "Ready!"

Holgate stepped forward and flipped the loop over St. Andre's head, gripped both ends of the cord between his hands and pivoted so that he stood back to back with the detective. Now the cord passed from Holgate's hands, up over his right shoulder and around St. Andre's neck. Bending forward, Holgate drew the loop tight. Only for an instant did Holgate keep up the tension, but St. Andre felt the knots bite into the sides and centre of his throat, blocking the windpipe and stopping his breath.

"That's how they do it," Holgate said, releasing the cord and turning fast. "Are you all right, lieutenant?"

Jerking the cord hurriedly from his throat, St. Andre sucked in a deep breath before he nodded and replied, "I—I think so. Do you know of any way one can break the grip of the cord, Captain?"

"None. The *thuggi* always tries to take his victim by surprise. Once the noose falls and is drawn tight, there is no escape."

"That's what I thought," St. Andre said quietly and turned to Calamity. "I've decided—."

"And so have I!" Calamity interrupted. "I'm still going through with it. So you'd best try that trick on me, Cap'n, and let me get the feel of it."

"On *you*?" gasped Holgate.

"On me. I'm the one the Strangler'll be doing it on."

Throwing an appealing glance at St. Andre, Holgate hoped for moral support in his refusal; but did not get it.

"When Calamity makes up her mind, we poor men might just as well give up and let her have her way," the detective stated. "She's seen enough to know how to make a *thuggi* cord, and she's stubborn enough to find help in practicing escaping from it. So we might as well help her."

"You might just as well," agreed Calamity, laying her cigar in the ashtray on St. Andre's desk.

Coming to her feet, Calamity stepped forward and took St. Andre's place before Holgate. After throwing another imploring glance at St. Andre, the captain took up his cord and stepped into position behind the girl. Calamity waited, tense and ready, watching for the cord to pass before her eyes. While watching the demonstration on St. Andre, she had seen what might be a way of breaking the hold and wanted to try it.

Down came the noose and instantly Calamity brought up her hands, palms outwards, sliding her fingers under the cord in an attempt at stopping it drawing tight on her. The try failed miserably. She felt the cord jerk tight as Holgate turned, and the leverage slammed her hands back into her throat, the knuckles sinking into her flesh. A sudden feeling of panic hit the girl as the way her breath was chopped off and she tried to jerk forward; which only made the grip on her throat tighten. Then the cord slackened and she staggered forward, tearing it from her neck.

St. Andre sprang forward and caught the girl in his arms, while Holgate spung around, concern showing plain on his face.

"Are you all right, *cherie*?" asked St. Andre, for he had seen the momentary panic on her face.

"Did I hurt you?" Holgate went on before Calamity could reply.

The concern for her welfare shown by St. Andre and Holgate jolted Calamity back to her normal self and she managed a weak grin.

"Yes for you, Sherry, and no to the Cap'n. Only I know one way I *can't* chance using now."

Yet while she fought to hide it, Calamity felt very worried. Holgate had moved slowly and with care, she had been ready and waiting for the noose too, yet he still managed to snap her hands back against her throat and prevent her from pulling the cord even a little free. Of course the leverage on the cord as it passed over Holgate's shoulder accounted for the strength of its grip, but the same would apply just as much when the Strangler wielded the noose. Another point to be remembered was that the Strangler would move neither as slowly nor gently as did Holgate when applying his killing cord.

Never one to avoid facing the truth, Calamity reviewed the situation in the light of what she now knew. One thing stood out clear and simple. If she hoped to stay alive long enough for the protective police screen to arrive and save her, she must find some way of breaking the hold of the cord around her neck. There now only remained one problem to be solved, the most important matter of all—how to do the breaking.

Taking off her bandana, Calamity spread it out flat, then folded it lengthways instead of re-rolling it. Carefully she wrapped the bandana around her neck to act as some slight protection against the cut of the cord. Giving a weak grin, she looked at the two men.

"Try again, Cap—Nope, you'd best let Sherry handle the rope this time, 'cause I'm going to try like hell to get free, and he's paid to take the lumps."

"Thank you for your concern, *cherie*," said the detective. "But let the Captain do it once more while I watch. I may be able to see some way of breaking the hold while watching."

On the first attempt, Calamity tried lashing with her right foot. She missed her mark, lost her balance and only the fact that Holgate instantly released the cord saved Calamity from obtaining a too thorough idea of how the cord worked. Without her hands on the cord, Calamity learned the purpose of the three knots. The lump of the central knot pressed on her adam's apple, the other two closing in from the sides so as to effectively clamp shut her wind-pipe. Even through the folds of the bandana she could feel the pressure of the knots, and guessed at the sensation caused when they bit into naked flesh.

A shudder ran through Calamity as the noose slackened, but she fought down her fears. Thinking fast, she came up with a possible solution.

"Kicking won't work," she said. "Try again."

On the next try Calamity made an attempt at stepping to one side. She hoped to pull the cord from Holgate's shoulder. However, she made a mistake by stepping to her right and this only drew the cord tighter.

"That won't work," St. Andre warned as the cord slackened.

"I kinda figured that myself," admitted Calamity.

"Try stepping to your left next time. It might pull the cords off his shoulder."

"Let me catch my breath first. Then we'll try it your way, Sherry."

An expression of admiration came to Holgate's face as he coiled the cord and watched Calamity pick up her cigar.

"If you don't mind me saying so, Calamity," he said. "You're the bravest woman I've ever seen or met."

"Feel free to say it any time," she replied, hoping she was not blushing at the praise. "Only I'm not being brave. I'm just a half-smart lil country gal trying to act all smart and save her fool neck."

"If you're a *half*-smart country girl," St. Andre put in, "I'd hate to come across a smart one."

"Or I," Holgate went on. "Any time you need a job, come and see me. I could use you as mate on my ship."

"Let's make another stab at escaping," Calamity put in hurriedly and knew she *was* blushing now.

Even stepping to the left did not provide the necessary solution to the problem, for the cord would not slide off of Holgate's shoulder and only drew tighter. Calamity let out an exasperated snort when released.

"Say, do you have that itty-bitty stingy gun with you, Sherry?" she asked.

"Of course," St. Andre answered, taking out his Smith & Wesson.

"Unload it. Let's try something else. Maybe if I'd a gun in my reticule, I could get it out and use it."

"It's worth a try," the detective admitted. "I've got the dead girl's reticule in my desk, seeing that you didn't bring one along."

"It don't go with pants and a shirt," explained the fashion-conscious Miss Canary and looked at Holgate. "You'll have to hold the cord a mite longer this time."

After St. Andre unloaded his revolver, he took the reticule from the desk's drawer, handing weapon and bag to the girl. Calamity double-checked on the empty condition of the gun, a safety precaution St. Andre approved of, then placed the revolver into the bag and drew tight the draw-strings which closed the neck of the reticule.

"Let's go," she said, standing with the reticule swinging by its strings from her left wrist.

Once more the noose dropped into place and even as it did, Calamity grabbed for the reticule with her right hand. She tried to move fast, but not fumble, yet for all that she barely slid her hand into the reticule before the cord around her throat drew tight. She found that the sudden cutting off of her breath, even though she expected it, induced a state of near-panic which prevented her thinking. Desperately she began to struggle against the choking of the cord.

"Let loose!" St. Andre yelled.

Holgate obeyed instantly and Calamity sank to her knees, hands jerking the cord and bandana from her throat. Both men moved to her side and gentle hands lifted her to a chair. The roaring in her head subsided and she saw two worried faces before her.

"That's all, *cherie*," St. Andre announced grimly.

"I just didn't move fast enough," she objected.

"And the Strangler will be moving much faster than I did," Holgate pointed out. "Surely there's some other way. Can't your men stick closer to her?"

"Not as close as they'd have to be to make it safe, or the Strangler would see them, especially in the Park."

"How well can Raoul Redon and the other boys shoot?" asked Calamity.

"Fairly well," answered St. Andre.

"Well enough to pick the Strangler off me from thirty yards at least on a moonlight night?"

"*Sacre blue*!" gasped the detective. "I doubt it. Hey, how about one of your friends with the freight outfit?"

For a moment loyalty to her friends warred with common sense and in the end common sense won. While Calamity hated to admit it, she doubted if even Dobe Killem could handle a revolver that well. A rifle maybe; but one did not see folks walking around in New Orleans with a rifle tucked under an arm. To have one of the boys do so would attract too much attention.

"None of 'em could do it. There's none of the boys can handle a gun that good."

"Or my men," St. Andre admitted.

"It's a pity you don't have one of those Western gunfighters here," Holgate remarked.

"Somebody like Dusty Fog, you m—."

St. Andre's sentence never ended. Giving a whoop like a drunk Pawnee coming to a pow wow, Calamity sprang forward, grabbed him by the shoulders and gave him a resounding kiss.

"That's it, Sherry!" she whooped. "If there's any way of getting out of the cord, old Dusty'll be the one to know it."

"Dusty Fog is not in New Orleans," St. Andre pointed out.

"Some detective," sniffed Calamity. "Don't they have a telegraph office in this fancy big city?"

"It's a chance," St. Andre admitted. "Captain Fog knows that strange way of fighting. He might be able to come up with the answer. We'll get off a message to him right away. But if he doesn't come up with the answer, we'll call off the whole thing."

CHAPTER TWELVE

Miss Canary Attracts Attention

ST. ANDRE turned to Calamity as they left the telegraph office after dispatching the request for advice to Dusty Fog in the Rio Hondo country of Texas.

"That is that, *cherie*," he said. "The answer will be sent over to my office as soon as it arrives."

"If Dusty's at the OD Connected, we'll get an answer right soon," Calamity replied. "What're you going to do now?"

"Make another tour of the Latour Street district and see if I can find anybody ready to talk about a missing girl. And you?"

"There's no use in my going with you. Happen the Strangler should see us together in daylight, he might be able to recognise me later, even through that blonde hair and paint."

"You could take up Captain Holgate's offer of a tour of inspection of the *China Star*," St. Andre suggested, for the captain had made the offer before leaving Headquarters to rejoin his ship.

"Sure I could. Might do that later. Only right now I've a hankering to see what kind of hosses the Army brought us down here to collect."

"Then I'll see you——."

"Tonight, same as last," Calamity finished for him. "We'll just have to play 'em as they fall until we get word from Dusty."

Seeing there was no chance of changing Calamity's mind, and knowing she would probably be stubborn enough to go without an escort, St. Andre surrendered. He hailed a passing cab and handed the girl into it, then gave the driver instructions where to take her.

"Until tonight then, *cherie*," St. Andre finished, taking the girl's hand and kissing it.

"Yep," agreed Calamity. "Hooray wah! Hey, what do you know, I talk French now."

Standing on the sidewalk, St. Andre watched the cab pull away. Maybe Miss Martha Jane Canary lacked most of the social graces, but there would never be another girl like her. With that thought St. Andre turned and looked for transportation to take him on what his instincts told him would be another dud quest to learn the identity of the Strangler's victims.

The cab carried Calamity towards the waterfront area. Cattle and other livestock came into New Orleans and an open section of the docks had been given over to pens. Leaving the cab, Calamity walked towards the largest of the pens and as she drew close, the wind wafted the smell of horses to her nostrils. Calamity sucked in the aroma as eagerly as a bluetick hound hitting hot cougar scent. In her imagination, she was carried back to her beloved West. Suddenly Calamity felt homesick for the rolling Great Plains country. She longed to feel leather in her hands as she handled the ribbons of her big Conestoga wagon's team, feel the sun on her head, the wind or rain in her face. The big city was not for Calamity Jane and never would be. She hated the never-ending rush and bustle of New Orleans, where folks hardly had time to stop and talk a spell. Out on the Great Plains everything seemed calmer, more friendly, cleaner. Even death came openly on the Plains, from bullet, arrow, knife or war-lance, not sneaking, unseen, silent and cowardly as the Strangler's whipcord noose.

"Now easy there, Calam gal," she told herself. "You've had some fun here too."

A young cavalry lieutenant, far more tidy and glittering than the junior officers Calamity had met on the Plains, stood by Dobe Killem's side at the largest of the coral-like pens. Turning from their study of the forty or so horses in the pen, both men looked in Calamity's direction and Killem raised his hand in greeting.

"Hi there, Calam gal," he said. "Come on up and get acquainted with Lootenant Bristow."

Trying not to stare too pointedly at Calamity's shapely figure and unorthodox dress style, Bristow bowed as taught at West Point.

"My pleasure, ma'am," he said.

"Reckon it is," grinned the girl and thrust out her right hand.

Hurriedly Bristow jerked off his right gauntlet and accepted the girl's hand. With the formalities tended to, Calamity turned and swung up on the pen's top rail to study the horses.

"What do you think of them, Miss Canary?" Bristow inquired.

"They look a mite small to me. Can't see one as goes fifteen hands even."

"We didn't buy them for great size, but for their hooves."

Ducking between the rails, Calamity entered the corral. Unlike Western horses, the animals in the pen showed no desire to avoid human beings, allowing Calamity to approach them. Although the girl had not worn her gunbelt that morning, the bull whip was thrust into her waist belt. Pulling the whip out, she made a loop of part of its lash and dropped it over the head of the nearest horse. Holding the animal, Calamity glanced down, then bent to take a closer look at its hooves.

Full of male superiority, Bristow joined Calamity in the pen and pointed down at what interested the girl.

"That's why the Army bought these horses," he explained. "They're called muck-ponies and bred between here and Florida. See the sizes of the hooves?"

"I'd be hard put not to."

"Despite the size, the foot is light, yet, tough," Bristow went on, lifting the horse's near fore leg to emphasise his point. "See the small size of the frog? It leaves a deep hollow into which mud can pack tight enough to support the horse's weight when crossing ground into which an animal with a normal hoof would sink belly deep. Why, I've seen muck ponies canter across swampy ground and quicksands that would mire down any other horse, and carrying weight too."

"That'd be real useful," answered Calamity, "in swampy country. Only we're a mite long on swamps on the Great Plains."

"You have snow there."

"Yep, reckon we do. It gets real de—Hey, you mean that the army figures using these hosses for a winter campaign again the Injuns?"

"Something like that," Bristow agreed. "You know as well as I do that the campaign against the Indians is almost brought to a halt with the snows of winter?"

"Reckon it is," the girl admitted, releasing the horse.

"We hope the muck ponies will enable us to carry on the offensive through the winter. That's why we bought them."

"Now me," grinned Calamity, "I thought that some general'd bred too many hosses and wanted to sell 'em fast."

Bristow eyed Calamity coldly and stiffened slightly, for he was still fresh enough from West Point to take himself and life very seriously. Before he could think up a sufficiently chilling response to her remark, he saw something which made him let the matter slide. A two-horse carriage driven by a grizzled infantry sergeant approached, in it sat a tall, slim major-general, a plump, motherly-looking woman and a pretty girl dressed to the height of fashion.

"Excuse me, Miss Canary," Bristow said stiffly, then turned and left the pen. Watching him go, Calamity coiled her whip and thrust it into her waist band. "Damn fool gal!" she told herself. "That big mouth of your'n'll get you hung one of these days."

Following Bristow from the corral, Calamity leaned on the rail and watched the young officer march smartly to the carriage and throw a parade-ground salute to the general.

"At ease, Douglas," the general said. "We came down to see that horse I had shipped in for Aileen's birthday."

"Mr. Killem cut it out for me, sir. I had it put in the smaller, empty pen."

"Good horse?"

"A fine animal, sir, but a touch high spirited."

"How about the others, Dobe?" asked the general, turning to the freighter.

"I've looked 'em over, General," Killem replied. "They're in good shape. I reckon we'll still have some alive when we reach St. Jo."

"They'd better be, or I'll be coming to you for employment," grinned General Furlong. "This idea is costing money and Congress hates spending *that* on the Army in times of peace."

"Reckon those muck-ponies'll do what you want?" asked Calamity.

"I hope so. The main idea came from Sheridan, I believe. If the ponies can take the cold, they might help us hit at the Indians during winter."

"May we see my new horse, papa?" Aileen Furlong asked.

"That's what we're here for," the General replied.

Although nobody asked her, Calamity accompanied Furlong's party to one of the other pens. Hooking a foot on to the bottom rail, Calamity studied the fifteen hand black gelding inside. She liked what she saw and to her way of thinking there stood a tolerable piece of horse-flesh, dainty, shapely, proud and spirited. The kind of animal one would pick as a go-to-town horse, yet capable of doing a hard day's work.

"He's a beauty, papa," Aileen gasped. "May I try him?"

"You're hardly dressed for riding, dear," her mother put in.

"And the horse is too much for a woman yet, Aileen," Bristow went on. "It needs gentling before you use it."

"Nonsense!" Aileen snorted. "I've been riding—."

"I'd rather see the horse ridden before we make any decisions," interrupted Furlong. "I'd ask you if you weren't in uniform, Douglas. How about it, Dobe?"

At which point Calamity put her bill in. While not setting up as a militant feminist who believed she could do anything a man could and better, Calamity took a dim view of Furlong and Bristow's display of arrogant male superiority. And with Miss

Martha Jane Canary to take a dim view of anything was to act in an attempt to clear her vision.

"Hell, Dobe totes too much lard to ride a hoss that size," she said. "I'll go in and 'three-saddle' it for you."

All eyes turned to the girl and grins creased the faces of the two older men, although Bristow clearly did not approve of Calamity's free and easy attitude. Having been on the Great Plains with her husband, Mrs. Furlong had lost any snobbish ideas of class-distinction she once possessed, so she smiled at the Western girl's speech. Aileen was young enough to regard Calamity as daring, modern and unconventional—in which she did Calamity an injustice—so must also be someone to respect.

"I could have one of the regimental horse-masters take it in hand, sir," Bristow suggested.

"And they'd spoil it for the gal," Calamity sniffed. "They're all right for busting a hoss so some lead-butted recruit can sit it, but that black wants gentler handling."

While General Furlong would not openly admit it, he knew army trainers were of necessity often heavy-handed in their training methods and tended to break rather than gentle a horse. Such treatment would ruin the black for his daughter's use. Anyway, it might be fun to see if Calamity Jane stacked up as high as Dobe Killem claimed for her.

"Do you have a saddle here?" he asked.

"The boys rode down this morning, their rigs are hanging on the rail at the big pen," answered Calamity. "Happen Mr. Killem'll act like a lil gentleman and fetch one over for me, I'll go catch me a hoss."

"I'll tend to it," grinned Killem.

Swinging into the pen, Calamity walked across the hard-packed ground towards the horse. However, the black did not wish to be caught and had room in which to manoeuvre. Showing a neat use of speed and the ability to turn on a dime, the horse refused to be caught for a time. This made Calamity use some choice language not often heard on the lips of a young lady and caused Aileen to jerk up her fan to hide her smile. A small crowd of loafers, the kind of men who gathered everywhere when given a chance of watching other people work, stood around the pen and sniggers sounded.

"All right!" Calamity snorted, coming to a halt and eyeing the horse. "If that's how want it."

Drawing her bull whip free, she shook out the lash then sent it snaking through the air to coil around the black's neck. Outside the pen Aileen gave a little shriek of dismay, while Bristow gave an angry snort aimed to let folks know his lack of faith in Calamity had been justified. General Furlong, a man with some knowledge of horses, noted that the black did not scream or show any sign of pain as the whip landed.

"Ooh!" gasped Aileen. "Did you see that?"

"It's—," her father began.

Before the General could say more, Calamity raised her voice in a lady-like plea for assistance.

"Dobe! You and that shavetail shove your tired butt-ends over here and lend me a hand to toss leather on this fool critter!"

"Be right there, gal," Killem chorused back and held the saddle he carried in Bristow's direction. "Here, bring this in. I'll toss a rope on that black."

From the quiet manner in which the horse stood after feeling the whip's lash coil around its neck, Calamity decided it had been rope-broke at least. However, her whip could not hope to equal a sixty foot length of hard-plaited manila rope when it came to holding a horse, so she raised no objections when Killem joined her and dabbed a loop on the black's neck. Calamity shook free, coiled and belted the whip. Clearly the horse did not intend to stand mildly and have the saddle fixed on it. In fact the black kicked up quite a commotion and attracted more loafers to see the fun.

"We'll have to ear him down," Killem stated, bracing himself against the pull of the horse and watching Calamity and Bristow's tries at getting the saddle in position.

"I'll tend to it!" whooped Calamity.

Watching her chance, the girl darted forward and grabbed to catch the rearing black by one ear. Making her catch, she reached around, took hold of the other ear and used her weight to get the black on to all four feet again. Calamity felt the horse strain against her grasp and as a further inducement to good behaviour took hold of the tip of the nearest ear between her teeth. Apparently the horse knew what Calamity's action meant, for it stopped struggling and avoided taking further pain. For all his smart and pompous manner, Bristow moved fast. Although he was more used to the Army's McClennan saddle, he wasted no time in swinging the range rig into place and securing it on the black.

While this went on, Tophet Tombes had returned from checking on the flatboats in which the horses would be transported north. He was on the opposite side of the corral to Furlong's party, but leaned on the rail among the loafers to watch the fun. A trio of burly, hard-looking men stood close by him. Brutal and coarse though they looked, all wore better clothing than the crowd around them. The tallest of the party had a livid weal running from the right temple across to below the lobe of his left ear. Nor were his friends clean of face, for one sported a swollen, cut lip and black eye, while the other's nose looked enlarged from some recent damage. Tombes noticed none of this, being more interested in watching the saddling of the black and awaiting Calamity showing those city folks a thing or two about the art of horse-handling Western style.

Never one to disappoint an audience, Calamity fixed herself to give the onlookers a good show. First she checked that the horse's saddle sat just as she wanted it, then fitted the bridle in place and cast off Killem's rope. Gripping the saddlehorn and reins, Calamity went afork the horse in a lithe bound.

"Yeeagh!" she yelled and rammed both heels into the horse's ribs, causing Killem and Bristow to make hurried dives towards the pen's rails.

It took but three bucking jumps to tell Calamity that the horse had already been 'three-saddled', ridden by a buster the three times which were all considered necessary out West for the horse to be ready to hand on to its regular owner. However, the black proved to be a show bucker, tucking its nose between its front legs, arching its back and going high but straight forward. While such a style looked highly spectacular, especially to an audience. who saw few such sights, it was not difficult for a skilled rider to handle. Calamity knew that as long as she did not fall asleep, she could stay afork the black and would not wind up eating pen-dirt without stooping for it.

Not that Calamity was content merely to take the conceit and bed-springs out of the black's belly in solid chunks. To whet the appetites of the crowd, she pretended to be losing her seat, waving as if off balance. A yell of applause rose as she fought her way back into control.

"Dang that Calamity," grinned Killem. "She'll bust her fool neck one of these fine days."

"I've never seen such a splendid rider," Aileen breathed back.

"Likely," grunted the big freighter, for he knew a show bucker when he saw one. "Stay with it, Calam gal!"

However, the horse decided to call it a day. Having been 'three-saddled', the black horse knew better than fight against the inevitable, and its snuffy nature sprang more from not being worked recently than out of a bad spirit. So, finding its rider clearly intended to stay afork, the black stopped fighting. Calamity fanned the horse's ears with her hat and jabbed moccasined heels into its ribs, but to no avail. Never one to punish a horse for showing a little spirit, she rode the black to the side of the pen and dropped from the saddle.

"There you are," she said to Aileen. "You've got a good hoss here, gal."

"I'll walk him until he cools, Aileen," Bristow put in and swung into the pen to take the black's reins from Calamity.

"Thank you for riding the horse, Miss—," Aileen began.

"Never been one for 'Missing', unless I don't like the other gal," Calamity interrupted. "Call me Calam."

"Thank you, Calamity," smiled Aileen. "I thought when you used the whip—."

Aileen's words trailed off again, for she did not know how to express her fears and wondered if Calamity might take offence at criticism.

Standing at Aileen's side, Killem let out a bellow of laughter. "The hoss wouldn't get hurt, unless Calam meant it to."

"But how could she—?" Mrs. Furlong put in.

Seeing that Aileen also appeared to have doubts about her ability to handle the whip, Calamity decided to demonstrate and prove her employer's words. The fact that a good-sized crowd also stood watching did not worry Calamity in the least, for she had never been a blushing violet seeking to hide her talents.

"Toss me my whip, Dobe," she said.

A grin creased Killem's face as he complied with his employee's request. Being a member of the bull-whip breed himself, Killem liked to see an expert at the art in action; and despite her age and sex Calamity was about as expert as one could be in the handling of a long lashed bull whip.

Catching the whip Killem tossed to her, Calamity shook out its coils and prepared to show the watching crowd how a Western freighter handled his, or her, most valued possession. The whip she held had been specially made for her by Tophet Tombes, who had a reputation for being something of an authority on such matters. Made of finest leather, the twenty foot lash was lighter than usual, yet that made the whip no less effective, handy—and deadly—in Calamity's skilled hands.

While knowing she was attracting considerable attention to herself and her unusual—for a female—talents, Calamity did not guess just what result her forthcoming demonstration of the ancient art of whip-popping would have.

CHAPTER THIRTEEN

Miss Canary Renews An Acquaintance

As a starter to her display Calamity worked the whip back and forward in the air so its tip gave out a series of cracks like a volley of gun shots. This in itself was not a particularly difficult trick, but always made an impressive commencement to a demonstration of the whip-wielder's art. While cracking the whip, Calamity pondered on which of her extensive repertoire would be best to use as opener to her show. She wanted something spectacular, yet which could be topped by a climax at her completion of the demonstration.

General Furlong remembering a trick performed by an Army wagon master and whip expert, took the matter of selection from Calamity's hands. Taking a silver dollar from his pants pocket, Furlong tossed the coin so it landed at Calamity's feet. Calamity grinned, guessed at the trick required by Furlong and accepted the challenge. Stepping over the coin, she advanced seven paces towards the centre of the pen and the crowd watched in silence, wondering what she planned to do. Calamity turned, sending the whip's lash snaking out the moment she faced where the coin lay. An explosive crack sounded, a spurt of dust rose from the hard-packed ground, and the coin spun high into the air. Having duplicated the Army expert's trick, Calamity next proceeded to improve on it. Striding forward, she caught the coin as it fell and flipped it back to its owner.

Never one to miss being in on any fun going, Tophet Tombes finished rolling a cigarette. Gripping the top rail of the pen, he swung himself up and sat astride the pole.

"Got a light, Calam?" he yelled and thrust the cigarette between his teeth.

Turning to face the speaker, Calamity saw an opening for a more spectacular trick. Without ever having been on a stage, or in a business that required a study of human nature, Calamity knew instinctively that her next trick would go down better if she showed folks just how dangerous it could be.

Instead of striking at the cigarette jutting from Tombes' mouth, Calamity aimed slightly ahead of the scout and let her lash coil around the rail on which he sat. Excited and unbelieving comments rose as the nearest of the audience saw the groove Calamity's whip carved in the stout timber. Having duly impressed her audience, Calamity went ahead with the trick.

Taking sight carefully, for a wrong move could be deadly, Calamity struck again. Crack! The whip made its noise and the cigarette in Tombes' mouth burst into a ruined cloud of paper and shreds of tobacco. Mutters and chatter rose as the watching crowd realised that Calamity had shattered the cigarette without also carving a sizeable divot out of the scout's face.

"I still think that whip hurt my horse!" Aileen stated as Calamity began another series of whip cracks.

"Do, huh?" grunted Killem. "Watch this."

Swinging up on the pen's rail, Killem rolled back his shirt's left sleeve and extended a brawny, bare arm shoulder high. Calamity nodded and moved closer. Once more she sent the whip licking out, its tip kicking a chip of wood from the rail and hacking a gouge in the timber. Drawing back her arm again, Calamity took careful sight and estimated the distance. Out coiled the long lash, headed straight at Dobe Killem's bared arm.

Aileen gasped and tried to look away. Even the river loafers, men with little or no interest in anything other than themselves, held their breath as the whip's lash, which had carved a groove in solid timber, curled itself around Killem's flesh. Yet Killem gave no sign of pain, his grin never flickered for an instant; and when the lash fell away Aileen could see no damage to the freighter's skin.

"But—But—!" she gasped.

"It's all in how you strike," Furlong told his daughter. "Used one way that whip would strip the flesh from a man's bones—."

"Charles!" yelped his wife.

"D—Don't, papa!" Aileen went on with a shudder.

"All right, honey. But used the other, and I doubt if Calamity would tell you how it's done, the whip just coils around and doesn't hurt."

Across the pen, Calamity's skin was attracting just as much attention, but for a different reason. The burly man with the livid weal on his face ran his forefinger along the groove left by the whip, then touched the ridge on his face. Twisting his face into what might be passed as a friendly grin, the man turned to Tombes.

"Who's that gal?"

"That's Calamity Jane, friend," Tombes replied, a touch of pride in his voice.

"Reckon you must know her real well, letting her take that cigarette out of your mouth," the man went on. "I sure as hell wouldn't want to chance it."

"There's no danger with a gal like Calamity handling the whip," Tombes answered.

"She's good with one, huh?" put in a second of the trio, fingering his side.

"As good as they come," Tombes stated.

The interest shown by the men did not strike Tombes as being strange. He knew that few city folks ever saw a member of the bull whip breed in action. Nor did the scout give a thought to the mark across the biggest man's cheek.

"I'd sure hate her to take into me with that damned thing," remarked the third man. "Don't reckon she would though."

"Wouldn't, huh?" grinned Tombes. "There's a bunch in town who don't reckon so."

"How's that?" asked the biggest man.

"Night we arrived ole Calam run across a bunch jumping a young feller and cut in to help him. Turned—."

"Hey, Tophet!" Calamity called. "Come on over and let's see what else we can show 'em."

"Why sure," Tombes replied and jumped down from the fence to walk over to where Calamity stood.

"Reckon it's her, Jules?" the second man asked, watching Tombes slouch away.

"She'd be the right size, and that damned thing sounded just like when whoever it was jumped us. Let's go tell Max about this."

"Danged lil show-off," grinned Tombes as he joined Calamity.

"Was just showing them how the other half live," she replied. "Anyways, I didn't want that gal thinking I'd hurt her hoss."

"Some fellers over that way was some took by you, gal," the scout remarked.

"Where they at?"

"Over there—Nope, that's them just walking away. Fact being, one of 'em looked like he might've tangled with a whip his-self."

Calamity stopped coiling her whip and looked in the direction indicated by the scout. Even as she looked, a fourth man joined the trio. A low hiss left Calamity's lips as she saw that the newcomer's right arm hung in a sling. The quartet stood for a moment, then began to walk away towards the waterfront.

"Go tell Dobe to come with you!" she ordered.

"Where to?" barked Tombes after the girl's departing back.

"After me!" Calamity answered over her shoulder and headed for the pen's rail, coiling her whip as she walked.

"Danged fool female!" snorted Tombes. "It's being in the city made her *loco*—or wuss'n she was afore."

Shaking his head, but also grinning as he thought of the many sterling qualities which sprang from Calamity's '*loco*' behaviour, Tombes crossed the pen and climbed out. However, before he could prevent his boss leaving and deliver Calamity's message, Tombes saw Killem and Furlong walk towards where Lieutenant Bristow returned from walking and cooling out the black horse.

"Where's Calam?" Killem asked when his scout arrived.

"Danged if I know," Tombes admitted. "Soon's as I told her about them three fellers, she took out like the devil after a yearling."

"Know the gal likes company," Killem remarked. "But them fellers must be real something happen *she* chases after *them.*"

"And me," drawled the scout. "They wasn't none of 'em what anybody 'cepting maybe their mothers'd think worth looking at. One of 'em looked like he'd already tangled with a whip."

On the night Calamity told her friends of how she rescued St. Andre, Tombes had been drinking; which always affected his memory. However, Killem, more sober at the time, took in Calamity's story and could remember enough of it to understand her present interest in a man with what might be whip-marked features. Despite her wild nature, Calamity was not a promiscuous girl who threw herself at every man she met. If Calamity took out after three men, she did not do so for sexual reasons but because she suspected them of being part of the quartet which jumped St. Andre.

"That danged lil fool hot-head!" Killem spat out. "Let's get after her."

"What's wrong, Dobe?" Furlong asked, but the freighter and scout already strode away at a good speed.

"Our lil gal's likely to find herself with some bad trouble," Killem called back over his shoulder.

On leaving the corral, Calamity passed through a crowd of excited admirers, grinning and acknowledging their approbation but keeping an eye on the departing quartet. The loafers, seeing there would be no more free entertainment, separated to go about their business. Ignoring the men behind her, Calamity strode through the waterfront area following the four bulky shapes. As she walked, she hoped to see a policeman who she might take into her confidence. Not that Calamity reckoned she would need help, but merely wished to have some official on hand to take over if the four men should be the same who attacked St. Andre. Even as she walked, Calamity found herself wishing that she had flouted New Orleans' rules and worn her gunbelt that morning.

After walking for a short way, the four men turned into an area given over to stacking cotton bales ready for shipment. The bales stood in high rows, separated by lanes through which roustabouts could move and handle the cargo. Reaching the corner, Calamity turned it, looked along the lane. She could see no sign of the quartet along the hundred or more yards length before her, but there were numerous side paths down which they might have gone. Figuring this would be as good a time and place as any to get in closer, Calamity strode along the lane at a better pace.

A movement caught Calamity's eye as she passed one of the side lanes. Fast though her reactions were, Calamity left things just a shade too long. Even as she started to turn, right hand reaching for her whip, she saw the big tough with the livid weal on his face, and a second hard-looking cuss standing concealed by the bales. Out shot the bigger man's hand, gripping Calamity by the right shoulder, digging in and pulping it so she could not make the arm muscles work. With a heave, the man plucked Calamity into the lane and his companion made a grab, catching the whip, pulling it from the girl's belt and tossing it aside. Neither of the men nor Calamity noticed that the whip fell in plain view on the path the girl had just left.

Before Calamity could make a move in her defence, the man who held her gave a shove which crashed her into one of the piles of bales. She hit it hard, but the nature of the bales' contents prevented her from serious injury. Seeing from the very bulk of the two men that fighting was out of the question, Calamity decided to try to bluff her way out.

"Hey!" she began. "Wha—."

For a big man that whip-scarred cuss could move real fast. His right hand came around in a slap that sprawled Calamity to the ground. Stepping forward, he touched the ridge on his cheek, and drew back his left foot.

"Hold it, Jules!" the other man snapped. "Max wants to see her first."

"Yeah?" Jules snarled. "She did this to me and I'll—."

"Max'll see to it," the other interrupted, bending, gripping Calamity by the hair and hauling her to her feet. "Don't make any fuss, gal, or it'll be worse for you."

Fighting down her inclination to use her knee on the man, Calamity raised a hand to rub her cheek. Then her eyes flickered to the lane down which she came. Where in hell had Dobe and Tophet got themselves to?

Feet thudded and the other two of the quartet made their appearance from among the bales. Although Calamity did not know it, she could hardly have found herself in worse or more dangerous company. Max Gravitch ran one of the most notorious bars in New Orleans; a place the police long sought to close, but failed through lack of evidence. While dressed better, and slightly more intelligent in appearance, Gravitch could not be termed an oil-painting and there was an expression on his face that boded little good for Calamity.

"So this's St. Andre's little friend," Gravitch said, coming closer.

"This's her," Jules agreed.

"Hey!" Calamity yelped. "What's with you bunch?"

Jules shot out his hand, thrusting the girl back against the bales and bunched his big fist ready to strike. Before the tough could move, Gravitch shoved him savagely aside.

"Hold it! This might not be the one. What do you reckon, Billy?"

"Don't seem likely a gal could do it, Max," the man who had been with Jules replied. "Only we saw what she could do with a whip."

"It's her all right!" Jules snarled and waved a hand towards his face. "Reckon I wouldn't recognise the bastard who gave me this?"

"I came out worse than you," Gravitch answered, "and I couldn't be sure."

"Why was she following us just now?" asked the fourth man.

"*Me* follow *you*?" Calamity spat out. "Hell, you might go over like a house on fire with these city gals, but you're sure nowhere with me."

"Then why'd you follow us?" Gravitch inquired.

"Who's following you? I hurt myself riding that hoss and aimed to go home to rest up. Come through here looking for a cab."

"I tell you she's the one, Max!" Jules bellowed.

"Hold your voice down!" Gravitch ordered. "Whether she's the one or not, we don't want the law coming down on us."

"Look," Calamity put in. "If you'd just—."

"Shut your yap!" growled Jules, then looked at his boss. "You didn't see her using that whip, Max, or hear how it sounded."

"That's right," Gravitch agreed. "I didn't. Where's the whip at now?"

"Right here, gents," said a voice from behind them.

Never had Calamity been so pleased to hear Dobe Killem's voice, or to see her boss and Tophet Tombes, than at that moment. The words brought Gravitch and his men spinning around fast. Freighter and scout stood a few feet apart, Killem holding his coiled whip in his right hand, Tombes gripping Calamity's whip in his left and holding his right hovering above the butt of the Army Colt thrust into his waist-band in defiance of New Orleans' disapproval of people carrying firearms.

"What do you pair want?" Gravitch asked, for there were few men on the New Orleans water-front who would dare cross him.

Unfortunately for Gravitch, Killem and Tombes were only visitors and as such unaware of how they should act in the tough's presence. More than that, they came from a country which held many hard men and so grew blasé about such self-opinionated persons. In the final reckoning Killem and Tombes were, in the range sense of the word, dressed and figured themselves capable of evening the odds against them. So Killem studied the men, noted that Jules still gripped Calamity's arm in one hand, and answered Gravitch's question.

"We'll start by having that feller take his cotton-picking hand offen Calam, *hombre*," said Killem, his voice mild and gentle as that first whisper which heralds the coming of a Texas blue norther storm.

At which Calamity showed a remarkable lack of tact. Later she would apologise for her actions and explain that the rough-handling dished out by Jules prevented her from thinking straight. Maybe that was true, for the man's treatment had been far from gentle, but for once in her life Calamity spoke in a serious situation without giving due care and attention to her words.

"They're the bunch that jumped Sherry!" she yelled.

A snarl of fury left Jules' lips. "It was he—."

His angry words came to an abrupt halt. Along the river front Jules had a reputation for being rough on women and at least two street-walkers carried scars to attest his brutality; the trouble being that at long last he had picked on the wrong girl. Calamity was no street-walker living in fear of Gravitch's bunch and so meekly submitting to Jules' maulings. In her wild free life Calamity neither feared nor took abuse from any man. Only common-sense prevented her from proving that to Jules earlier.

Then Calamity stood alone against the burly quartet. Now, two good friends on hand to back her, she figured the time for meekness had ended and Jules' education could begin.

Suddenly, even as the man spoke and without giving a hint of her intentions, Calamity pivoted around. Her first move took Jules, used to more complaisant girls, by surprise. What came next prevented him from recovering his composure and making use of his extra height and strength. Coming around to face the man, although still held by the arm, Calamity drove up her right knee. While Calamity had not found time to visit a *savate* academy, she still knew how to get the best out of her shapely but powerful legs. Up lashed her knee, catching her captor right between the legs. While Jules was a tough man with a body hardened to take punishment, no amount of strength could immunise him against a blow like that. Letting out a startled and agony filled croak in place of the 'r' at the end of his interrupted final word, Jules clutched at his injured region, doubled over and staggered into the nearest bales, retching and with sweat pouring out of his agony-twisted face.

Having taken a kick in the same area during the attack on St. Andre, Gravitch found that he gathered troubles of his own. The instant Calamity felt Jules release her arm, she prepared to perform the ancient and noble feat of getting the hell out of it. Like a flash, almost before Gravitch's men, with the exception of Jules, realised fully what she had done, Calamity spun around. Dropping her shoulder, she threw herself forward and butted hard into Gravitch's injured arm. Calamity heard the man yell as she bounced away like a billiard ball heading for a cannon. Pain ripped through Gravitch as he staggered under the impact of Calamity's arrival, but his left hand shot into his jacket pocket.

"Catch!" Tombes yelled, throwing Calamity's whip handle-first to her as she came bounding in his direction. At the same moment, the scout's right hand grabbed at the butt of his Army Colt.

Even as she caught the whip, Calamity skidded into a turning halt by her two good friends. Behind the girl, Gravitch's bunch made the foolish decision to fight with guns. Billy's right hand whipped under his jacket to emerge holding a short barrelled Colt Police Pistol, .36 in calibre and the one of the few easily concealed, *working* revolvers of the period. Whether Billy had skill in its use remained a moot point, for he was not given the chance to use it.

Up and down rose Killem's whip, its lash looping forward; and in matters of that nature Killem stood second to no man,

The result proved just as effective as when Galamity handled Gravitch on the night of the attack upon St. Andre, maybe even more so for Killem's whip was heavier than the girl's, though none shorter in length. Screeching as his wrist bones splintered under the constriction of the whip, Billy felt himself hauled forward. Killem let the man come close, then ripped a punch into his belly. With an agonised croak, Billy sank to his knees, clutched at his stomach, retched violently and lost all interest in the proceedings.

Which left Gravitch and the fourth man to uphold the honour of the New Orleans underworld, Jules still being more concerned with his own troubles. For an Eastern criminal, Gravitch could lay claim to being better than fair with a gun. Only he dealt with men trained in the handling of firearms and who knew much about gun-fighting situations. Even while staggering, Gravitch sent a hand into his jacket pocket. Closing his fingers on the butt of the waiting Remington Double Derringer, Gravitch fired through the coat and by instinctive alignment. For all that, his shot came mighty close to accomplishing what several aspiring Indian brave-hearts and a couple of white bad-men tried to do. The .41 bullet missed Tophet Tombes' face by inches on its way up, ripped a hole through the brim of his hat and sent the Stetson jerking back on its storm strap.

An instant later Tombes' Army Colt gave a deep-throated answer to the Remington's challenge and the scout shot in the only way he dared under the circumstances—to kill. Tombes did not know what kind of a gun Gravitch held in the pocket, and against a man who handled one that good it did not pay to take chances. Caught between the eyes by a .44 ball, Gravitch pitched over backwards and crashed to the cotton bales at Jules' side. For a moment the gang boss hung there, then he crumpled over and fell to the ground.

The fourth member of the quartet did not even get his gun clear. Whip in hand, Calamity completed her turn. Out flicked her lash biting into the man's sleeve and sending shocking pain through him. When he brought his hand from the pocket, it came empty.

"No more!" he screeched. "I quit!"

Feet pounded and a small crowd gathered, attracted by the whip cracks and shots. A pair of policemen come forward, halting and staring at the scene before them, but they did not have time to ask questions.

"Here, boys," Calamity said. "Lay hold of 'em. Lootenant St. Andre wants to see them."

CHAPTER FOURTEEN

Miss Canary Meets An Intellectual Gentleman

"NONE of the three can tell us anything," St. Andre told Calamity as he sat on the bed in her apartment and watched her dress for her role as decoy. "Max Gravitch, he was their boss, only told them they had work to do. It was a pity that Tophet had to kill Gravitch."

"He just wouldn't have it any other way," Calamity replied, drawing up her skirt and hooking one bare leg on the other, then reaching for a stocking.

"So Tophet explained. Not that I objected to Gravitch dying, our city will be a cleaner place without him. But I would rather have had him alive and talking. You see, *cherie*, it has long been my theory that there is a big man behind all the organised crime in New Orleans, a man who controls a dozen like Gravitch. One day I hope to get him."

The day would come, but not for almost two more years, when St. Andre got his man and finally solved the murder which indirectly brought him into contact with Miss Martha Jane Canary.

"No answer from Dusty yet?" Calamity inquired, drawing the stocking on and ignoring St. Andre's gaze at her legs.

"Not yet. And uncross your legs, we haven't time to think about *that*."

"This danged police work sure spoils a gal's fun," grinned Calamity.

"Then why not dr——."

"No. Sherry. We've got to get that Strangler afore he kills again and this's the only way we might do it. You didn't have no luck in tracing the last one he killed, did you?"

"None. It's the same story, the people who know won't help the police."

"Then me 'n' Jackie's going out again tonight."

Seeing from Calamity's attitude that there would be no changing her mind, St. Andre surrendered. "Very well," he said. "Go ahead. I'll tell Redon and the others not to get too far from you, and if you should meet anybody who might be the Strangler, to make sure they don't give him a chance to put that cord around your neck."

"Happen the boys are in too close, you might scare him off," Calamity pointed out.

"It's a chance we have to take, *cherie*," answered St. Andre, rising and laying a hand gently on her head. Bending over, he kissed her lightly on the lips. "I'd rather lose the Strangler than you."

"You're not getting all serious about me, now are you, Sherry?" smiled the girl, looking up at him.

"Would it be a bad thing if I did?"

"It'd be a plumb waste of both our time, and you know it. Hell, it'd never come to anything but trouble if we got too close, Sherry."

"We don't know that," St. Andre answered. "You could adapt into any society, if you wished to."

"I sure couldn't," Calamity contradicted. "And I sure as hell couldn't settle in a big city any more'n you could stop being a lawman and come West with me."

"We've—."

"We've done no more than I've done afore with men and expect to do again," the girl interrupted and gently took his hands in her own. "Mind you, Sherry, you're a long way from the worst I've known at happying up a gal. Now stop looking all solemn and go fetch my hat."

For a moment St. Andre did not move. If any other woman had spoken in the manner Calamity addressed him, he would have felt disgusted. But one did not judge Martha Jane Canary by other women's standards. Jerking her forward, he gave her a kiss, then shoved her away from him.

"Miss Canary," he stated. "You are an immoral young lady. But, Lord, there will never be another one like you."

"I'd surely be disappointed if there was," Calamity replied. "Now go get my hat while I plaster all this muck on my face. Darn it, Sherry, why do gals wear all that paint and powder?"

"To beautify themselves and attract men."

Calamity made a wry face. "Hell, I done all right without it all these years."

Before St. Andre could make any reply, a knock on the door heralded the arrival of Jackie and Redon. Both were dressed for the decoy assignment and tactfully overlooked the fact that Calamity still wore only one stocking.

"It's this boss of your's keeping me talking, Raoul," lied the unabashed Miss Canary. "You and him wait in the hall and leave a gal some privacy."

Within ten minutes a blonde Calamity, dressed as the previous night, came from her apartment with the ballet-dancing *savate* expert. Despite knowing, even more so than the previous night, the dangers facing them, the girls looked unworried and cheerful.

"Let's go," Calamity said, hooking her hand into St. Andre's arm. "Maybe we'll be lucky tonight."

Calamity proved to be a mighty poor prophetess. Although they made the rounds of the Latour Street district until past midnight, neither girl received an offer from any man resembling the Strangler's build and height. However, the night was not entirely wasted. Using her ability to make friends, Calamity started to gain the confidence of the street girls they met in the various places. While waiting for customers on one side and hoping to be selected as the Strangler's next victim in the other case, Calamity bought a few drinks, made jokes, lent a sympathetic ear to problems, and in general won over several girls. She worked for one purpose, to find out the names of possible Strangler victims.

While Calamity had never been trained for such work, she knew instinctively that she must not rush matters. One hint of suspicion would not only prevent the street-walkers taking her into their confidence, but almost might end her usefulness as a decoy. So, for the first evening, she confined herself to getting to know the other girls and persuading them that she followed their trade but did not regard them as business rivals or enemies. Buying a couple of rounds of drinks, and boasting how she had made a good sale that evening to explain where the money came from, started the thaw. From then on, once her bridge-head had been established, Calamity consolidated her position in a manner which any general would have admired. Always good company at such times, she soon had the girls laughing at her raw, unprintable jokes. In addition, she listened to the other girls' troubles, agreed that all men were lousy beasts and generally made herself agreeable. For the first time, while talking with the street-girls, Calamity learned just how rough company she had been in that afternoon. Already the story of the capture of Gravitch's gang had gone the rounds, and Calamity found that her *alter ego* stood high in the street girls' favour with only one complaint levelled at her head, that she had not treated Jules far rougher than she did. Not that the girls recognised this blonde obvious member of their profession as the famous Calamity Jane, but it made

Calamity feel good to hear their comments and receive their unconscious approbation.

However, apart from a boost to her ego, and making a lot of friends, Calamity achieved nothing that evening. No man even vaguely resembling the Strangler's height and build approached her, and shortly after midnight Redon attracted Calamity's attention with a jerk of his head.

"Well," Calamity said, shoving back her chair. "That's me for the night."

"And me," Jacqueline agreed. "If my man doesn't like it, he can do the other. What do you say, Jane?"

"Don't let *him* hear you say it," Calamity replied, winking at the others, "or the reds of your eyes'll be turning black. See you tomorrow, girls."

Calamity and Jacqueline left to the accompaniment of cheerful laughs and waves. Not until they were clear of the Latour Street district did they wait for their escort to catch up with them.

"You pair've been having fun," Redon remarked after sending one of the men to find a cab. "Did you learn anything?"

"Nothing much," Calamity admitted. "I didn't reckon rushing around asking if any of them was shy a pard or two'd get me any place. So I played it steady and maybe tomorrow I'll get me a few names."

"One of those gals, that big black-haired one, goes around with a couple of fellers we'd like to lay hands on," Redon said. "Why not—?"

"That's out!" Calamity snapped. "I'm in this thing to help you boys catch the Strangler, not go bounty hunting."

"No offence," grinned the detective, and strangely did not think any the worse of Calamity for her refusal. "Maybe we'll have a taker for you tomorrow."

"Maybe," answered Calamity. "I only hope that he hasn't got another gal tonight."

The Strangler had not struck again that evening, which did not surprise any of the decoy party. Next morning Calamity slept in late and on rising had barely finished breakfast when a messenger from St. Andre brought word that her presence was required at Headquarters. Calamity paused only long enough to collect her hat and whip before taking the cab St. Andre sent for her and driving across town. On her arrival, she found Jacqueline waiting and noticed that the slim girl wore black tights and a blouse. St. Andre sat at his desk and waved a buff-coloured telegraph message form as Calamity entered.

"This is from the Rio Hondo," he said. "It may give us the answer we need."

"Good for old Dusty," replied Calamity. "I knew he'd find the way and be only too pleased to help out."

"I have read the message and Lieutenant St. Andre showed me how the Strangler works, Calam," Jacqueline remarked. "We waited for you before trying, but I think it will work."

"Now me," grinned Calamity. "I'd be more surprised if it *didn't* work, knowing Dusty Fog like I do."

Taking the sheet of paper, Calamity read it, mouthing the words in the manner of one who spent but little time at such a pursuit. Within the limitations of using the telegraph services, Dusty Fog appeared to have done a fine job in explaining how he figured the Strangler's noose attack could be defeated. After reading the message, Calamity felt that her confidence in the Rio Hondo gun wizard had been more than justified.

"Danged if it don't look so easy you'd wonder how we missed it," she said and laid down the telegraph message form. "Let's give her a whirl, Sherry."

However, reading how to perform the counter to the attack and actually performing it, proved to be two entirely different things. Calamity's first two tries proved no more successful than her previous attempts at escaping from the constriction of the strangling cord. Much to Calamity's annoyance, Jacqueline was first to make a successful counter. With her fast dancer's reactions, she managed to perform the counter on her fifth attempt.

"It works!" she said delightedly. "I think if you did it slightly faster, Sherry, we would have a better chance."

On following the dancer's suggestion when trying the killer's hold with Calamity, St. Andre found that the counter worked much better. Previously he had been slow moving and braced for the counter. When working faster, he found less opportunity to prevent the girl escaping. The Strangler would be working fast and unprepared for resistance after so many easy kills.

"Reckon we've got the hang of it now," Calamity stated as she picked herself up from the floor after a successful counter to St. Andre's attack.

"Now that's what I call a poor choice of words," smiled the detective, also rising. "But I feel a whole lot happier now we know you've a chance of escape."

"Know something, Sherry?" said Calamity. "So do I."

That evening found Calamity and Jacqueline out on the streets

127

again. At ten o'clock Jacqueline had a likely taker. A well dressed young man of the right height and size, slightly drunk, made the usual advances and she departed with him. Redon followed with one of the men, while Calamity spent a quarter of an hour worrying over her friend's safety. At last Jacqueline returned, unmarked and unflustered, to take a seat at Calamity's side.

"No?" asked Calamity.

"No," agreed Jacqueline. "I thought it might be when he suggested we take a walk down towards the Park. But when we got to the outside, he wanted to go to my room instead of walking. Raoul and Vic came up then, explained matters and saw him on his way."

"Could have been the Strangler playing cagey," Calamity remarked.

"They searched him thoroughly and he didn't have as much as a piece of string in his pockets. He's a clerk in a riverboat company's office and wouldn't want word of his escapade to slip out. Where now?"

"Let's try the Blue Cat, shall we?" Calamity suggested.

"Suits me," answered Jacqueline. "I wonder if we'll learn anything there?"

Half-a-dozen street girls sat around a table in the Blue Cat, a saloon much favoured by their class, when Calamity and Jacqueline entered. Apart from one, Calamity and Jacqueline had seen all the girls around the Latour Street district during their visits and five were among those Calamity befriended the previous evening. Clearly Calamity was now regarded as being all right, for cheerful greetings came her way as she and Jacqueline crossed the room.

"This's Nora, Jane," one of the girls introduced, waving a hand to the only girl Calamity and Jacqueline had not seen around the district. "She's making her debut tonight."

Looking at Nora, a small, pretty, young-looking girl wearing a blue dress and sporting a large blue ring on her right hand's third finger, Calamity smiled. "Don't know what that is, but I hope you enjoy it."

"I will," answered Nora, touching her curly blonde hair and returning Calamity's smile.

From the way she spoke, Nora clearly imagined her new life would be one of leisure and pleasure. Watching Nora, Calamity wondered if she should break her habit of letting folks run their own lives and try to steer the blonde out of a dirty, unpleasant business.

However, before Calamity could make any moves in that direction, or start to make a stab at learning the names of a few possible Strangler victims, she saw a man enter the room from Latour Street. From the way Jacqueline stiffened in her seat, Calamity guessed that the dancer also spotted the man and shared her interest. The man halted just inside the doorway and stood looking around him. Although he wore good quality clothing, the material showed signs of lack of care. His hair was long, not in the manner sported by Wild Bill Hickok and other plainsmen but merely long enough to hint at a needed visit to a barbershop. Some folk might have called him good looking, but Calamity took note of his pallid features with the intense expression and did not like what she saw. What interested Calamity and Jacqueline about the newcomer was the fact that he had a slim build and stood slightly over five foot ten in height.

Glancing at the bar to check that Redon saw the new arrival, Calamity found that after one quick look the detective turned his back on the man as if wishing to avoid recognition. The newcomer left the door and strolled in the direction of the girls' table.

"Hi, girls," he greeted.

"Hello Browne," chorused five of the table's occupants.

Calamity, a keen student of human nature and facial expressions, noticed a flicker of a scowl crease the young man's eyes as the girls used his name, however, his mouth never lost the friendly smile. He nodded in Calamity's direction.

"And who are the new faces?" he asked.

"This's Jane and Jackie," one of the girls introduced. "They've come down river from Memphis. And this is Nora, she's just starting."

"It's one way of supporting your family, Nora," the young man remarked. "The kind of money they can earn isn't enough to keep you in anything but poverty."

"You're right," Nora gasped, eyes shining in delight as she found a good excuse for turning to this kind of life instead of staying in her previous employment as a maid.

"My dear child," smiled the man, though Calamity thought it nearer a condescending sneer, "I always am."

With that he walked away, followed by several admiring, and one critical, gazes.

"Who's he?" asked Calamity.

Shock and surprise showed on most of the other girls' faces. "Why that's Browne Crossman," one gasped.

"And who's Browne Crossman?"

"Just the greatest writer who ever lived," the other girl explained. "He wrote a book, but the aristocrats won't let it be published. Works for the *Intelligencer*. Even though he's got plenty of money, he comes down here a lot. He prefers our company and he's all for the workers."

Calamity was a poker player of some skill, so she concealed her feelings. However, she had met a few of the kind of politicians who were 'all for the workers' and, being a sensible girl, mistrusted them. From her study of Browne Crossman, she decided he would be like most of his kind, self-opinionated, despising the people he professed to be all for. There had been more than a hint of condescension about him as he spoke to the girls, a touch of annoyance during the familiar use of his Christian name.

It appeared that none of the other occupants of the room had any doubts about Crossman, for he was greeted cheerfully and familiarly as he walked towards the bar. On his arrival, Crossman saw and recognised Redon, guessed the detective must be on some duty which involved keeping his identity secret, so prepared to demonstrate his love of the down-trodden underdogs.

"Well, fancy seeing you in here, Sergeant Redon," Crossman said in a voice which carried around the room. "I thought the Police Department used you in the Bourbon Street district. Or isn't that area profitable enough for you?"

Anger glinted in Redon's eyes as he turned. He knew that the young reporter deliberately identified him. "I just came in for a drink, Mr. Crossman."

"You aren't dressed as well as the last time I saw you," Crossman went on. "Isn't business as good as usual?"

A nasty snigger rose from the crowd, for all knew Crossman hinted that the detective sergeant added to his pay by taking bribes. Under other conditions Redon would have taught some of the sniggerers a sharp lesson in respect for the law, but among its other activities the *Intelligencer* liked nothing better than to expose police 'brutalities'. Such a report always meant trouble for the officer involved, so Redon held his temper, finished his drink and walked out of the room.

At her table, Calamity sat squirming angrily. Only by exercising her willpower did she prevent herself rising, crossing the room and telling Crossman what she thought of him. Redon was an honest man who never took bribes, a brave man and one doing a thankless task. In Calamity's opinion he deserved better than have to put up with the sneers of a man not fit to lick his boots.

The other girls seemed both amused and pleased to see a policeman humiliated, so Calamity kept her thoughts to herself.

Having proved himself once more 'all for the workers', Crossman dominated the conversation in the room. He spoke well, but with only one purpose, and the customers listened attentively. With skill Crossman played on the greed and envy of his audience, condemning everybody who owned more than the people in the room, hinting that under his political party the world would be a gloriously happy place where 'the people owned everything'. To hear him talk, nobody would ever need to work if his party gained control of the country. While most of his audience drank this in eagerly, Calamity listened with a sceptical ear, wondering just what kind of world Crossman and his kind would make. Somehow she doubted if their world would be the pleasant, rosy place he painted it.

Just as Crossman started a tirade against the police as oppressors of the poor and tools of the rich, with Calamity hoping the rest of her escort would not tip their hands, screams and scuffling sounded in the street. Then the main doors flew open and a wildly excited man looked briefly in.

"Fight!" he yelled. "It's Annie Goldtooth and Louisa Duval!"

Instantly Crossman's audience came to its combined feet and headed for the door and windows at a rush. While it might be pleasant to sit listening to what a fine place the world would be when the workers got their rights, the crowd would much rather watch the exciting battle long awaited between two prominent rivals at the street girl trade.

Calamity went along with the others and saw as good a cat-fight as it had ever been her pleasure to witness from a spectator's angle. Fifteen minutes later the crowd returned to toast Annie Goldtooth's success, for she soundly defeated her rival. The first thing Calamity noticed was that Crossman had left the room. Next she glanced at where the intellectual young man had stood. A shattered glass lay on the ground; a glass which would not have broken by merely being dropped, and appeared to have been hurled furiously at the floor.

CHAPTER FIFTEEN

Miss Canary Meets The Strangler

SOLEMN faces greeted Calamity as she entered the office to find St. Andre and Redon waiting. After the fight the previous night, Calamity and Jacqueline stayed on at the bar, but excitement over the sight of the battling women rode high and they found no opportunity to bring the talk around to possible victims of the Strangler. On leaving the bar, the girls and their escort found a fuming Redon waiting along the street. It took some pretty strong talk on Calamity's part to prevent the furious detective from following his intention to find and hand Crossman the thrashing of his life. After cooling Redon down, they called off the decoy and returned to Headquarters. Calamity was called in from her bed the following morning and her every instinct told her something had gone badly wrong.

"I'd like you to come to the morgue, *cherie*," St. Andre told her. "The Strangler took another victim last night."

"Another?" she gasped.

"Two youngsters found her body in the Park this morning."

"I think I saw her last night, but it's impossible to tell from the face," Redon went on. "You might be able to—."

The words died away for Redon, while admiring Calamity, did not entirely approve of a girl doing such work and also thought the sight of that body nothing to show a woman. Calamity guessed at the sergeant's thoughts and did not feel any annoyance, but she gave her agreement to St. Andre's suggestion and went with the two lawmen downstairs to the basement morgue.

Although not given to being affected by atmosphere, Calamity could hardly hold down a shudder as she entered the lamp-lit morgue. Never a cheerful spot, the basement room appeared far worse when one thought of its purpose. Calamity fought down her thoughts and walked slowly towards the sheet-draped form on the centre table. Sucking in a breath, she drew back the sheet and looked down. Blonde hair; a hideously distorted mask that seemed vaguely familiar, showed in the light. Calamity bit down an exclamation and drew the sheet from the body. A blue dress inc eased her suspicions and she found confirmation when she saw the big blue ring on the right hand. Pulling back the sheet to cover the body, Calamity turned to face the waiting detectives.

"Name's Nora. She only started on the street last night. Was working as a maid for a Colonel Yaxley's family," Calamity said. "Poor fool lil kid! I meant to try to talk her out of doing it."

"Who did she leave with?" St. Andre asked, leading Calamity from the room.

"Alone, as far as I know. She went out back and didn't come in again. The other gals laughed and made a few jokes about her losing her nerve. Lord! If that had been all she lost."

St. Andre laid a hand on Calamity's arm. "Nora?" he said. "At least we have a start. Did she say where she intended to take her customers?"

"A room in a house on Garou Street. Goldberg's place," Calamity answered.

"I know it," Redon stated. "I'll see Goldberg."

"And I'll take the Yaxleys," St. Andre went on.

A string of curses left Calamity's lips. "That poor—!" she finished.

"Easy, *cherie*," St. Andre interrupted gently.

"Easy hell!" she spat back. "Why couldn't the Strangler've picked on me last night? Maybe he will tonight."

For once in his life St. Andre looked uneasy. He did not speak until they were standing on the ground floor. Then, shrugging his shoulders, he turned to the girl and said, "*Cherie*, we must call off the decoy for the next three nights."

He did not expect Calamity to take the news calmly, and was not wrong. Anger glowed in her eyes as she swung towards him. "Why?" she asked coldly.

"General Butler is paying New Orleans a visit and I have to use every man to guard him."

Which figured when one thought how the Union Army general treated Southern prisoners-of-war and people during or after the War Between the States. While Calamity had been born in the North and supported the Union, she did not regard Butler as a hero, or even desirable, and failed to see why his life should be more important than a street walker's.

"The lieutenant's hands are tied, Calam." Redon put in. "He tried to fight against the order, but was out-ranked."

"I know he would," Calamity replied. "But we sail in three days. That means you won't have a chance to use me again."

"Some girls would be pleased of that," St. Andre told her gently. "At least we now have the name of a victim. It might lead us to the killer."

133

"Yeah," answered Calamity. "It might at that."

If St. Andre had not been so busy following up the lead in the Strangler case, than helping organise the protection of the visiting general, he might have thought about Calamity's meek acceptance and decided that it was not in keeping with her character as he knew it.

On leaving Headquarters, Calamity took a cab to the river front and joined Killem's men. She said nothing about the decoy work being cancelled and, although she and Killem went to watch the arrival of General Butler, they did not have a chance to speak with any of their detective friends. However, Calamity saw why the Chief of Police insisted on maximum security. A large crowd of hostile demonstrating sufferers at Butler's hands during and just after the War swarmed on the river front, and it took a good force of club-swinging policemen to hold them back as the hated figure left the riverboat. (A noticeable side-issue was that the *Intelligencer*, usually so rabid in exposing police 'brutalities,' never said a word about the clubs cracking heads in defence of General Butler). The defence and protection of Butler had been left in the hands of the municipal authorities because various wise heads realised that the sight of Butler taken with Union Army uniforms might provoke serious trouble.

Having grown used to Calamity dressing and leaving on the decoy work, none of her freighter friends saw anything unusual in it that evening. Calamity debated whether she should take a gun or not, but decided against it. So she set forth into the night, walking through the Park and entering the Blue Cat to find only a handful of girls and a few riverboat men present.

"The Street's quiet tonight," she remarked, taking a seat with the other girls and ordering a beer from a bored waiter.

"There's a big crowd gone up to the Opera House to show that bastard Butler what folks down here think of him," one of the other girls answered.

After sipping at her beer, Calamity pretended to notice something. "Hey, has Nora got a taker already?"

None of the girl's answered for a moment, then a buxom blonde called Hetty said, "She's not been home all night, or today. I room next to her."

"Maybe the Strangler got her," another put in. "That Redon was around asking about her this morning. They came round just after Betty Muldoon disappeared."

"And when Sarah Gotz stopped coming here," a third girl

remarked thoughtfully. "I knew Sarah hadn't just run out like her man told the law."

Once the subject had been opened, the girls started to discuss it thoroughly and in doing so told Calamity all she need to know. Sitting quietly, she made a mental note of the various names mentioned. Not all would be Strangler victims but she reckoned she had learned enough to start St. Andre on the trail.

"I'm getting scared to go with a feller," Hetty stated. "Why in hell don't the police stop him?"

Only just in time did Calamity prevent herself answering that the police might have brought the Strangler's career to an end earlier if given assistance by various members of the public. She read the fear in each girl's face and realised it came through the detectives asking about a Strangler victim by name. Before the girls did not know if a friend be dead or merely missing, now they knew for sure. Calamity decided to get word to St. Andre as soon as possible to strike while the iron of fear burned hot, as he would find the girls more co-operative now.

All eyes jerked around as the main doors opened and Calamity detected almost a gasp of relief as the lank figure of Browne Crossman entered. The young man looked even more than usually sullen and moody as he crossed the room, but managed to greet the girls in a friendly manner. Taking a seat with them, he accepted Hetty's offer of a beer and joined in the discussion of the identity of the killer. Crossman expressed the view that the killer might be a religious bigot trying to improve the world by removing its undesirable fallen women. From the way Crossman spoke, Calamity decided that he did not approve of religion and was suspicious of anybody who followed Christian beliefs.

Then one of the girls, perhaps bored by Crossman's bombastic domination of the conversation, dropped in a remark about Butler's visit. With the exception of Calamity, every girl at the table had been born and raised in the South, so their views on Butler varied only by the speaker's power of invective. Watching Crossman, Calamity saw the anger in his eyes and in the way he gripped his glass between his fingers.

"Why doesn't your paper do something about Butler, Browne?" Hetty asked. "If it hadn't been for him letting his men loot my father's store, I'd never've had to go on the streets."

Normally such a story would have brought much sympathy from Crossman, but in other cases the girl's persecutor had been someone whose political or social views did not coincide with the young man's.

"I'll ask the editor about it," he answered.

At that moment the doors opened and a number of men entered. One of the men, sporting a bruised lump on his forehead gathered when trying to rush Butler through the police cordon, invited the girls to take a drink with him. At the bar, Calamity listened to the profane flow of ideas about Butler's morals, parentage, destination after death and general habits. Suddenly she realised that Crossman had not come to the bar and was not in sight. This surprised her, for Crossman had not been slow to accept free drinks from the girls and she expected him to take his chance when the newcomer offered to pay.

Deciding she would see where the reporter went, Calamity remarked, "Reckon I'll take a stroll and raise the rent."

Before any of the men at the bar could make her an offer, Calamity crossed to the door and passed out on the Latour Street. For a moment she stood at the door, undecided which way to go. Seeing no sign of Crossman, she turned and made for another gathering place for street girls.

Just as she passed a side alley, she saw a dark shape and heard Crossman's voice. "Hi there, Jane. Looking for trade?" he said.

"A gal has to pay for her room somehow," Calamity replied.

"If you come to my room, I'll see you don't have that problem."

"That's me you hear knocking on the door," Calamity said. "Let's go."

"Come this way," Crossman ordered. "I don't mind, but there are folks in town who would use my going with you against me."

"I reckon there are," agreed Calamity and walked into the alley.

Clearly Crossman knew his way around the back alleys behind Latour Street, for he did not falter as he led Calamity through the area. Although there was still a full moon, Crossman kept to the shadows and slowed his pace whenever he saw anybody ahead of him. In this manner he led Calamity down to the road which separated Latour Street from the City Park. Halting in the darkness of an alley, Crossman looked both directions along the street before turning to Calamity.

"My place's across the Park," he said. "Let's walk through to it, shall we?"

Acting her part, Calamity hesitated. "Well—I—."

"Scared of the Strangler?" asked Crossman mockingly. "Maybe I'm him."

"Aw! Don't say things like that, Browne," gasped Calamity. "You couldn't be the Strangler."

"Then let's go, or I'll go alone."

"Don't get mad. I'm coming."

More than three years of living with danger as a companion had given Calamity an instinct for trouble. She noticed the way Crossman hustled her across the street at a time when nobody either stood or walked nearby and it occurred to her that at no time had any person seen her with the young man. Uneasy stirrings gave Calamity a warning and she remembered that Crossman fitted the size which Tophet Tombes claimed for the Strangler. All too well Calamity knew Tombes' skill as a reader of sign, he would not make a mistake about so basic and important a matter as estimating the height and weight of the man he tracked.

Yet could this slim man, who preached such stupid ideas as making life easier for owlhoots and not hanging murderers, be the fiend who slaughtered nine girls in the Park?

Down on Latour Street, just as Calamity and Crossman entered the Park, men began chanting, "We'll hang that bastard Butler on a sour-apple tree."

Calamity felt Crossman's hand tighten on her arm and heard the sudden hiss of his breath.

"They sure don't like old Butler, do they," she said.

"The scum!" Crossman hissed back. "The lousy scum. Don't they realise that General Butler is a great man?"

"Maybe they remember how he treated them while he was down here in the War," Calamity answered. "He gave 'em cause to hate him."

After an unsuccessful career as a combat soldier, General Butler had been appointed Governor of New Orleans under the Union Army of Occupation. Amongst other acts, Butler siezed some eight hundred thousand dollars which had been deposited in the Dutch Consul's office, the money going into his personal bank account. His final act, which brought his recall to Washington, was an order stating 'If any woman give insult or offence to an officer or soldier of the Union Army, she shall be regarded and be held liable to be treated as a woman of the streets playing her avocation.' Crossman knew all that, regarding the theft of the money, and later stories of corruption, as lies spawned by Butler's enemies, and regarding Butler, currently a Radical Republican, as a great, noble and misunderstood man whose views almost coincided with Crossman's own.

Believing anybody he regarded highly must be perfect, Crossman's anger rose at the insults piled on General Butler since his arrival in New Orleans for a visit.

Taking his hand from Calamity's arm, Crossman allowed the

137

girl to move slightly ahead of him. He dipped his hand into his jacket and pulled out the length of stout, knotted whip cord which served him so well on other occasions when a member of the working class scum needed punishing. How he hated those stupid fools he came into contact with on Latour Street. Not one of them cared that he and his kind intended to make the world a better place for them. All they thought about was their pleasure. Take last night. Instead of listening to him and being prepared to follow his lead, those scum ran into the street to see two women fighting. Well, one of them paid the price for that insult. When Crossman and his party came into power, in addition to making the world a better place for the workers, he would see that those bunch from the Blue Cat paid for their indifference; just as this slut was going to pay right now.

Out flickered the cord, its deadly noose circling then dropping around the brim of Calamity's hat and down to her shoulders. Swiftly Crossman gathered the two ends of the cord, swinging so his back faced Calamity's and carrying the cord up on to his shoulder as he had done nine times before. Soon he would feel the cord tighten and the girl's frantic, but unavailing, struggles which would become weaker until she hung limp and dead.

"You're like all the rest!" he snarled as the noose flickered out and dropped into place.

Although Calamity partially suspected Crossman, and had practised escaping from the Strangler's attack until she felt it would be almost second nature to do so, the feel of the cord dropping around her gave her a nasty shock. It was like the first time she became involved in an Indian attack on the freight outfit. Sure she had known what to do in such conditions, but the actual happening handed her a hell of a jolt.

For all that Calamity did not freeze or panic. Instead she went into action fast, using the technique suggested in his message by Dusty Fog. Giving a fervent prayer that Dusty, as he mostly did, knew what he talked about when he sent off the instructions, Calamity made her move.

Thrusting herself back, instead of pulling away—as the other victims had instinctively done, thereby tightening the noose and speeding their end—Calamity rose on her toes and thrust her shoulders back against Crossman's. At the same moment her hands shot up, back over her shoulders, closed on and gripped the cords between her neck and Crossman's hands. Before he could lean forward and gain the extra leverage which made the use of the *thuggi* cord so deadly effective, Crossman received a shock. Swiftly

Calamity tightened her hold on the cord, then jerked both feet from the ground, bending her knees, and letting her dead weight hang on Crossman's back. Taken by surprise by Calamity's weight and the unexpected move, Crossman could not prevent himself being dragged over backwards. He lost his grip on the cord as he and the girl both went rump-first to the ground.

Following the plan she made while walking through the Park on her way to the Blue Cat earlier that evening, Calamity released one end of the cord and jerked it from around her neck. Hat and blonde wig went flying as she removed the cord, but Calamity did not care how she looked at that moment, being more concerned in summoning assistance.

"Help!" she yelled, and Calamity had quite a voice when needed. "The Strangler's here!"

Letting out a snarl, Crossman rolled on his side and rose. He swung to face the girl and stared at the sight before him. Gone were the hat and wig, and even through the paint and powder on Calamity's face Crossman recognised her. Fury ripped into him as he faced the girl he had seen with St. Andre on the night some fancied insult led him to take his eighth victim. It appeared that the stupid, inefficient, bungling police had out-witted him, laid a trap into which he fell.

Then shock bit into Crossman as he realised just how close to the edge of the Park he made his murder attempt. On every previous occasion the distance would not have mattered, for his victim struggled but died in silence. Success on nine occasions had made him lax, anger caused him to be unthinking.

Footsteps thudded on the path and Crossman looked by Calamity to where half-a-dozen brawny men raced in his direction. For a moment Crossman hesitated, then panic hit him and he started to turn to run. Maybe if Crossman had stood his ground he would have been able to talk his way out, but he lacked the kind of nerve to take such a chance.

Even as Crossman turned to run, Calamity sprang forward and grabbed him by his jacket's lapels. Desperation and terror flooded over Crossman as he heard the angry yells of the approaching men. Grabbing Calamity's wrists, he tried to drag her hands from him, but failed. Mouthing terrified curses, he lashed out wildly with a foot and caught the girl full on the shin-bone. Calamity screamed as the agony bit into her. Pain caused her to lose her hold and Crossman thrust her aside, whirled and prepared to flee for his life. He left it too late, the six men swarmed by the staggering Calamity and at him.

"She's ly—!" Crossman began.

But the men had seen the cord, read its message and knew the truth. Out shot a big fist, smashing full into Crossman's mouth and shattering his words half said. Crossman reeled backwards, more blows landed on him. No man could think of the nine dead victims of the Strangler without feeling an uncontrollable hatred for the one who killed them. Not even being 'all for the workers' could save Crossman from the fury of the men. He went down screaming, then a boot smashed into him and another came driving out to strike his temple with shattering force.

"No!" Calamity screamed, trying to walk on her kick-damaged leg.

Turning, one of the men came back and gently caught her by the arms. "Easy gal," he said. "The bastard won't harm you now.'

A policeman came racing up, blowing on his whistle as he ran. Skidding to a halt, he looked first at Calamity, then to where the men stood around the still shape on the ground.

"Just stay right where you are, boys," he said, walking forward to kneel by Crossman's side and examine the unmoving form.

"That's the Strangler," one of the men said. "We stopped him killing the girl there."

"I sure hope you're right about that," answered the policeman. "He's dead."

CHAPTER SIXTEEN

Miss Canary's Departure

ST. ANDRE sat by Calamity as she lay back on the bed in her appartment. It was the evening after Crossman's death and St. Andre came to visit the girl to give her the latest details of the affair. He found Calamity wearing her usual style of dress and nursing her injured shin, but otherwise none the worse for her experience.

"We searched Crossman's apartment last night," he told Calamity. "Among other things we found his diary, quite a document I can tell you. In fact it gives us complete proof that he was the Strangler."

"Does it tell you why he did it?"

"Patience, *cherie*," grinned the detective, then became sober again. "From what he wrote, Crossman believed himself to be ordained to make the world a much better place for the rest of we weak mortals to live in. He intended to change everything, improve the lot of the poor folks. Only he found that they didn't exactly fall over themselves with eagerness to let him improve their lot."

"Figured all along he didn't care for the folks down at the Blue Cat, no matter how he acted," Calamity remarked.

"You figured right. One night while he was there, he slipped and spilled a drink over him, and the customers laughed. They had the audacity to laugh at the great Browne Crossman, and I quote from his diary. He had been reading about the *thuggi* and made up a cord, this was before he went to the Blue Cat that night. The cord was in his pocket. Apparently he had been seeing a girl in secret and while they walked in the Park, she started teasing him about his accident. In a rage, he killed her. After that, she being his first victim, every time anything went wrong for him, or he detected insolence in the attitude of the 'workers', he picked up another girl and killed her."

"Why'd he pick on the gals, Sherry?"

"That he doesn't explain, but I believe he found it safer, less dangerous than trying it with men. He says that the girls never suspected him and went willingly into the Park with him."

"How'd you reckon he got that way?" asked Calamity.

"I don't know," St. Andre answered. "I've seen several of those young intellectuals in college and since. They're all the same, hating anybody who possessed more than they, despising the poor and under-privileged they pretend to wish to help. Crossman was that kind. When he found that people didn't regard him as their saviour he grew to hate them and took that way of getting revenge."

"What'll happen about the men who killed him?"

"That depends on the trial, *cherie*. But I can't see any jury convicting them for killing the Strangler. And now, what would you like to do tonight?"

"Aren't you guarding Butler?"

"He was recalled upriver this afternoon, and I have taken some much deserved vacation time. From now until you leave, I am at your service. Shall we go to the opera, or try gambling at one of the clubs on Bourbon Street?"

Calamity smiled. "Let's sit and call each other liars instead."

Standing on the river front, St. Andre watched the powerful paddleboat take up the strain and drew the trio of horse-loaded flat-boats from the quay. Suddenly a whip cracked by his ear and he looked to where Calamity stood at the stern of the last boat. The girl had been busy helping the horses and unable to speak to him before. Now she stood with one foot on the rail, the whip which saved St. Andre from a brutal beating held in her hand.

"Horray wah, Sherry!" she yelled.

"*Au revoir, cherie!*" he called back.

Not until the boats disappeared in the distance did St. Andre turn. His head throbbed from the previous night's celebration party at the Cheval D'Or. While he boasted being able to take his liquor, he had to admit those Western freighters made him look like a beginner. The party lasted late and Jacqueline danced herself into exhaustion. She had cause to celebrate. The New Orleans authorities offered a thousand dollars reward for the apprehension of the Strangler and with typical generosity Calamity insisted on giving the dancer half. At last Jacqueline had enough money to take formal ballet lessons and St. Andre arranged for her to meet with the head of the visiting ballet group.

After the excitement and happiness came the sorrow of parting. Calamity had gone and he doubted if they would ever meet again.

"Philippe darling!" a voice said turning St. Andre found a

142

beautiful young woman at his side. "I looked for you at the ballet last night, you naughty boy. Now I insist you buy me lunch to make up for my disappointment."

At one time St. Andre would have been very pleased to escort the girl anywhere. Now he regarded her with cold eyes. How pallid and insipid she seemed after knowing Calamity Jane. Then the detective shrugged. Calamity had gone from his life for ever. He might just as well take what was left, for there would never be another girl like Calamity.

Trouble Trail

CHAPTER ONE

MISS CANARY HOPES TO TAKE A BATH

THE air was warm and the sun's rays splashed through the trees on to the surface of the Witch Fork of the North Platte River. At one point a good-sized tree had fallen into the water, creating a large, deep hole beyond its effective brake on the current. In the big hole a large brook trout finned lazily, not actively hunting food, but ready to take any morsel carried to it in the swirling eddy beyond the dead-fall. The trout had grown large because it learned wisdom early. Once it had shared the hole with many of its smaller brothers and sisters, but cannibal tendencies exploited while young gave it growth and bulk until it reigned supreme on that stretch of river. Dwelling in the most choice spot, it lived on such smaller squaretails as ventured into its domain, while frogs, snakes, small birds and animals all fell grist to the big fish's mill.

However, like all tyrants, the big fish had enemies. The ubiquitous black bear and the rarer but even more deadly Great Plains grizzly had long been catchers and eaters of fish and were large enough to take even a big brook trout. Once a cougar tried to hook out the fish while lying on the dead-fall and slashing with its claws. Recently another menace had been added to the list of enemies. Soldiers from Fort Connel discovered the big trout early in their stay and many an attempt was made, the enlisted men dunking worms and other live bait, the officers trying their fancy artificial flies, to bring the fish to the bank. All failed, for the trout knew caution and had a secret advantage. At that point the bank was a mite overhung and some property in the bank's soil transmitted vibrations from any feet approaching the hole. Once such a warning had been received, the big squaretail faded into the depths of the hole and remained there unfeeding until the danger passed.

Just as the trout had engulfed an incautious little squaretail which ventured into the hole, it felt warning vibrations strike its lateral line. They were danger vibrations—the big trout ignored such harmless four-legged creatures as wapiti or white-tail deer—heralding the arrival of a two-legged, human animal. With a lazy flick of its powerful tail, the brook trout sank down into the depths and withdrew to its submerged cave under the dead-fall.

The figure which strolled along the Witch Fork's bank did not have fishing in mind—and if she had would not have wasted time trying to take a nine-pounder that was likely to be as tough as old saddle leather when in the frying pan. Miss Martha Jane Canary hoped to take a bath. For ten days she had been on the trail, handling the reins of a six-horse Conestoga wagon, eating dust and growing more dirty by the hour, for there had been too much urgency to reach Fort Connel to allow time out for ablutions. Her one desire in life at that moment was to strip off her clothing and soak away the dirt and dried sweat in the cool, inviting waters of a mountain stream.

The river lay ready, cool and waiting before her. She had not broken either of her arms and so stood full capable of stripping off her clothes. One way and another Martha Jane Canary reckoned she ought to be able to satisfy her whims.

The still waters behind the dead-fall reflected the picture of a girl in her late teens and who, wearing her Pawnee moccasins, stood maybe five foot seven in height. A battered U.S. cavalry kepi perched on top of her shortish, curly mop of red hair; and the face framed by the hair was good looking without being ravingly beautiful. Tanned and sprinkled with attractive freckles, the face had happy blue eyes, a slightly snub nose and a mouth which looked made for laughter and kissing, but which could cut loose with a hide-blistering flow of coarse invective when a situation called for it.

Laying down the small bundle of clean clothing she had brought to wear after her bath, the girl unfastened and removed her tight-rolled, dust-smothered old bandana. The man's shirt and jeans she wore looked like they had been bought a size too small and further shrunk during washing. Clinging firmly to her torso, the round full swell of her breasts straining against its material, the shirt's upper three buttons

6

lay open and revealed there was little other than girl under the cloth. Her waist slimmed down without the aid of a corset, then swelled out into shapely rounded hips which held tight the washed-out blue jeans. Nor could the jeans hide the firmly-muscled curves of her shapely and powerful legs.

A gun belt hung around the girl's waist, its holster tip lashed to her thigh by a pigging thong and supporting an ivory-handled Navy Colt butt forward at her right side. On some women such an outfit might have been regarded as a stupid piece of ostentation. Martha Jane Canary could handle her gun well enough to prevent folks laughing twice at the sight of her wearing it. Thrust into her belt at the left side was a coiled, long-lashed blacksnake whip; and, like the gun, she did not carry it just for decoration.

Taking off her kepi, the girl folded her bandana and placed it into the hat's crown, putting them down by her clean clothing. Next she unfastened the holster's pigging thong and unbuckled the belt, laying the gun and whip where she could reach one or the other's working end even while standing in the water. Again this was no affection; Martha Jane had been long enough in the West to know the folly of being out of reach of one's weapons.

With a wriggle, she extracted herself from the shirt's tight embrace and underneath it wore a man's sleeveless undershirt which revealed more than it concealed. Just as she reached to unfasten her waist belt ready to take off her jeans, she heard the dry pop a stepped-on twig made as it broke.

Bending down, the girl's right hand closed on the butt of her Colt, sliding the gun from its holster and thumb-cocking it even as she turned. Then she gave an annoyed grunt, lowered the Colt's hammer on to its safety notch and replaced the gun in its holster once more. Scowling her disgust, she studied the man who walked from the trees towards her.

'I might've known nobody but a shiny-butted, desk-scraping, blue-belly three bar'd make that much noise sneaking up on a gal,' she said contemptuously.

Coming towards the girl, Quartermaster-Sergeant Milo Hack worked his loose lips into what he fondly imagined to be a masterful grin; but which came out as a slobbering sneer. He was a man just over middle height, fatter than any hard-riding combat soldier ever became, and with a face that only a

7

mother could love—most folks thought Hack's face would show at its best advantage upon a tray and with an apple thrust between its teeth. If his uniform looked better and smarter than most soldiers on the frontier sported, it was only because his position in life gave him opportunities of augmenting his salary and enabled him to patronise a higher class of tailor than who served the needs of his fellow enlisted men.

'Figured you might like a guard,' he told the girl, 'seeing's how we're in Injun country.'

Actually Hack's intention had hardly been so noble and chivalrous, for he did not intentionally come into view at that moment—nor had he come to defend her from marauding Indians, but rather to watch her disrobing and had no desire to be noticed at such an early stage in the interesting process.

Hack figured himself to be gifted with intelligence beyond that of his enlisted comrades and reckoned he could think right smartly. So when he saw the girl talking with the boss of the freight outfit, he listened to the conversation. On hearing the girl say she aimed to find someplace to take a bath, he decided the sight would be worth seeing and possessed possibilities of amorous adventures. So he followed her at a distance until she reached the dead-fall and halted to commence her bath.

At first he decided to stay put and watch her preparations, but decided the view might be better closer up. Not being a man who went for such outdoor pleasures as stalking alert prey, he trod on a twig while moving up for a better view and the sound warned the girl that she did not have the woods to herself. Hack would never know how close he came to getting a ·46 calibre bullet in his favourite belly. In fact, only one thing saved him from a not undeserved fate.

'Mister,' the girl said, explaining the reason she did not shoot, 'the only Injuns in these parts are the Army's Crow, Arikara and Osage scouts—and *they* know better'n to bother me. Happen I'd not seen your uniform, you'd have knowed it, too.'

'Yeah!' grinned Hack, coming closer and his eyes staying like they were magnetised to the front of her undershirt. 'Well, how's about me'n' you getting to know each other better?'

'I know me, all I want to,' the girl answered. 'And I sure as hell don't want to know you.'

'Now that's not friendly, gal. I saw you come in with Dobe

Killem's freight outfit. If Cap'n Bigelow sees you, you'll be headed back for wherever you come from and fast.'

'Will, huh?'

'Sure will, gal. He's a real stickler for the rules, is Cap'n Bigelow. He lives by the good book, which to him's *Field Service Regulations*. And they says no unattached females is allowed on military trains.'

'Is that the living truth?' asked the girl.

'It sure is. Now me, I'm not as hide-bound and bow-necked as the cap'n when it comes to some things.'

'You wouldn't be.'

'Shucks, be nice, gal,' Hack warned, moving closer all the time. 'I'm nice to be nice to, but I'm hell to rile.'

Even as he spoke, Hack reached out his right hand, aiming to lay it where he had been looking all the time—and that was not at the girl's face. If he had studied the grim set of her features, Hack might have saved himself a fair piece of the trouble that was fast coming his way.

Up came the girl's hands, clamping hold of Hack's advancing wrist. Holding the trapped wrist, the girl carried her arms upwards, pivoting under them and bringing them down again. Hack found himself with the choice between going over or receiving a dislocated shoulder. He chose the former, his feet leaving the ground as he sailed into the air and then lit down heavily on his back. Snarling with rage, he forced himself up although the girl still held his wrist. Bracing herself, she suddenly heaved, catching Hack off balance. The man let out a howl as he shot forward and went head-first into the water.

Bending down, the girl scooped up her whip, its lash coiling out behind her as she watched Hack surface. He stood belly deep in the water and a fair way out.

'You cheap whore!' were the first understandable words to follow water out of his mouth. 'I'll——'

Out flickered the whip's lash, wrapping itself around Hack's fat throat and choked off what he aimed to say next. Bracing herself, the girl gripped her whip's handle in both hands and heaved back on it. Hack pitched forward and under the water's surface again. Coming up, he began to snarl out more curses until the girl jerked on the whip and returned him to beneath the water.

While underneath for the third time Hack gripped the lash

9

of the whip in both his hands and on surfacing gave it a savage jerk which shot the girl towards him. As he saw her coming, Hack's mind worked with its usual speed. Once he laid hands on her, he would half-drown her, maybe give her a damned good licking to boot as an added lesson not to resist the honourable intentions of Milo Hack in future. Then when she felt good and sorry for herself, he would stretch her out on her back upon the bank-strip——

At that point his day-dreams ended; although probably not in a fashion he would have selected had he been given his choice. Given his way, he would have preferred to carry on savouring the forthcoming rape of the girl rather than have his thoughts ruined by being kicked under the jaw with the full power of a young woman's shapely right leg.

Using a trick taught her by whip-fighting freighters, the girl permitted Hack to believe he was dragging her helplessly forward into his clutches, then when she came into range brought up a kick which learned him the error of his ways.

Returning beneath the water's surface with a churning splash, Hack found himself free of the whip's lash. His right hand went down and brought the Army Colt from its closed-topped issue holster. A wise fighting man would have known better and called the game quits at that moment. While Hack had the advantage of a reasonably good education and a certain shrewd, unscrupulous cunning, he was not and never had been a *fighting* man and so did not know the vitally important lesson of having the prime good sense to yell 'calfrope.' Lurching himself upright from the water, he began to raise the revolver.

If he expected the sight of a drawn gun to quell the girl into submission, or drive her into swooning helplessness, he would be sadly mistaken. Even as he rose from the water and began to lift his long-barrelled revolver, the girl dropped her whip and bent to scoop the Navy Colt from its holster.

'Drop it!' Hack snarled—or as near a snarl as his chattering teeth would allow him, the water being very cold for so lengthy an immersion. 'Drop it, you cat-house whore, or I'll——'

'Sergeant Hack!' roared a voice that was masculine, familiar to Hack's ears and which did not originate from the girl.

Both the girl and Hack turned to look in the direction of

the speaker. He had come hurrying along the river's bank unnoticed by either of them; a tall young man with a sun-reddened face sporting the latest eastern fashion in side-whiskers, and wearing a well-groomed Quartermaster Corps' captain's uniform. Letting the fishing rod he carried slide from his fingers and rest against the trunk of a tree, the captain stamped along the river bank and jumped over the dead-fall to halt before the girl and his soaking, still water-bound sergeant. Being Army, the captain directed most of his annoyance against the civilian element. Yet he had his duty to do and aimed to do it come what may.

'Get out of there and return to the fort, Sergeant!' he ordered. 'I'll attend to you later.'

'Yes—sir,' Hack replied sullenly, holstering his revolver.

'That's the first sensible thing you've done so far, Fatso,' the girl stated as she replaced her Navy Colt. 'An 1860 Army Colt's as good a gun as can be had, but even it won't shoot after that long in the water—and my old Navy's bone dry.'

'So?' snarled Hack, dragging his sopping wet form from the water.

'So happen you'd pulled that trigger, misfire or not, I'd've blowed a hole in your fat-gutted belly sure as they call me Calamity Jane.'

If the way Hack's eyes bulged out like twin organ stops went to prove anything, he knew the name the girl dropped out. So did the captain, for he glanced at the girl with cold, unfriendly eyes.

Calamity Jane. A name spoken of around the camp-fires throughout the West. In a man's world, Calamity Jane stood almost unique. Her father died on a wagon train and her mother, a bright and lively girl in her own right, left the Canary children in a St. Louis convent then disappeared into the West. Charlotte Canary figured she acted for the best, knowing a girl with her talents could not keep a family and that the kids would have a better life than she could offer them. However, Martha Jane had too much of Charlotte in her to take to the strict life of a convent. On her sixteenth birthday she pulled up stakes. Hiding out on a freighter's train, she had been twelve miles from St. Louis before making her appearance. Even then she might have been returned in ignominy if the cook had not been too drunk to make the men a meal. One of the things the nuns taught Jane was how to cook and she laid to and whomped up a mess of mouth-watering victuals for the freighter's men. From then there had been no thought of sending her back. Jane went the full trip with Dobe Killem's outfit, cooking, lending a hand with the stock and making herself useful. At the end of the trip Killem offered to take her on the next run and she agreed. How she picked up the name Calamity was not known. She learned to do a man's work in handling a six-horse wagon team. The freighters taught her to wield a whip with the best of them and through necessity she learned to handle firearms. After taking a licking from a saloon girl who rolled one of the boys for his poke, Jane added fist-fighting to her growing reper-toire. She returned the saloon-girl's licking with interest and developed a taste for fighting which often led her into throw-ing out a challenge to take on the toughest gal in the house when visiting a saloon. Nor did she lack takers, for saloon-girls prided themselves on their toughness and tried to put down that kid in the man's clothes. None of them succeeded in doing so and Killem's outfit made many a handful of money betting on Calamity.*

Many stories were told of Calamity's achievements in vari-ous fields, some of them exaggerated. One thing Hack did know for certain sure. If that red-headed girl was Calamity Jane—and he had every reason to believe she was—he had never been more fortunate than when Captain Bigelow arrived and prevented his trying to line his gun.

'You heard my orders, Sergeant?' Bigelow barked, scowling at Hack.

'Y-yes, sir, Cap'n Bigelow!' Hack answered, tearing his fascinated eyes from the girl and throwing up a salute which came straight off the pages of the drill training manual and disregarded the fact that his hat floated away on the river's current.

After Hack took his hurried departure, Bigelow turned and faced Calamity. A flush came to his cheeks as his study of the girl reached the undershirt and what lay beneath it. With an effort that showed the high standard of will-power West Point instilled in its cadets, Bigelow jerked his eyes up to the girl's

*Calamity finally met a girl who licked her, as told in 'The Wildcats' by J. T. Edson.

12

face. Like Hack, Bigelow had heard stories of Calamity Jane, but he discounted most of them as being mere fallacies built up around a rather unsavoury frontier woman. If anyone had asked Bigelow to describe what he imagined Calamity Jane looked like, he certainly would not have been within a good country mile of getting her right.

'And what, may I ask, are you doing out here?' he asked, fighting to keep his eyes on her face. 'I gave orders that nobody was to leave the post.'

'Figured to take me a bath,' Calamity replied. 'Only lardguts back there thought I needed somebody to wash my back, which same I don't.'

'And what are you doing at Fort Connel?'

'Driving for Dobe Killem.'

'You! A woman!'

'Me,' Calamity grinned. 'And I reckon that by now you're sure I'm a woman.'

The flush deepened on Bigelow's face as he jerked his eyes guiltily upwards once more. Being a red-blooded young man, under the *Manual of Field Service Regulations,* he found it hard to resist the temptation to glance downwards.

'I'll not have it!' he barked.

'Mister,' Calamity replied, 'you're some too late to stop me being born a woman.'

'I mean I'm not having Killem taking along his camp foll——'

'How'd you like to go into the river?' Calamity interrupted, anger glowing in her expressive eyes.

'I'm senior off——' Bibelow began, having been fed respect for his rank back east and reckoning it to be his God-given right.

Once again Calamity chopped off his pompous words. 'Dobe pays me as a wagon driver and that's what I'm here to do. No less—and no more, as that barrel-gutted shiny-butt just found out!'

Being a 'shiny-butt,' as the combat soldiers impolitely termed all office staff of the Quartermaster Corps, like Hack, Bigelow did not care for the name. A scowl creased his brow and he pointed in the direction of the fort.

'Get back to your wagons!' he barked.

While Calamity was an obliging girl most times, she had a

well-developed streak of mule in her when riled. She sure did not care for the way that bow-necked shiny-butt officer talked to her and objected to his giving orders to a civilian.

'I've not took my bath yet,' she stated.

'Damn it, woman!' Bigelow bellowed. 'Get g——'

Slowly, never taking her eyes from his face, Calamity drew the undershirt from her pants and began to raise it. For a moment Bigelow thought her to be bluffing and aimed to call her bet. However, the undershirt lifted to expose her navel and an even-widening strip of bare flesh. Give him his due, he stood his ground like an officer and a gentleman until the bottom of the undershirt almost reached the lower slopes of Calamity's breasts. Then he turned and headed into the trees as fast as his legs would take him, leaving his fishing tacle behind him.

Calamity watched him go, then grinned and continued her undressing. Somehow she did not figure there would be any further interruptions to her bath.

MISS CANARY MEETS AN OFFICER'S LADY

An hour later, on her return to the circle of six big Conestoga wagons which stood outside the log-walled confines of Fort Connel, Calamity found that some business must have detained Captain Bigelow, for the young officer stood with Dobe Killem and had just commenced the discussion on the subject of Miss Martha Jane Canary's return to wherever she came from.

Although Bigelow was a tall man, Killem towered over and bulked out on either side of him. The freighter stopped six foot three and weighed around two hundred pounds—none of them flabby fat either. He shoved back his dust-covered black Stetson hat; his whisker-stubbed face showed a kind of benign innocence that never left it even when anger filled him. From the hat, through his fringed buckskin shirt, levis pants and boots, Killem looked a typical hard-case freighter. A gunbelt hung around his waist, a James Black bowie knife, sheathed at the left side, an 1860, Army Colt in a contoured holster at the right.

Behind the two men stood a grinning quintet of drivers and Chan Sing, the outfit's cook whose lapse from grace gave Calamity her first chance of staying with Killem's crowd. All had heard enough to know, or guess what had happened at the river, and waited to hear how their boss dealt with the situation.

'So you figure Calamity's got no place out here,' Killem said mildly as Bigelow finished his demand for the girl's eviction.

'I do. Of course, the Army will pay her return fare to the East. But as commander of the train——'

Poor Bigelow, it appeared to be his day for having folks interrupt his well thought-out speeches and trample all over his flaunted military authority. Before he could state what he,

15

as commander of the train, thought, Dobe Killem interposed a statement.

'Mister, without *my* outfit, you don't have no train to command.'

Which, bitter and unpalatable as the thought might be to Bigelow, was the truth. While Bigelow had all kinds of important orders and instructions pertaining to the removal of his supplies from Fort Connel to Fort Sherrard in the Dakota Territories, he still needed those half-a-dozen civilian-owned Conestoga wagons to do the actual carrying. Nor could he get tough and commandeer the wagons. Handling a big six-horse Conestoga wagon took specialised training and even if his escort could supply men with that knowledge, he was not in a position to spare them.

'You signed a contract to deliver the supplies,' Bigelow pointed out in a desperate attempt to regain control of the situation.

'And to supply six wagons, teams and *drivers*,' Killem answered calmly. 'Which same, Calamity's one of my drivers. And afore you say she's a woman—don't. That gal handles a team as good as any man. If she don't drive, then my outfit goes back where we come from, there's work in plenty there.'

No man could ask for a plainer answer than that. However, Bigelow did not care for the idea of civilians laying down the law to him. While he must get the supplies to Fort Sherrard, he was just bow-necked enough to half-decide to make a stand and refuse to take Calamity along. In which case things would reach an hopeless impasse, with neither side willing to back down from the stand taken.

Fortunately, a face-saving sight made its appearance. A rider topped a distant rim, coming down the slope towards the fort. Then first one then more white-canopied wagons lurched up into view and trundled down in single file after the rider. A few women and children walked at the side of the wagons and men rode herd on a small remuda of working and saddle horses, or hazed along a bunch of cattle. There looked to be around forty wagons in the party, a good-sized, well-equipped bunch which amounted to being a complete town on the move.

'Looks like an immigrant train headed west,' Calamity remarked, strolling forward to join Killem and Bigelow.

'Now that's a real good guess, for a woman, ain't it, Cap'n,' drawled Killem, squinting at the leading rider. 'Feller up front looks kinda familiar.'

Bigelow could hardly make out more than the fact that a man rode at the head of the party. However, he had seen enough of the long-sighted ability of western men to know the freighter was not trying to job him.

'Looks like he's in a tolerable hurry to get acquainted,' Calamity went on.

A few seconds later Bigelow could see that the rider had spurred his horse and was galloping down the slope towards them, leaving his wagons to make their steady pace in his wake. The captain wondered why the man hurried, but felt it under his dignity to ask for suggestions from Calamity or Killem.

'Yep!' Killem remarked with satisfaction. 'Thought I knowed him. That's Beau Resin there.'

One thing was for sure; the man who rode towards them knew how to handle a horse. No immigrant traveller he, but a man born to the West. He rode a sixteen-hand, spot-rumped Appaloosa stud horse—one of the much sought-after breed reared by the Nez Perce Indians of the Pelouse River country and highly prized for speed, stamina and hardy nature. A wide-brimmed, low-crowned black Stetson hat trailed behind him on its storm strap, leaving his straw-coloured hair exposed to view. A scarlet bandana, tight-rolled around his neck, trailed long ends over his fringed buckskin shirt. He wore levis pants tucked into knee-high Sioux moccasins. Around his waist hung a gunbelt, a walnut-handled Remington Army revolver at the right balanced by an Ames Rifleman's knife with a spear-pointed, eleven and three-quarter-inch long blade sheathed at the left.

Watching the man come forward, Calamity noticed that he had wide shoulders that tapered down to a lean waist; and looked about as handsome as a girl could ask a rugged weather-beaten plains scout to be.

On approaching the party, he dropped from his horse's saddle and left the big Appaloosa standing with trailing reins. Calamity noticed that he rode a low-horned, double-girthed saddle of Texas cowhand pattern, with a coiled rope strapped to the horn and a Spencer carbine in its saddle boot.

17

'Howdy you-all,' he greeted, coming forward with a long-legged, mile-eating stride. 'Was I asked, I'd say you was Cap'n Bigelow.'

'I am,' Bigelow agreed stiffly, very much on his dignity as became an Army officer when dealing with a mere civilian scout; and a Southerner to boot or his voice lied badly.

'Got me a letter for you from General Sheridan. Lil Phil told me to look out for you and pass it on.'

Bigelow stiffened like somebody had poked his butt-end with a red-hot iron at the irreverent manner in which the scout addressed him and made use of General Sheridan's first name. Before he could make any comment, the scout reached into his shirt and extracted a much-crumpled, none too clean envelope from an inside pocket. Taking the envelope with a cold expression, Bigelow opened it and removed an official-looking sheet of paper.

'Says for you to give this train of mine an escort up as far as you go,' Resin remarked.

'I can read!' Bigelow answered.

'Yeah,' drawled the scout. 'I reckon you can at that.'

Turning, the scout left Bigelow reading the letter and walked towards Killem. The big freighter gave a broad grin and said, 'Howdy, Beau, ain't seed you——'

'Hey!' Resin yelled, interrupting his old friend's greeting as he saw Calamity walking towards his Appaloosa. 'He'll chaw your hand off up to the shoulder happen you give him half a chance.'

'Mister,' the girl replied, 'ain't nothing but something that's worse'n me could do that—and that I ain't met yet.'

'That's a lot of thats, gal,' grinned Resin, expecting to see his horse chase Calamity half-way back to the wagons.

Then the smile died off his face and surprise took its place. Calamity walked straight up the stallion without any hesitation at all and gave it a confident slap across the neck. Her very lack of fear warned the big horse to attempt no such liberties as kicking or biting. Also knowing better than take liberties, Calamity contented herself with just the one pat. Turning from the horse, she walked back to its amazed owner and her grinning employer.

'Don't reckon you've met Calamity, have you, Beau?' Killem inquired.

'Can't say I—are you Calamity Jane, ma'am?'

'Happen I'm not, somebody'd best watch out, I'm wearing her clothes,' Calamity replied.

'And you sure look good in 'em,' answered Resin. 'It's a pleasure to make your acquaintance, ma'am.'

'Then take hold and get pleasured some more,' grinned the girl, holding out her right hand. 'And for Gawd's sake stop calling me "ma'am." '

'What I like about Dobe here's the polite way he introduces folks,' Resin drawled, taking her hand. 'Anyways, I'm Beau Resin——'

'Best danged Injun scout, fighting man, poker player and gal chaser I ever come across,' Killem went on. 'Specially the last.'

'That I can well believe,' Calamity grinned. 'Happen a gal'd any sense at all, she wouldn't run too hard to get away.'

'Mind one time down to Kansas City——' Killem began.

At that moment—and before Killem could go into further details, probably to Resin's relief—Bigelow finished the letter. Folding it almost reverently, it being his first personal communication from anybody as high up in Army circles as General Phil Sheridan, Bigelow turned towards the westerners.

'This says you have an officer's lady aboard and we're to offer her transport to Fort Sherrard on the supply train.'

'So Lil Phil told me when he wrote it,' Resin replied. 'She's been using the front wagon, but I reckon she could finish the trip with Calamity here.'

From the sound of it, Resin would not be entirely displeased to relieve himself of the officer's lady's presence. However, his mention of her alternative accommodation brought to mind the subject of Bigelow and Killem's earlier disagreement. A solution, and a face-saver for all concerned, lay before them and Killem took the first step to grab it.

'Beau's got him a good idea there, Cap'n,' he said, unbending sufficiently to give Bigelow his formal title.

'Yes. Mrs. Tradle will need a chaperone,' Bigelow agreed.

'Is he insulting me?' breathed Calamity into Resin's ear. ''Cause if he is, I'll trample his fancy buttons in the dirt.'

'He's not. He means that she needs a wet-nurse,' grinned the scout. 'You'll get on with her real good, Calam gal.'

'I'd better ride out and meet her,' Bigelow said, neither confirming nor denying Calamity's presence with the supply train, but ignoring it in the best Nelsonian tradition.

'Why waste sweat and hoss-lather?' asked Calamity. 'She'll be here in ten or fifteen minutes at most.'

Giving a sniff which might have meant anything, Bigelow waited; partly because he did not have a horse with him and doubted if he could handle the Appaloosa even in the unlikely event that Resin offered to loan it to him. Without answering Calamity, he turned and watched the approaching wagon train.

'I'll go tell 'em to make their night cirlce down back of your outfit, Dobe,' Resin said.

Walking towards his horse, he went afork it in a lithe bound and caught up the reins. Turning the Appaloosa, Resin galloped back towards the line of wagons and called orders to the driver of the first in line, pointing towards the Killem outfit's circle.

Bigelow studied the woman seated by the first wagon's driver. At that distance he could tell little or nothing about her, but as the wagon came closer he discerned more. She looked to be about the same height as Calamity, with a small Eastern-style hat perched on her black hair. There was a haughty imperiousness about her beautiful face and it bore an expression of distaste as the wagon lurched along. The black Eastern travelling outfit she wore looked expensive, had been tailored to set off what must have been a marvellous body, but the clothes looked worse for wear and dust spattered.

All this Bigelow saw as the wagon rolled towards him, then it swung off to start forming the night circle. The following wagons kept on their leader's tail, swinging by the watching soldier, Calamity and Killem. With the exceptions of Mrs. Tradle and one other wagon, the travellers looked the usual kind to be making such a trip across the plains. Dirt farmers ever seeking a land which would sprout crops better than their last home; townsmen and their wives moving West in the hope of finding a land flowing with milk and honey; people in search of a new home and willing to sweat, bake, freeze or die in trying to find it. The other exception to the normal pattern was a smaller, two-horse wagon driven by a thin, short, rat-faced man who wore a derby hat and a loud check suit. No farmer or townsman him. He looked like the kind of jasper who roamed the West selling gold-bricks or peddling secret medicinal brews guaranteed to cure all ills. There were four women in the wagon or four in sight, one seated on the box and the other three standing behind her.

Calamity studied the women with knowing eyes. All wore low-cut, torso hugging dresses of louder colours than the other women of the train sported. From the way they dressed and made-up their faces, they worked at the saloon-girl's trade, but none were good looking and all packed considerably more heft than most men would care for—unless of course, there was no other female company to be had. All that applied to the girls in the body of the wagon counted even more so for the blonde on the front seat next to the driver. She was a medium-sized, stocky woman, dressed a mite better than the others, but with an age-coarsened face that rouge and powder fought to make look young. Studying the blonde, Calamity gained the impression that she would be a real tough cuss in a brawl. Calamity tended to study most saloon women on their potentialities as a fighting rival and she decided the blonde would take some licking.

'Fancy outfit,' she remarked to Killem; Bigelow stood slightly away from them as if wishing to assure the travellers that he did not belong to their outfit.

'Yeah!' Killem grunted. 'I've seed that red-faced jasper and the blonde someplace afore.'

'She's a hard-looking cuss,' Calamity said—just a mite too innocently to fool Killem.

Especially as he remembered where he had seen that particular bunch of travellers before and recalled how the blonde made her living. The very last thing Killem wanted was for Calamity to learn the blonde's identity, for Killem liked a peaceful life—and also did not want any of his drivers out of action even for a few days.

'Handle their wagons well,' he growled, changing the subject.

Calamity flicked a glance at her boss, knowing him as well as he knew her. From the way he replied, he knew that bunch—and did not want her to know them. In such matters Calamity had her full share of woman's perversity and curiosity. She reckoned it might be worthwhile to look into the identity of that bunch of travellers, if only to find out why Killem did not want her to know them. Not that Calamity mentioned that to Killem, but gave her attention to watching the handling of the wagons.

At last the circle had been formed and the lead wagon came to a halt almost before Killem's party. Striding forward in the best traditions of U.S. Cavalry's chivalry, Bigelow saluted the woman on the wagon box and removed his hat.

'Captain Wade H. Bigelow at your service, ma'am. I have the honour to command your escort to Fort Sherrard.'

Thrusting his hat on again, he reached up and swung the woman down from the wagon box. Calamity watched the move and noticed the way the woman's hands clung to Bigelow, testing the power of his biceps while her beautiful face studied him in a calculating, predatory manner.

'My pleasure, Captain Bigelow—or may I call you Wade?' Mrs. Tradle replied, her voice husky and cultured. 'You must forget formality and call me Eileen.'

'Thank you, Eileen. May I escort you to the fort. Colonel and Mrs. Ferris will wish to meet you.'

'Of course, Wade,' Mrs. Tradle replied. 'Oh, could you arrange to have my baggage transferred to one of your wagons?'

'I'll send my striker to attend to it,' Bigelow promised.

'Get my boys to move it over for you, Cap'n,' Killem said.

'It's marked with my name, they can't miss it,' the woman said, glancing at Killem. 'I trust the next wagon is more comfortable than the last, Wade. That one was an absolute horror —and the language of the driver!'

'Which shouldn't be any problem in future, Eileen,' Bigelow replied. 'Miss—Canary here will be your driver.'

Turning, Eileen Tradle looked Calamity up and down in the cold, impersonal manner of a farmer examining some poor quality animal. Always willing to be friendly, Calamity stepped forward, her hand going out.

'Howdy,' she said. 'Reckon we'll get on all right.'

'I'm sure we will,' Eileen replied, ignoring the hand and answering in her most chilling manner before turning to Bigelow. 'I believe I know your father, General Haywood Bigelow?'

'My uncle,' Bigelow corrected, taking the woman's offered arm. They strolled away chatting amiably and leaving a pot-boiling mad Calamity staring after them.

Shooting out a big hand, Killem caught Calamity by the waist-belt as she took a step after the departing couple.

'Hold it, Calam gal,' he warned. 'You start mean-mouthing her and you'll find yourself in bad trouble.'

'Danged snooty, high-toned old hag!' Calamity spluttered, her face getting redder by the second. 'I'd sure like to kick her right in the tail.'

'Blast your ornery side, Calam!' growled Killem, scooping her kepi off and running his big fingers through her hair. 'You're more trouble than a dozen bull-whackers. Danged if I know why I keep you on.'

As suddenly as it came the anger left Calamity and she grinned up at her boss. ''Cause I'm the best blasted hoss-handler you've got—and 'cause if you fire me I'll tell everybody your real name's Cecil.'

Digging his fingers into her curls, just stinging but not really hurting her, Killem scowled down at the girl. 'Happen you ever tell anybody that, Calam, I'll fix your wagon good. See if I don't.'

'Get your cotton-picking hands offen me,' she replied with a grin, then her eyes fell on Bigelow's fishing tackle which she had put down while approaching the wagon train scout's big Appaloosa stallion. 'I know one thing for sure. That two-legged man-trap's not having any fresh trout for supper.'

'Huh?' Killem grunted.

Crossing to the tackle, Calamity lifted up the wicker creel and opened it to expose a pile of plump, frying-size brook trout. An appreciative glint came into Killem's eyes as he looked into the creel and he ran a tongue tip over his lips.

'Now they look nice,' he said.

'Sure are,' the girl answered. 'Get them cleaned and I'll fry them up for supper tonight.'

'Where're you going?'

'Back to the river to put the rod and this fancy box down where he left 'em,' grinned Calamity. 'They do say the mink in this area'll steal a man's fish plumb away, happen he leaves it lying around unwatched.'

'Darn it, Calamity,' Killem chuckled. 'There's a mean streak in you when you're riled.'

'Why sure,' she replied and glanced at where Beau Resin

23

rode towards them. 'But I can be right loving with it.'

Saying that, she took up the fishing tackle and strolled off in the direction of the river.

At about the same time Bigelow was promising Eileen a treat, a speciality of the area which was a gourmet's delight, fresh-caught brook trout fried in butter.

CHAPTER THREE

MISS CANARY MEETS A SCHOOLMARM

WHILE strolling through the wagon train camp in search of Beau Resin, Calamity thought she detected a faint hint of disapproval from the womenfolk. While the men at the various fires and attending to their chores looked at Calamity with open admiration, the women clucked their tongues and gathered in peeking, talking groups after she passed by. Not that Calamity cared, she had met with disapproval in better places than a wagon train camp on the North Kansas plains. She dressed the way she did as being practical for her work and did not give a damn what other folks might think about it.

In passing Calamity studied the rat-faced man's outfit. They appeared to be accepted by their fellow travellers as being part of the train, but not of it. All the women looked to be busy setting up their camp, but the man sat on a box and watched them work. Even while Calamity passed, the plump blonde laid hold of a heavy-looking box and toted it to the wagon without raising any sweat. She looked to be a tolerable strong gal, Calamity mused, then regretfully decided the folks of the train would not approve of a female brawl. Not wishing to make any trouble for Dobe Killem, Calamity passed on without stopping to speak with the blonde.

After making almost a tour of the camp, Calamity decided Resin must be out of the circle. Most likely he might be visiting the fort, talking with the Army scouts and learning of conditions ahead. Calamity felt disappointed for she figured Beau Resin to be a man worth getting to know better. With that in mind she had planned to invite him to supper; working on the belief that the best way to a man's heart was through a mess of well-cooked brook trout.

Just as Calamity was about to return to Killem's outfit, she heard a considerable commotion among the trees outside the camp. Turning, she passed between two of the wagons and headed in the direction of the sound. She came into view of the cause of the commotion and one look told her she ought to insert her presence.

School should have been in progress among the trees. A small, very pretty blonde girl in her early twenties stood at the side of an erected blackboard and easel, trying to attract the attention of and bring order to a class of youngsters. Some twenty or so children aged between ten and fifteen were in the clearing, although not taking advantage of the educational facilities offered to them. All appeared to be making some kind of noise and the ring-leaders, a boy and girl alike enough to be fifteen-year-old twins, encouraged the others. With his thumbs hooked into his belt, the boy swaggered around and leered at the teacher, while the girl twisted a younger girl's ear and made her screech.

'Children!' the teacher called, her face showing desperation almost as she tried to control her unruly class. 'Children, sit down and take your slates. Come on now, please.'

Politeness got her nowhere and so Calamity figured to cut in and help the schoolteacher bring order to her class.

Swinging free her whip, Calamity flipped its lash forward, the end exploding with a gun-shot crack a couple of inches from the boy's left ear. Letting out a startled squawk, the boy clapped a hand to his ringing ear and leapt into the air as if stung by a bee.

All eyes turned towards Calamity as she walked forward, coiling the whip's lash one-handed. For a moment the twin sister stared open-mouthed, then considered her audience and stepped forward with the intention of making a grandstand play to show the others that nobody pushed her or her brother about. She was a big, plump girl with a mean glint in her eyes and a sullen twist to her mouth.

'What do you think you're do——!' she began.

Bringing up her left hand, Calamity laid it palm-first against the girl's face and pushed hard. Taken by surprise both by Calamity's temerity and strength, the girl staggered back a few steps and landed flat on her rump with a thud which gladdened at least one watcher's heart.

Springing forward, the boy yelled, 'Hey, you can't d——!'

Calamity showed him she not only could do that, but could

also improve on it. Swinging her right arm, she gave him a flat-handed slap across the face which knocked him staggering and made him howl in pain. Both he and his sister headed for the trees in the direction of the camp, screeching like they had been scalped.

A flush of red crept into Molly Johnson's cheeks as she watched Calamity's arrival and the hurried departure of the twins. Being on her first post as schoolteacher, Molly wanted to make a good job of it, but had found the theory gained in college proved little practical use when it came to handling the Bloom twins. From the start they had been the bane of her existence and although she approved of Calamity's actions in part, both her training and knowledge of the twins' mother made her wish the red-haired girl had not interfered.

'All right, you slab-sided, mis-shaped, yowling, caterwauling bunch of milk-soaked half-pints!' Calamity barked, swinging to face the class. 'Get sat and stay sat before I tan the hides off you!'

Never had Molly seen her class take their seats with such speed and silence. Almost before the words died away, every member of the class had taken a seat upon the ground and sat nursing slate and chalk in becoming humility.

'Want the other two back?' Calamity asked, turning to the teacher.

'I—I think you'd better go,' Molly replied, trying to hold down a smile. There was something refreshingly different about Calamity and Molly had not been long enough out of college to lose her fascination for anything or anybody new and unconventional. 'Mrs. Bloom doesn't approve of anybody punishing her children.'

'Yeah,' Calamity said dryly. 'I could see that.'

From the start Calamity liked the look of Molly Johnson. The girl stood at most five foot two, but had a shapely figure that a severe gingham dress and tightly taken back hair could not hide. Molly affected the dress and hair style to try to make herself look older and more in keeping with the popular conception of a school teacher.

'Thank you for your help,' Molly went on, glancing nervously at the camp.

'Shucks, these half-pints don't know what they've got, having a chance at book-learning,' Calamity replied, ignoring the glance and pleading look Molly gave her. 'Mind if I set a spell and listen to the lesson?'

At that moment Mrs. Bloom made her appearance, advancing through the trees like the battle-ram *Albemarle* steaming to war, and followed by the full conclave of her cronies. Since leaving St. Louis, those half-dozen women had ruled the train and put fear into the hearts of all the men. Mrs. Bloom led them, a commanding figure almost six foot tall and with a hefty build. When she bore down bust-first on some offender, the offender's heart quaked at the sight—usually. When she yelled, it sounded like the crack of doom and as a last resort she commanded a fine and spectacular burst of hysterics which drove her mild-mannered husband almost frantic with worry.

'Are you the one who struck my children?' she demanded in her finest aggressive manner, glaring at Calamity with an eye that had never failed to quell.

'Reckon I am,' answered the un-quellable Calamity calmly.

'You struck my little Rodney with that whip?' bellowed Mrs. Bloom, patting her son fondly upon the top of his head as he clung tearfully to her skirt at one side, his sister at the other.

'Nope, I popped it clear of his ear.'

'He said——'

'If I'd wanted to hit his ear, I'd've done it—only he wouldn't have any ear left now,' Calamity interrupted.

'How dare y——!'

'Wasn't nothing daring about it. I saw those pair of over-fed lard-heads fooling and making fuss for their schoolmarm instead of buckling down and learning what she could teach 'em. Figured from the hawg-mannered way they acted that they didn't belong to anybody to teach 'em better—so I took 'em in hand. Which same I didn't treat 'em too mean—the first time.'

Never had anyone stood up to Mrs. Bloom in such a manner. For a full minute she stood with her mouth open and working spasmodically while she tried to decide if physical assault or hysterics would be the best tactics to use. Behind her, the other members of her band stared horrified at Calamity and wondered why lightning did not strike down the girl for her blasphemy to their leader.

'Whup her good, Maw!' 'little' Rodney suggested and then ducked hurriedly out of sight behind his mother as Calamity

28

scowled at him.

'How dare you address me like that,' Mrs. Bloom gasped,
ignoring her son's words and disappearance. 'You——'

'Afore you say it—don't,' Calamity warned. 'I can name-call
and mean-mouth you and all your crowd to a stand-still without needing to draw extra breath.'

Just what might have been the outcome had the matter gone
further would never be learned. Even as Mrs. Bloom tried to
decide what course to follow, there came an interruption
which washed all thoughts of taking Calamity to task out of
the big woman's head.

A pallid-faced youngster maybe two years younger than the
twins, but clearly a member of the Bloom clan, staggered out
of the trees. He held his left wrist in his right hand, bawled
unmelodiously as he came and dripped blood over his right
fingers and pants legs.

'Hubert!' Mrs. Bloom screeched. 'Hubert! Oh, my Lord!
Fetch the doctor, one of you. Fetch help!'

'The doctor's with Mrs. Schmidt, she's in heavy labour,'
moaned one of the other women.

'Oh heavens! What can we do?' Mrs. Bloom wailed, realising her inadequacy to deal with the situation.

'You could try getting the hell out of my way and letting me
take a look for a starter.'

Calamity gave out that sage advice as she stepped forward.
Much to the surprise of the other women, Mrs. Bloom moved
aside. There was an air of confidence about Calamity that Mrs.
Bloom found reassuring at that moment and so the woman
stood aside and let the girl take charge of the situation.

'Oooh!' Hubert howled.

'Shut up, damn you!' roared Calamity.

Gripping the suddenly silent Hubert's left wrist in one
hand, Calamity pulled his right hand away from it. A long,
shallow gash showed in the flesh of his forearm, painful, messy,
but far from dangerous.

'It hurts!' Hubert groaned.

'Of course it hurts!' Calamity spat out. 'Anybody fool
enough to whittle with the knife's point sticking inwards asks
to get hurt.'

Surprise caused Hubert to stop his moaning and he stared at
Calamity. 'H-how'd you know?'

'Done the same fool trick when I was ten,' she replied, looking around her and seeing what she wanted.

'C-can't you stop the bleeding?' asked Mrs. Bloom; but for once it sounded like a mild request for help, not a royal command.

'Just now figuring to,' answered Calamity, hauling Hubert after her towards one of the trees. 'Where at's your knife, boy?'

'I dropped it back there.'

'Then soon's I've fixed this scratch, you're going straight out to find it. Hey one of you fellers loan me a knife.'

Several young hands darted into pockets and Calamity had the offer of half-a-dozen assorted knives. Taking a jack-knife from one of the boys, Calamity—who could never resist a chance to grandstand a mite—drew admiring gasps by opening its blade with her teeth. The tree had a number of blister-like swellings on its bark and the girl slit one open, allowing a flow of thick syrup-like gum to ooze out. Dipping her forefinger into the flow, Calamity coated the wound with the gum.

'Wh-what is that you're putting on?' asked Mrs. Bloom.

'The best damned wound salve you'll find anyplace,' Calamity replied. 'It'll stop the bleeding and help the wound heal. One of you girls haul up your skirt and tear a strip off your underskirts so's I can bandage this.'

Departing behind a bush, Molly Johnson followed Calamity's orders. She returned with a long strip of white cloth in her hands, giving it to Calamity and watching the other girl swiftly bandage the wound.

'That's as good as any doctor could do it,' one of the women remarked.

'Most times out here there's not a doctor around,' Calamity answered. 'Gal gets to know how to do her own doctoring. There, boy, now go find that knife and bring it back in here.'

'Shouldn't he be in bed?' inquired Mrs. Bloom.

'It's not night yet,' Calamity grunted. 'Anyways, it's no more'n a scratch. But there's an open knife lying someplace out in the trees, maybe some poor fool critter'll step on it and get hurt. You fetch it, boy, and don't waste time. You should be attending the class.'

Like his brother and sister, Hubert tended to be unruly and disobedient; but for once he did not argue. Turning, he scuttled off into the trees and his mother stared after him. Then she became aware that Rodney and her daughter, Beryl, were both pulling at her skirt and demanding her attention.

'How's about what she done to us, Maw?' Rodney asked.

'Yeah,' Calamity agreed. 'What about that. They was making fuss and stopping the class.'

'That's a l——!' Rodney began.

His words chopped off as his mother landed a ringing smack across his ear and sent him staggering. Then Mrs. Bloom brought her hand around to apply its palm in a slap to Beryl's rump that lifted the girl almost a foot into the air.

'Just let me hear of you misbehaving in class again!' she snorted. 'Miss Johnson is here to teach you. See that you behave and try to learn something.'

If somebody had walked up and handed Molly Johnson a diamond necklace, she would not have felt more pleased than she did at that moment.

'Take your seats, please,' she said.

Without fuss, noise or objection the youngsters hurried back to their places and prepared to start their lessons. Behind them Mrs. Bloom's party gathered around Calamity.

'What sort of tree is this?' Mrs. Bloom asked, indicating the one from which Calamity drew the gum.

'Balsam fir,' the girl replied. 'It's good for stopping bleeding. So's powdered witch hazel leaves, or a poultice made by stewing bark, buds or twigs of a slippery elm. Fact being, there's medicine for nearly all your ailments growing in the woods happen you know what to look for.'

'How can we tell which sort of trees to use?' a woman inquired; forgetting her earlier comments at the sight of Calamity walking through the camp.

'We've maybe four weeks travelling together. Likely I can show you most of what you'll need before Fort Sherrard.'

'Would you please?' said Mrs. Bloom.

'I'll make a stab at it,' Calamity promised. 'Not tonight though. You ladies most likely have food to cook for your men.'

Her words caused a hurried departure. Not because she shocked the women or failed to hold their interest, but because all of them remembered leaving food on their fires when coming to lend Mrs. Bloom moral support in defence of her mis-

31

treated children. Promising to see Calamity at the next camp, they hurried away.

'I'd like to thank you, Miss——' Molly said, coming to Calamity's side.

'Never been one for "Missing" with folks I like. The name's Calamity Jane. You can call me Calam, like most of my friends, or be real formal and make it Jane.'

'Thank you, Calam,' Molly smiled, taking a better liking to the other girl. 'They were getting out of hand and too much for me.'

'Try slapping their ears down a mite next time.' Calamity suggested. 'I'd say Mrs. Bloom won't mind.'

'According to Professor Strubacher "physical punishment arouses resentment and creates the desire to make more mischief",' Molly quoted.

'How many kids has he got?' asked the practical Calamity.

'The professor? He's a bachelor.'

'Then where in hell did he learn about kids? Way I see it, happen you treat a kid same way as you treat a hound pup, you bring 'em both up right. Praise him when he does right and take a switch to his hide when he wets on the wagon bed, only do it right off so he knows what he's getting licked for.'

A smile came to Molly's lips as she heard the wild, poorly educated young Western woman argue against the learning and instructions of the great Professor Strubacher. Or was the red-head so poorly educated in practical matters? Molly admitted that she, for all her college education, would have been helpless to deal with the cut on Hubert Bloom's arm. From a more personal point of view, Molly had only to look at her class's decorum to see that Calamity's views on handling children apparently worked better than had Professor Strubacher's.

'You could be right at that,' Molly smiled. 'Go cut me a switch.'

'Gal, you're the first eastern dude I ever saw who knowed good sense when she come face to face with it,' Calamity replied.

After the class ended, with Calamity sat by and listening as attentively as any of the pupils, Molly walked back to camp with the western girl.

'Are you coming to the dance?' Calamity asked as they entered the camp circle.

'Which dance?' asked Molly.

'The one they'll hold tonight.'

'I haven't heard of any dance.'

'There'll be one, you mark my words,' Calamity grinned. 'Do you reckon all those soldier boys down to the fort are going to miss a chance to come here and dance with you unattached females?'

'I'm not much for social life,' Molly admitted.

'Then it's time you started,' Calamity told her. 'Go let your hair down, put on your best party dress and you 'n' me'll celebrate until the last dog's shot and all the pups are hung.'

'Do you want my company?'

'Why sure,' Calamity chuckled. 'It's not every day I get a chance to go to a dance with a schoolmarm. Say, come over to our camp and I'll fry up a mess of brook trout. If you've not ate fresh-caught Kansas brook trout, then you've never tasted fish.'

CHAPTER FOUR

MISS CANARY ATTENDS A BALL

MOLLY JOHNSON caused something of a stir when she arrived with Calamity at Killem's camp-fire. In fact, she scared a group of tough, efficient and hardy men into stammering inarticulation and brought about a hurried disappearance in search of washing water and shaving tackle. Probably the fluster came about through Calamity insisting that Molly let down her hair from its severe schoolmarm style and wear a dress which showed off her figure. As a stout supporter of the newly started feminist cause, Molly tried to object to fancying herself up, but Calamity could be mighty persuasive when she wanted. Seeing the reaction her change of costume caused, and being pleased despite herself at it, Molly decided that Calamity might have a real good point in suggesting she changed.

With some amusement Calamity watched her male friends over the meal, as they strove to remember half-forgotten or hardly learned social manners. One man spilled his stew over his pants and turned red in the face as he fought down the words which rose naturally at such a mishap. Not even the pleasure of eating Bigelow's trout could break the ice.

'Colonel's having the Regimental Band come out this evening,' Beau Resin remarked, having joined the party for a meal. 'They've got a dance caller who'll set your feet to tapping, Miss Johnson.'

At that moment one of the freighters bumped into the man next to him and jolted a cup of coffee from his hand. Naturally the bumped one swung around and said, 'You clumsy——'

Then he flushed as he realised he stood close to a for-real lady who should never have her ears sullied by the last word he spoke in his haste. With this thought in mind, he turned to the girl and made amends.

'I'm sorry, ma'am,' he said, 'this bastard pushed me.'

34

For a couple of seconds silence fell over the group. Then Molly began to laugh. She could not help herself, the sight of the men's shocked faces, and the way the words came out, struck her as amusing. The nervous air of the men sagged off a mite as they realised the girl was not only human like themselves, but also had a real keen sense of humour.

Showing timing that a professional comedian might have envied, Calamity continued with the ice-breaking progress. With her usual gusto, she started to tell Molly how she humiliated the pious, sanctimonious boss of a freight outfit.

'Wouldn't let his boys stay on in town overnight to celebrate,' Calamity explained. 'So I runs up to him and throws my arms round his neck, like this,' she demonstrated on Beau Resin. 'Gives him a kiss, like this,' once more she gave a spirited demonstration. 'And then I says, 'Why, darling, don't you remember how you n' me set up drinks that night on the North Platte?" I tell you, Molly, gal, that feller looked sicker'n a skunk-stunk beagle. He tried to pull away from me and kept gasping about never seeing me, or there being some mistake. "Now that's not what you said that night, honey," I tells him. Then he jerked free from me and lit a shuck out of town like the devil after a yearling. Never did show up again that night and the boys had them a time.'

By the time the meal ended Molly found herself on friendly terms with the freighters and looked forward to a night's fun at the dance.

Just as Calamity predicted, the soldiers from the fort made their appearance as the day's work ended. By the time Calamity and Molly returned to the wagon circle, they found that practically everybody who could had left Fort Connel and come a-visiting. First to arrive had been the unmarried enlisted men, followed some time later by the single officers who had not wished to show ungentlemanly haste, but were just as eager to see some female company. Lastly came the families and the senior officers, mingling with the travellers and exchanging gossip.

One thing Molly noticed as she walked with Calamity through the wagon train circle was how like gathered to like. Without any hint of snobbery the senior officers and their families gathered with the better class citizens of the train; the Blooms and Molly's aunt and uncle among others. So it went

35

on through the camp, the different social levels finding equals among the travellers. A group of young officers swarmed around Molly and Calamity, gay blades fresh out of West Point or with only a few years service, all hot and eager to get better acquainted with the pretty little blonde. For her part Molly revelled in a chance to talk with somebody of her own age and class. Five minutes flashed by and the little blonde saw that Calamity had backed away. Excusing herself, Molly went after the other girl.

'Where are you going, Calam?' she asked.

'Back to my kind of folks. You stay there and have fun with yours.'

'But I——'

'Look, honey,' Calamity said with a smile. 'You wouldn't be happy down there with us when we start celebrating; and I sure as hell couldn't set down and enjoy myself among the brass.'

'But—but——'

'Hey, Molly, come on!' called one of the officers.

Laying her hand on Molly's arm, Calamity squeezed it gently, smiling. 'Go on, gal. Have your fun. Comes morning I'll visit and we'll "woman" over tonight.'

Without another word, Calamity turned and walked away. Molly could see no sign of dejection in Calamity's walk and the red-head called out cheery greetings to various people, being received with laughter and friendly attitudes that had not shown while the girl stood with Molly and the officers. Then Molly realised that her social chatter with the officers must have been over Calamity's head and probably bored the other girl. It was just another case of like calling to like. She and Calamity were worlds apart in social life and neither could be truly happy in the other's area.

Molly turned a head towards the young officers, glancing back over her shoulder. It seemed that Calamity must have been thinking about her, for the red-head had turned. Calamity gave Molly a broad grin, turned after waving and mingled with the crowd.

Music sounded as the Regimental Band approached. Night was falling and eager hands built up the various fires so that all who wished to dance would have plenty of light by which to do so.

Joining Beau Resin, who showed considerable pleasure at her company, Calamity headed for where the crowd of poorer folk congregated to have their fun. While heading for the dance ground, Calamity saw the piggy, sullen face of Sergeant Hack. His presence did not worry her any; having handled him once, she figured she could do so again, even without the help of the big young scout.

Watching the girl and Resin join the crowd, Hack gave thought to taking revenge on her. He knew something of his captain and guessed Bigelow would not be overkeen on taking Calamity along on the train. Nor would the train's women if it came to a point; a girl as unconventional as Calamity would be an anathema to them. If she became involved in some unseemly incident, the women would demand that she be expelled from the train.

Once having decided that, Hack put a smart and scheming brain to causing an incident. All he needed was the right sort of man to carry his plans out, for Hack was a thinker not a fighter and as such never put himself in a position of danger if he could help it. A booming roar of laughter from a group of soldiers drew Hack's attention to them. They were tanned, tough, hard-riding combat non-coms, fighting sergeants and corporals who had little but contempt for an office soldier of Hack's type—unless the shiny-butt showed up suitably supplied and equipped. Hack had just the kind of equipment he needed. Turning, he headed back to the fort and collected something guaranteed to sweeten the heart of any combat non-com.

Not knowing the fate in store for her, Calamity joined in the dances and threw herself into having a good time with her usual verve and spirit. She and Resin led the sets, urged more and more folks to dance and led the applause which came at the end of each dance. At odd intervals as the time passed Calamity saw Hack standing with the group of non-coms, but she thought little of it. There was some drinking being done and combat soldiers had always been known for sociability when bending their elbows. Catching the eye of one of the drinkers, a big, burly, red-haired man with a face that was so Irish it might have been painted emerald green, Calamity gave him a friendly wink, showing that she understood how he came to be in such company. Unfortunately, he read the sign

37

wrong.

Turning from his friends, the big sergeant came forward and joined the dance set being formed. With casual ease, he planted himself alongside Calamity and beamed down to her.

'The name's Paddy Muldoon, colleen,' he told Calamity in a brogue so thick it could have been cut with a knife. 'Sure and they say you're Calamity Jane.'

'Sure and they're roight,' Calamity answered, ever willing to be friendly at such a moment.

'And there's not another girl like you anywhere in the world.'

'If there is, I'll whip her so fast she'll think the hawgs have jumped her.'

'You could do it!' Muldoon bellowed. 'Let's get married and raise the finest fighting family that's ever been born.'

At that moment they separated and Calamity found herself partnering Beau Resin. She nodded towards Muldoon and grinned. 'I've just been proposed to, Beau.'

'By Paddy Muldoon?' asked the scout, showing a remarkable lack of concern. 'If you agreed, and he thought you meant it, he'd take off out of here faster'n a Neuces steer.'

'That's what I figured,' groaned Calamity. 'I no sooner get a decent offer than the feller heads out.'

'Don't let it bother you, honey-chile,' Resin drawled, giving her waist a squeeze. 'I'll allus love you.'

Another change in partners brought Calamity to Muldoon again, although under the rules she should not have met up with the sergeant in that set. They whirled around together, Muldoon dancing with gusto, abandon, but little skill. However, Calamity had long been spry on her feet and used to avoided being trampled on by her partner.

At the end of the set Muldoon started to head towards Calamity, but she went back to Resin and her freighter friends. The big sergeant stood watching her, not exceptionally bothered, when he felt a hand on his sleeve. Turning, he looked down at Hack.

'Now that's no way for a gal to treat a cavalryman, is it, Paddy?'

Normally Muldoon's reaction would have been to tell Hack where to go. However, pay day was a few days away and Muldoon had never been a man to look a gift-horse in the mouth, especially when it toted a load of good Old Stump-Blaster in its chubby hand.

Taking the offered bottle, Muldoon drank deeply, wiped his mouth with the back of his hand and scowled after the departing couple. 'It is not,' he agreed, then slapped Hack on the back in a friendly manner which almost caved his spine out through his chest. 'You're not as bad as I allus reckon you was.'

Three dances went by, with Muldoon joining in every set and imposing his bear-like scowl on anybody who tried to get near Calamity. Of all the crowd only Beau Resin ignored the scowls. The soldiers at the fort knew better than cross big Paddy Muldoon and the travellers on the wagon train recognised him as a dangerous when wet proposition. For his part Muldoon knew he possessed but one rival for Calamity's affections. Beau Resin, a *civilian*—normally Muldoon had respect for the abilities of a good scout such as Resin, but not when the scout became his rival for the affections of a real good-looking girl—was grabbing Calamity every time the caller announced a change of partners and Muldoon had never been a man to stand mildly by while the ground was cut from under his feet.

So Calamity found herself with only two partners, which had never been the intention of square dancing. She also attracted the disapproving glances of the other women. Normally such glances would not have worried Calamity, but they did that night for Calamity realised the delicacy of the situation.

'Let's go see how the other half live, Beau,' she suggested at the end of a set, taking Beau's arm and hauling him with her just as he aimed to walk over and settle matters with Muldoon.

'Damn it to hell, Calam!' Resin growled angrily. 'No bog-trotting Pat-lander's going to steal my gal.'

'Which same you can start worrying when he does,' Calamity replied calmly. 'If I start squalling and pulling you, he's surely going to come a-running to help.'

Calamity figured that Muldoon would have the good sense, and be sober enough, not to come making trouble in officers' country and so led Resin to where the upper classes celebrated. Officers and their wives mingled with the cream of the wagon train, talking, dancing the same kind of dances as the peasants performed—although with less vigour and more style —or gathered at the hurriedly-made bowl of punch before the Blooms' wagon.

Looking across the fire, Calamity saw Molly standing in the centre of a group of the younger bloods. Clearly the little schoolmarm was enjoying herself and it appeared to Calamity that Captain Bigelow had his sights set on Molly. It also became clear that Mrs. Eileen Tradle had designs on Bigelow. Eileen, wearing a fancy ball gown that trailed its hem on the floor, hung on to Bigelow's arm like she was scared it might fall off, showing great attention to every word he said and making herself agreeable in every way to him.

'Make up your sets, please,' the colonel's wife announced. 'After this dance we will break off and eat. Gentlemen, the lady with you at the end of the dance is your partner for the buffet.'

Watching the dance proceed, Calamity saw that Mrs. Tradle intended to wind up with Bigelow. Twice Eileen cut in front of Molly to grab the captain for a partner and Calamity's fingers itched to make some bar-room-style improvements to the officer's lady's elegantly combed and preened hair.

'Ease off, hot-head!' Resin growled in her ear. 'This's officers' country, not the Texas House in Dodge City.'

The gods of fortune decreed that Bigelow, Molly and Eileen should arrive before Calamity as the dance drew towards its close, the fourth member of their set being a stout, red-faced and middle-aged major. Whoever did not collect Bigelow as a supper date would wind up with him as an escort and it became clear Eileen did not intend to be the one. By what looked like the sheerest accident, Eileen placed her hip against Molly's side and shoved, staggering the smaller, lighter girl a couple of steps away from Bigelow. With a cat-vicious smile Eileen started to advance on her prey—then came to a sudden halt.

'Why, mercy-me!' Calamity gasped, looking down at the cause of Eileen's sudden halt. 'I got all clumsy and trod on the bottom of your dress.'

For all her apparent contrition, Calamity made no attempt to move her foot from the fuming Eileen's dress until Molly reached Bigelow. All the time Eileen glared over her shoulder in a manner that in saloon circles would have wound up in a cat-clawing brawl. Then the music came to an end and Calamity moved her foot. For a moment she thought Eileen aimed to turn and jump her, especially as Molly passed by laughing, on the young captain's arm.

'Come on, Eileen gal!' whooped the major, bearing down on the brunette. 'Dammit, I thought young Bigelow'd lick me to you, only it looked like he preferred a younger gal.'

Which proved that while the major might be a real brave man in action, and he was, and a fairly smart man at his work, he would never make a diplomat.

'So he did, Harold,' Eileen replied in a tone that would have sliced tough meat. 'How fortunate for me.'

'Sure was. Come on. I want to tell you how that husband of yours hung a chamber pot on the roof of the White House on the night of Grant's Inaugural Ball.'

Eileen Tradle allowed herself to be led off towards the buffet table, nor did she find another opportunity that night to get near Bigelow. The major, Bigelow and Molly all took their full share in making sure of that. By the end of the evening Eileen had worked up quite a hate for both Molly and Calamity.

Long before the evening ended Calamity had troubles of her own.

'Hey, Calamity!' whooped a voice as she and Resin walked back to their own section of the camp circle. 'Come on, gal, 'tis time we started dancing again.'

Walking up, Muldoon laid hold of Calamity's right arm in an insulting and proprietary manner. Before he could make a move to lead the girl anywhere, a cold Southern drawl cut in.

'Just take your hands off her, Muldoon,' Beau Resin ordered.

'So that's the way of it?' asked Muldoon, shoving Calamity gently to one side and facing the big scout. 'All right, bucko, 'tis time you civilians learned respect for us who're making this country safe for the likes of yez.'

'Start trying to teach me,' Resin replied and countered the soldier's claim with an old scout's insult. 'You'll find me a mite harder than tangling with a village full of squaws and kids.'

Silence dropped over the area. Cold chilling silence as everybody stared at the two big fighting men facing each other. As if drawn by magnets Killem's men arrived to move

41

in behind Resin and Muldoon's cronies appeared to form a half circle behind the big sergeant. Other soldiers and civilians showed interest in the affair and there was the makings of a good old-fashioned riot in the air. To one side, in a position which offered him a clear line of retreat, Hack watched his plan approach fulfilment. Once the fighting started, it would ruin the dance and the wagon train's women were going to look for somebody to blame. The blame would fall smack on Calamity's curly red head.

Hack knew that—and so did Calamity.

Although attending a range-country ball, Calamity was, in Western terms, dressed. Her Navy Colt rode its holster and her long whip hung coiled at the left side of her waist belt. Reaching down, Calamity jerked the whip free and measured the distance between herself and her two suitors with a practised eye. Resin and Muldoon were moving towards each other, crouching slightly in a manner which offered good defensive and offensive potential but did tend to stick out their butt-ends in a manner which looked mighty promising to provi-dence and Calamity Jane.

Drawing back her right arm, Calamity shot it forward and the whip's lash curled out. Beau Resin let out a yelp of pain and leapt almost three foot into the air as the lash's tip caught him. Before Muldoon or any of the other men could make out just what happened, Calamity struck again. Once more the lash hissed out and not even Muldoon's saddle-toughened butt could resist the impact of what felt like a king-sized bee-sting.

With the two main protagonists handled, Calamity pro-ceeded to damp down the ardour of any other mean-minded cuss who aimed to stir up a fight. Her whip's lash hissed and cracked like gun-shots between the men.

'I'll take the legs from under the first one to start anything!' she warned. 'Anybody's wants a busted ankle step right out and get one from Calamity Jane's dispensary.'

And she could do it, too. Every man in the two groups knew it for sure, or guessed it with enough accuracy to believe her. Yet Calamity knew she must settle the issue in a more per-manent manner and her eyes flickered around. In one glance she saw the way—and a possible reason for the trouble, taken with certain things she remembered from earlier.

Hack saw his chances of revenge on Calamity fading away

and decided to follow their example. Once Muldoon quietened down, he was going to start thinking; although thinking had never been the burly three-bar's strongest suit. While Muldoon might not be a mathematical genius, he could add up two and two and make the answer come out four. Hack had never been noted for generosity or mingling with the lower elements of society and Muldoon might suspect a nigger with a bottle of Old Stump-Blaster dwelling in the wood-pile of the shiny-butt's sudden flow of hospitality.

With that in mind, and knowing something of Muldoon's way when roused, Hack turned to take a hurried departure. Before he had taken two strides he found his progress halted as surely as Eileen Tradle's had been earlier, through the same person though in a less gentle manner. The lash of Calamity's whip coiled around his fat neck and dragged him back on his heels. Angrily he turned to face the girl as she bore down on him. His anger oozed from him when he saw her change the whip handle to her left hand and draw her gun. While Calamity could not truthfully claim to be *fast* with a gun—in the West one needed to be able to draw and shoot in at least three-quarters of a second and the best Calamity could manage was a full second—she sure as hell looked fast to Hack.

Stepping forward, Calamity stabbed out the barrel of her Navy and sent it deep into Hack's lard-soft belly.

'Talk, Fatso!' she said. 'Talk up a storm!'

'Huh?' Hack gurgled. 'Ooof!'

The first exclamation had been to indicate his lack of understanding, the second came when the Navy's barrel jabbed home again.

'Talk, you lard-gutted shiny-butt!' Calamity growled. 'Tell Paddy why you fed him rot-gut whisky and stirred him up agin me.'

'Now that's a good point, Hack,' Muldoon said thoughtfully, rubbing his sore butt-end. 'I never remembered you being generous afore.'

'Was I you, I'd talk up, *hombre*,' Resin commented, 'afore ole Calam pokes that Navy clear through your backbone belly first.'

'I—I don't—ooof!'

'I'll tell you why!' Calamity snapped, after ending his protests with another savage jab. 'It's 'cause of what happened on

43

the river bank this morning.'

'And what did happen on the river bank this morning, darlin'?' asked Muldoon eyeing Hack with renewed interest.

'Ask him,' replied Calamity.

'Now you've got a real smart point there, gal.'

On hearing Muldoon's reply, Hack decided the time had come to depart, and had been passed several belly-aching minutes before. The whip's lash had come free and so Hack turned and fled. Letting out a bellow, Muldoon took after him and most of the soldiers followed to see the fun.

The crisis had been postponed and Calamity decided to make an end to it. When he returned, Muldoon might still retain his amatory interests and Resin would not take kindly to that. So Calamity figured to remove temptation from Muldoon's way.

'That hurt?' she asked as Resin rubbed his whip-stung rump.

'Stings like hell.'

'I got me a real good cure for what ails you,' she told him, 'only I can't do it here.'

'Then let's go someplace where we can.'

'I thought you'd never ask.'

Together they walked from the camp circle and into the darkness. At dawn Resin returned to the wagon he shared with the wagon boss's outfit. His rump no longer hurt him and although he had missed the end of the dance, Resin had no complaints, Calamity's cure had been well worth it.

CHAPTER FIVE

MISS CANARY INCREASES AN OFFICER'S LADY'S ENMITY

'THOSE are my bags, the ones marked with my name,' Eileen Tradle told Calamity as they stood by the lead wagon of the train. 'I suppose you can read?'

Eileen would never know how close she came to getting hand-scalped at that moment. It was the morning after the dance and the wagon train's travellers prepared to move on. At such a moment Calamity's temper had never been the best and she did not take kindly to sarcasm. The harnessing of a six-horse team took time and Calamity wanted to get her guest's baggage loaded so as not to delay the start of Killem's outfit. Due to loading the stores on the previous day, Killem failed to collect Eileen's baggage earlier, but had sent Calamity and two of his men to collect it as soon as they hitched up their teams in the morning.

'Reckon I can,' Calamity answered. 'Only those do-dads are marked "Tradle," ' she pronounced the word to rhyme with 'saddle,' 'and everybody calls you "Tray-dell!" So I figured they couldn't be yours.'

Fortunately, the colonel's wife was present and had been out West long enough to have lost her preconceived ideas of superiority; and plenty long enough to read danger signs without needing spectacles.

'Now leave Calamity to handle the baggage, Eileen,' she said, stepping forward. 'It couldn't be in better hands. I talked with Dobe Killem last night and he left you a· space in the front of Calamity's wagon. I've had a camp-bed rigged in it and all you'll need.'

'Thank you, Monica,' Eileen answered. 'I suppose she is competent?'

Again Eileen had more luck than she deserved, for Calamity

had never heard the word 'competent' and did not know what it meant. The Colonel's wife did know and hurried to assure Eileen that Calamity was quite competent.

'You couldn't be in better hands,' she finished.

'Lay hold of those fancy do-dads, boys,' Calamity said. 'And don't scratch 'em up, they belong to a *lady*.'

'That woman is insufferable!' Eileen gasped as Calamity and the men walked away with her baggage.

'She probably feels the same way about you, although I don't think she'd express it in that way.'

'She's—she's——'

'She's unique,' the colonel's wife replied. 'There's only one Calamity Jane, my dear.'

'I would imagine that was one too many,' Eileen sniffed.

'Look, Eileen,' said the older woman, laying a hand on the other's sleeve. 'This isn't Boston. People out here don't care that you come from the best Back Bay stock, that your father is a Congressman and that you have two uncles who are generals. It's what *you* are that counts with a girl like Calamity. I don't often give advice, except to young wives going out to their first frontier post, but I'd advise you to make friends with Calamity. You could learn a lot.'

'I'll remember your advice,' Eileen promised coldly.

'I doubt it,' smiled the colonel's wife. 'Goodbye, my dear, and good luck—you'll probably need it.'

Stiff-backed and tight-lipped, Eileen stamped off after her baggage. Nor did her annoyance lessen when she found Molly Johnson standing by the side of the wagon into which her belongings were being loaded.

'Asked Molly here to ride with us this morning,' Calamity remarked in a tone which implied she did not give a damn whether Eileen objected or not.

'If you think there won't be room, I'll go back to my own wagon, Mrs. Tradle,' Molly remarked, being more susceptible than Calamity to atmosphere and realising Eileen did not approve.

'Shucks, there's more'n room for the three of us on *my* wagon,' Calamity put in. 'Ain't none of us that fat. Hop aboard, gals, and we'll be all set to roll.'

Turning, Eileen stared up at the wagon's box and found it to be higher than she imagined. Of course, the other wagon had been high, but supplied a step-ladder to allow her to mount. She watched Calamity climb the spokes of the front wheel and hop lightly aboard.

'Here, Molly, take hold!' Calamity ordered, extending her hand to the little blonde, then glared at the freighters who hung around in the hope of seeing a well-turned ankle. 'Get the hell to your wagons or I'll peel the stinking hides offen you.'

Which caused a rapid departure for the men knew better than to cross their Calamity at such a moment. Molly, with Calamity's help, made the climb on to the box and took her seat. Being on her dignity, Eileen declined assistance.

'I'll manage,' she stated as Calamity offered a none-too-clean hand.

'It's your notion, not mine,' replied Calamity calmly and sat down.

Eileen tried to climb aboard without help, but could not manage it. However her pride refused to allow her to ask for assistance.

'Hey, Calam!' yelled the man in the wagon behind them. 'Get rolling.'

'Do you want help, or shall I have a couple of the boys come boost you up?' Calamity asked and bitterly Eileen conceded defeat.

After being helped on to the box by a pull from Calamity's strong arms, Eileen sat down hard and looked into what would be her home for the next four weeks or more. Although the rear of the wagon carried a load of wooden boxes, a piece at the front remained clear, apart from her baggage and a camp-bed—and a war-bag, bed-roll and a wooden box of battered aspect which certainly did not belong to her.

'Don't worry,' Calamity remarked, seeing the way Eileen eyed the latter. 'I sleep under the wagon most nights.'

Already the wagon train had started to roll, following the wagon master's vehicle in single file. Killem's outfit would bring up the rear and it only remained for the cavalry escort to make its appearance. Which it did, bringing an exclamation of surprise and amazement from Calamity.

With Bigelow at their head, a force of twenty troopers under a lieutenant and Sergeant Muldoon swept from the fort. Only they looked like they were riding a general's review, not

47

handling an escort duty through wild country. Each man wore his regulation uniform blouse over his shirt and their short-legged boots had a shine to match the glint of their brass work. More than that, each man carried a sabre in addition to his carbine and revolvers; a thing which, artists' impressions or not, rarely if ever went into action against the horse-Indians of the plains.

'Land-snakes!' Calamity gasped. 'Just lookit old Paddy Muldoon there. My, don't he look right elegant and becoming all togged up in his shiny best. Say, they must be expecting good buffalo hunting, way they're toting them over-grown carving knives along.'

'Those are sabres!' Eileen answered.

'Do tell. What do they use 'em for, 'cepting looking fancy?'

'They fight with them!'

'Whooee!' Calamity gasped, although she knew well enough what a sabre was for. 'I'd sure as hell hate to tangle with a Cheyenne or Sioux buffalo lance with one of them things in my hand.'

Not wishing to encourage familiarity, Eileen let the matter drop and Calamity stopped talking as she prepared to start her wagon rolling.

'Wagon roll!' Killem roared.

'Hang on, gals,' Calamity warned. 'And don't blush if I have to do some cussing. These hosses are common cusses like me and don't take to soft talking.'

The wagon ahead started and Calamity swung her whip, yelling to her horses. She gave her full attention to the team as it took up the strain on the harness, and flicked the centre near-side horse with the tip of her whip to make sure it did not shirk its share of the load. With a lurch, the big wagon began to roll, but Calamity gave her horses a blistering string of profanity just to let them know she was still around. At last the team settled down and Calamity relaxed, turning with a grin to Molly.

'Wasn't that a party last night?'

'Did you enjoy it?' asked Molly.

'I always enjoy a good—dance,' Calamity answered with her reckless grin. 'That Beau Resin's got his points, Molly, gal. If you see what I mean and I reckon you don't.'

An angry flush crept to Eileen's cheeks as she read an implication into the words that Calamity had not meant to be there. On the way West Eileen had shown some considerable interest in Resin and thought Calamity knew of this. Eileen took it that Calamity knew of the friendship and tried to annoy her by hints at a *very* close relationship with the big scout.

'I really enjoyed myself last night,' Molly admitted, seeing the expression on Eileen's face and changing the subject—or so she hoped—to safer ground.

'Sure,' grinned Calamity. 'I saw you and that bow-necked shiny-butt.'

'Wade's not bow-necked, or a shiny-butt!' Molly put in hotly. 'He's just unfortunate in having been assigned to the Quartermaster Corps, but he's hoping for a transfer when he reaches Fort Sherrard and——'

Molly's defence had come just a shade too quickly and her cheeks reddened as she saw the tolerant smile on Calamity's face, so stopped her details of the life of Wade H. Bigelow, frustrated captain of the Quartermaster Corps.

Once more Eileen breathed her annoyance; for she had hoped to become much better acquainted with Bigelow during the trip to Fort Sherrard and saw her chances going out of the window in the face of the pretty, *single* schoolmarm's competition. Naturally Bigelow would prefer an unmarried girl, with its attendant possibilities, rather than squiring an officer's lady which could only pass mild, innocent flirtation with the gravest risks to his career.

To give her credit, Eileen had no intention of extending her friendship with either Resin or Bigelow beyond the mildest flirtation. She loved and was loyal to her husband and reared in the strictest Back Bay Boston traditions—which were about as strict as one could get. So her interest in both men was more mercenary than licentious. Resin had been third from the top in the wagon train's hierarchy during the trip from the East and the two higher members of the social scale were both married, with their wives along. Bigelow, as commander of the military escort, now was the head man. All her life Eileen had tried to be around the top people, not out of snobbery but because she had been born into that class. She knew the value of friendship with men in high places as an adjunct for obtaining her own way. So she planned to be known as the escort of the leader of the train; it was always a good thing to be.

Only it appeared that Molly, who Eileen had previously regarded as a rather plain, sexless little mouse, was cutting the ground from under her feet one way and the coarse, common, vulgar Calamity Jane taking her place in the other.

All in all the earlier stages of the drive were not happy for Eileen. In the course of her talk, Calamity let it slip out that she had appropriated Bigelow's trout; which further annoyed Eileen who had been offered a supper from the fish and was disappointed not to receive it after hearing so much about the taste of fresh-caught squaretails. She resisted all attempts to make peace, snapping out chilling answers until Molly's even temper started to wear thin and Calamity sat debating to herself whether to boot the officer's lady from the wagon box.

Fortunately for Eileen, before Calamity reached a decision on the matter there came an interruption. Muldoon galloped his horse up from the rear and pulled in alongside Calamity's wagon. After mopping his sweat-streaked face with an enormous bandana, he grinned at the girls.

'The top of the morning to yez, ladies,' he greeted.

'Sure and 'tis elegant yez look, Pathrick, me darlin',' replied Calamity. 'If 'twas Indian country, sure they'd see yez coming five miles off with the flash of yez fancy buttons.'

'*Elegant!*' answered Muldoon, snorting like an old bull buffalo faced with a pack of Great Plains wolves. 'It's the idea of that bow-neck——'

'Now hush up there, Paddy,' grinned Calamity. 'Can't you see I've got a *lady* aboard. Anyways, that shavetail from Connel's been out enough to know better.'

'And so he does, for hasn't he had the teaching of Pathrick James Muldoon to show him what's right. Sure, we'd be riding in comfort but for that——'

'Sergeant!' Eileen snapped. 'Do you usually cut down your officers before civilians?'

Stiffening into a brace, Muldoon looked at the young woman. 'No, ma'am. Only Calamity isn't a civilian at all——'

'Aren't you going somewhere on duty?' Eileen interrupted coldly.

'That I am, ma'am,' Muldoon answered.

Anger glowed in Calamity's eyes as the burly sergeant sent his horse along the line of wagons. Eileen met Calamity's stare without flinching and it appeared that an open clash could not be avoided.

'Will we see any buffalo this trip, Calam?' Molly asked mildly.

'Huh?' Calamity grunted, then smiled at the little blonde. 'We might.'

Eileen decided that having two enemies might be a mite more than she could handle, so reckoned she ought to make her peace with one of them. Of course, there could only be one choice. While Molly Johnson was in employment, schoolteaching stood on a different plane to other kinds of female labour; and Molly was socially acceptable both by birth and education. With that in mind, Eileen turned and smiled in her most winning manner at the blonde.

'My father came out here hunting last year, with *another* congressman,' she said, deciding to show Calamity that she possessed a string of imposing relatives, 'and my uncles, Generals Brackstead and Porter. They all shot several buffalo.'

'Never could stand these dudes coming here and gunning down poor fool critters then leaving the meat to rot,' Calamity put in.

'Nobody asked you!' Eileen spat out. 'I'll thank you to continue driving and mind your own business.'

'Yeah!' snorted Calamity. 'Well, you can g——'

'I think I'll go to my own wagon.' Molly interrupted. 'It's humiliating to see two grown women acting like children.'

'I assure you, Molly——'

'Danged if she didn't start——'

Both girls started to speak at the same moment, stopped and glared at each other then relapsed into silence.

'Of course, I could talk with one of you for, say ten minutes, then turn to the other,' Molly remarked, hoping the introduction of a light note would break the hostility.

'Don't put yourself out for me!' Eileen snapped.

'I got work to do!' Calamity snorted. 'Blasted dudes coming out here and shooting up the country.'

'I always say a woman should dress like one!'

'Yeah? Well, let me tell you something, you high-and-mighty Boston——'

'Don't you insult Boston, you—you——'

'I'll insult what I want on *my* blasted wagon!'

Fortunately, Captain Bigelow rode up at that moment and Eileen, somewhat red in the face, turned to speak with him. Although he prevented any further rift between the girls, he did not bring peace. For the rest of the day's travel Calamity and Eileen ignored each other.

After being dismissed by Eileen, Muldoon galloped his horse to the head of the train, paying little attention to its occupants. Once clear of the train, he brought his horse to a halt and let out a long chuckle.

'Pathrick James,' he said, 'happen she gets some of that Boston fuddy-duddy knocked out of her, that gal'll make a real fighting officer's lady.'

'Always reckon it's the first sign when they start talking to themselves,' drawled a voice from behind Muldoon.

Turning, the big sergeant grinned at Beau Resin and showed no sign of animosity over the previous night's affair.

'Sure and I've always been after having an intelligent and superior person talking with me, and having an intelligent and superior person to talk with, Beau,' he explained.

'You've got a right smart point there, or a damned good excuse. You boys are sure fancied up.'

'That we are. He'll learn, Beau, he'll learn. There's a man's heart under that shiny-butt's uniform.'

'He'd best learn; and fast!' Resin stated. 'Word has it that Sand Runner's gathering the Cheyenne bad-hats.'

'Which's why they sent us soldier lads to defend all you civilians,' grinned Muldoon. 'Say, where'd you and Calamity go last night, I was looking for to apologise for me unseemly behaviour and give her a little something to remember Fatso Hack by.'

'We were around, and how we were around,' the scout drawled. 'What happened to Hack?'

'The poor darlin' fell over something. The fort surgeon says he'll be right as ever in a week or so. Sure though, isn't that Calamity a lil darlin'?'

'She thinks the same about you.'

'Then she shows good taste.'

'Yep,' drawled Resin. 'Couldn't stop talking about you offering to marry her. Asked me if you'd want a white wedding in a church.'

'Holy Mother of God!' croaked Muldoon, horror replacing

the delighted beam on his face. 'I hopes you stood true by an old friend, Beau lad, and persuaded her what a lousy husband I'd make. Sure 'tis no use I'd be to any woman, I drink, never save a dime——'

'Reckon I talked her out of it,' grinned the scout.

'Then 'tis me thanks you have, Beau, lad,' said Muldoon, gripping Resin's hand in a heart-felt manner. Letting out a shudder, Muldoon went on, 'Faith, a gal as strong-willed as Calamity might've—hey, just look who's there.'

While the two men sat talking, the wagons passed them and the outfit belonging to the rat-faced jasper with the four hefty girls was just going by. It was to the buxom blonde not the man that Muldoon nodded.

'Joined us on the Kansas line. Keep to themselves and pay their way,' Resin replied. 'Which's all we ask.'

'Does Calam know who *she* is?'

'Lordy-lord, I hope not. If she does——'

'Yeah,' grinned Muldoon. 'It'd be a sight to see though, happen Calamity finds out.'

CHAPTER SIX

MISS CANARY TAKES A CHANCE

'COFFEE, Mrs. Tradle?'

'If you please, Miss Canary.'

A week had passed since leaving Fort Connel and the association between Calamity and Eileen was in the dangerous stage of studied politeness. Each tried to out-do the other in avoiding giving reason for a further clash—which brought them closer to it many times than would more ordinary behaviour.

In several ways Eileen had changed. On the first night Calamity growled an order for Eileen to start a fire while the freight outfit's crew tended to their chores. It had been on the tip of Eileen's tongue to refuse, but a further comment from Calamity to the effect that Eileen would not know how to make a fire without a flock of Boston servants to help brought a change of plan. Angrily Eileen went to the rawhide possum belly under the wagon and drew out dried buffalo-chips and wood. Refusing Molly's help, Eileen made a fire as her father taught her in the days of her rather tomboy youth. Next day Eileen lent a hand to harness the team and each day since had taken more and more of a share in the work load. Her soft white hands hardened with washing dishes and doing other manual labour that had for years been the prerogative of her family's servants.

Both Calamity and Eileen looked for an excuse to bury the hatchet, but each time the way opened something would happen to start them feuding again.

As an onlooker, Molly found the situation highly diverting and amusing. Although the British writer Rudyard Kipling was still many years from writing about the under-the-skin kinship of the colonel's lady and Sarah O'Grady, Molly was in an ideal position to understand what he would mean.

Calamity's energy amazed Molly. Not only did the girl rise in the first light of dawn, tend to and harness her team, drive all day; but after caring for the six horses in the evening would visit the class Molly taught, then organise a lecture on various western subjects for the women of the train and throw herself wholeheartedly into any festivity she found herself invited to attend after dark.

Eileen helped Calamity around the wagon and attended all the girl's lectures although always standing at the back and pretending not to be listening, or showing her disbelief if the red-head happened to glance her way.

Storm clouds were gathering in the sky as the two women stood by the fire and drank their coffee, after eating the breakfast Eileen had helped cook. Killem slouched over to them and nodded his head.

'Looks like rain,' he said.

'Tastes a mite like coffee though,' Calamity answered.

Once more the possibility of burying the hatchet went flying by. Calamity's joke had been harmlessly meant, but it was Eileen's coffee—and well-brewed at that. Giving an angry snort, Eileen doused the fire by up-ending the coffeepot and pouring out a good three mugs full, one at least of which Calamity had hoped for and looked forward to drinking.

In angry silence the two girls prepared to travel and neither spoke as the wagon rolled. Molly had not joined them that morning, finding the situation on the wagon too disconcerting and, having taken a liking to Eileen, wished to avoid antagonising either of her friends.

Each morning the order of travel changed so that the same people did not spend all their days eating the dust at the rear of the column. On this day Calamity found herself in second position behind the wagonmaster's vehicle which always took the lead. Before they had gone a mile, dust was not the thing the travellers needed bother about.

Suddenly the blackened skies split with a flash of lightning and rain began to gush down, coming in slanting sheets that drove towards the wagons. There was no chance to take precautions and almost everybody on the train found themselves soaked to the skin.

'If you'd any sense you'd get in there and put your slicker on,' Calamity told Eileen, hunching miserably on the box and sending her whip's lash flickering out to keep the idle centre near-side horse doing its share.

'When I want your opinion I'll ask for it!'

'So soak and the hell with you then! Easy there, you stab-gutted, spavined crow-bait. You're not on Boston High Street.'

For fifteen minutes the two girls sat side by side, soaked to the skin and both too damned hog-stubborn to give in. At last Eileen decided to call it quits and turned to slip through the dawn-down canopy into the lurching wagon. Although her oilskin coat and hat hung ready for use, she doubted if she could change while the wagon rolled, jerked and pitched. Donning the coat, she was about to climb back on to the box when she saw Calamity's wet-weather clothing lying on the battered box.

Picking up the Stetson hat and yellow oilskin slicker, she opened the flap and climbed out.

'Here!' she said.

It was on the tip of Calamity's tongue to tell her to go to hell, then sit out the storm unprotected, but she changed her mind.

'Thanks.'

'I'd have done it for a dog,' Eileen sniffed. 'Let me take the reins and you get dressed.'

'*You?*'

'You've been boasting about how good your team is, so I should be able to manage them—if they're that good.'

'Don't you insult my horses!' Calamity squealed, but handed over the reins and donned her protective clothing.

Suffering a mutual discomfort might have brought peace to the two girls, but the fates decreed that before they could forget their differences a fresh cause of strife would arise.

Beau Resin came galloping through the rain towards the wagonmaster and Bigelow as they rode at the head of the column. The rain had been slashing down for over an hour and the ground under foot grew soggy and uncertain.

'We got trouble, Sam,' Resin drawled, water trickling from his Stetson brim in a steady stream.

'When did you ever come back like that and not have trouble?' asked the wagonmaster calmly.

'That's what you pay me for, to bring you bad news.'

'What is it?' Bigelow asked, slightly irritated even after a week at the way Resin failed to respect his rank and position.

'A damned great valley, Cap'n. Come on ahead and take a look at it.'

On riding some three miles ahead with the two civilians, Bigelow saw the cause of the trouble. A wide valley stretched ahead of them, its left slope sheer, the right, on which they sat, fairly gentle and the bottom along which the train planned to move turned into a roaring torrent by a storm-flooded stream.

'That'll be hell to get by,' remarked the wagonmaster.

'Plumb hell,' agreed Resin.

'We could go along the top there,' suggested Bigelow.

'Could,' Resin answered. 'Only there was a big burn-out up there a few years back and its grown over with thick young stuff and loused out with fallen dead trees. It'd take us a month to cut a way through.'

'How about the other side?'

'Happen we could cross that stream, which same's not likely, there's a fork down the valley about half a mile, you can't hardly see it for the rain. It'd take us near a hundred mile out of our way to get round that fork and back on to our line and there's no way we could cross.'

'Do we wait it out?' asked Bigelow, which showed that something of a change had come over him. He now asked for advice instead of giving orders.

'Now that's a good question, Cap'n,' answered the wagonmaster. 'I only wish to hell I knew the answer.'

'If one wagon broke the ground across this slope, the others could follow,' Resin remarked.

'Sure,' agreed the wagonmaster dryly. 'Only I'd hate like hell to be the first one.'

None of the party spoke for a few moments for both Resin and Bigelow knew that if it came to the point, the wagonmaster most likely would be the one who made the pioneer trip across the treacherous mile or so of slope.

Riding forward with Bigelow at his side, Resin found the slope's soil to be soft, soggy and slick. Yet their horses found little or no difficulty in keeping their feet. Of course, the Appaloosa and Bigelow's bay did not haul a damned great Conestoga wagon behind them. On returning to the wagonmaster's side, the two men found Killem and the train's segundo present.

'Means going a good two mile along the slope before it's clear to hit the top,' Resin remarked, glancing at the halted wagons behind the men.

Jumping down from her wagon, Calamity slouched forward and looked at the scene ahead, reading its implications. Her eyes went to the lead wagon from which the wagonmaster's family were climbing.

'Way I see it,' she said, joining the men, 'my wagon's carrying the least important stuff. Right, Cap'n?'

For a moment Bigelow thought then nodded. 'If it comes to a point, your load is the most easily replaced.'

'I've got the best danged team, too,' the girl said calmly. 'Have all the stock pushed across ahead of me, and let them with hosses ride across. Sam, get your kids back in your wagon out of the rain.'

Five startled pairs of male eyes stared at Calamity. In a way she spoke the truth. Of all the wagons hers could probably be most easily spared; every other carried a family's home and belongings or vitally needed military supplies. Yet the men could not risk a girl's life on the dangerous task ahead; not even a girl like Calamity Jane.

Without waiting for their permission, Calamity returned to her wagon and climbed aboard.

'What's the delay?' Eileen asked.

'Nothing. Get out.'

'*What?*'

'I'm taking the wagon across that slope ahead and can't tote extra weight,' Calamity growled, her nervous tension preventing her from explaining that she could not risk the other girl's life in the crossing.

'But how do I get across?' asked Eileen, the rain making her temper rise.

'Look down there!' Calamity snapped, pointing to the bed of the wagon. 'See them things sticking out from under your dress? They're feet, use 'em.'

'But I——'

'Get out or I'll throw you out!' Calamity screamed.

Something in the girl's voice warned Eileen not to push Calamity any further. While Eileen willingly swapped word-warfare, she drew the line at physical conflict and so climbed from the wagon. A squeal left her lips as she sank ankle-deep into the mud. Hearing the sound of men approaching, Eileen turned. The wagonmaster, Bigelow and the other men came towards Calamity's wagon but one look at their faces warned Eileen not to worry them with petty troubles. One thing Eileen had learned young and early was when not to trouble the men-folk and such a time was at hand.

'All right, Calamity,' Killem said. 'I'll take your wagon over.'

'Like hell you will,' she replied.

'Come on, Calam,' Killem growled. 'Let me handle it.'

'Nope!'

'I said I'd take it!'

'And I said go to hell!'

'Damn it, Calam!' Killem barked. 'You're fired.'

'Swell!' she answered. 'Then I don't have to take your orders any more.'

Giving an angry snort, Killem stepped towards the wagon. Then he came to a sudden halt, he and the other men who started to follow him with the intention of lending their moral support. While Calamity's Colt rode under her fastened slicker, a Winchester carbine lay in a boot on the side of the wagon— or did lie there for Calamity jerked it out and fed a round into the chamber.

'Get your hand off the wagon, Dobe!' she warned as her boss reached for the wheel to climb aboard. 'Damn it, I mean it. Get your hand off or I'll put lead into you.'

And she meant it, too, every man present knew that. Calamity had pride in her work and nobody, not even her boss, took over her wagon no matter how dangerous the situation.

'It's damned risky, gal,' Resin pointed out.

'Reckon I don't know it?' she snorted. 'Dobe, Sam and all the boys have kin depending on 'em. You're needed as scout and the cap'n doesn't know how to handle a six-hoss team well enough to take it across there. I've got nobody needing me to support 'em, so I'll take her over.'

'All right, you blasted ornery female,' Killem said, his voice gentle. 'Go bust your fool neck and kill yourself. Only don't you come blaming me when you do.'

On receiving his permission, Calamity booted the carbine, leaned over to remove Killem's hat and planted a kiss on the top of his head. 'I love you, too, Cecil!' she whispered, then raised her voice. 'Get that stock run across, Beau.'

Even with all the spare stock run across the slope so as to churn up the ground a mite, Calamity could see her task was anything but a sinecure. She started her team moving, conscious that almost every member of the train stood behind and watched her. The story of what Calamity hoped to do passed around and Eileen forgot her position to watch the girl, realising why Calamity ordered her from the wagon.

Ignoring the crowd, Calamity sat her wagon's box and concentrated on handling her team. She kicked off her moccasins and sat with bare feet on the wagon bed, the better to feel the vibrations of movement under her. With her eyes on the horses, she gave low-voiced encouragement.

'Slow and easy, blast you!' she said, gripping the reins between delicate yet strong fingers to steady or urge on as the situation demanded. 'You make me trouble, Muley, and I'll skin your hide tonight.'

This last came as a warning to the near-side centre horse as she felt it slack its pull. Usually the horse tended to idle and needed the spice of a whip-flick to keep its attention on work, but it sensed the danger of the situation and buckled down to pull its weight.

Never would Calamity forget that trip across the slope. Once she felt the rear wheel begin to slide and her fingers controlled the reins, giving the horses confidence while keeping them pulling. Although the rain beat down and she was wet to the skin, Calamity felt sweat soaking her and the few seconds during which the wheels slid downwards seemed like an hour. Then the great horses' strength held it and the wagon rolled on once more. Behind her Calamity heard a roar of cheers that followed on the concerted gasp of horror which rose as the slipping started. She ignored the crowd's approval, knowing that she was far from being in safety.

'I sure hope they mark that place down,' she breathed. 'Pull, boys, pull!'

On went the horses, fighting their way along. Ahead of her, where she could turn to safety on top of the slope, Calamity saw Resin, Muldoon and a number of the biggest, strongest men of the train gathering. So intent had been her concentration before that she could not remember them passing her and wondered what they were doing. Then she got the idea and gave a sigh of relief. After a pull like they had just been through, the horses would find difficulty in hauling a heavy Conestoga to the head of the slope. The party of men had come to lend a hand at a time when their aid would be of the most use.

Even with the aid of the men, Calamity felt her wagon's wheels skid and saw the horses straining and fighting to move it. For a long moment everything hung in the balance and then Calamity felt the wagon inching forward and upward. Then the horses topped the slope and her wagon lurched up and on to level ground.

'Yahoo!' Resin whooped, coming alongside the wagon and grinning up at the girl. 'You done it, Calam!'

'It looks a mite that way,' she replied. 'Hey, get some hosses up top here and ropes, the others won't have teams like mine. I'll head down to the bed ground and settle in.'

'Sure thing, gal. Go on about half a mile, you'll find a big clearing. Stay there, the stock's down there already.'

After moving her wagon on to the appointed bed ground, Calamity attended to her horses. The rain, having made things as dangerous and awkward as it could for the travellers, eased off and, by the time Calamity had halted her wagon, finished to allow a watery sun to creep through cracks in the clouds. Calamity ignored her own soaked condition as she worked on her horses, drying their coats and then taking them to water in the brook at the edge of the camp. After watering and feeding the horses, Calamity headed back to the slope to see if she could help out. On her way she found that Eileen had crossed and was also very busy.

Although she slipped once and slid several feet in the mud of the slope, and lost both shoes in the process of crossing, Eileen had come to the other side on foot. She forgot her own discomfort as she watched the others straggling across; men, women and children walking so as to relieve the weight on the wagon teams and lessen the risk if anything went wrong. Something stirred inside Eileen, the spirit which lifted her family above the rest of the herd and made them leaders instead of staying among the led.

Finding Molly Johnson, Eileen made her suggestions and the two girls started a fire. Then Eileen bustled around the women, making them work and taking their minds off their misery. The results of her drive showed quickly enough in the other fires that appeared and then in the smell of brewing coffee and cooking food. By the time half of the wagons had made the still dangerous crossing, hot coffee and food awaited the hard-working men. Not until everybody had been fed did Eileen manage to get to the wagon and start to change her clothes.

The flap of the wagon lifted and a naked Eileen gave a gasp, swinging around and hiding as well as she could behind the towel she held. Calamity swung in and looked at the other girl. Tossing aside her hat and slicker, Calamity unfastened her bandana and removed it.

'Come out from behind there,' she said testily as Eileen continued to hold up the towel. 'I've seen all you're likely to show me and got about the same.'

'I'm not used to sharing a changing room,' Eileen replied, cold and exhaustion bringing an edge to her voice.

'Yeah, well in that case you go out of the wagon, I don't aim to,' Calamity snapped back. 'I'm getting sick to my guts of you!'

'The feeling is quite mutual!' snorted Eileen, turning her back and continuing her drying.

Calamity tried to peel the sodden shirt and undershirt from her, but the already tight material stuck. Giving a harder tug, she jerked them over her head but the force of the pull sent them slapping on to Eileen's back. A squeal of fury left Eileen's lips and she swung around, dropping the towel.

'You did that deliberately!' she hissed and drew back her hand.

'Don't try it!' Calamity warned angrily. 'You start slapping and I'll take you apart, you Boston hoity-toity.'

Commonsense warned Eileen that Calamity spoke the truth. While Eileen could more than hold her own in a slanging match, she knew that Calamity had the advantage in any other kind of brawl. Then she realised how she was—or was not—dressed. Blushing, she bent hurriedly and grabbed up the towel, rubbing herself savagely with it. Once dry, she dressed and pushed by Calamity, leaving the wagon. Calamity stared after Eileen, gave an angry snort and finished her drying, then put on dry clothing and went in search of Beau Resin.

Once again a chance mishap had ruined their hopes of peace for both girls had formed a respect for the other during the day. With luck they might have ended their feud in the wagon, but things went wrong and both were pot-boiling mad at the other.

Leaving the wagon, Eileen went in search of Bigelow, but he was at supper with the Johnsons. In her loneliness, Eileen fell into conversation with Muldoon who she met on his way to inspect pickets. While walking through the camp, he told her much of Calamity, expressing his admiration for a number of most unfeminine talents shown by the girl.

'Now there's an outfit for you, ma'am,' Muldoon remarked as they passed the rat-faced dude's wagon. 'You'd never guess what they do.'

'Are they actresses of some kind?' she replied.

On hearing of how the outfit made its living, Eileen first thought that Muldoon must be joking. Then she saw he appeared to be very serious and listened to what he said about the blonde in particular. Nothing might have come of it, but after separating from Muldoon and walking back to her wagon Eileen saw the blonde away from her friends hanging clothes to dry.

For a few minutes, Eileen tried to fight down the temptation, then she gave an angry snort. Calamity had asked for it, and needed to lose some of her conceit. With that in mind, Eileen walked over to the blonde and started talking. It seemed that Muldoon told the truth about the blonde, and she was willing to help Eileen out.

CHAPTER SEVEN

MISS CANARY MEETS A LADY PUGILIST

THE wagonmaster and Bigelow declared the day after the rains a rest period in order to allow the travellers a chance to dry out their belongings. Men went out to cut timber and the women did their chores.

During the morning, after having slept on the matter all night, Eileen felt tempted to call off the arrangement she had made with the blonde. However, a trivial incident which neither of them could be blamed for sparked off a blazing quarrel and so Eileen went to see the blonde, taking money with her to finalise the arrangements. In these Eileen showed considerable planning skill that might have been worthy if applied to a better cause.

In the late afternoon Eileen walked over to where Calamity sat cleaning her carbine, watched by a couple of admiring youngsters.

'There's some trouble down at the stream, Miss Canary,' she said. 'Molly——'

'Is Molly needing help?' asked Calamity, laying aside the carbine. 'I'll go right along.'

'I'll come with you.'

'That'll be as much help as an udder on a bull,' Calamity sniffed.

While listening to Calamity's haste to go to Molly's aid, Eileen had come almost to the verge of calling off her scheme, but Calamity's sneer changed her mind. Tight-lipped and angry, Eileen turned and walked off through the camp. Behind her, Calamity told the two boys to 'scat and keep out of mischief' then followed on Eileen's heels.

The boys headed back to their wagons and on the way they met Molly returning from conducting a class.

'Gee, Miss Johnson,' one said. 'We thought you was in trouble.'

'Now what gave you that idea?' Molly smiled.

'Mrs. Tradle told Calamity you was and they went out of camp together.'

Molly stared at the boy in horror. 'Quick, Pete!' she said. 'Which way did they go?'

'Down by the edge of the stream, following it down river.'

'The fools! But Eileen Tradle wouldn't——'

'Wouldn't what, Miss Molly?'

'Nothing. You boys had better go back to your wagons and see if there are any chores for you.'

Leaving the boys, Molly hurried out of the camp and through the woods, keeping to the banks of the stream. She covered almost a mile, well past the last working party and began to wonder if she was the victim of a schoolboy prank. Then she heard noises ahead. Moving forward, Molly saw there really was trouble on the bank of the small stream.

Neither Calamity nor Eileen spoke as they walked through the trees along the bank of the stream. Eileen had learned the futility of trying to appear well-groomed and attired to the height of Eastern fashion and she wore a cheap old gingham dress instead of her fancy outfit; apart from her wedding ring, she had stored away all her jewellery, and her hair hung in a tidy fashion instead of being piled up in formal style.

'Are you sure it's this far?' asked Calamity after they had passed the last of the train's working parties.

'I'm sure.'

'I hope I'll not need my medicine bag,' Calamity went on, looking down at the buckskin bag containing various herbs and items for rough-and-ready frontier doctoring.

'You probably will,' Eileen answered.

'I hope to hell you haven't got lost,' Calamity sniffed.

'I haven't. It's just around the bend here.'

Turning the bend, they came through the bushes into a clearing. Calamity saw a blonde woman sitting under a tree, but it was not Molly. On seeing Calamity and Eileen, the blonde rose, a long, flowing black robe hanging around her from neck to ankle.

'What is this?' Calamity growled. 'Where's Molly?'

'I don't know,' Eileen replied.

'But you said——'

'I started to say that Molly wasn't involved, but you never gave me a chance. Anyway, I thought you'd jump at a chance of meeting Miss Petrosky.'

'So who the hell is she?' asked Calamity, looking at the buxom blonde who had aroused her interest earlier.

'Her professional name is Russian Olga,' Eileen replied. 'She's a lady pugilist.'

'A *what*?'

'Fist fighter, girlie,' the blonde answered. 'I'm champion of the world and never been licked.'

Then Calamity saw what had been worrying Killem and the reason he changed the subject every time she mentioned the rat-faced dude's outfit. Killem thought that if Calamity learned of Russian Olga's claim to fame, she would go hell-blatting out looking for a chance to disprove the blonde's statement. Calamity had heard of girl fist-fighters—they enjoyed a vogue much as girl wrestlers in later years—but had never connected the buxom blonde with the name Russian Olga.

'Never been licked, huh?' said Calamity thoughtfully, remembering something she had heard some time before.

'Never, girlie.'

'How's about with that German gal up to Quiet Town?'

A scowl creased Olga's face at the mention of the incident, for her defeat still rankled. Yet she had met a defeat at the hands of an erstwhile member of the troupe while supposed to be fighting a fixed bout to cheat a rich miner out of his wager money.*

'I just aimed to whup you a mite, girlie,' Olga growled, unfastening her cloak. 'But now you've riled me and I'm going to lick you good.'

On removing the cloak, Olga showed that she had come prepared for a fight, for she wore the outfit used in the ring. Calamity studied the woman, noting the powerful fat legs in black tights, the firm condition of her torso under the upper part, which resembled a man's sleeveless undershirt, and the muscular state of her arms. There might be fat around Olga's middle, but under the fat lay hard muscles or Calamity missed her guess.

* Told in 'Quiet Town' by J. T. Edson.

'You fixing to tangle with me?' Calamity asked.

'If you don't shoot me first,' Olga answered.

'I'll soon settle that,' Calamity said, the light of prospective battle glowing in her eyes.

She removed her bandana, a simple precaution for a saloon-girl once almost choked her by grabbing it in a brawl, and placed it in the crown of her kepi, putting them under a tree. Next Calamity removed her shirt, figured that if Olga could fight in an undershirt, so should she, and lastly she unfastened the pigging thong and unbuckled her gunbelt, placing it by her hat.

Turning to face Olga, Calamity grinned. 'Ready or not, here I come!' she said, then looked at Eileen. 'Is this how you do your fighting in Boston, with somebody else to take the bruises?'

A flush crept into Eileen's cheeks. 'I—I thought you might like to show me how tough you were and I wouldn't be a match for you.'

'Which you wouldn't. But when I've whupped the champeen here, I'm going to whale the tar out of you.'

Eileen felt that she deserved the 'whaling,' although she doubted if Calamity would be in any condition to do it. Standing under the tree by Calamity's clothes, Eileen watched the red-head move towards the blonde.

Much to Calamity's surprise and amusement, Olga adopted the fighting stance used by male boxers of the period. Calamity had tangled with several saloon-girls at different times in her hectic young life, she had never seen one adopt such a posture.

The amusement did not last for long!

Out stabbed Olga's left fist to crash under Calamity's unprotected and offered chin. Taken by surprise both by the speed and force of the blow, Calamity went back on her heels. Olga came in fast, her left slugging Calamity in the stomach and folding the gasping girl over to take a right behind the ear. Down went Calamity in a winded, dazed heap on her face. Through the whirling mists that filled her head she heard Eileen and Russian Olga talking.

'That will be enough, Miss Petrosky.'

'Like hell. She reckons she's tough. I aim to see how tough.'

A hand gripped Calamity by the waistbelt and another dug

67

into her hair. She felt herself being dragged along and then
dropped. The ice-cold shock of landing face down in the
stream drove the mists from her head and she rolled over,
sitting up. Standing on the bank, hands on hips and a grin on
her face, Russian Olga looked down at Calamity.

'Had enough, girlie?'

Slowly, Calamity rose, spitting out a mouthful of water. She
put up a hand to feel at her chin and winced. Then she
climbed from the water and swung a punch which ripped into
Olga's cheek. On the heels of the first, Calamity brought
around a second blow and the blonde staggered back putting
up her hands again.

Watched by Eileen, Calamity and Olga slugged it out like
two men for almost three minutes. Although Calamity landed
good punches, she lacked Olga's skill and training, which gave
the blonde a distinct advantage. Twice Calamity went down
and each time, much to her surprise, Olga moved back to let
her rise. While on their feet and slugging, Olga's skill went
against her in one way; when she threw a feint to draw
Calamity's guard, the girl ignored it for Calamity had never
learned such tactics. Blood trickled from the blonde's nose and
Calamity's left eye was swelling when Olga sent the girl down
for the third time. Rolling on to her face, Calamity tried to
force herself up and shook her mist-filled head.

'Calam, gal!' she told herself. 'You've got to fight her your
style, not her'n, or get the licking of your young life.'

With that in mind Calamity levered herself up into a one-
knee crouch. She saw Olga advancing and flung herself forward, head ramming into the blonde's middle and arms lock-
ing around the fat thighs. To the accompaniment of Olga's
gasp of pain, they went backwards and crashed to the ground.
Now Calamity held the advantage for Olga was not used to all-
in, roll-around bar-room fighting. For all that the blonde gave
a fair account of herself in the hair-tearing, thrashing session,
but soon she realised it would be to her advantage to be on her
feet. Unfortunately, Calamity also understood Olga's point
and determined to keep the fight on the ground.

Eileen watched the fight with growing horror. For the first
time she realised just what she had started—although to be
fair to her, she had expected to see Calamity decline the challenge or be speedily defeated. Back Bay, Boston, being rather

sheltered from the rawer side of life, Eileen had never seen two women fight before and had no conception of how rough they could get. Suddenly scared, she moved forward to try to stop them; which showed a considerable lack of experience on her part.

With Olga trying to rise and Calamity struggling to get her back on the ground, the fighters had almost made their feet when Eileen reached them.

'Stop it!' Eileen gasped, trying to push them apart. 'St——'

Feeling a hand on her shoulder, Calamity swung at its owner, driving her bunched fist into Eileen's nose. The force of the blow brought a squeal of pain from Eileen and she staggered back. Freed of the hindrance, Calamity hooked a leg behind Olga and tripped her, dropping to kneel astride her. Holding her nose, Eileen howled in fury. Her Back Bay training left her and she became a primeval, hurt woman. Springing forward, she grabbed a double handful of Calamity's hair and heaved at it. Calamity squealed, feeling as if she was being scalped. Just as she was about to turn and deal with the fresh menace, Olga, bucking wildly to free herself, grabbed hold of Calamity's waistbelt and prevented Eileen from dragging the red-head from her.

At that moment Molly came on to the scene. What she saw brought her to a shocked and sudden halt. Like Eileen, Molly had been brought up in an area where women fought with catty remarks not fists and Molly made Eileen's mistake.

'Eileen, Calam!' Molly said, running forward and catching Eileen's arm. 'Stop it, bot——!'

Releasing Calamity's hair with the arm Molly held, Eileen thrust the smaller girl away. Then Eileen used the free hand to land a slap that Calamity would remember for some time across the red-head's ear. Once more Molly came forward and caught the back-hand swing from Eileen's blow at Calamity. It landed hard enough to stagger Molly back again.

Then Molly changed from a pacifist to an active and enraged belligerent. With a wild squall of pain and fury, she threw herself bodily at Eileen, landing with flailing fists and hair-grabbing fingers. Locked together, Eileen and Molly sprawled over Calamity and went down together. For a Boston-bred officer's lady and a sedately-reared college-educated New England schoolmarm, Eileen and Molly put on a highly spirited rendition of a hand-scalping bar-room brawl. Nothing fancy like the Calamity Jane–Russian Olga fracas, but fast, lively and with plenty of spirited hair-tearing, slapping, kicking and general female battling tactics.

For almost ten minutes the two separate fights carried on, then the four of them rolled into an unholy mixed-up tangle during which Olga gave Eileen a black eye, Eileen tore one shoulder strap from Olga's outfit, Calamity completed the destruction of Molly's blouse and Molly sank her teeth into Calamity's leg as it waved before her face; all this in addition to whatever they did to their opponents.

Somehow they managed to untangle themselves still fighting the same opponent and Calamity gained a momentary advantage on Olga. A wild-swung punch sent the fat blonde sprawling on her back and Calamity dropped down to sit on Olga's belly to end the battle.

Whether by accident or a desire to help, Eileen lashed out with a bare foot, she and Molly having lost their shoes earlier. The kick caught Calamity at the side of the head and knocked the girl off balance just as Olga gave a heave. Lurching up, Olga reversed the position by diving on to the dazed Calamity.

Shoving Eileen backwards, Molly was about to attack when she saw Olga knelt on Calamity, one knee on the red-head's belly and a hand dragging her head up to be hit. Dazedly, Calamity saw what was coming and waited for the end. The blow never came. Instead Olga suddenly let out a screech and jerked backwards, dragged by the double handful of hair Molly held.

Freed from Olga, Calamity started to rise, saw Eileen rushing forward and tackled her around the waist. Down they went and for a couple of minutes got a whole belly-full of dislike out of their systems. Give Boston her due, Calamity thought as they thrashed over and over fighting, she had sand to burn and could sure fight. Nothing fancy mind, but she packed a mean slap, could punch, kick, yank hair and use her knees as good as many a saloon-girl who had had the advantages of a correct upbringing in such matters.

However, Back Bay social life did not compare with western freighting as a training ground for a fight and Calamity would have finished Eileen off had she not seen that Molly needed help.

At first Molly's speedy, furious attack prevented Olga from doing anything effective, but weight and strength were on the fat blonde's side. With a heave, Olga threw Molly backwards and started after her. Pure instinct caused Olga to put up her fists boxing style and Calamity knew Molly would stand no chance once Olga started slugging. Leaving Eileen with a slap that knocked her staggering, Calamity headed towards Olga. Linking her fingers, Calamity slugged the fat blonde behind the neck and knocked her sprawling by Molly, then followed to bound on to Olga's back and bring her down.

Calamity had expected that after the roughing-up Eileen received, the brunette would be only too pleased to get away. Not so. Eileen managed to rise and staggered after Calamity, then swerved and re-tangled with Molly.

Just how it happened none of them would ever know; but Molly caught Eileen by the wrist and swung the girl, meaning to throw her. Instead, Molly retained her hold, swinging right round in a circle, making Eileen stagger on the end of her arms. Once more Molly swung the gasping Eileen around and the sigh gave Calamity an idea. She and Olga were struggling weakly on their feet and she caught the blonde's wrist then heaved her around in a circle, going the opposite way to Molly.

Gasping in saw-scraping croaks, Molly brought Eileen around again, just missing Olga's swinging body in passing. Calamity moved a step closer and the two bodies swung towards each other. Olga's squeal of fear mingled with Eileen's wail of exhausted realisation and merged in a thud as they collided. On the impact between Back Bay, Boston, and Lower Eastside, New York—from which sprawling slum area Olga originated—New York came off slightly the better. Eileen went down, collapsing backwards and dragging the little blonde after her, Molly falling over Eileen's body and lying across it. Olga sank to her knees and Calamity threw a punch that caught the fat blonde's ear and draped her across Molly. Then Calamity staggered and collapsed, falling face down over Olga.

Back Bay socialite, New England schoolmarm, New York lady pugilist and western female freighter lay in a pile on the ground. A philosopher once said that war was a great leveller and from the look of the girls he spoke the truth.

Almost a minute passed before any of the girls showed any

sign of getting up. Apart from a little involuntary movement of arms and legs, they lay still, until as last Calamity levered herself on to her knees, then managed to rise. Looking down, she saw Molly weakly attempting to rise but falling due to the weight on top of her. Reaching down, Calamity gripped the still motionless Olga and rolled the fat blonde from Molly. The little schoolmarm came up trying to fight and Calamity caught her by the wrists, steering her to the edge of the stream.

Reaction flooded over Molly and she started to cry hysterically, but Calamity splashed cold water over her and the sobs died off.

'Easy, gal,' Calamity said.

'Wh-what happened?' gasped Molly.

'We licked 'em is what,' grinned Calamity. 'Let's go wake the sleeping beauties, shall we?'

Anything less beautiful than Eileen and Olga would have been hard to imagine as they lay side by side, half naked, bruised, bloody and with their hair in matted tangles over their faces. Not that Calamity and Molly could feel superior for they were in no better condition.

Dragging first Olga then Eileen to the edge of the stream, Calamity dumped them into the water. While she bathed her face and torso, Calamity watched the two women recover and sit up gasping.

'If you want any more,' she told them, 'my pard and I'll be pleased to hand it to you.'

'I've had enough!' Olga gasped, much to Molly's relief, for the little blonde did not relish the thought of another fight.

Or did she? Much to her amazement Molly found herself thinking that the fight had been exciting. In it she worked off a number of frustrations and petty inhibitions which had troubled her all the way West.

'How about you, Boston?' asked Calamity, but for once the name did not come out as a sneer.

For a few seconds Eileen could not speak, she managed to catch her breath and nodded her head, agreeing she was satisfied with the result.

'Get my medicine bag, Molly,' Calamity said, helping Olga then Eileen out of the water. 'Hey, Boston, you was right, I do need it.'

Taking the bag from Molly, Calamity extracted a horn of

72

the type usually employed to carry gunpowder. She shook some powder from it on to her palm and sniffed the grains up her blood-trickling nostril. Tipping some more out, she offered it to Molly.

'Sniff her up, Molly, gal,' she ordered. 'It's that powdered witch-hazel leaves I told you about.'

All four nose-bleeds were treated with powdered witch-hazel and Calamity turned her attention to the other injuries. She found a balsam fir and punctured one of the bark blisters then smeared the gum on a nick upon her cheek and over a gash on her arm.

'You'd best let me put some on that nick on your forehead, Boston,' she said, turning to the others.

'Thanks, Calam,' Eileen replied.

Not until she had treated the gash did Calamity realise what Eileen had called her. A grin came to her face and she held out her hand. 'Friends, Eileen?'

'Friends, Calam, only make it Boston.'

For the rest of the time—and it covered twenty years— Eileen was on the Great Plains country, she was affectionately known by all who met her as 'Boston.'

'How about you, champeen?' asked Calamity after attending to Eileen's cut.

With a bitter frown on her face, Olga allowed Calamity to apply the gum to her minor abrasions. It hurt the woman to think that a kid had whipped her in a fight. From a mercenary point of view, she knew that her boss would not hesitate to offer Calamity a place in the troupe when he heard. Olga held her position as boss's favourite because none of the other girls could displace her, but that would soon change should Calamity become a member.

'Whooee, gal!' Calamity said, smearing gum on a scratch on Olga's back. 'I see how you got to be champeen. I tell you, Olga, if Molly there hadn't helped me, and I'd stayed on my feet instead of rough-housing, you'd've whipped me for sure.'

Apart from the piece about Molly's aid, Calamity spoke the truth and her words relieved the bitterness Olga felt.

'How'd you like to be a fist-fighter?' she asked.

'I wouldn't, if it meant tangling with gals near-on as tough as you,' Calamity replied and she saw Eileen wink. It appeared her words had not fooled the officer's lady at all.

'We'd best get back to camp, I think.' Eileen said.

'Oh my lord!' Molly gasped, staring at Eileen and Olga's tattered clothing, and knowing she was not more completely attired. 'How can we get to camp like this?'

'It'll be dark afore we get there,' Calamity replied. 'We'll sneak in and get into me 'n' Boston's wagon, then see about getting clothes for you two. What's wrong, Boston?'

Eileen had been touching her blackened and puffed-up left eye with a delicate forefinger. Giving a wince, she replied, 'Can't our native medicine woman do any thing for a shiner?'

'A lump of beef-steak'd help, which same we can get back to the camp,' Calamity replied, then looked at the other girls' battle-marked faces. 'It'll fix 'em a mite, but we'll sure as hell cause some talk when folks see us in the morning.'

CHAPTER EIGHT

MISS CANARY HANDS OUT ADVICE

'GOOD morning, Mrs. Tra——' Dobe Killem began as Eileen limped stiffly towards the camp fire after coming up from the river. Then his words trailed off as he saw her face. Fine poker player though he was, Killem could not prevent his surprise showing as he studied the condition of her face.

'I walked into a door, Dobe,' Eileen said and put a hand to her temple. 'Ooh! Must the cook make so much noise?'

Yet it was not her usual imperious complaining. From the slight scraping noise being objected about and Eileen's obvious headache, Killem might have suspected a hangover, but that could not be in her case—or could it?

Just then Calamity came up, throwing a towel into the wagon as she passed and Killem found his day for surprises instead of ending had only just begun. Taking in Calamity's battle-scarred features and adding them to Eileen's fist-marked face, he reckoned there must have been the expected explosion between them—No, that could not be. That hoity-toity Boston gal could never have marked up Calamity in such a manner, and yet the signs showed plain enough.

'I bumped into two doors,' growled Calamity before her boss could ask the questions buzzing in his head. 'Now get the hell out of my way and let me at the coffee. Hey, Boston, pour out a cup for a gal.'

Which same, from past experience, told Killem that Calamity had tied on one of her still rare benders and carried a whisky-head to show for it. Yet she addressed Eileen in a friendly manner.

'Go to hell and pour your own, you idle slut,' Eileen replied, but not in her usual tone; and she poured out a cup of coffee before Calamity reached her.

Killem wondered if he ought to go back to bed and see if he

had got up that morning. Anyway, he thought, nothing more could surprise—— At that point he saw Molly hobble up from the river sporting as fine a brace of shiners as he had ever seen and a nose to match them—and showing much the same hungover symptoms as the other two.

'Who gave you them eyes?' he gasped, long past politeness and western waiting to be told about private affairs.

'Nobody,' Molly replied. 'I had to fight like hell for them.'

That was when Killem decided to call it a day. Turning, he slouched away from the girls and met Muldoon coming with more puzzlement and news. Apparently Russian Olga was hobbling round her fire, looking like her face had been tromped by a mule and mean-mouthing her friends like she toted a hell of a sore head which did not come from a bout of fist-fighting.

'Reckon Calem might know anything about it?' asked Muldoon.

'I reckon she might at that,' agreed Killem.

'You mean that Calam went and took Olga on and never told all her good friends, so let us miss it?'

'From what I just saw,' Killem replied in a dazed manner, 'you don't know the half of what we must have missed—and neither do I.'

The previous evening the four girls sneaked unseen back to camp and into Calamity's wagon. Being the only one at least acceptably attired, Calamity visited the Johnson wagon, keeping in the shadows, and collected a change of clothing for Molly, saying the blonde would be staying with her for the night. In doing so, Calamity kept her face out of sight and Molly's aunt did not even know that her favourite niece had been acting in a most unladylike and unschoolteacherlike manner.

On her return, Calamity produced steaks—to be applied externally to bruised eyes—and completed the deflation of Eileen's Boston ego. Nobody could even attempt to maintain frigid superiority when sat on the floor of a wagon wearing the tattered remnants of a cheap dress and holding a steak to either eye. Calamity produced a jug containing, she claimed, a cure for what ailed them. It worked. Neither Eileen nor Molly had ever tasted raw home-brewed whisky until that night and did not know its deadly power. Luckily, the freighters had

76

been invited to the Army lines for a meal or they might have heard some remarkable confessions from Calamity's wagon as the four girls got quietly, happily, but completely drunk.

Molly had quoted Professor Strubacher, said to hell with him and gone to sleep, leaving Eileen telling Calamity and Olga about her best friend who she hated like the devil hates holy water and wished had been in the clearing. At which point Eileen joined Molly. Half an hour later Olga, having told Calamity the story of her life, joined the majority of the party and Calamity decided not to bother sleeping under the wagon that night.

In the very early dawn the girls recovered. Olga returned to her outfit and the other three crept to the river to bathe their stiff, aching bodies and compare headaches. Any intention Eileen might have possessed about returning to her old behaviour departed in the hangover. It never returned.

Speculation ran rife through the wagon train when word and sight of the four girls' appearance went among the travellers. The four participants maintained silence over the affair and appeared to be on the best of terms. Nobody ever did really discover what had happened the previous evening and two days later they left the woodland to start crossing the Great Plains. The change of scenery and conditions took interest away from the cause of the girls' injuries.

A week later an informal gathering of the leading members of the train met around Killem's fire after the day's journey was over. Killem, the wagonmaster, Beau Resin and both Army officers stood by the fire drinking coffee handed out by Eileen and Calamity, when a scared-looking youngster dashed into camp.

'Injuns!' he howled, pointing back up a rolling slope above the camp.

Bigelow dropped his cup and swung around, his right hand going to the flap of his holster.

'Easy, Cap'n,' Resin said calmly. 'I been watching 'em for the past ten minutes.'

'Te——!' Bigelow squawked, and no other word could describe the sound. 'Then why didn't you say something?'

'Figger they was watching, not fighting.'

Every eye turned towards the top of the rim a good half mile away from the edge of the camp. Even as they watched

77

the group of Indians on top grew larger until they numbered around fifty, all braves and wearing war-paint with arms to match.

This was the moment Bigelow had been waiting for—hoping for, too, maybe. A successful encounter with a band of Indians would greatly enhance his chance of obtaining a transfer to a fighting regiment and out of the dreary limbo of being a shiny-butt. Ever since leaving Fort Connel he had been preparing his strategy for such a moment and presented his subordinate with plans for almost every conceivable circumstance. He would have arranged practice circle-forming and other drills for the travellers, but found the idea met with a point-blank refusal when he put it to the wagonmaster.

Some confusion showed among the travellers as they watched the Indians gather on the rim. Weapons were caught up and women and children sent scuttling to the safety of the wagons. In a bull-voiced bellow that rang around the camp, the wagonmaster ordered that there be no shooting; beating Bigelow to the command by a good thirty seconds.

Bigelow used the breath drawn to give the no-shooting order to snap a command to the young lieutenant at his side.

'Mr. Grade, parade the troop twenty yards outside the circle and facing the hostiles.'

The tall, slim lieutenant threw an appealing glance at Bigelow, then relayed the order to Muldoon as the sergeant brought up the men. Not so well-disciplined, Muldoon growled out a startled curse, but long training caused him to obey orders.

'On the double, mister!' Bigelow barked. 'We'll impress them with our numbers. Mr. Resin, would you come and act as interpreter, please?'

'Reckon so; but——'

Whatever Resin wished to 'but' over did not get said. Bigelow led off his men, filing through the wagons and out of the circle to halt a single line facing towards the Indians. The young captain glanced at the line of blue-clad troopers, each extra-well armed if one counted the sabre he wore in addition to his Army Colt and the Springfield carbine, and decided they would impress the Indians. In that he was right. He impressed the watching braves with the inadequacy of numbers of his force and also with his own inexperience.

Calamity, Eileen and Killem followed the soldiers to the edge of the wagon circle and stood watching. Turning her head, Calamity exchanged a knowing glance with Killem. While not setting themselves up as great minds—which invariably think alike—Calamity and Killem had the same thought in mind; neither of them cared for Captain Wade H. Bigelow's version of tactics.

'What are they, Mr Resin?' asked Bigelow, maintaining his pose of the cool, calm and polite officer in a crisis.

'Fox, Owl and Pony Lodge Cheyenne,' the scout replied. 'I don't like Cheyenne war lodges any time and even less when they're all mixed together. You watch 'em good, Cap'n.'

'They're under a white flag,' answered Bigelow, pointing towards a war-bonnet chief who rode out of the party holding a flapping piece of white cloth on the tip of his buffalo lance.

'Which same's another I don't like. Injuns in general and Cheyenne in particular don't put no trust in white flags after what Yeller-Hair Custer done to Black Kettle's village on the Washita back in '68.'

A flush of annoyance crept on to Bigelow's face at the scout's flat-spoken condemnation of a man the captain regarded as the *beau idéal* of cavalry leaders. Bigelow tended to regard the Washita business in the light of brilliant strategy on the part of the 'Boy General,' George Armstrong Custer, instead of, as it had been, a bloody, treacherous massacre of innocents.

'We'll respect their flag of truce!' he snapped.

'Sir——!' croaked the lieutenant.

'Call them in, Mr. Resin!' Bigelow barked, ignoring the possible warning.

'What in hell's he doing?' asked Calamity.

'Inviting the Indians to come in for a truce,' Eileen replied.

'Like hell!' spat Calamity. 'Boston, that officer-boy's going to get us all massacred way he's going on.'

All the Indians rode slowly down the slope, following the flag of truce with an apparent trust in its protective powers that worried Beau Resin more than he cared to admit even to himself. With each approaching pony-stride, Resin's worry increased; those Cheyenne brave-hearts had a feller among them who could read military character and had a shrewd idea of the kind of man they dealt with.

79

'Hey great soldier-coat chief!' yelled the war-bonneted flag-of-truce bearer in passable English. 'We good Injuns, make peace with white brother. We come into your camp, trade with your people.'

'Certainly!'

'Not on your scalp-taking lives!'

Bigelow and Resin spoke at the same moment. Swinging towards to tall scout, Bigelow let out an angry hiss. 'I'm in command here!'

'Then for gawd's sake command right!' Resin snapped back. 'Didn't they teach you nothing at West Point?'

Just what might have come of the exchange had the two men been left to their own devices is uncertain for at about that moment Calamity and Eileen took a hand in the matter.

While watching the approach of the Indians, Calamity let out a blistering string of curses which might have made Eileen blush a few days back but that now merely made her inquire what caused the profanity.

'What the hell's he doing letting them red-sticks come down like that?' asked Calamity.

'Answering their flag of truce,' Eileen replied.

'I don't like it,' Calamity stated. 'Happen they come much closer, they'll be *in the camp*!'

From the way Calamity emphasised the last three words, having Indians—even apparently peaceful and under a flag of truce—in the camp struck her as being mighty undesirable. Yet Eileen knew that the objection did not stem from mere racial prejudice; for Calamity treated all races and creeds to the same cheerful, friendly open-handed courtesy, unless they riled her. So there must be some deep-seated reason for her objection to allowing the Indians to enter the camp.

'Why not?' asked Eileen.

'And *you're* Vint Tradle's wife?' Calamity answered.

'So they tell me, but we don't have many hostile Indians in Boston.'

'Likely. One thing you never want to forget, Boston, gal. Feed an Injun, give him some presents—but never, *never* let him come into your camp. That way you'll stay alive long enough to go home and whup that Back Bay dame you told us about.'

'I see,' said Eileen.

'But ole shiny-butt don't,' Calamity growled as the shouted conversation between the men reached their ears. 'Land-sakes, don't let him do i—Hey, where in hell are you going, Boston?'

Eileen had strode determinedly between two of the wagons and headed across the open towards the soldiers. After throwing a startled glance at Killem, Calamity went after her friend, more out of curiosity than for any other reason.

Just as Bigelow opened his mouth to give permission for the Indians to enter the camp, he heard a cool feminine voice at his side.

'Captain Bigelow, may I speak to you?'

Now whatever faults Eileen Tradle might have shown in the early days of their acquaintance, stupidity had not been one of them. So Bigelow found himself staring in some surprise to see her committing the apparent folly of leaving the wagon circle and approaching him at such a time.

'Not now, Bo—Mrs. Tradle!' he answered. 'Return to the——'

'Right now!'

Although a bachelor, Bigelow knew enough about women to recognise the futility of arguing with one when her voice held that tone. He glanced at the Indians who had come to a halt, threw an imploring look towards Resin who ignored him, then walked towards Eileen as she drew away from the men. Showing surprising tact, Calamity moved clear of the other girl and waited to see what Eileen aimed to do.

'Wade,' Eileen said in a voice pitched low enough for his ears alone. 'I know *you* are in command and don't wish to interfere, even if that's just what I'm doing, but Vint wrote me more than once on the matter of never allowing Indians to enter one's camp. Of course, the safety of the train is *your* responsibility and I don't wish to impose——'

Bigelow sucked in a long deep breath and thought fast. All too well he knew that Eileen's husband was known and respected as a real smart Indian-fighter and had won his promotion in the field for untangling the mess a glory-hunting fool led a battalion into. Even the Army scouts, who would give few officers credit for being able to breathe air in and blow it out again, had high regard for Vinton Tradle's Indian-fighting skill and knowledge of the hostile's ways. Advice, even at second-hand, from such a source was not to be lightly ignored.

'Thank you for your concern, Mrs. Tradle,' he said stiffly.

'Let your brace slip, Wade,' she smiled. 'It was Boston when you wanted another cup of my coffee.'

Marvelling at the Calamity-wrought change in the formerly snooty Mrs. Tradle, Bigelow returned to his men. Above them the Indians were getting restless and the war-bonnet chief called out another request to be allowed to come down and trade.

'How about it, Mr. Grade?' Bigelow asked.

'Keep them out, sir,' the lieutenant answered immediately and Muldoon could not hold down his mutter of agreement.

'Hey, soldier-coat chief!' yelled the flag-bearer. 'You let us come in and smoke-um peace-pipe?'

'Where's your chief to light it?' Resin yelled back.

'I am chief!'

'I mean where's your big chief!' Resin countered. 'Where's Sand Runner?' and without turning, he spoke over his shoulder. 'Calam, Boston, get the hell back to the wagons. Cap'n, get set to fight or run. If she's due, she'll pop real soon.'

'The hell's being got,' Calamity replied, taking Eileen's arm and heading at an unladylike run towards the safety of the wagon circle.

Up the slope considerable consternation showed among the assembled Cheyenne brave-hearts. They came posing as friendly Indians and if there be one certain thing in the world, it was that Sand Runner had never been anything like friendly to the white men. So none of the Indians offered to reply, but sat their suddenly restless horses and cast sheepish glances at each other. The flag of truce lowered, but the expected attack did not come and Resin pressed his advantage.

'What's wrong?' he bellowed. 'I thought I spoke with Cheyenne brave-hearts who do not hide true words. Or am I wrong, are these before me Crows, Arikara, Pawnees, or,' he paused and gave the conventional spit to one side before mentioning the lowest of the Plains Indians low, 'Osages?'

The insult brought results. While the war-bonnet chief had been to mission school and knew the value of lying and deceit, none of his party had received the benefits of a white brother's education. One of the braves jumped his paint horse from among his lodge brothers and waved his buffalo lance over his head. He was a tall young buck wearing three eagle feathers in his hair and sporting as his war-medicine a U.S. cavalry blouse, its front smothered with dried blood from the lance-thrust which smashed through the chest of the original wearer. Such a brave had a high pride in his tribal honour.

'Know you that Sand Runner is over there beyond the hills behind your camp and waiting for the time!' he announced. An exclamation of annoyance left the war-bonnet chief's lips for, as has been mentioned, he bore the results of white man's education and knew that, despite tribal traditions of truthfulness even to an enemy, there were times when a good lie licked the pants off telling the truth. However, the rest of the party gave out their deep-grunted, old-time Cheyenne approval for the young brave's spirited and honest reply.

'How many brave-hearts ride with him?' called Resin.

Bigelow fidgeted at the apparently pointless delay in negotiations. Just as he opened his mouth to insert a comment designed to bring the subject to a conclusion, he heard a whisper that contained a thick Irish brogue in his right ear.

'With the Cap'n's permission, sir. I'd not be interfering was I him. It might sound long-winded, but we'll learn plenty from them red varmints afore we're through.'

'What do we do while this goes on then, Sergeant?' Bigelow inquired over his shoulder and trying to avoid showing his mouth working.

'Stand and look dignified, sir, which if yez'll pardon me for saying, you should be pretty good at.'

A smile flickered to Bigelow's lips, one of some pride, for never before had Muldoon treated him with anything but strictly *Manual of Field Regulations* military courtesy, although the sergeant often made unmilitary comments to the shave-tail lieutenant. Bigelow remembered a lecture from his West Point days on the subject of officer–senior non-com relationship. It appeared that he was winning the burly sergeant's respect and he hoped to could live up to Muldoon's high standards. One way to do that was to take advice when given it by reliable sources and he had already proven capable of doing that.

'You talk well, white brother!' boomed the war-bonnet chief before any of his men answered Resin's question. 'Are you Indian?'

Like the white man, the Indian believed that Indian blood made a man full native stock, but unlike the white man allowed the Indian blood made its owner a mite more trustworthy than the forked-tongued pale-faces.

'I lived three years with them after the big war of the white men to the east,' Resin replied.

'What tribe?' asked an elderly warrior, hefting his powerful war bow and eyeing the rank of soldiers to select a worthwhile target should the fun begin.

'The *Tshaoh*!' Pride rang in Resin's voice as he boomed back the answer.

'The *Tshaoh*!' muttered a dozen Indian voices and even at that distance Bigelow could see the warriors on the slope were impressed.

'Who are the *Tshaoh*?' he asked over his shoulder.

'The Enemy People, sir,' replied the lieutenant.

'That's right, sir,' Muldoon confirmed. 'You'd know 'em as the Comanche.'

Tshaoh, Enemy People, Comanche: if a rose by any other name smells just as sweet, those stocky fighting raiders from the Texas plains spelled the same by any name—bone-tough warriors with few peers and no superiors. The Osage might be low men on the Plains Indian totem-pole, but the Comanche stood way up the top. Even the race-proud Cheyenne admitted that and found no shame in so doing.

Having duly impressed the Cheyenne warriors with his right to ask questions as became a member of a noble, brave-heart tribe contemplating war against an equally brave and honest enemy—and three years among the Comanche made a man part of the tribe,—Resin repeated his request for information.

'Ten hands,' replied the war bonnet chief.

'Which's a hundred at least, them heathen savages not having learned to count with accuracy, sir,' Muldoon remarked. 'And took with that bunch up there, a hundred and fifty no less.'

'Not many against a party this size,' Bigelow answered.

Yet more than enough for a surprise assault, especially with a third of the fighting force mingling with the people of the train, lulling their suspicions and ready to change from peaceable traders to savage killers on a signal. A shudder ran through Bigelow as he visualised the scene. The sudden rush

84

from outside the circle, the change among the Indians in the circle. His people would have been demoralised, panic stricken and fallen easy meat to the Cheyenne band.

And the matter went deeper than that, although Bigelow did not know it. Nothing succeeds like success, even among unlettered savages. Should Sand Runner's strategy work, he would have loot and coups to flaunt before his more peaceably inclined brothers, living proof that the white man was far from being invincible and that even a large wagon train guarded by soldier-coats fell before Sand Runner's medicine-inspired thought—no chief dare claim he made up any plan without the divine assistance of the Great Spirit's medicine.

'How many men have you?' asked the chief, as Resin knew he would.

'Over seven hands,' the scout replied. 'Many of them with repeating rifles.'

A low mutter ran among the braves and they studied the wagon circle's condition of readiness to meet any attack. Everything appeared to be prepared in a most unsatisfactory manner from the Indian's angle. The wagonmaster was no novice at Indian-fighting and knew better than to relax or concentrate all his attention on the bunch which showed themselves. So he did not allow his people to relax and, aided by his blistering tongue, made the men watch their front instead of standing gawking at the conference on the slope and ignoring what went on in other directions. Any attempt at making a sudden rush upon such a ready train would be repulsed with much bloodshed among the rushers, for any hope of surprise had gone.

An Indian might be brave, but he was no fool and could add up odds with the ease of a professional gambler. One hundred and fifty to seventy meant the Indians possessed a two to one advantage, but the repeating rifles and other firearms owned by the white men reduced those odds and changed them out of the Cheyennes' favour.

'Can we make talk?' asked the chief.

'Who?' asked Resin.

'You, the soldier-coat chief and me.'

'Where?'

'Half-way. On my lodge-oath there will be peace while we talk.'

85

When a Cheyenne war-bonnet chief swore on his lodge oath, he aimed to keep his word, even if he had been educated at a mission school and in the face of knowledge of innumerable times when the white man gave peace-words and broke them.

'How about it, Cap'n?' Resin asked, knowing the above. 'He's got something else on his mind. Some tricky lil game Sand Runner thought up in case his idea for sneaking in on us didn't work.'

'Let's talk then,' Bigelow replied. 'If this is a formal truce, do we remove our weapons?'

'Not less you want to insult him. He's treating us as men of honour who can be trusted.'

'What's happening, Calam?' asked Eileen, watching the scout and captain walk up the slope after the shouted conversation.

'Them Injuns, and that includes Beau Resin, dang his Comanche hide, are smart, Boston, gal,' Calamity replied. 'Happen two different tribes come up against each other they don't just bust in head down and guns roaring. They talk a mite first, learn how much power the other side's got and how ready they are for war. Then they figger their chances and happen they don't like the way the other side stacks up, they allow their medicine's gone bad on 'em and pull out. It sure saves a heap of grief.'

'But do they always tell each other the truth?'

'Only Indians I ever seed as liars were the ones we *civilised*,' Calamity answered, spitting out the last word. 'Don't reckon there'll be no war today. What'd you tell ole shiny-butt?'

'Oh, a little white lie,' smiled Eileen. 'But it worked.'

On reaching the half-way point between his men and the soldiers, the war-bonnet chief dropped from his horse, strode forward a couple of paces and went into a heel-squat. At a sign from Resin, Bigelow sank on to his haunches and the big scout sat Indian-style. Bigelow knew enough about diplomatic tactics not to open the jackpot, but waited for the Indian to break the ground.

There appeared to be no hurry to get down to business. Resin took a pipe from his pocket, primed the bowl with thick black Burley shag tobacco. With the bowl full, he handed the bag courteously to the chief and glanced at the officer.

'Got anything to smoke, Cap'n, there's going to be some

time to pass.'

'Will a cigar do?' asked Bigelow.

'Light her away,' drawled the scout, rasping a match on his pants seat and firing the tobacco in his pipe.

For almost five minutes none of the trio spoke, but smoked in quiet enjoyment. At last the chief removed his pipe, knocked out the remaining embers and doused them in the hard palm of his hand. Although Resin did not move, Bigelow could almost feel the big scout sense in a manner which said, 'This is it.'

'This is Cheyenne land,' the chief announced.

'Not by treaty,' Resin countered. 'The Cheyenne old man chiefs gave their sacred oath that this area would be left open to passage of white man's wagons. Are you going against the oath to the Great Spirit?'

'Great Spirit sides man with most warriors,' answered the chief.

Bigelow stared as he heard the Great Plains version of Napoleon's statement that God favoured big battalions. However, the captain did not speak, but left the handling of the matter in Resin's hands.

'We have the most guns,' Resin pointed out.

A pause followed while the chief digested the unpleasant and unpalatable fact that the white men carried superior arms in a long-distance fight. He gave a low grunt, spat reflectively and remarked. 'Sand Runner war chief, not make any treaty with white brother.'

'So?'

'So *Tshaoh*, Sand Runner make fresh treaty with soldier-coat chief here. If he can make-um that is.'

'How about it, Cap'n?' asked Resin.

'I'm permitted to negotiate temporary terms to ensure the safety of the train.'

'That means "yes" or "no?" ' asked the Cheyenne.

'Yes,' answered Bigelow.

'You make-um talk in small words so I know 'em. Talk best left to Tshaoh, him savvy what Indian understand.'

'What does Sand Runner want?' asked Resin, hiding the grin which rose inside him and getting down to business.

'Him want tribute from wagon train. Get it, not make trouble, leave 'em alone all time.'

87

'That can be arranged. But no guns, powder, bullets or lead.'

'Ugh! Not want-um. Want money.'

'*Money!*' grunted Resin, coming as near as Bigelow had seen to showing any emotion.

'Fifty dollars for each wagon,' replied the chief and went on with a touch of pride, 'At mission school me learned to count white-man style.'

'We've forty-six wagons,' Bigelow breathed. 'That would be two thousand, three hundred dollars.'

'Yeah,' answered the scout. 'But what in hell does a bunch of Cheyenne want with *money?*'

'You pay-um?' asked the chief.

There was one possible reason why the Cheyenne wanted money, although Resin doubted if it could be. However, a man did not hand over such a vast sum to Indians, or anybody else, without giving the matter plenty of thought.

'We'll give you blankets, see-yourselves,* some knives, axes, decorations for your women and shoot you forty-six horse-loads of meat,' Resin said.

'No good. Want money or make-um plenty hell same as teacher feller told us at mission school.'

'No money!' Resin said flatly. 'And that's final. You can tell Sand Runner I said so.'

'I tell him. Him not like. That plenty good tobacco, *Tshaoh.*'

Taking out his tobacco pouch, Resin handed it to the chief. 'Help yourself. They don't have it in the Spirit Land and that's where you and plenty of your men'll be headed happen you try forcing us.'

Helping himself to half the tobacco, the chief returned the pouch to its owner. 'Think well before you refuse and ask no more questions.'

'Which same stops us asking why they want the money, Cap'n,' drawled Resin. 'How about Sand Runner's offer?'

'You already gave my answer.'

'We don't pay and that's final.'

'Not think Sand Runner's plan would work when he made it,' admitted the chief calmly, and with just a hint of satis-faction in his voice. Sand Runner was a mite too much of the bright-idea Johnny-come-lately to suit his taste apart from the

* Mirrors.

88

other detail about the aspiring Cheyenne war leader. 'Speak long to the Comanche Great Spirit, *Tshaoh*, and make your war medicine. You'll need it.'

'*Ka-Dih* favours those with repeating rifles,' Resin replied, mentioning the Great Spirit of the Comanche. 'Remember that well, brother.'

A grin twisted the Indian's lips. 'You sure you not full Indian?' he asked and came to his feet.

Turning, the chief walked back to his waiting horse and went afork it in a single bound, plucking the buffalo lance from the ground where he had stood it. He gave a wild whoop, whirled the horse in its own length and rode back to his party. Swinging their horses away from the train, the Cheyenne galloped out of sight over the rim.

'Will they tell Sand Runner not to attack?' asked Bigelow as he and Resin walked back towards the waiting soldiers.

'He'd know near on as soon as we did,' Resin replied. 'There'd be wolf-scouts watching the camp from the moment the others appeared, only you don't spot wolf-scouts, that's their job.'

'Lord!' Bigelow breathed. 'And I nearly let them walk into camp. You must think I'm a helluva fool.'

'Nope, just inexperienced. We all make mistakes, that's why they put them big, burnable mats under spittoons in fancy saloons. You ever figger how me, or young Dave Grade'd make out handling the kind of work you've come to do natural—until we learned how to do it?'

'I never thought of it like that.'

'Shucks, making a man captain don't turn him into an expert on every blasted thing under the sun,' grinned Resin. 'Not until he's been out and learned some about it.'

'Take the men into the circle, Mr. Grade,' Bigelow ordered. 'Rendezvous with me at Mr. Killem's fire after standing them down, and you, Muldoon.'

'Yo!' Muldoon replied.

On entering the wagon circle, Bigelow walked to Eileen and smiled at her.

'Thanks for passing on Vint's knowledge.'

'I've a confession to make, Wade,' Eileen smiled. 'And take your hand off my arm, Molly's coming and I don't want to annoy her, I've just lost the marks from the last time.'

'So you and Molly did tangle?'

'Never you mind. Vint never mentions his work, not to any great extent, in his letters, Wade.'

'Then how——?' Bigelow began.

'Calamity gave me some of her sage-advice and I acted on it. Only I thought that——'

'That I'd be too bow-necked a shiny-butt to take *her* advice.'

'Something like that,' Eileen admitted.

'You probably guessed right,' grinned Bigelow. 'Anyway, Miss Canary's sage advice was well worth having. She's quite a girl—and so are you, Boston. I wonder what Molly would do if I kissed you right in front of her?'

'I don't know what she'd do,' Eileen answered. 'But I know what I'd do. Calamity gave me some sage advice on that, too.'

CHAPTER NINE

MISS CANARY GOES TO WAR

A COUNCIL of war gathered around Killem's fire, with the same men attending as had been present before the Indian-alert and augmented by the presence of Muldoon. After serving coffee, Calamity, Eileen and Molly kept tactfully in a woman's place in the background. Bigelow outlined Sand Runner's proposals and then awaited his more experienced subordinates' comments.

'That's the first time I ever heard of a free Indian asking for money, sir,' said Lieutenant Grade with all the wisdom of twenty-three years of age at his back.

'Or me,' Muldoon agreed. 'Happen they was tamed Injuns on a reservation I'd like it some better.'

'Reckon you refused, Cap'n?' asked Killem, idly whittling a stick, which was a sure sign to those who knew him that he regarded the situation as being grave.

'I did.'

'So we'll likely be having fighting soon, sir?' asked Muldoon.

'Possibly, Sergeant.'

'Then could I make so bold as to suggest we start wearing our campaign hats, sir? 'Tis shady to the eyes they are when doing fine sighting along the barrel of a carbine.'

'You're officer of the day, Mr. Grade,' Bigelow said with a wry smile. 'Make whatever dress arrangements you feel are needed.'

'Yes, sir!' answered Grade eagerly. Wearing official blouse and kepi might look smart and formally soldier-like, but they were sure hell to fight in under the hot plains sun.

'What do you think Sand Runner will do now, Beau?' asked Bigelow.

After relaxing his stand on the subject of *Dress Regulations*, Bigelow figured he might as well go the whole hog and adopt a less formal attitude towards the big scout; whose knowledge and aid might prove invaluable.

'Fight!' came the one word but encyclopaedic reply.

'Right now?' asked the captain, looking around the camp and noting its condition of readiness.

'Nope. Night's too near on us. Most Injuns don't fight in the dark, figure a man gets killed at night might not be able to find his way to the Spirit Land. 'Sides, it'll be long gone dark afore they whomp up another mess of war-medicine, us having spoiled their last boiling.'

'Sand Runner may not be able to persuade the others that his medicine holds good after his failure to get into the circle, sir,' Grade remarked.

At that moment the men heard a distant crackle of shots, the deep booming of a Dragoon Colt and the sharper crack of a carbine, the Dragoon's roar sounding again after the carbine's shot. Silence dropped on the men and Bigelow remembered that none of the party he had spoke with carried firearms. His eyes went to Resin and the scout gave a low grunt.

'Happen all I heard's true,' Resin drawled, 'Sand Runner's just done some persuading. They do say that he uses an old Colt Dragoon that throws flame like a cannon.'

'Who is this Sand Runner?' asked Bigelow.

Slowly Resin filled his pipe and lit it, while none of the others offered to make any reply. Sucking in a lungful of air, he breathed it out again and then answered the captain's question, without helping any.

'Don't ask me. I've never seen him. Nor have any of the scouts at the fort.'

'That's true enough, sir,' Grade admitted. 'We know most of the Cheyenne war leaders: Wooden Leg, Two Moons, Iron Thunder, Wolf Voice. But not Sand Runner. He came into prominence two years ago when he led a bunch that wiped out a company of infantry up along the Rosebud. Since then his name's grown bigger every month, but he never shows at any of the peace meetings.'

'He's always in the background and out of sight when white men are about, sir,' Muldoon went on. 'I was with the colonel when he went to talk with the old man chiefs. We'd orders to try and speak with him, but the others allowed it was his medicine not be seen by white folks. Far as I know, every white who's seen him wound up dead.'

'Won't the Cheyenne talk about him?' asked Bigelow.

'Not if it's medicine business,' Resin replied. 'They take their religion a damned sight more serious than most white folks do.'

'And what was the shooting about?'

'Likely somebody reckoned Sand Runner's medicine'd gone bad on him,' Resin guessed. 'Which'd be the same's calling a real proud gun-fighter a liar; fast and deadly. From the sound, Sand Runner done made his point.'

'So he's still their leader?' asked Bigelow.

'I'd say that,' agreed the scout.

'Then he'll attack us.'

'Likely.'

'When?'

'Dawn, maybe. That's a favourite time for Injuns to attack, when folk's good and slowed down from just waking,' Resin replied. 'It all depends on how many Sand Runner has to convince his medicine's still strong. Only that Sand Runner's a smart cuss, he'll likely have something slick up his sleeve.'

'Like what?' asked Bigelow.

'That, Cap'n,' drawled Resin, 'is what we'll have to wait to find out.'

'You figuring to sit talking, or going to do something?' asked Calamity, coming forward with the coffeepot.

'Just talking for now, Calam, gal,' Resin replied. 'No point in figuring or doing until we know what's happening.'

'Are they still watching us?' Bigelow inquired after drinking his coffee.

'Sure,' Resin answered, jerking a thumb in the direction of the slopes at the rear of the camp. 'I got two of their wolf-scouts spotted now.'

'Are there more of them?'

'Likely two more at least.'

'Could you find them in the dark?' asked Bigelow.

'The two I saw, happen they stayed in the same place after dark, which same they won't. A man don't get to be a wolf-scout without he's slicker'n a bad-hunted buffalo-wolf.'

'Hum! I thought we might get rid of their scouts and pull out during the night, travel as fast as we could through the darkness——'

'Which'd be twice too slow for a Cheyenne war-relay to follow, and follow they would. Then hit us at dawn, when all our folks were tuckered out.'

'Amen!' drawled Killem piously.

'Then what do we do?' asked the wagonmaster, 'sit and wait?'

'Yeah,' agreed Resin. 'That's just what we're going to do—or so it looks to them scouts.'

Calamity came forward and squatted by Resin's side. 'Tell us about it,' she suggested. 'I've never knowed you flap your lip unless you aimed to do something at the end of it?'

'How good are our folks with their wagons, Sam?' the scout asked the wagonmaster.

'Good as any I've seen.'

'Good enough to harness their teams in the dark, without making a helluva noise doing it?'

The wagonmaster did not reply for a few seconds as he thought out the implications of the question. Then at last he nodded. 'I reckon they could.'

'Then I say we get every thing ready to roll in the morning afore daylight,' Resin said. 'And as soon as it's light enough to see start them rolling out.'

'Will that help?' asked Bigelow.

'Injuns are funny. They get a plan all figgered out and stick to it. But happen things go wrong, they're plumb likely to get discouraged and give it up. So they all plan an early morning rush on the circle and expect us to fight from it. When they come in, find us pulling out fast, they could get to thinking their medicine's gone bad on 'em. Won't be so eager to push home their attack then.'

'It could work,' Grade remarked.

'Can't think of a better idea off-hand,' Killem went on. 'Them scouts won't be too all-fired eager to stay out on the places when they see us settle down for the night.'

'I'm counting on it,' Resin replied, then stopped his next words and looked at Bigelow. 'The final decision lies with you, Cap'n.'

Bigelow did not answer immediately. Never had he been faced with such an important decision. The fate of well over a hundred lives, including one which had become very important to him, depended on the decision he made. If they

94

stayed in a defensive circle the Indians might not attack, but they would hang around the camp, pin down the travellers and this area did not have water for a prolonged stay, nor did the train carry sufficient food for an extended siege. Yet if they broke the circle and Resin's plan failed, they would be vulnerable to a mass assault that might easily cost every person—including his Molly—their lives.

Looking at the scout's face, Bigelow tried to read something from it but could not penetrate the inscrutable mask. Yet Resin would never suggest an idea he did not expect to have a better than fair chance of succeeding.

Some officers, as Bigelow knew, might have asked their subordinates to take a share of the responsibility, even to the extent of requesting Grade and Muldoon to sign statements to the effect that they took the share of arranging the plan. Bigelow could not bring himself to do that. If the decision had to come, he intended to make it himself.

Then his eyes met Eileen Tradle's and he saw the way she smiled and nodded. Eileen must guess at his problem, but was signalling to him that she thought he could safely follow Resin's plan.

'We'll give it a whirl,' Bigelow said. 'Now let's get down to arrangements. The more we plan now, the less confusion in the morning.'

After the men separated to pass word of the arrangements, Calamity, Molly and Eileen fetched in the six-horse team and hobbled it close to the wagon. While they worked none of them spoke, but at last the work ended and they had time to stand and think.

'Will it work, Calam?' asked Eileen.

'Could do. Like Beau says, Injuns are funny critters. If they see we're doing the plumb unexpected they may not make a solid attack. If they do make it——'

Calamity let her words trail off and the other two girls realised just how serious she regarded the situation. Six eyes looked at each other and then Eileen gave a shrug.

'Oh well,' she said, which if not very explanatory, covered her feelings.

'Can you shoot, Boston?' asked Calamity.

'A little.'

'Got a gun?'

'Papa sent Vint a shotgun and shells along. I can use that.'

'Less chance of loosing off and missing with shot,' said Calamity calmly. 'How about you, Molly?'

'I've no gun and can't shoot, but I know how to reload.'

'That'll do us then,' Calamity grinned. 'We're riding my wagon tomorrow.'

'But my aunt and uncle?' asked Molly.

'They'll be all right. One of ole shiny-butt's soldiers'll be with 'em.'

'Come with us, Molly,' Eileen said in a pleading tone. 'I—I know it sounds silly, but I feel sure we'll be lucky if we stick together.'

Calamity laughed. 'Damned if I wanted to admit it afore you well-eddicated city gals, but I feel the same way.'

'And what if the plan fails?' Molly asked.

Slipping an arm around the little schoolteacher's shoulders, Calamity gave her a gentle squeeze.

'Then we'll know *our* medicine's gone bad on us, gal—and I'll make damned good and sure the Injuns don't get either of you alive.'

'Will the Cheyenne destroy everything if they succeed?' Eileen asked.

'Likely,' Calamity replied.

'Oh!'

'Hey, now, cheer up, Boston, gal. Hell, we're not licked yet.'

'I know,' Eileen smiled. 'Now you children be good and go play while I write a letter.'

'A letter?' Molly gasped.

'A funny, silly letter to my husband,' Eileen explained. 'Telling him how much I love him, how sorry I am that I never gave him children to carry on our family name, how I've been a prideful fool, and how a girl I wouldn't have thought fit to hire as a scullery maid, much less call friend, taught me humility and—oh, a lot of silly things. I know Vint will probably never get it. But I feel that if I write it, all will go well with us.'

'Go write it,' Calamity said gently, slipping her other arm around Eileen's shoulders. 'We need all the luck we can get going for us. How about you, Molly?'

'I—I'm frightened, Calam,' Molly replied. 'Afraid of death, of dying before I fulfil myself as a woman, before I even know

96

what *it* is like.'

'There's a way of finding out,' Eileen told her. 'I'd talk to old shiny-butt and see what he can do about it.'

'Before we're married?' Molly gasped.

'Happen things go wrong tomorrow, gal,' Calamity said dryly, 'you won't need to worry about *that*.'

Without another word Molly turned and walked off into the darkness. Eileen left Calamity's side and went to the wagon where she found a pencil and paper. Sitting in the light of the fire, she wrote her letter. For a time Calamity stood alone, for Killem's men were all preparing for the next day. A brooding silence hung over the camp, oppressive when one remembered the laughter and noise that usually rang out around the fires. At last Calamity gave a shrug and walked towards Eileen.

'To hell with it, Boston,' she said. 'So we're due to be massacred comes morning. I aim to enjoy life while I can.'

'You may have a point, Calam,' Eileen replied, folding the letter and placing it in the bosom of her dress. 'Unless these folk are livened up, they'll be licked before they even start in the morning.'

'Old Jack Topman plays a mean fiddle,' Calamity remarked.

'Have you heard the Deane boy play a jew's harp?'

'Nope, but I figger it's time we did.'

Together the two women from such different environments went around the camp and brought to bear the force of their personalities. At first the musicians they found did not seem inclined to perform, but were bullied and cajoled into doing so. Inside ten minutes of the music starting, the people of the train had forgotten their troubles and started dancing as if they had no cares.

'Calamity's a living wonder, so's Boston,' Bigelow told Molly as they stood side by side in the shadows and watched the dancing.

'And me?'

'You're a darling,' he said and his arm slid around her waist. 'Molly——'

She looked up at him, then her arms went around his neck and her mouth met his hungrily, passionately, far different from the gentle pecks handed to him on other nights.

'Molly!' he breathed once more.

'I spoke to Calamity and Eileen earlier,' she breathed. 'Just

97

after the dance started.'

'Well?'

'Calamity's wagon will be empty all night,' she whispered and took his hand to lead him towards the wagon.

Half an hour later Molly knew what *it* was like.

At ten o'clock the dancing ended for Resin did not want a sleep-drugged force on his hands in the morning. The scout wondered where Bigelow might be, seeeing Grade making the rounds, and so went to find Calamity to see if she could offer any suggestions.

'Let's go look down by my wagon,' she replied.

'Sure,' he answered, but on reaching the side of the girl's wagon could see no sign of the captain. 'Where's Boston at?'

'Gone to spend the night with Molly's aunt. Johnson's on guard and she don't cotton to being alone.'

'Molly'd be there.'

'Nope,' Calamity answered and something in her tone stopped any further questions Resin might have felt like asking on that subject.

'In the wagon?' he asked.

'Underneath,' Calamity replied. 'There's no room inside.'

'Huh huh,' said Resin.

Although he had never owned a watch, Resin woke just after half-past two in the morning. As he moved in the blankets, Calamity stirred beside him and her bare arm slid around his neck. Hungrily her mouth crushed up to his.

'Time we was thinking about moving, gal,' he said.

'So move,' she replied sleepily.

Fifteen minutes later Resin sat on the blankets, drawing on his shirt and ignoring a pair of cavalry boots which swung down from the wagon. Calamity hurriedly buttoned her shirt and reached for her gunbelt as Bigelow walked away from the wagon carrying his weapon belt in his hands.

'Get going, Beau,' she breathed. 'And good luck.'

All around the camp people were stirring as the sentries went around waking them up. The fires had been allowed to die down, except for one in the centre of the circle and that did not give much light. However, the travellers had been handling harness for long enough to know how to hitch up their teams whether they could see properly or not. Of course, the business could not be done in absolute silence, but it was handled with the minimum of noise.

Following Bigelow's orders, the men and older boys handled the harnessing of teams and saddling of horses while the womenfolk stayed in the wagons and kept the children quiet. Everything went according to plan, with only minor, easily handled problems coming up.

Carrying a darkened lantern, Eileen arrived at Calamity's wagon and found one of her friends spluttering *sotto voce* curses while harnessing the six horse team. As for her second friend—on climbing into the wagon and removing the cover from her lantern, Eileen found Molly seated glassy-eyed on the bed and still wearing her underclothes, her frock lying on the floor with her stockings and shoes.

'It was wonderful, Eileen,' she sighed.

'So I recollect,' Eileen replied dryly. 'Come on, kid, get dressed while I see if Calamity needs any help.'

However, Calamity needed no help for she had harnessed her team and was already swinging aboard. All around the camp leather creaked and silence fell as men finished their work and prepared for the departure that would come with the ever growing light. Soon it would be light enough for them to see and when that happened—well, maybe it would be the last dawn any of them saw. Somewhere in the darkness the Cheyenne were gathering and already their coyote-yip signals began to ring out.

'Got your gun ready, Boston?' asked Calamity, uncoiling her whip and shaking the kinks out of it.

'Right here,' Eileen answered, lifting a magnificent Purdey shotgun from a walnut and brass case.

'Load it,' Calamity ordered. 'Is it clean?'

'I did it while you pair were lolly-gagging around last night.'

'You scared, Boston?' grinned Calamity.

'I'm scared, are you?'

'Sure. So scared that I reckon I'll do every blasted thing right when the time comes, same as you pair will. You did last time there was a mite of fuss. Say, I wonder how the champeen's making out?'

'She was doing all right last night when I saw her,' smiled Molly, her fear dying at the other pair's example. 'She and Muldoon disappeared into the darkness.'

'There was a lot of that going on,' Calamity remarked.

'Break open a box of shells for my carbine, Molly, gal, and stop blushing.'

Bigelow and Resin appeared, leading their horses. Looking like butter would not melt in his mouth, and acting as formal and polite as if attending a ball at the White House, the captain touched his hat brim.

'Everything all right, ladies?' he asked.

'Right as the off-side of a hoss,' Calamity replied. 'And for the Lord's sake climb up here and give the gal a kiss afore you go. Me 'n' Boston'll look the other way.'

'Calam!' Molly gasped, blushing like a schoolgirl.

'I'll tell you what,' suggested Eileen. 'I'll close both my eyes, Beau can come up the other side, that way you'll both get kissed.'

'Go on, Wade,' grinned the scout. 'Kiss your gal, or damned if I don't.'

'Let's both kiss Boston,' Bigelow countered.

'Now that's what I call a *real* good idea,' smiled Eileen. 'Only hurry and do it or we'll have to start without.'

Both men climbed into the wagon, each kissed his girl, then both gave Eileen a resounding smack at the same moment. With the service rendered, and their innocence of favouritism established, Resin and Bigelow jumped from the wagon box, took their horses and rode off.

'Damned if I ever thought I'd be kissed by a pair of unshaven men before breakfast, neither of them my husband, and like it,' Eileen stated.

'Reckon you've done a lot of things you wouldn't've thought possible afore you left Boston,' Calamity answered.

Thinking of the fight on the river bank, Eileen smiled. 'You can say that again, Miss Canary.'

The sky grew brighter by the second. Hands lifted reins, coiled around whip handles, gripped weapons. Men threw glances at their loved ones and silence lay like a cloud over the wagons. This time Calamity did not think about music, her eyes kept flickering towards the slopes around them as she waited for the signal to roll. To one side the cavalry mounted their horses and drew the Springfield carbines from their saddleboots ready for use. Other mounted men gathered around the train's livestock and spare horses ready to start them moving when Bigelow gave the word. From beyond the rim came coyote-yips which did not originate through four-legged throats.

'Now?' asked Bigelow.

'Not just yet,' replied Resin, gauging the distance to the coyote-yips.

Suddenly the Cheyenne appeared, topping the surrounding rims and racing their ponies down towards what they hoped was as helpless a bunch of white brothers as could be found. The drumming of something over a hundred and fifty sets of hostile war pony hooves rumbled out but as yet the war yells had not started, they were being reserved to shatter the travellers' sleep, to jar them into awoken confusion and add to the certain defeat of the hated people who had taken the Cheyenne lands.

Which would have worked a treat if it had not been for Beau Resin's plan.

'Let 'em roll,' Resin hissed in Bigelow's ear.

'Charge!'

Out rang Bigelow's command, sent forth on the expelled air from a powerful pair of lusty young lungs. Echoing the shout came the wild war scream of the Comanche and that whole column sprang into movement.

Up rose the wagonmaster's arm, then his whip lash snapped out to crack over the expectant heads of his team. The horses, waiting restlessly for their signal to go, thrust into their harness and the wagon lurched forward, turning from the circle and off in the direction of the west coast. Showing his attendance to orders, the driver of the second wagon started his team moving an instant later and the herd handlers closed in to move the stock into wakefulness ready to go. Wagon after wagon, as its turn came, rocked forward, urged on by cracking whip and bawled out profanity. The Cheyenne braves' wild war shouts rose and faltered in confusion as they saw the exodus begin.

'Fire!' roared Bigelow to his men as half the circle disintegrated and became a moving line.

Flame lashed from the barrels of his men's carbines, lead ripping into the exposed Cheyenne line. Two men and three horses went down; not bad shooting from the back of a fiddle-footing horse, aimed at a fast-moving target, with the notoriously inaccurate singleshot Springfield carbines the U.S.

Government saw fit to issue to their loyal cavalrymen.

'Yeeah!' screeched Calamity and her whip's gun-shot crack exploded over the heads of her team. 'Get to running, you slab-sided crow-bait.'

'Imagine you're on Boston High Street!' Eileen squealed, clutching the Purdey in hot, sweaty little hands. 'Pull!'

With a heave that almost lifted the wagon's wheels from the ground, the six great horses pulled; even the centre off-side critter for he had been around long enough to know when he might slack with impunity and when he must pull his guts out.

On the heels of the preceding wagon and last in the line, Calamity's outfit rolled out. Miss Canary was going to war.

CHAPTER TEN

MISS CANARY RECEIVES A COMPLIMENT

EVEN as Resin cut loose with his Remington, he could see the surprise tactic had caused some consternation among the attacking Cheyenne. Having planned all their strategy on raiding a sleeping camp circle, it shook them to their breechclothes to suddenly see the circle break up and the wagons pull out like the devil after a yearling, their occupants anything but bewildered and half-asleep.

Resin's bullet flipped a hard-riding brave backwards off his war pony, although it must be admitted that the scout did not take deliberate aim, singling out one special man. Rather he threw a ·44 bullet in the direction of the thickest concentration of hostiles and hoped *Ka-Dih* would still look kindly on his adopted follower. Thumb-cocking the Remington, Resin fired again but without result.

The deep bellow of a Dragoon caught Resin's ears—its forty grain powder load gave a distinctive sound, deeper than the cough of a lighter charged revolver, different from the sullen boom of a shotgun or muzzle-loader and unmistakable in comparison to the sharper crack of a cartridge-firing rifle. Instantly Resin became all attention for only one man he knew around that area toted a Dragoon—Sand Runner showed preference for the four pound, one ounce, thumb-busting old Colt giant. If Sand Runner died, his followers were sure to break and would not come back to a place which harboured so much medicine-breaking power.

Before Resin could locate the mystery leader, he found himself engaged in a shooting match against a group of fast galloping bucks who were coming rapidly into buffalo-bow range.

Over to Resin's right and towards the rear of the column a wild shape in the dress of a Cheyenne war-bonnet chief, his face covered with yellow ochre and hands concealed under much decorated U.S. cavalry gauntlets, fired another shot from his old Dragoon Colt. Caught by the smashing impact of the ·44 ball, Lieutenant Grade's horse went down. Grade managed to kick his feet free of the stirrups and lit down running, spitting curses as he looked for the man who killed his horse. If ever a young shavetail lieutenant had found trouble, it was Grade at that moment. The wagons went streaming by him and unless he could make it to one of them, he would be unlikely to see noon that day. With that in mind, he ran towards the wagon line, making for the second from last and hoping like hell that he made it. His chances did not look any too good for a young brave bore down on him, buffalo lance tip dropping ready to split him like a chicken on a roasting stick.

'Mr. Grade!' roared a voice from behind him and he saw Bigelow charging in his direction, only the captain had further to travel than had the Cheyenne. Twice Bigelow fired, emptying the last two chambers in his gun, without hitting the brave. An Army Colt was probably the finest percussion-fired revolver ever made, but like all its kind it could not be quickly reloaded; and time was something Grade was fast running out of.

On Calamity's wagon the girls saw Grade's danger and it threw Eileen into one hell of a predicament. She held a loaded shotgun, nine buckshot in each barrel just waiting to be turned adrift. Yet Eileen felt scared. She remembered conversations heard when her husband and father—both keen shooting men—discussed something called the spread of the shot. According to them, the buckshot balls would spread about an inch apart for every yard of range. Which meant that in shooting the Indian, she might also catch Grade with one or more of the ·32 calibre balls.

'Cut loose, Boston!' Calamity screeched, although the Lord only knew how she managed to see what was happening and guess at Eileen's problem. 'He's dead if you don't!'

And that, as Eileen well knew, was the living, gospel truth. Muttering a prayer, Eileen sighted the gun and pressed the trigger. The shotgun kicked like a Missouri mule and black powder obscured the girl's view; nor, if the truth be told, did she want to see the result.

Calamity let out a wild 'Yahoo!' as the Indian tipped backwards over his pony's rump and she overlooked the sight of Grade's hat being ripped from his head by one of the buckshot balls. However, Grade was on his feet still and Calamity allowed he would rather lose a replaceable hat than his irreplaceable life.

'Calam!' Molly screamed, catching the red-head's arm and pointing to the other side of the wagon.

Unnoticed by Calamity, one of the braves had cut in and headed his horse alongside her team. He lowered his buffalolance and aimed it at the heaving sides of the lead horse. If he thrust home and tumbled the horse, he would effectively bring the wagon to a halt.

There was no time for Eileen to try her shaky aim, nor for Calamity to draw and fire her Navy Colt, nor with any chance of making a certain hit. Yet she did not care, for in her good right hand she held as deadly a weapon as either shotgun or Colt under the circumstances.

Taking aim, she sent the whip's lash licking forward to curl around the man's neck. Then she heaved back on the handle and, taken by surprise, the man came jerking backwards off his horse. He lit down on the ground between his horse and Calamity's team. A steel shod hoof smashed on to his head and unconsciousness came down on him. Which might be claimed fortunate, for the wagon's wheels passed over his body.

Then as suddenly as it began, the attack came to an end. Demoralised by the white men's unusual tactics of running and fighting instead of allowing themselves to be slaughtered, the Cheyenne had no heart in the battle. Nor did the spirited opposition from the travellers do anything to increase the Cheyenne desire for war.

Bigelow had come alongside Grade, caught the young shavetail's hand and heaved him up on the rump of the horse. Swinging the double-loaded animal towards the wagons, Bigelow headed for the nearest.

'Jump for it, Dave!' he said, dropping the formal 'Mr. Grade' in his excitement, then seeing whose wagon he made for, went on, 'And keep your hands off the little blonde gal. She's mine, boy—and how she's mine.'

Which, as Eileen was married and Calamity appeared to be well hooked by Beau Resin, did not give Grade much of a chance in the romance line, even if he had the time or inclination for it at such a moment.

Even as he let his burden off in a flying leap that carried Grade to the box of Calamity's wagon, Bigelow saw the Cheyenne attack break and warriors go streaming up the slopes taking their dead and wounded with them.

At the other end of the train Beau Resin achieved one of his objects. He picked out Sand Runner, guided by the bull-roar of the Dragoon as the mystery chief cut down one of the soldiers. Unfortunately, Resin was not in much of a position to do anything about the chief for his Remington hung empty in his hand and Sand Runner raced his fancy palomino stallion up the slope to safety.

Holstering the empty revolver, Resin bent down and jerked the Spencer carbine from the saddleboot, drawing back the side hammer as the gun came to his shoulder. He took careful sight and touched off the shot. Although Sand Runner's attack medicine had gone sour, it seemed that the Great Spirit still looked with favour on his fair-haired boy. Just as Resin touched off the shot, a young buck swung between Sand Runner and the lined barrel of the Spencer. At that range even the forty-five grain powder charge which powered the gun could not throw its ·56 calibre bullet through the brave and into a man several yards beyond. The annoying thing to Resin's mind being that the point of impact on the brave showed he held true and Sand Runner ought to have become, in Western terms, a good Indian.

Instead the buck went down and Sand Runner raced on unharmed up the slope. The Spencer was a good gun, easy to reload with a further seven rounds, accurate and far more powerful than any of its repeater rivals, but it had faults. One of the worst being that after working the loading lever to eject an empty case and feed a loaded round into the chamber, one had to manually draw back the hammer before being able to fire—which proved to be one of the reasons the gun fell by the wayside in competition with the less powerful but more easily operated Winchester Model of 1866. Before Resin could complete the reloading process, Sand Runner had passed over the rim and out of sight. With him went the remaining members of his band.

Tearing his horse up the slope, Bigelow, flush-faced and excited, brought it alongside the scout's Appaloosa and yelled,

'Let's run them back to the hills.'

'Nope!' Resin replied. 'Least-wise, I wouldn't, Wade.'

'We've got them on the run now——'

'Sure. But take after 'em and dog-my-cats if you afore you know it you don't catch up with 'em.'

'Would that be bad?' asked the captain, holding in his restive horse where a few short weeks, days even, ago he would have gone head down and hell bent for glory without thinking of asking for any advice.

'Not if you caught 'em on ground of *your* choosing,' admitted the scout.

'But we wouldn't do that,' Bigelow stated rather than asked.

'Put yourself in Sand Runner's shoes. Would you stop and make a fight against men better armed than you unless the ground suited you and your weapons—And don't throw West Point training at me, Wade. There's hoss-Indians out here who've forgotten more than most cavalry officers know about light cavalry tactics. You might that happen you get to be a line officer and I reckon you'll maybe stay alive long enough to call Molly "Grandma."'

A slightly red tinge crept back into cheeks that had lost the flush of eager excitement. Then Bigelow grinned and slapped the big scout on the shoulder.

'All right, blast you,' he told Resin. 'I'll accept your advice and plead insanity at the court martial.' He paused then looked into Resin's eyes. 'Your plan worked, Beau.'

'*Your* plan, Wade,' the scout corrected. 'If it'd gone wrong, they'd've held you responsible, so damned if you don't get the credit now it's come off. It was a fool notion anyways, just how risky you'll get to know when you're handling your own company out here.'

From the way the usually unemotional scout spoke, Bigelow gained some slight inkling of how serious the risk had been. Surprise had been the plan's sole virtue; and even so it had been a desperate gamble. While the gamble came off that time, such a plan could hardly be written into the books as offering a standard guaranteed safe method of defeating an Indian attack.

Even so victory had not come without cost. Three soldiers and two civilians died during the hectic mêlée, several more had wounds of greater or lesser severity. Yet the toll might

107

well have been higher and probably would have been, even to the death or capture of every man, woman and child present, had they fought in a circle.

'What now?' asked Bigelow, watching the line of wagons drawing to a halt, his eyes anxiously searching the team and box of the last in line.

'Call up a few of your boys, then me 'n' you'll go up there and see Sand Runner's boys on their way.'

Already Muldoon's bull-voiced roars had gathered and formed up his men and an order from Bigelow brought a corporal's escort of four troopers to his side. Not enough men to tempt the captain into rashness, but plenty to fight off an attempted ambush by the departing Cheyenne. On reaching the top of the slope, they saw the last of the Indians disappearing over slopes and down valley bottoms ahead of them.

'And that's that,' said Bigelow.

'You sound a mite regretful,' answered the scout.

'Do I? I reckon I might be, a little. Terrible as it sounds, Beau, an officer can win more distinction in one day's Indian fighting than by working like a dog for years behind a desk. And in the final estimate, distinction carries the promotion in the end.'

'Yep,' drawled the scout. 'Only there's ways of getting that distinction, Wade. Way Custer does it is charging in head down, flags flying, band playing—and civilian newspaper writer friends looking on, and to hell with planning——'

'You don't sound to like General Custer,' Bigelow interrupted.

'He's either the bravest man in the whole danged U.S. Cavalry, or so damned stupid he ain't got the sense to be scared. And, whichever way, one of these days he's going to wind up getting him and a lot of his men killed.'

On June 28, 1876, while watching and listening to the Crow scout, Curly, bring the news of Custer's defeat and death on the Little Bighorn River—Bigelow being aboard the steamboat Far West with the reserve troops—the captain was to remember Beau Resin's words.

'And the other kind who gain distinction?'

'Oh them. They don't get their names in fancy dude newspapers. But they come out here willing to admit some hawg-dirty, grease-stinking civilian scout who's lived among 'em

108

likely knows more about Injuns than they do. So they listen to advice, ask questions, learn and use what they learn. Maybe they never have the glory of wiping out a whole damned great village, but happen they do, it's warriors and not old men, women and children they kill. Which's what Custer killed in, how'd they call it, his "signal success" against Black Kettle's village on the Washita. Nope, the other kind don't do that. Young Dave Grade's one of the other kind—and so are you.'

A flush of pleasure tinged the young captain's face. 'Thanks, Beau.'

'For what, speaking true? I lived among the Comanche long enough to get so I reckon the truth never hurt nobody. If I don't like a man, I tell him, stay out of his way and expect him to keep clear of mine. So why'n hell shouldn't I tell a man when I like what he is?'

'Damned if I know why not, Beau,' replied Bigelow, grinning like a schoolboy. 'And I'm not objecting; especially as it's me getting praised. Did you see the mysterious Sand Runner?'

'See him?' growled Resin and for a couple of minutes spat out a comprehensive flow of invective, finishing with, 'I'll say I saw him. That jasper's got more luck than a man's got good right to. I had him meat-in-the-pot under my sights and a damned young buck rode 'tween us just as I touched off the shot. If Sand Runner knows about that, he'll use it to claim his medicine can't be all bad.'

'Then we might still have trouble with him?'

'Might do. There's something about that Sand Runner I can't savvy, and it worries the hell out of me. We'll have no more fuss with him and his boys today, and that's for sure.'

'Then let's head down to the wagons and see about cleaning up. I want to make sure M—everybody's all right.'

'Everybody being a lil blonde schoolmarm,' grinned Resin. 'Was I you, I'd be real polite and well-behaved when she gets fool enough to marry you. I don't know who handed who a licking that night back there afore we reached the plains, but she'd been plumb in the thick of it and that was mighty rough company.'

'There are times you civilians think you're so smart,' sniffed Bigelow. 'Head back to the train, Beau, we'll move on for a mile or so, then make camp and attend to the burying.'

At the end of the attack Calamity started to slow down her

racing team. It was no easy job, even for one as skilled at horse-handling as Calamity, for the big horses ran hard and packed power to spare. Spluttering curses, she hauled back on the reins with both hands, a moccasined foot ramming down on the brake to hold it fully home. With a casual disregard for the safety of his limbs, young Grade bounded from the wagon box and sprinted to the heads of the slowing team. Grabbing the two lead horses, he lent a hand at getting them under control and helped Calamity halt the wagon within a foot of the preceding one.

'Are you pair all right?' Calamity asked, looking at the two pallid faces at her side.

'I'm going to faint,' Molly answered.

'Drop first so I can land on you,' Eileen told her in a strained voice. 'I—I—I killed a man.'

'Lean over the side of the wagon and let it go, Boston,' Calamity said gently. 'There's no disgrace in it.'

Neither girl did faint and although badly shaken by the experience of taking another human being's life, Eileen did not need to follow Calamity's advice. With an effort, she controlled her rising stomach and then settled down on the wagon box to await orders.

The wagons moved on for a mile, halting upon the banks of a pleasant stream and forming a defensive circle. Bigelow sent out pickets around the area to watch for any return of the Cheyenne and then started to organise the burying; and care of the injured.

Towards evening Eileen sat with Calamity at the freight outfit's fire. Molly had departed earlier to take her school class and the two girls were conscious of the brooding air that hung over the camp. Before either could speak of the situation, they saw a deputation approaching. One look told Calamity that Sergeant Muldoon, the corporal and two oldest troopers did not come on a social visit, nor to see her.

'I'll just go check the horses, Boston,' she said, rising. 'Stay put, gal, I can manage.'

Eileen opened her mouth to object, followed the direction of Calamity's gaze and closed it again. One look told her that something unusual was in the air. The men all appeared to have taken extra care with their appearance, not only by trying to clean up their uniforms, but taking the trouble to shine their brass work and polish their boots.

'Asking your pardon, Miz Bos—Tradle, ma'am,' Muldoon said, coming to a halt in a parade ground brace and throwing her a salute straight out of the drill manual. 'Could we speak with you?'

'Certainly, gentlemen. Would you care to sit down?'

' 'Tis a formal thing, ma'am,' the burly sergeant replied. 'You'll be knowing we lost three men in the fighting.'

'I know,' Eileen agreed.

'T'would be the senior officer's lady's place to write to their kin, ma'am, only the cap'n's not married, yet. So we wondered if you'd do it for us.'

A lump rose in Eileen's throat as she realised the honour the men gave her. She saw young Grade standing to one side of the men, clearly having given his permission for them to approach her with the request.

'Have I the right to do so?' she asked.

Taking off his hat, the young lieutenant looked at the hole in the top of its crown and thought of the hooves of the attacking brave's pony as they sounded behind him. He knew what Eileen must have gone through deciding whether to chance shooting with the risk of killing him while trying to save his life.

'Yes, ma'am, Boston,' he said. 'You've *earned* the right.'

'We'd take it kind if you'd do it, ma'am,' put in one of the troopers, a grizzled veteran who had joined years before the Dragoon Colt appeared to be damned as a new-fangled contraption that would never last.

'Gentlemen,' Eileen replied and, had he been there to see it, her husband would have marvelled at the quiet, genuine humility in her voice. 'I'd count it a privilege to do it.'

Coming to her feet, Eileen went to the wagon and returned with pen, ink and paper. Muldoon produced a box for her to sit upon and the men gathered around her. While she had known none of the dead men, except as familiar faces among Bigelow's troop, Eileen wrote letters to their next-of-kin which would long be treasured. She wrote simply, sincerely, without mawkish sentiment; and the wet-caused wrinkles the distant readers found on the paper were not placed there as an affectation but came from the tears which trickled down Eileen's cheeks as she wrote.

'Damned smoky fire,' she said, wiping a hand across her eyes after finishing the last letter.

'Yes, Miz Bos—Tradle.'

'Make it Boston and save your spluttering, Muldoon,' Eileen said.

'Yes, ma'am, Miz Boston, ma'am!' grinned the burly sergeant. 'And thanks.'

'You could have asked Miss Johnson to write the letters,' Eileen pointed out. 'She and Captain Bigelow are engaged.'

'Aye. But she's not Army—yet.'

'Stick your chest in, gal,' Calamity said, walking up after Muldoon's party threw Eileen salutes and marched away. 'You look like to burst.'

'I've become accepted as Army, Calam,' Eileen replied.

'Sure, I always knew you would. Soldiers always go for mean, ornery gals like you and me. Which's why you 'n' me never got on at first, we're too damned much alike.'

'Time was when I wouldn't have taken *that* as a compliment,' smiled Eileen, then the smile died. 'Everybody looks miserable, Calam.'

'Sure do,' agreed Calamity. 'Most of 'em, especially those who lost somebody, or got wounded on their hands, are asking themselves why the hell they came West. Happen they come up with the wrong answer most of them'll be licked right now.'

'Then we have to make them forget today, or get them over it,' Eileen stated firmly but grimly.

'You're the eddicated one, Boston, gal. You tell me how.'

Eileen explained her plan and together the Boston socialite and the wild Western girl went around the train. Using the power of their combined personalities, they gathered every man and woman who could walk, calling them all together around the main fire in the centre of the camp. There Eileen addressed them, speaking as she had earlier written, saying the things those gloom-ridden travellers wished to hear and urging them to carry on. Then Eileen stopped talking and Calamity stepped forward. In a quiet voice, she told them of the future, the land ahead of them, the new life waiting for them and of the importance of looking forward instead of back.

'By cracky, ladies,' said an elderly man whose youngest son died with a Cheyenne arrow through his chest. 'You're right.

My Jimmy wouldn't want us all to sit grieving for him and letting everything we all worked for go.'

'Thank you, Mrs. Boston, Calamity,' a woman who had lost her husband went on. 'You've given me heart to finish the trip.'

Once more Calamity and Eileen had helped hold the wagon train together and given it their strength at a time when such strength stood badly needed.

Molly came through the crowd followed by her children, forming them up in a neat block facing her two friends. Raising her right hand, she halted the crowd as it prepared to break up.

'Before you go,' she said, 'the children and I would like to pay a tribute to two gallant and for-real ladies. In doing this, Boston, I don't want you to think I'm belittling you, or holding a grudge for our little contretemps at Battle Creek——'

'If that means when you had the fight, who won?' called a man.

'We'll say it was a stand-off,' Molly answered, her eyes sparkling. 'Anyways, here is a little tribute to two real game girls. You would have been included in this, Eileen, but who in the world could make a rhyme with Boston.'

Turning, she motioned to the children and they began to sing:

> 'Calamity, Calamity,
> The best danged gal you ever did see,
> There'll never be, there'll never be,
> Another girl like Calamity.'

And Miss Martha Jane Canary, that rough, tough reckless and unemotional hard-case frontier girl stood blushing like a house on fire and promising herself what she would do to a certain little blonde schoolmarm when they were alone.

While the song would not cause Stephen Foster to turn in anxiety in his grave at a threat to his position as America's greatest song writer, it went down well with its biased little audience and by morning when the wagons rolled the words rang out from mouth to mouth across the plains.

CHAPTER ELEVEN

MISS CANARY HUNTS BUFFALO

'No sign of the Cheyenne,' Beau Resin announced, halting his Appaloosa by Calmity's fire and looking at the three girls, Bigelow and Killem who sat around it. 'But I saw a fair-sized herd of buffalo not a mile off.'

It was two days after the fight with the Indians and the wagon train had made good time. However, Bigelow knew that fresh meat would come in very handy, saving the train's depleted food supply. Hunting had been restricted for the past couple of days due to the chance of a further Cheyenne attack. If such an attack came and wiped out a hunting party, it might give Sand Runner's followers heart to make a further attempt upon the train.

'Buffalo!' Calmity whooped. 'Boston, gal, you've got to try roast buffalo hump.'

'I was supposed to try fresh-caught brook trout fried in butter, I seem to remember,' Eileen replied, 'but somebody else wound up eating them.'

'Shucks, didn't Molly and me apologise for that?' asked Calmity.

'You didn't.'

'Must've been so busy we forgot,' Calmity remarked.

'Calmity tried to catch some. I saw her throw a couple of worms into a river one night,' Molly went on.

'Want me to fetch Russian Olga for a partner, Boston?' asked Resin hopefully. Then he swung round from his horse and looked at Bigelow. 'Do I take a small party out and collect us some meat, Wade?'

'We sure need it,' Bigelow replied. 'Is it safe out there?'

'Like I said, there's no sign of the Cheyenne—and I looked careful.'

'Then how about you and I doing the hunting? I reckon Dave Grade can handle things at this end, with Muldoon helping him.'

'Reckon they can. Muldoon's so lucky that if they got the train lost, they'd wind up in San Francisco,' grinned Resin.

'If it's that safe, why not take Molly along, Wade?' Eileen asked. 'In which case I will have to come along as chaperone.'

'I think that's why you suggested it,' grinned Bigelow.

'It is. It is,' chuckled Eileen.

'Declare a school holiday, Molly, gal,' Calamity ordered. 'We're going buffalo hunting in the morning.'

'Hold hard there, red top!' barked Killem. 'I ain't said you can go yet.'

'If you don't, you'll wish you had,' Calamity threatened.

'Eileen and I will see to that,' Molly warned.

'Danged if one of 'em wasn't more'n enough!' groaned Killem. 'Now I got three to pester and bedevil me.'

'We'll fetch back a wagon-load of meat,' Calamity promised. 'And I'll save you the two biggest tongues.'

Which was a prospect Dobe Killem could look forward to with pleasure. No food in the world appealed to his palate as much as buffalo tongue prepared as only his cook could handle it.

'All right, Calam, we'll empty our chuckwagon. Take a couple of fellers along to do the butchering,' Killem said. 'And make damned certain sure that I get them tongues or I'll tan your hide for sure—all three of you.'

'Love those masterful men,' smiled Eileen.

At dawn the following morning the party prepared to go on their buffalo hunt. Calamity used two of her team horses in the now empty chuckwagon and a couple of the train's men who were skilled butchers had agreed to go along and attend to cutting up the meat. After some discussion the previous night Molly and Eileen elected to travel on horseback for the trip, especially as if the hunt proved successful the wagon would be piled high with meat on the return trip.

The remainder of the wagon train would continue on its way under Grade's guidance and the hunters expected to join up with it at its next camp ground, or during the day's march whichever came first.

'I've never been on a buffalo hunt,' Molly said, although her

115

enthusiasm stemmed more from going with Bigelow than because she liked the idea of hunting.

'I have,' Calamity grunted, sounding anything but excited.

'My father and his friend, the *other* congressman, both killed their buffalo on a straight run,' Eileen stated and smiled as she remembered the last time she had mentioned her father and his influential, important friends.

'That's one way of doing it,' Calamity answered, refusing to be drawn into an argument about dudes hunting for fun and sport.

'How do you mean, on a straight run?' asked Molly.

'When the herd is started running and you ride after it, pick the animal you want, gallop alongside it and shoot it on the move,' Bigelow explained, his eyes gleaming with the thought of the thrill to come.

'That's how *they* do it,' agreed Calamity and in his excited anticipation Bigelow overlooked the emphasis she placed on the word 'they.'

'It's the only sporting way, ladies.'

'Huh huh!'

'And what might that mean, Calamity?' Eileen asked.

'Means "huh huh",' explained Calamity. 'Let's get moving.'

Having told Calamity the direction to take, Resin had pulled out earlier to locate the herd. The rest of the party showed considerable faith in Calamity's judgment and skill, for none objected as she led them across the range. Mostly the talk dealt with various types of hunting and was carried out between Bigelow and the other two men for Calamity did not say much and Eileen and Molly appeared to be quite content to enjoy their ride while listening to the men's conversation.

'There's ole Beau wig-wagging for us,' remarked Calamity after they had covered almost two miles at a tangent from the train.

All the others stared ahead, searching for some sign of the big scout and his spot-rumped Appaloosa stallion on the rolling, bush and tree dotted range. Much to their surprise, they could see nothing of Resin.

'All right,' Eileen sniffed. 'So you can see him and we can't. But I can embroider better than you.'

'And I can write a better song,' Molly went on. 'Where is he?'

'See that clump of bushes ahead there, on top of the hump-backed rim we're coming to?'

'Yes,' replied Eileen doubtfully, squinting her eyes.

Raising her hand, Calamity waved it over her head. Not until the scout gave an answering wave did any of the others pick out his position, for his clothing tended to blend into the background. Once he moved, all could see him and wondered how they ever managed to overlook anything so obvious.

'Keeping still's the best way to stay hid,' Calamity commented when the others complimented her on her keen sight. 'And the best way to find something's to look for it all the time.'

'I'll go on ahead,' Bigelow told the others and sent his horse forward at a faster pace.

'My mother warned me not to marry a hunting man,' smiled Eileen, glancing at Molly.

'What happened?'

'I married one and spent most of my honeymoon on a deer hunt in the Adirondaks. It was wonderful.'

Molly glanced at Eileen, caught the other girl's wink and started to blush as she remembered using the same words in much the same tone on the morning of the fight with the Cheyenne.

Bringing his horse to a halt by Resin's side, Bigelow reached for the rifle in the saddleboot. An exclamation of annoyance left his lips as he found that his striker, usually a most reliable man who obeyed orders to the letter, had mistakenly given him the single-shot Remington Rider rifle instead of his Winchester.

'Damn the man!' he growled, although mostly he would never think of his striker in such terms. 'He's given me the Remington.'

'I know,' drawled the scout. 'I told him to.'

'You?'

'Why sure. I come across him taking your Winchester to the hoss lines and told him you'd need something with more power and range, so to get that fancy Rolling Block rifle you showed me.'

'But the Winchester is handier to use from the saddle,' Bigelow objected.

'Sure is,' agreed Resin, glancing to where his horse stood

concealed among the bushes, 'if we aimed to shoot 'em off a hoss's back that is.'

'That's the only sporting way to do it.'

'Yep. Only we're not here for sport, we're shooting meat for the train, so we want the critters down close together not spread out over a good country mile.'

After Bigelow secured his horse, Resin led him up the slope. Flattening down on the top of the rim, they looked to where a small herd of black, shaggy-humped Great Plains buffalo grazed some three hundred yards from their position. A trophy-hunter's gleam came into Bigelow's eyes as he studied the herd and picked out a big old bull as his first target. Bringing up the rifle, he aimed at the old bull; but, before he could squeeze the trigger, Resin caught him by the arm and gave a warning head-shake.

'Not yet,' breathed the scout. 'And don't drop that big old cuss, he'd be tougher to eat than old leather. This's how we do it—and I tell you now, there'll be damned little sport in it.'

'Tell on, good mentor,' replied Bigelow.

'First we lung-shoot one of the bulls. Yeah, we go out to wound him instead of taking a straight kill. He'll die in minutes anyway. The smell of blood and the way he staggers'll hold the attention of the others. I figured four'll be enough for what we need. Never took to shooting a critter just to see it fall and leaving its body to rot. Another thing, shoot for the head——'

'That will spoil his skull.'

'Sure, only we don't eat the skull, so hit there instead of the body where we'd lose meat.'

The system, worked to perfection by hide hunters like Frank Myers—who frequently shot up to fifty buffalo at one stand by using it—produced good results. On Resin's first shot, using a Sharps rifle borrowed from Killem, one of the young bulls gave a lurch and started to stagger, coughing frothy blood. Instantly the rest of the bulls gathered, hooking viciously with their horns at their wounded companion and ignoring the sound of the shot. With two bullets Bigelow tumbled over a pair of average-sized young bulls and Resin dropped the fourth. Then the remainder of the herd took fright at the noise of the shots and fled across the plains at a fair speed, considering their bulk and ungainly build.

'Get the hosses and wave the others up,' Resin suggested, rising to his feet and finishing the lung-shot bull with a bullet through the head.

However, there proved to be no need to go. Calamity knew enough about the principles of buffalo hunting to stay back until she heard the shooting start. Once she heard shots, she gave the signal to her party and brought them up the slope then down towards the killing ground.

'You got 'em,' she said, eyeing the four bodies on the ground.

'Naw!' scoffed Resin. 'These bunch up and died of old age. Them we shot at's still running.'

'The way you pair shoot, we can believe that,' Eileen remarked and looked with interest at the dead buffalo. Somehow they seemed larger and more impressive than the mounted heads her father and his friend brought home from their hunt.

Not only Eileen looked at the bulls and took note of their size. The two butchers stared at the animals with growing concern. While both were skilled at their trade, neither had ever been called on to perform a piece of major butchery under such primitive conditions. Looking at the huge shaggy shapes, the two men could not even decide how to set about removing the skins. An average-sized Great Plains buffalo, such as Resin and Bigelow had shot, stood around five foot nine inch at the shoulder and weighed well over seventeen hundred pounds. To handle such bulky creatures the two men would expect to make use of block and tackle, which they possessed but had not brought along. Yet both knew enough about their work to realise that the hides must be removed quickly or would set like iron upon the flesh underneath and be almost impossible to peel off.

'You gals had best go back over the rim,' Calamity said, jumping down from her wagon. 'We've got some skinning to do.'

'Is it as bad as that?' asked Eileen.

'Bad enough, Boston, gal.'

Neither Eileen nor Molly argued for they knew Calamity was giving them a frank, honest warning and not flaunting her superiority over Eastern-born women in a practical, if bloody, piece of Great Plains business.

Watched by an interested Bigelow and the two butchers, Resin drew his Ames knife and approached the buffalo. First the scout cut through the skin in a circle around the neck and just behind the horns, rolling some of the freed hide back. With that done, he slashed through the hide from neck to the end of the belly and opened the leg skin up to join the belly cut. Turning, he looked to see if Calamity was ready to do her share.

Telling the butchers to bring out the rope, spike and hammer with them, Calamity uncoupled the double-tree from the wagon but still left her horses harnessed to it. One of the butchers sprang down from the wagon and handed her the coil of stout rope, then stood back to see what she aimed to do with it. Securing one end of the rope securely to the clevis of the double-tree, Calamity carried the other end to where Resin had started to do his part in the skinning.

With his cutting done, Resin took the sledgehammer and stout, pointed iron rod from the other butcher. He drove the spoke through the buffalo's nose and deep into the soil so it held firm, then took the other end of Calamity's rope, gathered up a roll of skin on the animal's back and lashed it firmly and securely to the rope. Testing the knot's hold, he looked at Calamity.

'Let 'em go, gal!' he ordered.

Cracking her whip with one hand and controlling the reins with the other, Calamity started her horses forward. She watched the rope grow tighter and made sure the knots would hold before giving her next order. On a shout and whip crack from Calamity, the two horses started forward, thrusting into their harness to get more power as they felt resistance. With a sickening, soggy, rending sound, the hide peeled backwards over the rump of the carcase and trailed on the ground behind Calamity's horses.

All in all it had been a neat piece of skinning in the manner devised by buffalo-hunters. However, there was one difference between Calamity's party and the buffalo-slaughtering hide-hunters; where the hide-hunters left all but the skin to rot—unless they happened to take a tongue or other choice part—Calamity's party planned to take along every piece of meat, hide and bone, leaving as little waste as possible.

'There's your hide, Wade,' Resin remarked after unfasten-

ing the rope and rolling up the skin with the deft touch of a
master.

'Thanks,' replied the captain, not showing the interest one
might have expected at being presented with a prime buffalo's
hide; especially as he particularly wanted one to make into a
carriage-rug for Molly. 'I reckon I'll go join the ladies.'

Resin and the other two men did not regard that as a show
of weakness. Fact being the two butchers looked a mite green
around the gills and Resin hated the sound of stripping off a
hide in such a manner. So did Calamity and she wanted to get
the work done as quickly as possible.

The other three hides were removed, though each took a
longer time as the body under it cooled. A cursing Calamity
watched the last hide come free and stopped her horses. Even
though she felt sickened, Calamity's first thought was for her
team. She unhitched the two horses, watered them from the
five-gallon keg fastened to the wagon, then left the animals to
graze. Walking up the slope and passing over it, leaving the
three men to handle the butchering and loading of the wagon,
Calamity found Eileen lazing by the bushes, but no sign of
Molly and Bigelow.

'Hey, Boston,' she said, shaking the dozing girl. 'Where're
the love-birds?'

'Huh? Oh, they went for a ride.'

'They did what?' gasped Calamity, staring in disbelief at the
tracks of two horses leading from the bushes. 'Didn't reckon
they was headed for the wagon train, did they?'

'No,' Eileen replied, standing up as she saw the concern on
Calamity's face. 'They said they'd take a short ride and join us
in an hour or so.'

'Danged fools!' grunted Calamity. 'Wade's a nice feller and
smart in a lot of ways. Only he's no plains scout and it's hellish
easy to get lost out here. I reckon I'd best go look for them.'

'Shall I come along?'

'Nope. I don't want to fuss with that mean Appaloosa and
there's only one other hoss.'

'Why not tell Beau and let him go?' asked Eileen.

' 'Cause he's more use down there helping with the butchering and loading than I would be. And the sooner we get back
to the train, the better me 'n' him'll like it.'

'I thought you said there had been no Indian sign?'

'Time to start worrying about Injuns is when you don't see 'em,' Calamity answered. 'Can I take the hoss?'

'Do you need to ask?'

'Sure do, with a gal who fights as good as you do,' grinned Calamity. 'And don't worry, gal. I'll bring that lil schoolmarm of our'n back safe and sound.'

'You see you do,' Eileen replied. 'Or you and I'll take another walk in the woods.'

Eileen had been wearing a divided skirt and riding astride, which was fortunate, for Calamity had never been on a side-saddle such as was popular among female riders back East. The way Calamity looked at the situation, she might need all her riding skill before the day was out.

Collecting Eileen's horse, Calamity saddled and bridled it. For a moment she thought of borrowing one of the rifles from the wagon, but discarded the idea. If any Indians had been in hearing distance, the sound of the shots fired at the buffalo might bring them in. Not even settlers were hated by the Indians as were hide-hunters; and the Indian did not draw any distinction between slaughter for hides and folks hunting food. If a bunch of Cheyenne came on the party, they would attack and having three rifles could mean the difference between life and death for Calamity's friends.

While Eileen walked down to the wagon to tell the others, Calamity took the departed couple's trail. Although Calamity found little difficulty in following the tracks, she could not make even as much speed as Molly and Bigelow raised; and from the sign they had not been pushing their horses to any great extent. As she rode along, Calamity decided on just what she aimed to say to Captain Wade H. Bigelow when she caught up with him; it would not be ladylike, that was for sure, but aimed to tell him in pungent, profane terms just what she thought of his stupidity. Hell, not even being in love gave old Wade the right to take such damned fool chances with his and Molly's lives.

'Dang that Wade!' she spat out after trailing the couple for almost three miles. 'Why in hell don't he stop acting like a gentleman and take her off some place cool and shady?'

A flutter of white caught the corner of Calamity's eye and brought her twisting around in the saddle, right hand turning palm out by the butt of her Colt. One glance told her two things: first, she would not have need for the gun; second, that Bigelow appeared to have taken Molly some place cool and shady. The little schoolteacher stood on the edge of a fair-sized clump of bushes and waved as happily as if on a New England Sunday-school picnic.

'Hey!' Molly greeted as Calamity rode up.

'Where in hell's shiny-butt?' growled Calamity in reply, seeing no sign of the gallant captain.

'I thought we'd dropped that name!' Molly said a trifle stiffly.

'We dropped it when he stopped acting it. Which same he started again, or he wouldn't've taken you lolly-gagging off like this.'

'We only took a ride!' Molly answered, a blush creeping to her cheeks as she dropped a hand to the blouse, discovering its buttons to be fastened in the wrong holes—which they had not been in leaving the meat-hunting party.

'Sure, honey,' Calamity replied gently. 'Where's he at?'

'He's just like a boy,' smiled Molly, although a few minutes before Bigelow's actions had been anything but boy-like. 'After we—Well, we went through the bushes and saw a herd of those little pronghorn antelope. I said I would like to examine one of them and Wade insisted on trying to ride one down for me.'

'He went chasing a pronghorn on hoss-back?'

'Yes.'

'Danged if he's not worse'n I thought. That's like trying to out-swim a trout going up-stream.'

The fact that Calamity said 'danged' and nothing stronger told Molly that her friend had partially forgiven Bigelow.

'They are fast,' Molly admitted.

'He's not slow his-self,' grinned Calamity. 'Only he's got about as much chance of catching one of them white-rumped streaks of lightning as I have of becoming a for-real lady.'

'Calam!' thought Molly, knowing better by now than ex-pess it in words. 'You may not dress the part, but you're a for-real lady now.' She went on aloud, 'Are they that fast?'

'Danged fastest thing on *four* legs on the plains,' replied Calamity, seeing Bigelow ride into sight. 'Here he comes, without a pronghorn.'

The girls walked together through the bushes and halted at

the other edge to wait for Bigelow's arrival, keeping under cover for Calamity never liked to be unduly exposed when out on the Great Plains. Riding up, Bigelow came to a halt in the bushes and threw a glance at Molly.

'He got away, darling. Say, while we're waiting for my horse to cool out why don't we——?'

'Reckon I ought to close my eyes?' asked Calamity who had been standing to one side and behind a bush.

'Hey, Calam,' Bigelow greeted. 'We've just been resting Molly's horse and I thought——'

'Yeah,' Calamity said dryly. 'I know it. Only—Hell fire, Wade, we got us some real trouble!'

From where they stood, Calamity had a good view of the country traversed by Bigelow in his fruitless chase after the pronghorn herd. Turning, Bigelow saw what had turned Calamity's voice from faintly ironic to dead serious. A cold, sick feeling hit Bigelow in the pit of his stomach as he saw the deadly danger into which he had brought the girl he loved.

They came into sight over a rim not half a mile away, riding slowly as one of their number followed Bigelow's trail—almost twenty Cheyenne warriors led by a tall war-bonnet chief with a yellow-ochre covered face, wearing much-decorated cavalry gauntlets and with an old Colt Dragoon revolver thrust into his waistband. At that distance Bigelow could not pick out the details of the chief's dress and Calamity had not heard a description of Sand Runner. So, although they did not know the great war-leader was present, both knew for certain sure they had found about as bad trouble as three palefaces ever came across upon the Great Plains.

One thing—and it was not much—remained in their favour. So far the Indians only knew of Bigelow's presence. The bushes prevented the approaching Cheyenne from seeing the girls. No Indian would have contented himself in riding at so leisurely a pace had he known that two prime white-brother squaws stood just ready for the taking. However, that thought did not give Calamity any great joy. Happen they tried to run for safety, the Cheyenne could not miss seeing them and each man rode his war-relay. Using their spare, fresh horses, the Cheyenne could ride down the three palefaces before covering a mile, especially as Bigelow's mount had been hard-ridden.

Yet if they stayed, Calamity, Molly and Bigelow would be in no better shape for one man and two girls—even if one be Calamity Jane—could not hold off the attack of a score of war-wise Cheyenne braves hot and eager for coups or glory. Calamity knew that all too well. So, it seemed, did Bigelow.

He had dismounted on arrival and swung to face Molly, placing his hands on her shoulders. Lowering his head, he kissed her.

'Molly,' he said gently. 'I love you, my darling. I love you. Never forget that.'

Without any warning of what he meant to do, Bigelow bunched his right hand into a fist and drove it against Molly's jaw. The little blonde collapsed, but Bigelow caught her and lowered her gently to the ground. Then he looked up at Calamity expecting to find her showing amazement, anger or curiosity. Instead all he could read was admiration and realised he did not need to explain his action or what he aimed to do next.

'Let me go,' Calamity said.

'I'd never find my way back to the others, Calam,' Bigelow replied. 'Don't argue, there's no time and I don't want to leave you lying by Molly. Take care of my little girl, Calam.'

'I'll do that,' Calamity promised, gripping the man's hand. 'Try to get that damned war-bonnet chief there. Drop him and the rest *might* pull out. Good luck, shiny-butt.'

'And you, red top. Tell Molly I love her.'

Vaulting on to his horse, Bigelow kicked it into movement and sent it charging out of the bushes, headed off at a tangent from the Indians. Even as he went, Bigelow realised that for the first time in his experience the words 'shiny-butt' had not been used as an insult, but came out full of Calamity's un-expressed pride.

On seeing the captain burst out of the bushes, every Chey-enne voice lifted in a wild, ringing yell and each man started his horse forward at a gallop. In doing so, they swung clear of the bushes and headed away from the girls, just as Bigelow hoped they would.

He rode his tiring horse for almost half a mile, hearing the enemy hooves drawing closer. Pulling the Army Colt from his holster, Bigelow swung his horse to face the Cheyenne. His face grew set and grim as he went to meet them. Twenty against one. Yet he must face them for Molly, his darling, loving little Molly's life hung in the balance.

Twice Bigelow fired as the men closed on him, but he did not find opportunity to take Calamity's advice. Sand Runner's name as a warrior had been long established and he did not need to take chances. So the chief hovered in the background and allowed the young bucks to bear the brunt of the attack. His bull voice roared out a deep-throated order and, to Bigelow's surprise the attacking braves made no attempt to use their guns or bows even though one of their number slid from the back of his pony.

Then one of the braves cut loose with his buffalo-bow, sending its arrow into the chest of the soldier's horse. Feeling his mount going down under him, Bigelow kicked his feet free of the stirrups. His luck ran out for the horse landed awkwardly and threw him off balance. Down he went, rolling over as the hooves of the horses churned around him. Just as he reared up to try to shoot, the butt end of a buffalo lance crashed down on to his head and everything went black.

Calamity had watched everything and a shudder ran through her as she saw Bigelow taken alive. Even without being conscious of the action, her Colt slid into her hand. Just as Calamity prepared to charge out and attempt a rescue, or to kill Bigelow and save him from torture, a moan from Molly brought her to her senses.

'Not a sound, honey!' she whispered, dropping to her knees and laying a hand over Molly's mouth. 'Can I trust you?'

Surprise, puzzlement came to Molly's glazed eyes, then realisation, remembrance and understanding cleared them and Molly nodded.

'Where is he, Calam?' she asked when the hand moved from her mouth.

'Out there—Keep still, gal, we can't help so don't let it be in vain.'

'I—I don't want to live without W—him.'

'I do, and he wants you to!' Calamity growled, holding her voice down. 'The red-sticks took him prisoner, gal. Now hold yourself. For gawd's sake don't go all woman on me, or I'll have to quieten you.'

'C—can't we do anything?'

'Only one thing. Get back to the others, head for the train

and get help to go and rescue him.'

For once in her life Calamity had told a deliberate, *serious* lie to a friend. She knew in her heart that there was hardly a hope in the world of rescuing Bigelow.

CHAPTER TWELVE

MISS CANARY HEARS AN ULTIMATUM

A WHITE-FACED, dry-eyed Molly Johnson stared at Calamity as the full impact of the horror of the situation hit her. Yet she did not go 'woman,' turn hysterical. Moving cautiously, the two girls crept to the edge of the bushes and peered out, watching the Cheyenne ride away with Bigelow's body draped across the back of a horse. Calamity could feel Molly trembling and laid a hand upon the girl's arm.

'We must do something, Calam!' Molly moaned.

'Sure, Molly, gal. We'll let those red scouts get clear, then ride like hell to the wagon.'

'Couldn't we follow them?'

'No.'

'You mean I couldn't!' Molly gasped. 'Leave me here——'

Turning to face Molly, Calamity gripped her by the shoulders and shook her gently but firmly.

'Don't act *loco*, gal. And don't say that I can go and leave you to find your way back to Beau. You'd be lost in a mile. The quicker we get back to Beau, the quicker he can decide what to do.'

Molly nodded. Tears trickled down her cheeks and her shoulders shook with silent sobs. Taking the little girl into her arms, Calamity soothed her like a child, showing a gentleness which might have surprised many people who made an acquaintance with Martha Jane Canary at happier moments. When the flow of tears had passed and Molly regained something of a hold on herself, Calamity turned to look after the far-distant Cheyenne.

'Let's go, honey,' she said, helping Molly to rise.

Taking their horses, the girls rode cautiously from the bushes. Clearly the Cheyenne believed Bigelow to be alone for none of them even offered to look back in the direction of the bushes. For all that Calamity forced the pace; for protection and also to make Molly believe there might be a chance of rescuing Bigelow.

By the time they returned to the wagon, they found that most of the butchering and loading had been completed. Eileen and the three men watched the girls ride up and all showed some curiosity as to why Bigelow did not come with them.

'Where's Wade, Calam?' Resin asked.

'Cheyenne got him.'

'Huh?'

Quickly Calamity outlined the situation. None of the others spoke while she gave Resin every detail that came to her mind and described Bigelow's gallant action to save the girl's then his capture.

'Poor bastard,' said Resin quietly at the end of Calamity's explanation.

Something in the big scout's tone and attitude struck Molly with the impact of a mule's kick. Suddenly she realised just how little hope there was of rescuing Bigelow from the Cheyenne's clutches.

'I'll never see him again!' she moaned.

'Sure you will, honey,' Calamity answered.

'I won't! I won't!' Molly screamed, turning on the other girl. 'You lied to me! I could have gone to him. I hate you!'

And she threw herself at Calamity, little fists striking the girl's face. Calamity just stood there like a statue, letting the blows land although they were far from light taps. Like Resin, Calamity hated to lie and she hated it even worse when dealing with a friend.

Resin caught Molly's hands, drawing the girl gently away from Calamity and Eileen moved forward to take the blonde in her arms. After the rage-hysteria, the reaction set in and Molly collapsed sobbing into Eileen's arms.

Slowly Calamity lifted a hand to wipe the blood that ran from the corner of her mouth. She looked at the red streak upon her hand, then turned and walked towards her horse.

'Where the hell are you going?' Resin growled, catching the girl's arm before she could mount the horse.

'Molly's right,' Calamity replied. 'I lied to her. I'm going to see if I can rescue him.'

'Damn your fool hide, Calamity!' the scout snapped. 'You know better——'

'Let go! Get your goddamned hand off my arm!'

'When you stop acting like a fool kid I will. You know damned well that *you* can't handle a chore like that.'

'Can you?'

Lifting his hand from Calamity's arm, the scout rubbed his jaw. 'I don't know, gal. But I sure as hell aim to find out. It's the only thing we can do, and at best I'll make sure he doesn't suffer.'

Resin and Calamity's eyes went to the Sharps rifle which leaned against his saddle. That gun would carry accurately at ranges of up to a mile and packed the power to knock down a bull buffalo with one shot at the end of the distance. Both knew to what end the accuracy and killing power might be put. If the worst came to the worst, Resin intended to use it to cut short Bigelow's sufferings at the hands of the Cheyenne—even if doing so led to the scout's presence being discovered by the same Indians.

'I—I'm sorry, Beau,' Calamity said contritely. 'Times I act like a woman.'

Suddenly scooping Calamity into his arms, Resin kissed her hard, passionately and savagely. He felt no embarrassment at the act, nor did the girl. Way they saw it, a man who might not be alive at dawn the following day had a right to kiss a gal happen he felt that way inclined.

'Yeah,' he said, releasing Calamity. 'Times you sure do—I'm right pleased to say.'

After that no time was wasted in preparing to leave. Resin intended to use all three saddle horses, riding relay on them and so having something in reserve if it came to a run for his life. While he saddled his Appaloosa, the two butchers finished loading the wagon and took the saddles from the two reserve horses, for Resin did not wish to have them toting extra weight. Calamity hitched up her team to the wagon, marvelling at the way Eileen soothed and cared for the still sobbing Molly and kept her out of the men's way.

'Get aboard, all of you,' Resin ordered when all was ready.

'Calam!' Molly said. 'I—I——'

'Get aboard, honey,' Calamity replied gently. 'There's nothing we can do here and folks need this meat.'

Camp was being made for the night when Calamity's party arrived. A crowd quickly gathered but Calamity told them to start unloading and sharing the meat among them. In this she prevented any questions being asked, for she wished to give her story to the men who ran the outfit instead of wasting time answering a lot of fool questions.

'What happened, Calam?' Grade asked, coming up fast, Muldoon, Killem and the wagonmaster on his heels.

'We found trouble,' she replied.

'Bad trouble?' inquired the lieutenant.

'As bad as it comes, Dave. Wade got took alive by the Cheyenne.'

'The dirty, murderin' spalpeens!' Muldoon growled, sounding as mean as a winter-starved grizzly bear. 'How'd they do it?'

Quickly Calamity told most of what had happened, finishing with, 'Beau took out after them—with the Sharps.'

Her words met with cold, blank, guarded stares for the men knew exactly what she meant. Behind them, Eileen was already leading a sobbing Molly to the Johnson's wagon, driving off any inquisitive spectators with cold stare, or brief, concise words if the stare failed.

'Do we try to get him out, Paddy?' asked Grade.

'If there was only us to be thinking about I'd be after saying yes,' the burly sergeant replied; and wondered what his reply might have been had the question been put at the start of the trip. 'Only there's these good folks to take care of and see through—and precious the little chance of finding the cap'n alive.'

'First sight of the cavalry coming and he's dead for sure,' Calamity remarked.

'We'll wait for Beau.'

They waited and over an hour later, just after sundown, the scout rode in on his leg-weary Appaloosa; having left the other two horses behind as they tired. Dropping from his saddle, the scout slouched to Killem's fire and the freighter sent one of his men to tend the Appaloosa.

Coming up with a pail of water, Calamity handed it to the scout and Resin dropped to his knees to sink his face in, drinking thirstily. At last he raised his wet face and looked at the silent circle around him. Grade, Muldoon, the wagonmaster,

Killem and Calamity all stood waiting to hear what the scout could tell them.

'He's still alive,' Resin said. 'I trailed 'em and found their camp. Moved in close, soon after they arrived and saw them get to talking. Some of 'em wanted to get started on him, but Sand Runner did some yelling and hollering and they pushed Wade into a tent, tied like a hawg for slaughter. From what I could hear, they don't aim to make a move until tomorrow.'

'Then we might——' Calamity began.

'Yeah,' Resin agreed. 'We might. Like I said, they held a pow-wow. Seemed like Sand Runner was having to convince 'em about something. Don't know what, he don't speak that distinct.'

'And they aim to keep Wade alive?' asked Grade eagerly.

'That's how it looked to me. There's something about that damned Sand Runner gets me. I can't put a finger on it, but he's the weirdest Injun I ever saw.'

'How's about——?' Muldoon started to say.

'Hold hard, Paddy,' Resin interrupted. 'I've been all day without food. Let me eat, then we'll decide. You boys get pickets out, tend to your work and come back here in an hour and we'll say our pieces.'

Before any of the others could object, even if they aimed to, Calamity had come on them and hazed them away, leaving the big scout to eat his meal in peace. Eileen returned with news that the train's doctor had attended Molly and left her under sedation. Then for the first time Eileen heard the full story of what occurred on the plains.

The hour ended and the same party gathered around Killem's fire watched by almost everybody from the train.

'What we fixing——' began Muldoon, but once again found his question interrupted.

First a rifle shot cracked out from the darkness well within the ring of cavalry pickets but beyond the wagon circle; then a voice boomed out ventriloquially so that nobody could say for sure from where it came.

'*Tshaoh!* I come in peace to your camp-fire!'

'Easy folks!' Resin roared as travellers grabbed for their guns. 'Just simmer down and don't nobody make any moves. It's all right.' Then he raised his voice and called, 'Come and go in peace, brother!'

Gasps and mutters rolled up as the same war-bonnet chief who had acted as spokesman for Sand Runner rode into the camp circle. He came proudly, sitting erect and with a Winchester rifle held by its foregrip in his right hand high over his head, its lever down, showing he came in peace and unable to defend himself.

'How!' he greeted, riding towards where Resin's party stood.

'How!' Resin answered, watching the chief drop from his horse.

Johnson had joined the party for the conference and he said, 'Ask him——'

'All in good time, friend,' Resin drawled. 'You can't rush these things.'

Once again the two men went through the formality of charging, lighting and smoking their pipes, squatting by the fire. People gathered around, staring with fascination at their first close-up sight of a real, genuine hostile Cheyenne war chief. There was some muttering among one section of the party and a burly man slouched towards Muldoon.

'How in hell did that red devil get past your damned sentries?'

'Rode by 'em, darlin',' answered the burly sergeant, for he did not like the man; one of a bunch of political agitators fleeing to the West. 'If you reckon you could do better, get out and do it.'

'I ain't hired to stand no guard.'

'Nor do anything 'cepting moan about any man's got more than you have, watch to see that nobody does less than you and do damned little yourself,' growled Muldoon.

'Yeah?' snarled the man. 'Well, that damned Injun might not find it so easy to get back out again.'

Thrusting his sun-reddened face to within an inch of the other man's sullen features, Muldoon growled a warning. 'Don't try it, darlin', or I'll take pleasure in stopping ye meself, even if Beau Resin don't lick me to it.'

'You make plenty good fight last time,' remarked the chief, sucking appreciatively at his pipe. 'Spoil Sand Runner's medicine.'

'It was a trick that won't work twice,' Resin replied.

'Good enough trick this time anyway. You Comanche plenty

smart fighters.'

At that moment the pipes ended and the serious business commenced. Both men knocked out their tobacco remains, placed their pipes away and the chief said: 'We took the soldier-coat chief.'

'Is he still alive?' Johnson asked.

'Leave it to me,' Resin ordered. 'Do you still have him, or do the women?'

'He brave man, chief among his people. Not go to women.'

'What does that mean?' Johnson breathed in Muldoon's ear.

'Mostly they let the women torture the prisoners. But if they respect the man they catch, they don't hand him over, keep him themselves. There's devil the bit of difference in the end.'

'Why tell me this?' asked Resin.

The chief did not answer for a moment, but sat with his head hanging. Something appeared to be bothering him. At last he spoke.

'These are the words of Sand Runner. He says he want five thousand dollars for soldier-coat chief. You give-um, soldier-coat come back. No hurt except for sore head.'

'I've got the money in my wagon!'

'I'll get the money, Beau.'

Johnson and Eileen spoke at the same moment, but Resin shook his head.

'Not yet,' he said and turned back to the chief. 'Is this the Cheyenne way of making war? Do they now sell their brave enemies like they were *Comancheros* who will trade their own mothers?'

Hanging his head in shame, the chief answered, 'This is the word of Sand Runner. We will meet you by the place where you killed the buffalo tomorrow at dawn, you have money, get soldier. Try tricks, he gets dead.'

'This is a big matter,' Resin drawled.

Yet worry nagged him. Again had come the request, *demand*, for *money*. No hostile plains Indian had ever before demanded money and Resin mistrusted any change in the smooth order of things.

'You still take Sand Runner's orders?'

'His medicine not all bad,' replied the chief. 'It guided a young brave-heart into your bullet when the bullet would have taken Sand Runner.'

'So he knows about that,' growled the scout. 'A man who is a man does not blame a warrior for taking his chief's orders, even though they be bad orders.'

'My thanks, *Tshaoh*,' said the chief, gratitude plain in his voice. 'I am one called Bear Trailer. Someday I repay you. Now, for the matter of the soldier?'

'We must talk on it among the council. Tomorrow you will know.'

'It is well. I do not care for this way of Sand Runner's.'

'Why didn't he come, don't he speak English?'

'Speak it good enough. Medicine say him not come near white man. I go now.'

'That murdering red devil's not leaving!' yelled the man who spoke earlier to Muldoon and his cronies muttered their agreement. 'We aim to string——'

Which was as far as he got. Muldoon's huge right hand clamped on to the front of a greasy civilian shirt and jerked its wearer bodily forward.

'Now don't be a fool, darlin',' warned the sergeant. 'Sure, I'd hate to be seeing your blood spilled. *Look!*'

The man looked, gulped and turned pale. Facing him, the Ames knife looking twice as long as a cavalry sabre as it lined on his favourite belly, stood Beau Resin.

'The chief came here at my word,' the scout growled. 'He's leaving with honour and unharmed.'

'You're as bad as h——' began one of the sullen man's friends.

His stoppage came as something landed lightly on the toe of his boot. Looking down, he saw the thing to be the lash of Calamity's whip. The girl stood with legs braced apart, right arm holding the whip handle ready for use.

'Now all of you back off there,' she ordered. 'I aim to start practising whip-cracking right where you're standing.'

Being well-versed in political agitation, the sullen man knew better than ever place *himself* in a position of danger; and attempting to harm or impede the departure of the Cheyenne would be dangerous as hell. Turning, he slouched away and his gang followed him, being shepherded by a grim-eyed corporal who knew enough of Indians to respect them and did not intend any murder attempts to be made.

'You're free to go now,' Resin said. 'This soldier-coat chief

135

will take you through our picket line.'

'There is no need for them, Tshaoh,' grunted the chief. 'We do not attack you again.'

'May as well fetch the boys in then, Dave,' Resin suggested and it may be said that Grade took the chief at his word.

'When do we go?' asked Calamity.

And when her voice took on that note, no amount of arguing would move her. Knowing that, Resin did not even bother to try. Anyway, he reckoned Calamity could handle herself as well as any man on the train.

'We'll give him a couple of hours start,' he said. 'You, me 'n' Muldoon'll be about enough.'

'If Muldoon'll volunteer,' said Calamity, coiling her whip.

'I never volunteered for anything in me life, Calam,' Muldoon replied. 'So happen Mr. Grade don't order me to go, I'll order meself.'

On his return Grade gave permission for Muldoon to accompany the rescue party. Instantly preparations were made. Not plans; Resin, Muldoon and Calamity knew better than try to plan ahead when on such a dangerous and practically impossible mission. When they reached the Cheyenne camp area, they would play the cards as they fell, make any arrangement necessary on the spot and hope that whatever Deity they subscribed to looked with favour on their endeavours.

'Want to take my bowie knife, Calam?' Killem asked.

'I'd as soon tote along a camp-axe,' she replied with a grin.

Instead of the bowie, Calamity borrowed from the cook his highly-prized, seven-inch-bladed spear-pointed and razor-sharp Green River knife strapping its sheath on the left side of her belt. Being shorter and lighter, Calamity could handle the Green River better than the bowie and find it just as deadly for she knew something of knife-fighters even though she had never tried her hand at it seriously. Calamity figured she could handle the knife well enough for her needs.

'I'll use my Appaloosa, like a hoss I know I can trust,' Resin drawled. 'So go pick the three best hosses you've got Paddy.'

'Like me life depended on it,' replied Muldoon cheerfully. 'Which it does.'

Men moved fast, collecting and saddling the three horses selected as best by Muldoon. None of the party carried rifles, or anything but the bare essentials for they realised that an ounce saved on the horses' backs might mean the difference between life and death to them.

At last all was ready. Resin ordered everybody to act normally, not to come fussing around, just in case the Cheyenne had wolf-scouts watching the camp. The horses stood waiting in the darkness and the rescue party made their way to the waiting animals separately.

Eileen and Calamity walked together to the horses. Neither spoke until they arrived. With a catch in her voice, Eileen said:

'Good luck Calam.'

'We'll need it,' replied Calamity. 'Eileen, happen we don't make it back.'

'Yes?'

'Tell Molly I tried.'

137

CHAPTER THIRTEEN

MISS CANARY TAKES A WAGON RIDE

THEY rode through the darkness, two men and a girl who might not see the dawn of the following day. First Resin led them out of the camp in the opposite direction to the one they must take, swinging in a circle well beyond where any Cheyenne wolf-scouts might be hiding and watching the wagons. Guided by his plainsman's instinct, Resin brought his party on to the correct line and led them through the night in the direction of Sand Runner's hidden camp. None of the trio spoke much as they rode, for more than one reason. With the possibility of death in a painful manner close ahead of them, conversation did not come easily. Also all knew how sound carried on the still air of the night and of all sounds, none would be more likely to attract unwelcome Cheyenne attention than that of white folks' voices.

Holding their horses at an easy pace that retained a reserve of energy in case it should be needed, they rode on. Although Calamity and Muldoon kept their eyes open, neither saw any sign of the Cheyenne camp-fires, which surprised them for more than one Indian encampment had been betrayed by the red glow rising from it. Then, topping a rise and looking down towards the wooded area, they caught the glimpse of a faint red flicker among the trees. Whoever picked the location for the Cheyenne camp knew his business. A raiding party might have ridden by the area a dozen and more times without seeing the tree-masked fires.

On riding closer, they could hear voices raised in war chants. At last Resin raised his hand, bringing the others to a halt.

'This's as far as we take the hosses,' he said. 'Paddy, stay here and keep 'em quiet. Me n'n Calam'll go in on foot. If you hear us yell for you, come like a bat out of hell.'

'Huh huh!' grunted Muldoon and took an obvious precaution. 'Where at's their hoss herd?'

'With the camp, on the other side of that stream that runs through the wood and out beyond the trees. You'll have no trouble from them.'

Being gregarious beasts, horses were inclined to signal to any others of their kind that they located. A stray horse whinnying would be likely to attract the attention of the Cheyenne horse herd and one of Muldoon's duties was to make sure his horses did not sound an alarm.

'Good luck, the pair of yez.'

'Thanks, Paddy,' replied Calam, suddenly throwing her arms around his neck and kissing him. 'I'll tell you now, I never intended to marry you, so you didn't need to shy away from me like a rope-burned hoss all these weeks.'

'Me father told me never to take chances with women, and according to me troop, he stayed a bachelor all his life,' answered Muldoon, gripping Resin's hand after being released by Calamity. 'I'll be right here when you comes back.'

'We'll let you know, happen they get us,' promised Resin. 'See you around.'

Side by side Resin and the girl faded into the darkness, moving on silent feet. They entered the wood and moved through with all the care possible, although from the noise rising from the camp excessive caution might not be needed. At last Calamity and Resin reached the banks of the stream and moved along it.

'He's in a tipi just about here,' Resin said, halting by a tree on which he had carved a blaze in the bark and pointing straight towards the camp. 'Only it's on the inner circle, facing towards that danged council fire.'

'From the sound of that pow-wow there'll not be many folks missing from it,' Calamity replied. 'We could sneak through the camp, cut our way in the back——'

'And what if there's a guard in the tipi?'

'You got a right smart point there. Sand Runner got the full tribe along?'

'Only bucks and a handful of young gals to keep his boys happy.'

'Other tipis ought to be empty then. Or if anybody's being kept happy in 'em, they won't notice us tippy-toeing by. Or don't Injuns get kept happy same way we do?'

Resin's teeth glowed white in the darkness as he grinned at the girl. 'You got a low 'n' vulgar mind, Calam, gal.'

'I'm loving with it.'

'Happen we get out of this alive, gal,' the scout whispered, 'I'll——'

Whatever he aimed to do did not get said. They had waded through the stream while talking and both froze on the other shore as they saw a torch flickering in the hand of an approaching Indian. Swiftly and silently Calamity and Resin took cover, two hands holding knives; guns making far too much noise for dealing with such a situation.

The torch-bearer came into sight; a girl wearing Bigelow's campaign hat on her head, the braids of her hair trailing from under its crown, and with his blouse on over her doeskin dress, carrying a pinewood torch in one hand, a pitcher in the other. Clearly she was coming down to the stream to collect water. The sight of the girl's dress, particularly the hat and hair, gave Calamity an idea. Sheathing the knife, she turned to Resin and whispered :

'I'll take her.'

'Do it fast and quiet, these Injun gals are tough.'

While the girl might have been tough and capable of giving Calamity a hard and rowdy fight, she did not have the chance. There was no time to think of fair play or giving the other girl an even break. Calamity timed her move just right and watching it, Resin had to admit he could not have done better.

In dealing with the girl, Calamity used her head—literally. She hurled herself forward as the Indian approached, ramming her head in a vicious butt full into the pit of the other girl's stomach. So suddenly and unexpectedly did the attack come that the Indian could not scream or even think before Calamity's head caught her in the belly, dropping her in a doubled-over, winded heap, the hat flying from her head and the torch and pitcher falling from her hands as she went down. Calamity followed the girl down, digging fingers into her hair and flipping her on to her back, then dropping to kneel astride her. Drawing up the girl's head, Calamity brought around her other fist, driving it into the girl's jaw. One blow was all Calamity needed and the Indian girl went limp, then flopped to the ground. Seeing no further action would be needed, Calamity rose to her feet.

'What now?' breathed Resin, catching up the torch and tossing it into the water, then scuffing out the blazing ground it left.

'Got me a right fool notion,' Calamity answered, dragging the girl into a sitting position and starting to remove Bigelow's jacket.

'Such as?'

'How can we find out if there's a guard in Wade's tipi. I aim to go in and look; dressed like a squaw—this one.'

While he claimed that it took plenty to surprise him, Resin could not hold down his startled grunt.

'How'd you mean, gal?'

'Easy enough. I'm fixing to wear her clothes, walk around the side of the tipi and through its door. You be waiting out back and when I signal you'll know you can come in. Now turn your back while I undress her.'

'Spoilsport,' grinned the scout.

'Likely, only I hate competition, as Eileen would say.'

Calamity found little difficulty in undressing the other girl, for an Indian's doeskin dress was simply made and its wearer never bothered with underclothing. Dropping the naked, still unconscious body back to the ground, Calamity looked at the dress. A further thought came to her and she drew the Green River knife. Bending, she slashed off the girl's two hair braids over their fastenings. Then yet another thought came, the solution of which ought to please Resin.

'Cut the legs of my pants off over the knee,' she ordered. 'Move it. The squaw's stirring and we want her hawg-tied afore she wakes.'

Working fast, Resin slit Calamity's pants legs up the seams, then around the leg maybe a mite higher than was necessary. One could not blame him for that. However, he wasted no time in admiring the view, but turned to make a start at tying up their prisoner, using the trouser legs as rope and his own bandana as a gag.

'Sure hope she's not loused out with seam-squirrels like most Injuns,' Calamity stated as she drew the dress on over her clothes. 'And stop looking like you're enjoying your work, damn you.'

'Me, honey?' replied the scout, just as quietly as Calamity. 'Now do you reckon I'd enjoy hawg-tying a gal?'

'Likely,' Calamity sniffed, putting on Bigelow's jacket over the dress.

After slitting the dress to allow access to the knife or Colt, Calamity donned the campaign hat and thrust the two severed braids into position so they hung down from under it in a nearly natural manner.

'Legs are a mite pale,' Resin told her, having completed the securing of the Indian girl. 'Happen you keep to the shadows, it might work. You scared?'

'As hell.'

'And me. Let's go.'

Carrying the pitcher, Calamity headed towards the camp, Resin drifting on silent feet behind her. On entering the rough cluster of tipis which surrounded the open circle around the council fire, Calamity and Resin decided their guess had been correct, that all the camp were attending the pow-wow. At last they reached a buffalo-hide tipi on the very inner edge of the cluster and came to a halt.

'This's the one,' Resin breathed in Calamity's ear.

'I'll go 'round the front and in,' she replied no louder. 'Reckon boys and gals do in heaven, Beau?'

'Happen things go wrong, gal, we stand a fair chance of finding out. If you get there first, stay clear of them boy angels.'

'First gal angel looks two ways at you get's hand-scalped and wing-plucked,' Calamity warned and sucked in a deep breath. 'See you, Beau, one place or the other.'

Lifting the pitcher on to her shoulder so it hid her face, Calamity walked around the curve of the tent and into the fire light's glow. This was the moment of truth, the supreme testing time for her simple disguise. In seconds, Calamity would be into the tent—or well on the way to being dead.

Somehow, illogically, perhaps, Calamity did not expect to be detected. So far luck had gone their way. The finding of the camp; the capture of the girl; the fact that this was a raiding party and did not have married squaws, children or dogs that might not have been at the council fire and so could have seen the intruders and raised the alarm; all those things seemed to be good omens to Calamity. Even the very fact that Wade H. Bigelow still lived might point to destiny not wishing him to die yet awhile.

Yes; one way and another Calamity reckoned luck was on their side. Which, while comforting, did not make the long—it seemed hellish long to Calamity—walk around the side of the tipi and to its door through the fire-light any the shorter or more pleasant.

Her eyes flickered to the council fire and the Indians gathered around it. At any second one of them might turn and see her, but none did. Every Cheyenne eye stayed on the war-bonnet chief with the yellow-ochre-covered face and the Dragoon Colt in his waistband. Sand Runner stood addressing them, but Calamity did not know enough Cheyenne to understand his message to his assembled people.

The entrance to the tipi lay ahead, four strides, three, two—she was there! Now Calamity would really see how her luck was going. If there should be a guard in the tent, she must silence him before he could give any outcry. Lowering the pitcher, she slid the Green River knife from it and ducked into the tipi.

Clad in his shirt, pants and boots, Bigelow lay in the centre of the tipi. He was trussed like a fowl for cooking—no Indian ever gave a prisoner a chance to slide free of his bonds—and his face showed the suffering the tight cords caused him. But, and this was most important, he had the tipi to himself. Clearly the Cheyenne figured that he could not escape and so did not bother to guard him.

'Hold it down, Wade, boy!' Calamity breathed, crossing the tipi and kicking its rear side.

Much to his amazement, Bigelow saw a knife blade drive through the tipi side near where Calamity kicked, cutting downwards. Even before Resin made his entrance, Calamity was slashing Bigelow's bonds.

'Want a gag, Wade?' Resin asked. 'It'll hurt like hell when the blood starts flowing again.'

Weakly Bigelow shook his head. He might have been a damned fool to get into this mess in the first place, but he reckoned he could show courage. Within seconds of the circulation starting normal pumping Bigelow began to wish he had taken the gag. However, he gritted his teeth and held down the moans which welled in him. Calamity knelt by him, chafing his limbs, soothing him and whispering encouragement of a profane and uncomplimentary nature.

'We'll stay on a spell,' Resin told the other two, seeing Bigelow would be in no shape to travel anyway. 'Likely nobody'll bother you for a spell. They been at you yet?'

'No. Sand Runner's girl-friend helped herself to my hat and jacket, as you seem to know. The rest of my belongings are there. The war-bonnet chief who acted as Sand Runner's interpreter insisted they were left and returned with me. He and Sand Runner don't get on very well.'

'Bear Trailer's a Cheyenne of the old school, even if he's been to mission school,' Resin explained, moving to the door and cautiously peering out. 'He——'

'What is it——' Calamity breathed, moving to Resin's side and listening to Sand Runner's voice.

'He's asking where Fire-Rose is. That'll be the gal we caught. Calam, gal, it looks like old *Ka-Dih* done stopped siding us.'

Any moment now the search for the missing girl would begin. Once she was found, it was unlikely to take Sand Runner long to figure out why she had been caught and hog-tied.

'Get your gun, Wade,' Resin ordered and the captain crawled to where his weapon belt lay.

A yell went up from among the Cheyenne and one pointed off into the darkness. For a horrible, shocking moment Calamity and Resin thought that the Indian girl had escaped from her bonds. Then they realised that the man did not point in any direction from which the girl might be expected to come. Sick and sore as she was likely to be, the girl would have headed straight for the camp, not swung around in a half circle.

Hooves clattered, shod hooves as a clink of steel striking a rock told the listeners, harness leather creaked and wheels rumbled. The sound told a grim story to Calamity and Resin, range-wise in such matters. While an Indian might ride a stolen or captured shod horse until its shoes fell off, he would never bother to shoe one; once in a while the Indian might even use a white man's saddle; but he never troubled to harness a horse to a wagon.

So who came towards the Cheyenne's hidden camp in a wagon?

One thing was for sure. The visitor appeared to be expected, or at least friendly, for the Cheyenne showed no fear, only eager anticipation.

A two-horse, light wagon entered the camp, passing from the trees through the tipi circle, by where Calamity, Resin and Bigelow crouched watching and came to a halt just beyond the entrance to their hiding place. In passing, the wagon's driver gave Calamity's party a chance to study him. He was a tall, bulky, bearded man wearing buckskins and having the appearance of a hide-hunter. Yet he did not make his money shooting buffalo; such a man would never be welcomed into an Indian camp.

'Howdy, Sandy Runner,' the man greeted, standing up and lifting a small keg from the box at his side. 'Got you a fine selection of rifles, bullets, powder and lead.'

'A lousy renegade!' Bigelow hissed, fortunately being drowned out by the mumble of anticipation which rose from the watching Cheyenne.

Before the young officer could burst from the tent, Resin had caught him by the arm and held him.

'Not yet, Wade, happen you want to get back to Molly.'

Despite his professed disinclination to meet and speak with white people, Sand Runner rose and advanced to greet the renegade.

'They'd best be good rifles this time, Bernstein.'

'You got the money for them?'

'We'll have it tomorrow,' promised Sand Runner, speaking in good and remarkably accent-free English.

Fact being he appeared to handle the English language with greater facility than he spoke Cheyenne. At that moment everything became clear to Resin; the reason for Sand Runner's apparent un-Indian ways and mannerisms; his reluctance to meet white people; the repeated requests for money; all were now explained.

Sand Runner was a white man!

Maybe a deserter from the Army, fleeing from some real or imagined injustice; perhaps a criminal on the run from the law; perhaps; even an ideologist who regarded the Indians as down-trodden martyrs. Whatever the reason, in some way he had become adopted by the Cheyenne and risen to war chief by virtue of his fighting prowess and skill in the arts of killing the hated white brother.

Not that any of the watching trio wasted time in trying to

decide why a white man should turn against his own people in such a manner; being more concerned with thoughts of escape —if possible after destroying the wagon-load of firearms and ammunition.

Jumping from the wagon, the bearded man slouched towards the fire, carrying the keg in his arms.

'I'll see you made comfortable for the night,' Sand Runner told him. 'Got some cute lil gals. Hey, where in hell's Fire Rose?'

'Forget her and have a snort of redeye,' growled the renegade. 'I'll throw in the first barrel free, just to give your boys the taste.'

'Do that. And when they're good and likkered, I want to see my bank account book to make sure you paid in the last money I sent east.'

'It's in the wagon. I'll get it for you. Anybody'd think you didn't trust me, or something.'

'I don't. Come on, let's open the barrel.'

'This's our chance,' Resin hissed as the two men returned to the fire and opened the top of the keg. With the prospect of free whisky, none of the Indians were likely to take their eyes away from the liquor's owner and container.

'Let me go first,' Calamity suggested.

Before either of the men could confirm or deny the request, Calamity slipped from the tipi and to the rear of the wagon. The canopy at the rear had been lashed down, but the Green River knife made nothing of the securing ropes and she quickly lifted the cover to look inside. Despite having a pair of good, fast and powerful horses harnessed to it, the wagon did not carry a heavy load. Which did not entirely surprise Calamity. A man following the dishonourable business of trading whisky and guns to the Indians never loaded his wagon to the extent of slowing it down and rendering it incapable of outrunning pursuit.

Swinging up into the wagon, Calamity removed the hat, jacket and dress, then crept towards the box. Just as she expected, the bearded man's whip lay upon the seat and the reins curled around the canopy's forward support. A faint scuffling sound behind her heralded the arrival of Bigelow and he crept forward to the girl's side, crouching down by her, his eyes following the direction of her nod. Deftly he drew his Colt and checked it was still loaded and capped in four chambers. A couple of minutes dragged by before Resin saw his chance and ran to the wagon, climbing in and crouching by the other two.

'I'll slash the ribbons, grab them and the whip, and start this old wagon rolling,' Calamity suggested.

'Hold hard there, gal!' Resin whispered, moving back along the wagon and bending over the kegs. 'Let me find one with powder in it, then run us close by the fire.'

'Sure,' Calamity replied.

An inch at a time, moving slowly and cautiously, Calamity drew the whip into the wagon and shook it loose. While it weighed a mite heavier than her own, she reckoned she might be able to handle it with no trouble. Next she unfastened the reins and gripped them between the strong capable fingers of her left hand. Now Calamity was all set to do her part and just waited for the word.

Resin had found what he wanted, a twenty-five pound keg of gunpowder. Taking out his Ames knife, he tried to separate a couple of the keg's staves but the cooper who made it knew his business and they held firm. Which meant he had to drop it right on, or very close to the flames if he hoped to create the desired diversion. Still holding the knife, Resin hefted the keg in his hands and turned his head.

'Let her go, Calam!'

'YEEEAH!'

Letting out a screech near on loud enough to wake the dead, Calamity bounded on to the wagon box, swung the whip in an explosive pop over the head of the team and booted free the brake. Already restless, the high-spirited team horses lunged forward with a heave that jerked the wagon into motion like a cork plucked from a bottle.

Instantly pandemonium reigned around the camp fire. Few if any of the Cheyenne had other than knives with them at the pow-wow and even those who bore arms did not find a chance to use them in the confusion. Women screamed, clung to their men, or fled. Warriors bounded to their feet, cannoning into each other like so many pool balls and none knew for sure just what to do.

Bigelow added to the confusion by starting to throw lead with both hands. Not that he went in for any fancy aiming,

147

but merely sprayed into the brown in the direction of Sand Runner and the renegade. Once more the gods of war favoured the white folks, for a bullet from the Army Colt in Bigelow's right hand tore through the renegade's throat. Sand Runner's own luck held. A brave at his right went down with a Navy ball in his chest, the renegade fell at the other side, a bullet ripped a couple of eagle feathers from his hair, but he remained unharmed and Bigelow was carried by him on the rushing wagon.

A naked brave, knife in hand, sprang from a tipi followed by a screaming, naked girl. Howling his kill-or-die shout, the brave hurled himself forward, meaning to try to halt the wagon by knifing the nearer of the horses. He came on the side away from Bigelow and Calamity knew there would be no time to attract the captain's attention and change his target. Being a resourceful young woman, Calamity did not waste time. Back drew her whip hand, sending the lash flying forward. The borrowed whip had a different feel from her own, but she let fly just the same.

Although Calamity's aim proved to be a mite off, she could not argue against the results. Actually the Indian might have counted himself *real* lucky, for the whip curled around his knife wrist and snapped it like a rotten twig—instead of circling his neck and hauling him forward under the wagon's wheels.

With the menace handled, Calamity concentrated on driving the team. Already they had passed the fire and were headed for the darkness.

At the rear of the wagon Resin stood gripping the powder keg and his knife in between his hands. A Cheyenne brave sprang for and caught hold of the rear of the wagon, swinging himself up. Without releasing the keg, Resin brought up his foot and stamped on the red face, pitching the brave over backwards. Then, with a swing of his powerful arms, the big scout hurled the powder keg in the direction of the fire. However, the awkward manner in which he held keg and knife prevented him getting quite enough distance in his throw. The keg landed, bounced and rolled into the embers, but not on to the naked flames.

Just as Resin decided to speed the explosion by shooting into the keg, he saw a familiar figure. A yellow-ochre face twisted into a devil-mask of hatred glared at Resin and a hand raised an old Dragoon Colt. There was no time to draw a gun. Resin whipped back his hand, gripping the Ames knife for a throw. Down came the hand, fire-light glinted on flying steel and the knife sped at Sand Runner's body. If he had been less interested in trying to stop the wagon, Sand Runner might have avoided the throw. So intent was he on stopping the departure of the arms—and his bank-book, that he took a chance. Which was when his medicine ran out. The Ames knife drove down just over his waistbelt and sank almost hilt deep in his belly. Even so, he triggered off one shot that fanned wind by Resin's ear in passing on through the top of the wagon's canopy. He doubled over, clutching the knife to jerk it from his body and hurl it aside. Turning, he staggered blindly towards the council fire.

Then the powder keg blew!

With a roar like thunder and a sheet of flame that lit up the night and was seen at the distant wagon train, the keg, heated by the fire, exploded. It threw flaming wood into the air as the fire shattered, and pitched Indians off their feet by the blast. The wagon's team hit their harness so hard in their panic to get away from the noise that they lifted its wheels from the ground and almost threw the three occupants out; then, man, did those two horses run, tearing through the wood like the devil after a yearling. Nor were they the only horses to run. The Cheyenne remuda came from sleeping to terrified wakefulness and the herd boys had no more chance of stopping the wild stampede than they would have had of stopping water flowing downhill. One thing was for sure, there would be no Indian pursuit that night.

Muldoon heard the explosion and fought to restrain his panic-stricken horses, but could only hold the Appaloosa and one more. Curses spluttered from his lips as the other animals raced away. With old cavalry skill, he brought the two remaining horses under control.

'Muldoon!' roared a voice. 'This way, as fast as you can come.'

Leaping afork his horse, and leading the Appaloosa, Muldoon galloped into the night, heading for the distant sound of a wagon travelling at speed. He did not even start to imagine how Resin and Calamity came to be using a wagon, reckoned he might learn soon enough.

Calamity would never know for sure how she managed to steer the fear-crazed horses through the wood. Yet she did so. They crashed through the stream, flattened a few bushes, scraped a tree or two, then were out on the open range.

'I got the renegade,' Bigelow announced with some satisfaction as Calamity brought the team under control.

'And I got Sand Runner, me'n' the explosion between us,' Resin said.

'You sound a mite sad, Beau,' Calamity remarked.

'Am a mite, gal. I'll never be able to replace that old Ames knife.'

'I've just thought,' Bigelow went on, his voice flat and emotionless. 'I will have to face a court of inquiry to explain how the hell I was captured.'

CHAPTER FOURTEEN

MISS CANARY IS A WITNESS

'WADE!' Never would Calamity forget the sound of Molly's voice as the wagon came to a halt outside the circle in the early light of the dawn. Nor the sight of the sedate, modest little schoolteacher springing from her uncle's Conestoga and running forward clad only in a flimsy nightdress which did not conceal as well as the more conventional flannel bedwear what lay underneath.

The explosion had woken the camp and people peered from their wagons, then started to climb out and make their way towards Calamity's party. Molly, oblivious of everything except that her beloved Wade had come back to her, flung her arms around the captain's neck and kissed him. Nobody could blame Bigelow for grabbing a good double armful of his sweetheart and kissing her back.

'All right, folks,' Calamity snapped as people began to gather and stare at the lovers. 'Let's get back to our wagons, shall we?'

Her orders received backing from Resin and Muldoon, both of whom could turn a blistering phrase when needed and were used to enforcing their will on other folk. While the men held back the crowd, Calamity managed to separate the lovers and haze Molly back to the wagon with orders to get dressed afore she started every man on the train going love-sick.

Not until some time later did Calamity remember her own appearance. She had headed for Killem's fire and noticed the way the men glanced down at her feet, as she thought, and grinned broadly.

'As a fashion I can't see it ever catching on,' said Eileen's voice from the wagon.

'Huh?' Calamity grunted.

151

'The new style pants.'

Looking down, Calamity realised that she still wore the leg-less levis and for once in her life felt embarrassed. With an angry, squealing blanket curse at the grinning men, she dashed to the wagon and changed into a more conventional—-Calamity's own convention, that is—pair of pants.

Over breakfast Resin told the wagonmaster, Killem and Grade what had happened at the Cheyenne camp.

'Get your boys out to take a good look 'round,' the scout suggested. 'It's my reckoning that the explosion stampeded the Cheyenne remuda to hell and gone and they'll not get enough hosses back to come and try to re-take the arms wagon.'

'Probably,' Grade agreed. 'You know, Beau, the colonel at Sherrard's not going to look too hard at why Wade got himself captured when he hears what you've accomplished between you.'

'That's likely,' agreed Resin. 'Happen Sand Runner had come through with all these arms, he could have set this whole damned territory on fire.'

'And he was a white man.'

'Yep.'

'I'd like to take a look through that book he mentioned,' Grade said.

'Wade's got it, though how in hell he expects to find time to read it and convince Molly he's all right, I'll never know.'

Scouts went out and made a thorough search of the area, seeing no sign of the Cheyenne. So the wagon train resumed its journey at the usual hour, carrying on westwards. Eileen sat on the box of Calamity's wagon, handling the ribbons and allowing the red-head to catch some sleep. With the well-trained team, Eileen found no difficulty in keeping the wagon moving over the gently rolling, open plains through which they travelled.

Along towards noon there came an interruption to the journey.

A shot roared out from behind a rim and Bear Trailer, the interpreting war-bonnet chief rode into sight, his rifle held in peace fashion. Leaving the wagon where he had been sleeping, Resin borrowed a horse and rode to meet the advancing chief, wondering what had brought the other to the train.

'Damned Comanche!' grunted the chief, a twinkle in his

eyes that belied his expressionless face. 'You plenty spoiled Sand Runner's medicine this time.'

'You found him then?'

'All over the camp.'

Neither man spoke for a time, but sat facing each other; hereditary enemies from the days when the white men first began his abuses against the Indian yet each capable of admiring the other as a fighter and a man.

'Didn't hurt you, did we?' asked Resin.

'A few bruises, nothing more,' answered the chief and reached behind him to pull something from his waistbelt. 'Reckon maybe you'd want this.'

For once in his life the taciturn, unemotional scout almost let out a whoop of joy as he stared at the object in Bear Trailer's hand. Only a thousand Ames knives had been made and were issued to the 3rd Cavalry back in the days when they went under the name of the Regiment of Mounted Riflemen, Resin had obtained his from a dead trooper at the Battle of Shilo during the War Between the States, taken a fancy to its heft and balance and retained it. One grew used to a good knife and Resin thought his Ames to be gone for ever and irreplaceable as the company no longer existed. Yet there the knife lay, in Bear Trailer's hand, its hilt pointing towards him.

'You treated me with honour, *Tshaoh*,' the chief said. 'I bring your knife.'

'My thanks, Bear Trailer,' said the scout, taking and sheathing the knife. 'What do you do now?'

'Go back to our people. The men have no wish for war and we must think of the future. Goodbye, *Tshaoh*, one called Bear Trailer will not forget you.'

'Ride warily, brother,' Resin answered and took out his filled tobacco pouch. 'May the smoke remind you of me.'

With that the two men parted. Maybe the next time they met one or the other would die, but that did not mean they would ever lose their respect for a bold, noble, fighting man.

Although Bigelow listened to Grade and Eileen telling him he had nothing to fear, each mile he came nearer to Fort Sherrard the more he thought of the court of inquiry he must face. It was all very well for Grade and Eileen to say the colonel would overlook his capture and think only of the death of the renegade, recovery of arms and ending of a major raiding party of hostile Cheyenne. Neither of them gave a thought to the fact that Bigelow belonged to the Quartermaster Corps and had hoped to obtain a transfer to the cavalry regiment at Sherrard. No colonel would willingly take an officer stupid enough to let himself be captured by the Indians.

Then one day the fort came into sight. A cavalry escort had come out the previous day and a rider returned with Bigelow's full report. It also took a letter from Eileen to her husband and a second from the young lady to the colonel. The results of Eileen's letters showed when the train pulled in at just before noon.

'Captain Bigelow?' said the officer of the day. 'The colonel presents his compliments, and asks you to dine with him. The court of inquiry into your report will be held at three o'clock.'

'Well, Molly,' Bigelow said, taking the girl's hands in his. 'We'll know by four whether your husband is still in employment or not.'

'You won't be my husband until five,' she replied. 'And I don't care which way things go, as long as we're together.'

'We'll be that. Here's Eileen and her husband now.'

Captain Tradle, tall, handsome and more masterful than Eileen could ever remember, exchanged salutes with Bigelow and grinned. 'You're a blasted nuisance, Wade, why didn't you hold back your report for a few days, Eileen and I were going —deer-hunting—for a three-day pass and now we've got to wait until after the court of inquiry. Congratulations, we've been after that renegade for some time now, and expecting Sand Runner to blow the whole territory apart and you've nailed them both. Come on, we're all invited to dine with the colonel and his wife looks disapproving if her guests don't arrive promptly.'

'Is Calamity coming?' Molly asked Eileen as they walked off together.

'She excused herself,' Eileen explained. 'Said she was so damned scared at having to go witness at the court of inquiry that she daren't come.'

For a scared girl Calamity looked mighty cool, calm and collected as she sat at the long table and faced the board of officers assigned to investigate Bigelow's report. There was none of the awe-inspiring ceremonial seriousness of a court martial, the officers did not wear their best parade dress but sat in their working clothes, and the evidence was not given on oath. Anyhow, Calamity had never been a girl unduly worried by atmosphere. So she gave her evidence in a clear voice that bore the ring of pure, driven truth.

'So you say that *you* and Miss Johnson went for a joy-ride while the men skinned out and dressed the buffalo,' said the major in command after hearing the girl's 'truthful' account of the incident, 'and that Captain Bigelow came after you, then sacrificed himself to prevent the Cheyenne finding you.'

'Yep!' she replied, meeting his eye without flinching.

'That is not what Captain Bigelow told us.'

'Likely. He's an officer and a gentleman, so wouldn't want to show a couple of gals as having made a damned fool mistake. Nor would any of you!'

Grins flickered on to at least three faces and Captain Tradle went so far as to give Calamity a quick wink. However, one of the board of officers had to be a green young shavetail second-lieutenant on his first court of inquiry and full of remembrance of lectures on court procedure received at West Point. Being more inclined than the others to treat the matter seriously—after all, they were *cavalry* officers dealing with a mere shiny-butt—he did not smile.

'Would Miss Canary give the same evidence under oath?' he asked.

Grins died away and frowns took their place, promising extra officer-of-the-day and other onerous duties in the near future.

'There is no need to go into extremes, Mr. Bolroyd,' the major growled. 'I accept Miss Canary's st—evidence.'

Even a green shavetail with the mud of West Point hardly worn from his boots knew better than argue with a major, especially one holding the brevet rank of brigadier-general and next in line for command of their mutual regiment.

'Yes, sir,' Bolroyd said.

Taking up Bigelow's report in one hand, the major extracted a pipe from his blouse, thrust its stem into his mouth and produced a match which he lit on his trousers seat.

'Our friend Sand Runner appears to have made a fair profit over the past two years, according to his bank-book, but it gives no clue to his real identity. I think we will leave the disposal of his ill-gotten gains to the Adjutant-General's department.'

While speaking, the major accidentally allowed the light of his match to come into contact with Bigelow's neatly-written report. Even as the paper took fire, Tradle threw over his chair and came to his feet. First he rammed his elbow hard into the eager young Bolroyd's ribs and staggered the young gentleman to one side; then, to make further sure of the safety of the report, grabbed at and knocked over the water jug.

'That *was* clumsy of me,' said Captain Tradle. 'I'm afraid your report's gone, Wade.'

'The moral of which, gentlemen,' the major went on, 'is never smoke on duty. Now, I think we can say that no further action need be taken against Captain Bigelow and that he acted in the finest traditions of the U.S. Cavalry. I would also suggest that when he re-submits his report, he keeps it to matters of military interest, such as the death of the renegade and Sand Runner, the capture of the arms wagon and the disbanding of the Cheyenne war band. Anything else smacks of self-advertisement and I object to any officer assigned or transferred to my command acting in such a manner.' He paused and ground the ashes of the report to powder under his thumb, then took out his watch. 'Gentlemen, the time is four o'clock and I have it on good authority that my wife and Mrs. Tradle plan to give us all hell if we make Captain Bigelow's wedding start late. Dismissed.'

Outside the building used for the court Bigelow left his fellow officers and walked up to Calamity.

'Calam,' he said. 'I've never kissed a bare-faced liar before. But I aim to right now.'

'Then get to kissing afore either Beau or Molly gets here,' Calamity challenged, and much to her surprise he scooped her in his arms and gave her a kiss.

'Now get the hell to the colonel's house. Molly's got a surprise for you,' Bigelow ordered when he released the girl.

Which proved to be one hell of an understatement as Calamity discovered on entering an upstairs room of the colonel's house. She found herself surrounded by Molly, Eileen, Russian Olga and Mrs. Bloom and something told her she was not going to like what they had in mind. Her eyes went to a white dress lying on the bed, it looked a mite too large for M——

'Oh no!' Calamity yelped.

'Oh yes,' Eileen replied, rolling up her sleeves in a determined manner. 'We've decided you're going to be a bridesmaid. Do you put on the dress, or do *we* do it the hard way?'

Seeing the grim determination on each face, Calamity had the good sense to yell 'calf rope.' So it came about that, looking all sweet, innocent and virginal in a white gown, Calamity joined Eileen as bridesmaid and matron-of-honour at the wedding of Miss Molly Amelia Johnson and Captain Wade H. Bigelow, recently, very recently, transferred to the 6th U.S. Cavalry. If anybody noticed that a pair of Indian moccasins hid under Calamity's gown, they did not mention the fact. There were some sacrifices Calamity refused to make.

Being its first ever wedding, Fort Sherrard set out to celebrate it in style and make sure it be an event never forgotten. There was entertainment, dancing, all the liquor anybody, even the mighty Muldoon, could handle and a good time was had by all. However, the bride and groom disappeared before midnight—and who can blame them. Roughly at the same time Captain and Mrs. Tradle left to start a three-day deer-hunting trip based on the cabin which would be their home while at Sherrard. Two other noticeable absentees being a lady freighter called Martha Jane Canary and a bone-tough plains scout by name Beauregard Chesley Ryan Resin.

At nine o'clock the following morning Mrs. Tradle, Mrs. Bigelow and Miss Canary gathered in Eileen's new home's dining-room for breakfast.

'It was wonderful,' Molly breathed, sinking into a chair with a blissful sigh.

'It sure was,' agreed Eileen, dreamy-eyed at the thought of two more days of—deer-hunting.

'Yep,' Calamity finished. 'If the good Lord made men for anything better, he kept it to himself. Not that *I'd* know about it, of course.'

'Of course,' chorused the other two. Then Eileen went on, 'How about you and Beau?'

'His train goes on to California, they can't spare him, and Dobe's outfit's headed east, which same he needs me to handle my wagon.'

Calamity's friends thought they detected a wistful note in

her voice and felt a married woman's superior pity for an unmarried friend. Before they could start to express their thoughts, a knock came at the door and Eileen opened it to admit Dobe Killem. The big freighter held a sheet of paper and his face bore a wide grin.

'Rider just come in from Connel, Calam, gal,' he said, after greeting the assembled ladies. 'The Army's done give us a contract to go back to St. Jo and down river to New Orleans to collect 'em a bunch of hosses.'

'New Orleans!' whooped Calamity. 'When do we start?'

'So much for our concern over the poor girl losing her man,' sighed Molly.

From outside came the rumbling of a wagon, then others as the train started once more on its way west. Calamity did not offer to rise and walk to the window to see them go. Sure they had been her friends, maybe Beau had been a mite more than a friend. Likely she and the big scout might never meet again. Neither of them went much for saying goodbye and had parted that morning knowing their paths could cross again or not, depending on fate.

Already Calamity was thinking of the old French city of New Orleans, she had never been to such a fancy place and wondered what it held in store for her. That was ever Calamity's way. Never live in the past. Yesterday was gone forever, only tomorrow lay ahead and who knew what tomorrow would bring?

At the head of the train Beau Resin thought of Calamity and grinned. Now there was a gal to remember. He sure hoped old *Ka-Dih* would fix it so their paths crossed again some time while both were young and lusty enough to enjoy it. Slouching easily in his saddle, he listened to the voices of the train's children lifted in a mighty appropriate song.

> '*Calamity, Calamity,*
> *The best danged gal you ever did see,*
> *There'll never be, there'll never be,*
> *Another gal like Calamity.*'

The Cow Thieves

Author's note:

The term 'rustler' did not come into use until long after the period the story is set in. Even to this day in Texas, people prefer a blunter and more accurate term than 'rustler' – they say 'cow thief.'

CHAPTER ONE

BAT GOOCH'S MISTAKE

THERE were many types of marks by which the ranchers of the old west established ownership of their cattle, ranging from straightforward initial or number brands to John Chisum's Long Rail, a line burned along the animal's side from rump to shoulder.

A box brand had a square outline around letters or numbers; a connected brand meant that one of the letters in it touched the other; barbed brands carried a short projection from some part of them; a bench brand stood on a horizontal bracket with legs extending downwards like a bench; a drag brand carried lines sticking downwards from its bottom; should a brand have a small extension from each side it was said to be 'flying'; a letter suspended from or connected to a quarter circle bore the title 'swinging'; a tumbling brand meant that its letters leaned over at an oblique angle; a walking brand bore twin small extensions like feet at its lower extremities; a rafter brand sheltered under an inverted V-shape; a forked brand carried a small V-shaped prong on one of its sides; a running brand meant that flowing lines trailed from it; a bradded brand had a large termini; a collection of wings without a central figure bore the title 'whangdoodle.' *Haciendéros* below the Rio Grande used such large and complicated brands that a man might read them by moonlight, but could make no sense of them. The Texas cowhands called such brands 'maps of Mexico,' 'skillets of snakes,' 'greaser madhouses' and other less complimentary names.

A red-hot branding iron alone served the purpose of applying such a mark of ownership to a man's stock. This consisted of a three-foot-long iron rod with a handle at one end and a reversed facsimile of the outfit's chosen brand at the other. Such a

5

branding iron, when heated correctly and applied to the animal's hide, left a plain, easily read sign by which all men knew who owned the critter bearing it.

While riding the range on their lawful occasions cowhands often toted along one of their outfit's branding irons so as to be able to catch, tie down and mark any unclaimed stock they came across. It might be a grown animal overlooked in earlier roundups, or a new-born, late-dropped calf running at its mother's side. Either way the application of the outfit's brand set the seal of ownership upon the animal and added more potential wealth to the cowhand's ranch. So a cowhand who carried his outfit's iron was regarded as being a good worker, industrious and a man to be most highly commended.

But when a rider carried a rod without a stamp-head upon it, man, that was some different. Known as a running iron, such a rod could be used to change the shape of a brand, or for 'venting,' running a line through the original mark so as to nullify it, then trace another brand upon the animal—done legally this was known as counter-branding and was used when a critter be wrongly branded or sold after receiving its owner's mark. So a man carrying a running iron was not thought of as being praiseworthy or commendable. Folks called him a cow thief.

For almost six months past the range country around Caspar County, Texas, had been plagued by cow thieves. Stock disappeared in numbers that were too great to be put down to inclement weather or the depredations of cougar, wolf or bear; besides, not even the great Texas grizzly ate the bones of its kills and no sign of animal kills led the ranchers to blame *Ursus Texensis Texensis* for their losses. No sir, a human agency lay behind the disappearances and the ranchers decided it to be long gone time that something was done. A man who worked damned hard, faced hunger, danger, gave his blood and sweat to raise himself above his fellows, and took the responsibility of ownership and development instead of being content to draw another's wages did not take kindly to having his property stolen from him. So the ranchers decided to strike back.

Of course there were ways and ways of striking back. Vic Crither's hiring of Bat Gooch struck most folks as going maybe a mite too far, even against cow thieves. Few bounty hunters ever achieved a higher social standing than Digger Indians and

6

the Digger was reckoned as being the lowest of the low. Bat Gooch had a name for being worse than most of the men who hunted down fellow humans for the price their hide carried. For all that, Bat Gooch came to Caspar, called in by the mysterious, but highly effective prairie telegraph. Crither let it be known that Gooch would receive a flat wage for prowling the Forked C's range and a bonus of two hundred dollars each time he brought in a proven rustler—alive or dead.

The threat appeared to be working, for Gooch had ridden the ranges of the Forked C each night during the past fortnight without finding any sign of the cow thieves who preyed on the other ranches. While Vic Crither felt highly pleased with his strategy, the same could not be said for Gooch. So far his trip did not meet with his idea of the fitness of things. The potent quality of Gooch's name appeared to have scared the cow thieves from Forked C and not a single two hundred dollar bounty had so far come his way.

Being a man who liked money and all the good things it brought. Gooch decided, although he had never heard of the term, that if the mountain would not come to the prophet, then he would danged well go right out and find it for himself.

So it came about that on a clear, moonlit night Bat Gooch left the Forked C range and rode into the Bench J's domain. There was something about Gooch which warned of his chosen field of endeavour; a hint of cruelty and evil about his dark face and strangely pale eyes; the perpetual sneer on his lips, that silent way of moving, all hinted at something sinister. He wore dark clothing of cowhand style and Indian moccasins on his feet. In his saddleboot rode a Sharps Old Reliable buffalo rifle with a telescopic sight, but no bison had ever tumbled before its bullets. An Army Colt hung at his right side, a sheathed bowie knife on the left of his belt. Men had died through each of his weapons. In many ways Gooch was a man ideally suited to his work. He could move in silence through the thickest bush; shot well and possessed that rarest ability of being able to squeeze the trigger and kill another human being without a single hesitative thought. In addition to keen eyesight and excellent hearing, Gooch possessed a nose as sharp as a hound dog's.

On this occasion it was the nose which served him first. For four hours he had been prowling the Bench J land, eyes and

7

ears alert for any sound that might guide him to a cow thief engaged in illegal operations. Once found, the cow thief would die and be taken on to the Forked C's range where his body commanded a price of two hundred dollars. Yet, though he searched with care and used a considerable knowledge of the working of cow thieves to direct him, Gooch found no sign during the first four hours.

Then it happened!

The wind carried a scent to him. Not the pleasant aroma of jasmine or roses, but one just as sweet to Gooch's keen nostrils. Raw, acrid and unmistakable it came, the stench of singed hair and burning cow hide as a branding iron seared its irremovable mark on to an animal. Yet no sound followed the stench. No sudden bleat of pain such as one heard when a brand as applied in normal circumstances. Not that folks branded cattle by night under normal circumstances—especially on a range troubled by cow thieves.

Two things were plain to Gooch: first, from the stench of burnt hide somebody had just branded an animal upwind of him; second, the fact that the branders worked at night and took the trouble to muffle the branded critter's head and stop its bellow of pain told that they had good reason for not wishing to attract attention to themselves. Add one and two together, and the answer came out as a chance of picking up at least two hundred fine old U.S. dollars over and above Gooch's regular wages.

Keeping his big, wild-looking dark roan horse to an easy walk, its hooves hardly making a sound in the hock deep grass, Gooch rode up wind like a blue-tick hound going in on a breast-scent instead of running the line by the smell on the ground. Faint sounds came to his ears, then he saw a small glow of light flickering through the bushes and down a slope ahead of him. Once again his nostrils detected the smell of burning flesh and he brought his horse to a halt. Swinging from the saddle, he moved forward on foot. The big horse followed on his heels, stepping with all the silent caution of a whitetail deer in hard-hunted country. Give Gooch his due, he could train a horse and the roan ideally suited his purposes. Moving silently through the bushes, man and horse came into sight of a scene which did Gooch's money-hungry heart good to see.

At the foot of a small hollow six hundred dollars worth of cow thieves worked at their trade. The ground at the bottom of the small basin was clear of bushes, although its sides and the range around was liberally dotted with them and offered good cover which hid the light of the fire from all but the closest inspection. If Gooch had not caught the tell-tale smell of burning hide, he might have ridden right by the place without noticing anything. Instead he looked down at the three shapes around the fire. All wore cowhand clothes, although Gooch could only see two faces, the other having a wide-brimmed hat that effectively shielded the features. The two Gooch could see, he identified as young cowhands who worked for the Bench J; a brace of cheery, happy-go-lucky youngsters typical of hundreds across the length and breadth of the Texas range country. Although both of them wore holstered Colts, Gooch did not figure them as dangerous with the weapons—even if he aimed to give them a chance to fight. The third figure was smaller, not more than five seven, and slim under the wolf-skin jacket. Gooch studied all three noticing first that the slim, boyish third member of the party did not appear to be wearing a gunbelt.

Bending, the third figure thrust a running iron into the flames of the fire where a second iron lay heating. One of the other pair released a freshly branded calf and stripped the slicker from around its head.

'Go get another,' said the third cow thief, nodding to where half-a-dozen calves stood hobbled.

Excitement appeared to be affecting that one, making his voice almost as high pitched as a soprano woman's. Gooch gave little thought to the voice, being more concerned with deciding what course of action to take and which of his armament best suited his purpose. The single-shot Sharps would not serve, nor the bowie, so he must handle things with his Colt. At that range, with his targets illuminated by a fire, he figured to be able to down all three. If he knew them, they would panic when the first one went down, giving him a chance to tumble the other two before they could make for the trio of horses standing at the far side of the clearing. He reached down a big right hand, drawing the 1860 Army Colt from its holster.

'I don't like this,' the taller of the trio stated, standing with his back to Gooch—although he did not know of the bounty hunter's presence.

'Nor me,' the second cowhand went on. 'Buck Jerome's been a good boss.'

'Shucks, he'll not miss a few head, and anyways you know you can slap a brand on any unbranded critter you see,' the third member of the party answered.

'Sure,' agreed the second rider. 'Only this bunch were with Bench J cows.'

'So?' snorted the third cow thief. 'That doesn't mean they had Bench J mammies. And anyways, how'll you and Dora ever save en——'

The words ended unsaid as flame spurted from the darkness of the bush-dotted slopes around the basin. Caught in the middle of the back by a .44 calibre soft lead round ball—so much more deadly in impact and effect than a conical bullet— the tallest member of the trio pitched forward and just missed the fire as he fell. Just as Gooch figured, the second cowhand showed shocked indecision for an instant before trying to turn and draw his gun. By that time Gooch had cocked the Colt on its recoil and, before the young cowhand completed his turn or made his fumbling draw, fired again. Lead ripped into the cowhand's head, dropping him in a lifeless heap on the ground, his gun still in leather.

At which point Gooch saw that his plan had partially gone wrong. Instead of being in a state of panic, the third member of the party acted with speed and a show of planned thought. Spinning around, the figure left the fire and sped towards the horses in a fast, swerving run. Twice Gooch's Colt roared, but his bullets missed their mark. With a bound, the escaping cow thief went afork one of the horses. Range trained, the horse had been standing untied, its reins dangling before it. Scooping up the reins, the cow thief set the horse running, crashed it through the surrounding bushes like they were not there.

Still holding his Colt, Gooch turned and vaulted into his saddle. Knowing its work, the roan leapt forward, racing down the slope and across the open ground. A glance in passing told Gooch that he had earned four hundred dollars and that if not already dead the two cowhands soon would be. Knowing he could safely leave them where they lay, and find them there on his return, Gooch gave his full attention to riding down the last member of the trio.

Through the bushes and out on to the open range tore the horses, one ridden by a cow thief with the fear of death, the other carrying the same death in human form, wearing range clothes instead of a night-shirt and toting a .44 Army Colt in place of the more conventional scythe. For almost half a mile Gooch chased the cow thief, his roan closing the gap with every raking stride, although the other's mount was not exactly slow. While the bounty hunter held his Colt, he did not attempt to shoot. Gooch knew the folly of trying to shoot from the back of a running horse, at least over anything but short range. Sure, he had two loaded chambers left, but recharging a percussion-fired revolver could not be done from the back of a racing horse, and he had no wish to approach the other when holding an empty gun. So he aimed to get closer in and cut loose from a range where he could not miss; or if the worst came to the worst, take the fleeing rider from the ground and using his heavy calibre rifle.

Once the fleeing cow thief twisted in the saddle and looked back, gauging the distance between them and guessing there was no chance of out-running that big roan. Turning to the front again, the rider reached up with a hand to open the jacket and do something else that Gooch could not see. The bounty hunter grunted, not unduly worried, for he knew shooting backwards from a galloping horse to be, if anything, even less accurate than firing in a forward direction. However, a man did not care to take chances on catching a stray bullet; he could be killed just as long, permanently, dead by a blind-lucky shot as through one taken after careful and deliberate aim.

Before the bounty hunter could make his move, either to start using the Colt or stop the roan, dismount and make use of his Sharps, he saw what appeared to be a stroke of bad luck take the fleeing rider. Ahead of the cow thief stood a noble old cottonwood; the spreading branches of which no stealer of cattle ought to look on without a shudder and thinking of the hairy touch of a Manila rope around the neck. However, the rider appeared to be mighty insensitive to atmosphere, for the horse's course took it under the low, wide spread branches of the tree.

Suddenly the cow thief jerked backwards, apparently struck

by a branch, and slid over the horse's rump to crash to the ground. Gooch brought his roan to a halt, gun held ready for use as he studied the shape on the ground. Swinging from his saddle, Gooch advanced and the shape moved slowly, rolling on to its back. Gooch's Colt had lined at the first movement, its hammer drawn back ready and his forefinger on the trigger. Before he could send lead crashing into the near-helpless shape, he saw something that made him hold his fire and brought a broader sneer than usual to his lips.

In falling the cow thief's hat had gone from his head and the shirt under the thrown-open jacket appeared to have been torn apart to expose the flesh below. The first thing Gooch noticed was long hair trailing around the head. Hair far longer than even Wild Bill Hickok sported, and framing a beautiful, most unmasculine face. Next the bounty hunter's eyes strayed downwards, to the open shirt and what it exposed. Apparently the cow thief did not go in for wearing underclothing and what Gooch could see rising from the open shirt most certainly did not belong to any man.

Holstering his gun, Gooch walked forward and drank in the sight of those round, full and naked female breasts. Never a pleasant sight, his evil face looked even more so as he advanced on the moaning, agony-moving figure. While watching the trio by the fire Gooch had been aware that this third member of the party appeared to be the boss. Maybe she was the boss rustler of the area. Stranger things had happened and from what Gooch had seen of her in Caspar, she had the brains to be the big augur and nobody would ever suspect her. Only now she had been caught in the act and would bring in at least two hundred dollars same as the other two—dead.

Only before she died, Gooch figured he might as well pleasure himself a mite. He had a keen eye for a beautiful face and good figure; and, man, that gal on the ground afore him possessed both. Once dead, which she would be as soon as he finished his fun, the girl could not tell any tales of what happened before she met her end.

'Gal,' he said, dropping to his knees besides her and reaching down towards the open shirt front, 'if you enjoy it, you'll sure die hap——'

Which same concluded his speech, although he had not

entirely finished it. Suddenly the girl jerked her right hand into sight, it having been hidden under her jacket, a Remington Double Derringer gripped firmly in her fingers. Taken completely by surprise, Gooch looked death in the face. Shocked horror crossed his features and wiped the leering lust from them. Even as he tried to force his brain into positive, cohesive thought, to lurch erect, grab out his Colt, try to knock aside the wicked, deadly .41 calibre hideout gun, do anything at all to save his life, the sands of time ran out for Bat Gooch.

The Derringer spat once, its bullet taking Gooch just under the breast bone and ranging upwards. While the Double Derringer's three-inch barrels, comparatively weak powder charge and large calibre bullet did not have great carrying or penetrative powers over a range of thirty yards. Gooch was well within its killing area. A tearing, numbing agony ripped through Gooch, stopping his hand even before it could claw out his gun. Again the Derringer roared, its second bullet slicing into Gooch's body. Rearing to his feet, Gooch stood for a moment and then tumbled over backwards.

Coming to her feet, the woman reloaded the Double Derringer and dropped it into her jacket pocket. Without a glance at the dying man, she buttoned her shirt and closed the jacket over it.

'I figured you'd fall for that, you lousy murdering skunk,' she remarked, picking up and putting on her hat.

Her horse had come to a halt a short distance away and she walked to it. Taking the reins, she set a foot into the stirrup iron and swung gracefully into her saddle. Ignoring Gooch as if he did not exist—and he no longer did except as a lump of lifeless flesh—the woman rode back in the direction from which she fled.

Back at the hollow, the woman showed no more interest in the two dead cowhands than she had for Gooch's welfare. Swinging from the saddle, she stood for a moment and thought out the situation. First those half-a-dozen calves must be released. It was a pity they had only branded three of the animals. Alone she could not handle the branding of the others. Besides somebody might have heard the shooting and even now be riding to investigate. Shots in the dark on the Caspar County range would attract more attention under the prevailing conditions than normally and she had no wish to be caught. Being a smart woman, she did not regard the ranchers as fools, or figure they could not think things out. Maybe they might not be able to prove anything against her, but they sure would be suspicious to see *her* of all people riding the range at night and dressed in man's clothing. She would be watched too carefully in future to carry on with this profitable side-line to her normal business and that was the last thing she wanted.

Taking up a knife one of the cowhands had tossed into the dirt so as to be handy for hurried freeing of the calves, the woman walked forward and released the unbranded animals. As she expected, they wasted no time in heading off through the bushes, blatting loudly and looking for their mothers. She collected the two dead cowhands' ropes and with her own secured the three branded calves to her saddlehorn. After cutting the calves' hobbles, she mounted the horse.

'Hard luck, boys,' she said, throwing a glance at the two shapes by the dying fire. 'That's life for you.'

And with no more sentiment than that, the woman rode away, leading the three calves behind her. She left behind two dead cowhands—and two running irons.

CHAPTER TWO

SHE'S A MIGHTY SMART WOMAN

STANTON HOWARD, Governor of the State of Texas, was a busy man who could quite well have done without the cow thief problem of Caspar County being dumped in his lap. Brought in after the Texans' forcible ejection of Carpetbag Davis' corrupt, vicious Reconstruction administration, Howard found enough work to last him a solid twenty-four hours a day—he could have worked twenty-six hours a day if that be possible and still find work to do in plenty the following morning.

The disbanding of Davis' State Police had brought problems in its wake. For several years there had been little State law enforcement in Texas, Davis' men being more concerned with lining their own pockets in the guise of elevating the Negro to the status of a citizen with equal rights. With the departure of the State Police commanders—or such of them who did not meet not undeserved fates on the end of a rope—the coloured policemen slipped back to their homes, or wandered northwards in search of a land flowing with milk and honey. In the place of the State Police, the Texas Rangers returned from their Davis-inspired removal. Honest men, many of whom could have earned far more than their Ranger's wages in other, less dangerous walks of life, joined. The Texas Rangers asked little of its recruits other than loyalty, courage, ability to ride anything with four legs and hair and the knowledge of how to handle firearms.

However, with every Ranger working full time, Howard could well have done without receiving the letter from Caspar County. Yet one of the Governor's most pressing duties was to appease those Texans—and there were many—who had developed a hearty hatred of authority as represented by Washington's appointed head of the State. Knowing Texans, for he belonged to the Lone Star State himself, Howard could read between the lines of the letter. He smelled trouble in the air, far more trouble than one might expect from the theft of a few cows.

A jerk on the bell cord hanging behind him brought one of Howard's hard-working secretaries into the well-furnished room.

'Get Captain Murat for me,' the Governor said.

Five minutes later the door opened and a tall, slim, dark man in his early thirties entered. Although Captain Jules Murat, commander of Troop 'G,' Texas Rangers, wore town clothes, he carried himself with the swing of a horseman. One might almost imagine him wearing a plumed, cocked hat, a cloak over a Hussar uniform, a sabre at his side instead of a brace of holstered 1860 Army Colts, for there was a Gasconading air about him, a hint of controlled, deadly recklessness. Tanned, handsome, very rich, Murat was still one of the best Ranger captains under Howard's command.

'Trouble, Jules,' Howard said, waving Murat into a chair and offering his cigar case.

'No thanks,' replied Murat, taking a cigar. 'We've plenty of our own.'

'I hate a humourist at this hour of the day,' grunted the Governor.

'And me. What kind of trouble have you for me this time, Stan?'

'Cow thieves.'

Clipping the end off his cigar, Murat looked down at the weed. Although he showed nothing of his emotions, Murat had been sweating out the thought that the trouble might be yet another blood feud sprung out of the hatreds left behind by Davis' administration. Man, there you had real Texas-size trouble. With an entire county taking one side or the other, it was surely hell trying to discover the rights and wrongs of the affair, locate and arrest killers from either faction and pacify the rest before more blood spilled.

'There's plenty of them around,' he remarked, showing remarkable tolerance for a man who owned a good-sized spread and large herd.

'Small stuff,' stated the Governor. 'It's gone beyond being small up to Caspar County, Jules.'

Watching Howard, the Ranger captain felt his usual admiration. Sigmund Freud had not yet got around to presenting his views on human mentality to the world so, not knowing he should subconsciously hate his employer, Murat was willing to respect Howard as a brilliant man doing a difficult task. No matter what happened in Texas, sooner or later—and mostly sooner—Howard heard of it. More than that, the Governor formed his own conclusions from what he heard and mostly those conclusions proved to be correct. Mostly Howard left the Rangers to their own devices. When he called in one of the captains commanding the various companies, it meant Howard felt more than usually concerned about some incident or other.

'I smell bad trouble brewing up there, Jules,' the Governor went on. 'Vic Crither's passed word for Bat Gooch.'

'That *is* asking for trouble,' Murat admitted, almost showing the concern he felt. 'What's Gooch been fetched in to do?'

'Get the cow thieves—at two hundred dollars a head.'

Murat did not hold down his low whistle. 'That trouble you smell, I can get scent of it now. Gooch'll not be content just to ride Crither's range and let his name scare off any festive jasper with a running iron. He'll go out looking for the cow thieves no matter whose land they're working on.'

'You're right,' Howard agreed. 'With a man like Gooch riding the range, trouble's just over the rim and in peeking out ready to come boiling over. Bringing Gooch in's like turning loose a rabid dog to hunt down coyotes.'

'No man likes to see his property stole from under him,' Murat remarked.

'Which same I'll give you,' Howard replied. 'But there are better ways of stopping it than fetching in professional killers. Like you say, Gooch's not going to be content with just scaring the cow thieves off, he's there after a bounty. Only if he goes on to some other range, or downs an innocent man, he'll blow up all hell. I want action on this, Jules—and I want it fast.'

When Murat nodded his agreement he was not merely giving lip-service. After nine months in office together, Murat had learned to respect Howard's judgment and knew the Governor's insistence on immediate action did not spring from either panic or vote catching. Howard knew Texans, knew their high temper, their loyalty to kin or ranch. Already two bloody feuds

17

and range wars ripped at Texas counties and none knew the cost in lives and misery they brought to the suffering citizens of the areas involved. Another such affair could start those fools in Washington thinking about trying to reinstitute Reconstruction and, by cracky, that might be enough to restart the Civil War. Texas, least affected Southern State in the war, a nation of born fighting men who learned to handle weapons almost before they could walk, had never taken kindly to Reconstruction or having the 'if he's black he's right' policies of the Radical-Republicans up North forced on them. Another non-Texan governor, such as Davis might see the entire State torn apart by further civil conflict. Other than the most bigoted, Southern-hating, liberal-intellectual Yankees, no man in his right mind wanted that.

'It needs action,' the Ranger captain drawled.

'But?' asked Howard. 'There's a "but" in your voice.'

'I've only three men in camp out of my entire company. One with a broken arm, one with a bullet-busted thigh and the third's flat on his back with lead in his chest cavity.'

'Three—out of twenty?'

'The rest are all out handling chores,' Murat explained and went on hopefully, 'Shall I go?'

'I can't spare you, Jules. You're needed here, organising and attending to enlisting more recruits.'

'Danged if I don't resign and re-enlist as a private. I'll send off the first of my men to come in. Although the Lord knows when that'll be.'

'Let's hope it will be soon,' the Governor answered.

Clearly the interview had ended and Howard never wasted time in idle chatter. Coming to his feet, Murat turned and walked from the office. Before the Ranger reached the door, Howard had taken up a report from an Army commander and started to study the problem of controlling the Comanche Indians.

On leaving the Governor's office, Murat collected his horse and rode down town towards the Ranger barracks which housed Company 'G.' Once clear of the State Capital's area, Austin looked pretty much like any other cattle town. Rising along the wheel-rutted, dirt-surfaced street, Murat gave thought to his problem. No matter how much he wished to take action and, if possible, prevent another range war blowing up, he could do nothing until one of his men returned from the various tasks which held their attention.

A small, two-horse wagon came slowly along the street towards Murat. In passing, its driver—a tall, thin, dirty-looking bearded man in a frock coat, top hat, dirty collarless white shirt and old pants—caught Murat's eye and gave a slight jerk of his head. So slight had been the motion that a less observant man than Murat would have missed it. Even seeing the nod, Murat gave no sign but rode slowly on. After passing Murat, the man turned his wagon and drove it along an alley between two buildings. Murat rode on a short way before swinging his horse into the space between a saloon and its neighbouring barber's shop. Beyond the buildings lay a small, deserted street and the wagon had halted along it. Riding up to the halted wagon, Murat looked down to where its driver stood examining a wheel.

'In trouble, Jake?' he asked.

'Danged wheel's near on coming off,' the man replied.

'Let me take a look.'

Swinging from his horse, Murat walked to the wagon and bent down to inspect its wheel. Doing so put his face near to the man and the stench of unwashed flesh wafted to his nostrils. Murat wondered if Jacob Jacobs ever took soap and water to his hide, but did not ask. Jacobs was a pedlar, but who augmented his takings by acting as a gatherer and seller of information garnered in his travels around the range.

'You interested in running irons, Cap'n?' Jacobs asked in a low voice, bringing up the matter in the middle of a louder tirade about the poor quality of workmanship in the fitting of the wheel.

'Depends where they are,' Murat answered.

'Up to Caspar County.'

'I'm interested. What do you know?'

'I'm a poor man, Cap'n. There's no money to be made by a poor old Jewish pedlar these days.'

'Or a Ranger captain,' Murat countered.

'Heard about all the trouble and went up there special, me being a public-spirited citizen and all,' Jacobs put in. 'It's allus been poor trading country up there and I lost business.'

'Who's behind the stealing?' Murat asked, cutting off any

further descriptions of Jacobs's self-sacrifice.

'A woman.'

It said much for Murat's self-control that he showed no emotion at the words even though disbelief welled in him. His eyes studied Jacobs's face, but he read nothing in the pedlar's expression.

'Does she have a name?' Murat asked.

'Like I said, Cap'n, I'm a poor man.'

Taking out his wallet, Murat peeled off a ten-dollar bill and slipped it into a grimy palm that engulfed it like a large-mouth bass sucking in a shiner minnow.

'Who is it?'

'Name of Ella Watson. She runs the Cattle Queen.'

'Can you prove it?' asked Murat.

'Proof the man wants!' yelped Jacobs in what, if possible, was a *sotto voce* wail of protest. 'I tell him who is—I tell you, Cap'n, you Rangers should ought to arrest the feller who sold me this wagon.'

The last words came out in a much louder, complaining tone as a man walked from an alley behind them and passed by. Like all informers, Jacobs knew full well the delicate nature of his position and the danger it involved. He had no wish to become known as one who passed on confidential information to law enforcement officers and took all precautions possible to avoid raising suspicions. Not until the man had passed out of hearing distance did either the pedlar or the Ranger captain resume their conversation.

'I sure as hell haven't had ten bucks worth yet,' Murat warned as the other seemed inclined to edge around the question of proof.

Which same proved to be a powerful argument and one which Jacobs could understand right well. He knew Murat paid high for information, but expected service and accuracy in return for the money spent.

'I don't know much about it,' Jacobs admitted. 'Wasn't there for more than two days, pulled out as soon as I learned who was behind it. I figgered you'd want to know as soon as I could make it.'

'Likely. Who-all's in it with her?'

'She gets some of the fool young cowhands to do the stealing.

The young 'uns who haven't got too much good sense but like to feel a gal's leg now and then. Pays them for what they steal and gets the money back in her place when she's paid them. She's a might smart woman, Cap'n.'

'Sounds that way,' Murat grunted. 'Nothing more you can tell me?'

'Not about her. Don't know where she gets shut of the stuff once it's been stolen or even where she keeps it while she's waiting to sell.'

That figured to anybody who knew Jacobs. While the man willingly sold his information, he never took any extra chances in gathering it. However, Murat decided he had a start, a point where whichever man he sent up to Caspar County could make a beginning in breaking the spate of cow stealing. There was another point, a matter of some importance which Jacobs failed to mention.

'How about Bat Gooch?'

'He's been there for just over a week and—how'd you know about him?'

'My mother had a voodoo-mama nurse,' Murat answered, cursing the slowness of the mails. When Governor Howard's letter was dispatched Gooch still had not arrived in Caspar. Not that Murat intended to enlighten Jacobs; it did the Ranger captain's prestige no harm to have Jacobs think he knew more than his actual knowledge. 'Has he done anything?'

'Not much. Hasn't made him a bounty yet that anybody knows about. Crither's saying his losses've been cut already though.'

Strange as it may seem, the news did not relieve Murat's anxiety as much as one might expect it to. If the fear inspired by Gooch's name and evil reputation had scared the cow thieves off the Forked C range, the bounty hunter ought to be spreading the sphere of his activities real soon. From what he knew of Gooch, Murat reckoned the man would not be content with just wages and was likely to seek out victims on the neighbouring ranges. Sure, Murat wanted to drive the cow thieves off the range and stop their activities, which Gooch's presence might do—but there was such a thing as the price being too high. The sooner the Ranger captain could send one of his men to Caspar, the better he would feel. Even one Ranger on the ground might

21

act as a steadying influence and prevent Gooch from going too far in his bounty-hunting search for wealth.

'There's a couple more gunhands hanging around town,' Jacobs remarked. 'Are on Ella Watson's pay-roll, I think. They don't say much, or do much. 'Course, they only came in the day afore I left.'

Once again the pedlar gave Murat worrying news. Hired guns always meant bad trouble. If Ella Watson had brought in a couple of guns, it might be for the purpose of nullifying the threat Gooch offered to her cow-stealing business—always assuming that Jacobs had his facts right and she did run the she-bang.

Without letting his concern show, Murat slipped another five dollars into Jacobs's hand. 'If you go south, see if you can learn anything about those stage robberies they've had down that way,' he said.

'Sure, Cap'n. How about that Caspar fuss?'

'I'll send word to the sheriff up there and let him do what he wants.'

'Aren't you sending your men in?' Jacobs inquired.

'Only if the local law asks for them,' replied Murat cagily.

While Jacobs had proved himself a reliable source of information on more than one occasion. Murat did not trust the man. Knowledge of the coming of a Ranger, or a party of Rangers, would fetch a good price from the right area and Jacobs might just as easily sell his news to the cow thieves as he had to Murat. So Murat did not intend to give too much away; not with the lives of his men at stake.

'Don't reckon he'll ask,' grinned Jacobs. 'Sheriff Simmonds ain't the best, or smartest, lawman in the West.'

'He getting paid for sitting back and doing nothing?'

'I couldn't say, Cap'n. Only he's sure dressing better now than he did last time I saw him, before the cow stealing started.'

'I likely won't hear anything from him then,' Murat grunted. 'Which same I've paid out fifteen iron men for nothing.'

'News is always valuable, Cap'n,' answered Jacobs.

'So they do tell me,' agreed the Ranger. 'See you, Jake.'

'I'll be around,' promised the pedlar. 'You wanting me to go down south and see what I can find about the stage hold-ups?'

'If you're headed that way—and afore you ask, don't. You've

22

made fifteen bucks off me for something I might not be able to put to use.'

Turning, Murat walked to his horse and swung into the saddle. Jacobs watched the Ranger captain ride away and then swung aboard his wagon. With an annoyed sniff, the pedlar started his team moving. He felt disappointment at not learning more about Murat's plans. The Ranger captain most likely aimed to send at least one of his men to Caspar and to be able to identify the man might have proved profitable. Ella Watson would have paid well to know of her danger and be able to recognise it when the Ranger arrived. One thing Jacobs learned early was never to try to sell half information to criminals. While Ella Watson might be interested to know that the Rangers were coming, she was unlikely to pay for the information—at least not enough to make a return trip to Caspar worthwhile—unless Jacobs could also tell who exactly to watch for.

Murat rode between the two buildings and back on to the street once more, turning over the problem and Jacobs's information in his mind. A worried frown creased his face as he continued his interrupted return to his company's barracks. One thing was even more sure now. The Governor had been right to worry about the developments in Caspar County. Cow stealing was bad enough; but when both sides started importing hired killers the situation became far worse.

Hoping against hope, Murat swung his horse through the gates into the compound of Troop 'G,' Texas Rangers. No imposingly military structure lay before him. The compound had no parade ground, for the Rangers did no drill and wore no uniform. Just an adobe office building and cells, three wooden cabins, a long stable and barn, and a pole corral made up the company's headquarters. Murat glanced hopefully at the corral, but found it to be empty. The company's remuda had been taken out on to the range beyond the compound to graze and any horse in the corral would mean that one of his men was back from a chore.

Even as a youngster, one of the trio who acted as wranglers for the Rangers' horses, dashed up to collect Murat's mount, a tall man in cowhand clothes and with his right arm suspended in a sling left the office building. The man walked towards

Murat and the captain asked:

'No sign of any of the boys, Sid?'

'Nope. I'm near on fit though.'

The injured Ranger knew a summons from the Governor meant something urgent and wondered what further trouble had been heaped on Murat's shoulders.

'Near on's not good enough, Sid. I can't send you out until you can handle a rifle as well as a Colt.'

'Danged spoilsport,' growled Sid, but he knew Murat to be right. A Ranger with a bullet-busted wing sure would be at a disadvantage in handling any risky law work. 'It bad?'

'Bad enough,' admitted Murat. 'Let's go in and I'll tell you about it.'

Following Sid into the office, Murat made a decision. Unless at least one of his men had returned by sundown the following day, Murat intended to disregard the Governor's orders and head for Caspar himself.

CHAPTER THREE

MISS CANARY IN DISTRESS

MISS MARTHA JANE CANARY expected to be raped and killed before fifteen more minutes went by. Already the sweat-stinking fat cuss had finished his food and started opening the drawers of the side-piece, grinning slyly at her and waiting for her objections. The handsome jasper, if you cared for swarthy features and a drooping moustache, the others called Choya still sat eating; his black eyes studying the girl as if trying to strip her with his gaze. After finishing his meal, the short, scar-faced *hombre* named Gomez had left the cabin on a visit to the back-house and the fourth member of that evil quartet, Manuel, sat wolfing down a mess of victuals like it was going out of style. When they all had finished eating and no longer required her services as cook, the ball was sure as hell going to start.

From the first moment she saw the four Mexicans riding towards the cabin, the girl expected trouble. One saw plenty of Mexicans in this part of Texas, but the quartet struck her as being wrong. While they dressed to the height of *vaquero* fashion, they showed a mean-faced, slit-eyed wolf caution which did not go with the behaviour of such Mexican cowhands she had seen on her travels. The backwards glances, the careful, alert scrutiny of the place as they rode towards it, each told the girl a story. She knew instinctively the four men riding towards her were bad. Outlaws of some sort; maybe *Comancheros*, those human wolves who preyed on both white and Indian, leaving a trail of carnage wherever they went. All but smashed by the Texas Rangers before the Civil War, a few small bands of *Comancheros* had avoided capture, or sprung into being during Davis' incompetent administration. It seemed in keeping with the girl's general lousy luck of the past few days that she should run across one such bunch under the present conditions.

Way she looked at it, only one good thing could be said of

25

the situation. Those four snake-eyed greasers did not know her true identity. They must take her for the wife or, as she wore no rings, daughter of the house; easy meat for their evil purposes once she had filled their bellies. Most likely they would not have been so relaxed, or taken such chances, had they known her to be Calamity Jane.

Not that Calamity looked quite her usual self. She had seen to that on taking stock of her position in respect of the approaching riders. Her hat, a faded old U.S. cavalry kepi, hung behind the door instead of perching at its usual jaunty angle on her mop of curly red hair. Nothing about her tanned, slightly freckled, pretty face gave a hint of her true identity; the eyes were merry most time, the lips looked made for laughing and kissing, but could turn loose a blistering flow of team-driver's invective at times. The man's shirt she wore looked maybe two sizes too small as it clung to her rich, round, full bosom and slender waist, its neck open maybe just a mite lower than some folks regarded as seemly, the sleeves rolled up to show strong-looking arms. However, she wore a black skirt from the waist down, effectively covering her levis pants; the latter, like the shirt, fitted a mite snug and drew sniffs of disapproval from good ladies when Calamity passed by. Not that Calamity usually gave a damn about how folks regarded her style of dress. She wore men's clothing because she did a man's job and only donned the skirt as a piece of simple disguise which appeared to have fooled the four Mexicans.

Calamity had been on her way to Austin with a wagon-load of supplies, handling a contract for her boss, Dobe Killem, and decided to call in to visit with her friends, Dai and Blodwin Jones. On her arrival she found the Jones' had gone into Austin that morning, but with frontier hospitality they left the house open and food around for any chance-passing stranger to take a meal. Being hungry and trail-dirty, Calamity decided to night at the house. After caring for the team which drew her big Conestoga wagon, Calamity took a bath in the Jones family's swimming hole behind the house—leaving her gunbelt with its ivory butted Navy Colt, Winchester carbine and bull whip in the boot of the wagon. Like a danged fool green kid fresh out from the East, she did not collect the weapons before entering the house and cooking up a meal.

Not until she heard the hooves of the Mexicans' horses and looked from the window did Calamity realise the full gravity of her mistake. Once glance told the range-wise Calamity all she needed to know about the visitors and she did not like the thought. The Jones' had taken their weapons with them when they headed for town. Nobody left guns, ammunition, powder and lead around an empty house. Even so close to Austin, capital city of the State of Texas, there was always a chance of an Indian raid and no Texan wanted to present a bunch of hostiles with free firearms. Calamity did not even consider using one of the butcher knives to defend herself. Mexicans were a nation of knife-fighters and she would have no chance against them using cold steel. Nor did she commit the folly of dashing out to her wagon. Before she could make it, the *Comancheros* would be on her.

Thinking fast, Calamity headed for the Jones' bedroom and grabbed one of Blodwin's skirts. Blodwin stood a few inches taller than Calamity and the extra length of the skirt hid the fact that Calamity wore men's pants and Pawnee moccasins. then she waited for the Mexicans to arrive.

On their arrival, the four men had been all politeness. Choya, he appeared to be their leader, greeted her in fair English, asking if the *señorita* could feed four poor travellers. All the time he spoke, his three men scanned the place with careful eyes, searching for sign of the male members of the household and sitting with their hands on gun butts. On receiving Calamity's permission to enter, the Mexicans left their horses standing outside, not fastened but with trailing reins to prevent the animals straying. Calamity cooked up a meal of ham and eggs, conscious of the evil, lust-filled eyes watching her every move. There had been a knowing, mocking sneer on Choya's lips as he listened to her remarks about the ranch's crew being due back at any moment; he knew her to be alone and, as he thought, real helpless.

Carefully avoiding turning to where the fat man searched the side-piece's drawers, Calamity watched and waited. With the meal all but over, she figured it would not be long before the men decided to make their play. If she hoped to come out of the affair with her life, she must act soon, fast and right.

'There's nothing here, Choya,' the fat man stated in Spanish.

27

'No money, no guns. Nothing for us.'

'She may know where there is something,' Choya answered. 'It will be amusing to find out, hey, Manuel?'

Swallowing a mouthful of food, the fourth member of the party ogled Calamity with evil eyes. 'It will,' he agreed. 'Who is first?'

'Me,' said the fat man.

'You was first last time, Ramon,' Manuuel objected.

Calamity knew it was now or never. While the conversation had been in Spanish, which she did not speak, her instincts warned her of its meaning. One did not need the powers of a Pawnee witch-woman to figure out what lay in the Mexicans' minds, it showed too plainly on their faces for that.

Slowly she lifted the lid of the coffeepot, as if to check on the level of its contents. Among other unladylike things, her freight outfit friends had taught her a thorough working knowledge of the game of poker, including the art of hiding the emotions; and she used all her skill to prevent herself giving any hint of her intentions. Ramon still stood at the far side of the room by the side-piece and, if Calamity be any kind of judge on such matters, his holster did not look to be the type from which a Colt could be drawn speedily. Of the two men at the table, Choya struck Calamity as being the most dangerous and the one to be taken out of the game first.

With that thought in mind, Calamity acted. Suddenly, and without giving a hint of her intentions, she hurled the contents of the coffeepot into Choya's face. Almost half a pot full of very hot coffee caught the man, temporarily blinding him. Jerking back, hands clawing at his face, Choya threw over his chair and crashed to the floor.

Manuel gave an explosive Spanish curse, shoving his chair back and starting to rise. Even as the man's hand went towards his gun, Calamity, moving with the speed of urgent desperation, turned from Choya and met the fresh menace. Pivoting around, Calamity swung her arm at and crashed the bottom of the coffeepot into Manuel's face. Calamity had worked hard ever since her sixteenth birthday and had real strong arms. So as she hit to hurt, Manuel knew the blow landed. Blood gushing from his nose, Manuel went over backwards smashing the chair under him and sprawled on to the floor.

With the two men at the table handled, Calamity gave Ramon her full and undivided attention. The fat man had been taken completely by surprise by the unexpected turn of events and, as Calamity figured, could not get out his gun with any speed. Not that he bothered; instead his hand dropped and drew a wicked, spear-pointed knife from its boot-top sheath. Whipping back her arm, Calamity hurled the coffeepot at Ramon's head and for a girl she could aim mighty straight. Even at the width of the cabin, the flying coffeepot landed hard enough to hurt and slowed down Ramon's attempt at retaliatory measures. The coffeepot's blow did little actual damage, but it brought Calamity a vital couple of seconds time—and at that moment every second gained was precious.

Snarling with rage, Ramon sprang forward. Not at the girl, but towards the door of the cabin; meaning to block her way out for Calamity was heading towards it. Only Calamity had already thought of and discarded the idea of using the door as a means of egress. Instead she headed for the window nearest to her. Covering her head with her arms, she hurled herself forward, passing through the window and taking both glass and sash with her. The way Calamity saw things, the Jones' window could be far more easily replaced than the damage those four yahoos would inflict should they lay hands on her.

Sailing through the window, Calamity lit down rolling like she had come off a bad horse. She went under the porch rail and landed on her feet beyond it. Wasting no time, she headed on the run for her wagon. From the corner of her eye, she saw the cabin door fly open and Ramon appeared. The Mexican came knife in hand, a trickle of blood running from his forehead where the coffeepot struck him.

Calamity reached the wagon and despite the awkwardness of wearing a skirt, leapt for the box. Even as she swung on to it, a glance to the rear told her how little time she had to save herself. Ramon had halted and already changed his hold on the knife, gripping it by the point of the blade instead of the hilt. While not the brightest of men, he could figure out that the girl did not head for the wagon in a state of blind panic. She must be after a weapon of some kind and he aimed to throw the knife, downing her before she reached whatever she sought in the wagon.

Grabbing for the nearest of her weapons. Calamity caught up the long bull whip's handle. Even as Ramon prepared to throw his knife, Calamity struck out. Her right hand rose, carrying the whip up and flicking its lash behind her. Down swept the arm, sending the whip's lash curling forward. An instant before Ramon made his throw, the tip of the lash caught him in the face, splattering his right eye-ball as if it had been struck by the full force of a .44 bullet. Ramon screamed, the knife falling from his fingers as they clawed at his injured face.

For a moment Calamity thought that her luck had changed for the better. While she could handle her bull whip real well, there had not been time to take a careful aim. She just let fly and hoped for the best. Having a bull whip give its explosive pop within inches of one's head did not make for steady nerves or accurate aim when tossing a knife; so Calamity merely hoped to put Ramon off his aim, causing him to miss his throw, and give her the short time needed to change whip for carbine. From the way that fat jasper screeched and blood spurted between his fingers, she had done a whole lot better than just put him off by a near miss.

A bullet ripped the air by Calamity's head even as she swung around to drop the whip and grab up her Winchester. Once again, as she had several times before, Calamity decided there was no sound in the world she hated as much as the flat 'splat!' sound of a close-passing bullet. Throwing a glance at the shooter. Calamity found she was not yet out of the woods. Gomez stood at the corner of the cabin, holding up his pants with one hand, lining his gun at her with the other. He stood well beyond the range of her whip and handled that smoking Starr Army revolver like he knew which end the bullets came from. What was more, he took careful aim, not meaning to miss again.

Letting the whip fall, Calamity prepared to make a grab that would see the twelve-shot Winchester Model '66 carbine in her hands—unless she took a .44 Starr bullet between the shoulders first. It had been her original intention to make the wagon, collect the carbine and fort up some place where she could have a clear field of fire at the front of the cabin. If the plan had succeeded, Calamity reckoned she ought to be able to hand those jaspers their needings.

Only she had forgotten Gomez and it seemed that her lack of foresight would cost her dearly. She doubted if he aimed to miss a second time. Nor would there be time for her to grab the carbine and stop him.

Even as death stared Calamity in the face, while the Mexican aimed his revolver and pressed its double-action trigger, a shot rang out. Not the deep boom of a handgun, but the crack of a Winchester rifle. For an instant Calamity thought her unseen rescuer had struck a flour-sack, for something white sprayed up from Gomez' head. Then she realised that the Winchester's bullet, on striking the skull, had shattered the bone, spraying slivers of it and pulped out brains flying into the air. The Starr fell from Gomez' hand as his body collapsed in a limp, boned-out manner to the ground.

Not that Calamity wasted any time in thinking about the sight. Already Choya and Manuel were coming through the cabin door and they looked mean as all hell. Each man held a gun and had murder in his heart, with Calamity as the one they aimed to kill.

Bending down, Calamity jerked the carbine from its boot fitted to the inside of the wagon box. The move saved her life for both Mexicans fired at her and the lead passed over her head. The roars of the revolvers mingled with yet another shot from her unseen rescuer's rifle. Swivelling around, carbine in hand, Calamity saw the effect of the second rifle bullet. Choya leaned against the door jamb, sliding slowly down. A trickle of blood ran from his chest and his Remington had fallen out of his hand.

Manuel saw Calamity swing towards him, the carbine held with practised ease in her hands. For a moment he hesitated, wavering between handling the girl and locating the as yet unseen rifle-user. That indecision cost him his life, it gave the girl a vitally needed second or so in which to throw up and sight the rifle. Even as Manuel started to bring his revolver in her direction, Calamity shot him dead. She knew the *Comanchero* breed, knew the only way to stop their evil ways was to kill them, and felt no remorse at taking Manuel's life.

Which same left Ramon. Badly injured though he was, with an eye that he would never see through again, the Mexican still drew his gun and started shooting as he made for his horse.

31

Twice he fired and, even though pain misted his eyes, he sent the bullets into the wagon box. Splinters kicked into the air but Calamity's luck, now changed again for the better, held, and the bullets missed her. Yet she knew she must shoot back for Ramon had other charges in his gun and clearly aimed to use them. Her rescuer appeared to judge the situation in the same light for his rifle spat out at the same moment as Calamity's carbine cracked. Struck by two flat-nosed, Tyler Henry-designed .44 bullets, Ramon whirled around twice, crashed into the nearest horse and went down.

Silence dropped after the thunder of guns, the wind wafting away the burnt powder's smoke. Calamity let out a long shuddering sigh and lowered her carbine. She felt that the last half hour or so put years on her life and, sure as hell's for sinners, was about as close a call as ever came her young way; up to and including the time she acted as human decoy to lure out of hiding a murderer who had strangled eight girls in the old city of New Orleans. And *that* time had been mighty rough, for she wound up taking the Strangler alone; due partly to her own cussedness and mule-headedly going out without a police cover. She reckoned that not even the feel of the Strangler's killing cord around her throat had been as bad as waiting for those four Mexicans to jump her.

'Are you all right, ma'am?' called a male voice.

For the first time Calamity saw her rescuer. He stepped from the shelter and cover of the bushes some fifty yards away, his rifle held in both hands down before his body yet ready for instant use. Although he wore no badge of office he handled himself in the manner of a trained lawman. Despite calling out the question about her welfare, he never took his attention from the four Mexicans.

Calamity studied her rescuer with interest. There appeared to be something familiar about his features; as if she should know him, yet could not place him. He stood maybe six foot one, with a good pair of shoulders that trimmed down to a lean waist. An expensive black Stetson hat, low crowned and wide brimmed in the Texas fashion, sat on the back of his dusty-blond head. He had an intelligent, handsome face made even more grim-looking by trail dirt and a three-day stubble of whiskers, but it looked like it might relax under the right conditions. The tight

32

rolled green bandana which trailed long ends down over his blue broadcloth shirt, his brown levis pants with the cuffs turned back and hanging outside his high-heeled, fancy-stitched boots, all were trail-dirty and showed hard wear. His gunbelt hung just right, a brace of matched staghorn butted 1860 Army Colts in the contoured holsters. The guns rode just right for a fast draw and in a significant fashion; the right side's Colt pointed its butt to the rear, that at the left turned forward. Such a method often being used in the days before metallic-cartridge revolvers replaced the percussion-fired guns. Due to the slowness of reloading a cap-and-ball revolver, many men carried two guns, although few learned to be ambidextrous in the use of their weapons. Most folks toted their left gun so it could be drawn with the right hand. In a tight spot which called for sustained fire from his weapons, the young man who rescued Calamity most likely drew and emptied his right side Colt first, then either holstered it or made a border-shift—tossing the gun from right to left hand—and drew the second weapon cross-hand so as to continue shooting.

'Dang it though,' Calamity mused, studying the young man. 'I should know this feller from someplace. Now who in hell does he remind me of?'

Quickly Calamity thought of some of the men who passed through her hectic young life, trying to decide which of them the young Texan reminded her of most. She discounted Wild Bill Hickok right away. Nor did her rescuer remind her of Beau Resin, the Indian scout she met while freighting supplies to a fort in the Dakotas and with whom she shared some mighty stirring times. Her thoughts went next to Mark Counter, that range-country Hercules from the Texas Big Bend country. No, handsome though he was, the young man did not come up to Mark's standards, nor resemble the blond giant enough to remind Calamity of Mark. Yet he for sure looked like somebody Calamity knew.

Even as the girl decided to ask, she saw something that jolted all thoughts of who the young Texan resembled clean out of her head.

'Look out!' she screamed.

Clearly Choya, leader of the *Comancheros*, had not been hit as badly as they imagined. Suddenly, his eyes opened and his right hand scooped up the Remington in a fast-done move. He had been playing possum to lure his unseen attack in close enough to be shot down. The move came fast, deadly and un-expected as the strike of a copperhead snake, and was typical of a *Comanchero's* way of fighting. Even as Choya fired, and almost before Calamity screamed her warning, the young Texan acted. He moved with commendable speed, going into a crouch and lining the rifle hip high. Three times he fired, working the lever in almost a blur of movement. Choya got off one shot which fanned the Texan's cheek in passing and might have hit if the *Comanchero's* hand had been steadier. Twice splinters erupted from the wall, drawing closer to Choya. On the third shot no splinters flew, but the *Comanchero* jerked under the impact of lead. For an instant he struggled to keep his gun lined. The Texan levered another bullet into his rifle and prepared to shoot again. The precaution proved to be unnecessary. Opening his hand, Choya let the Remington fall from it. This time when the gun landed on the ground, Choya would not be picking it up again.

CHAPTER FOUR

YOU'RE DUSTY FOG'S KID BROTHER

'RECKON you feel up to covering them while I pull their fangs, ma'am?' asked the young man who had saved Calamity's life, his voice an easy-sounding Texas drawl.

Maybe Calamity did feel just a little mite shaken by her experience, but the words stiffened her like a hound-scared cat.

'Naw!' she replied. 'I'm all set to start swooning and like to pee my tiny pants.' She hefted the carbine for him to see. 'Go pull their teeth, friend, they're safe covered.'

Watching the way the young man moved. Calamity once again felt struck by the calm, competent and efficient manner in which he handled himself. One thing was for certain sure, he moved like a well-trained lawman. His route to the bodies took him by the front of Calamity's wagon. In passing, he rested the Winchester against the wagon's side and took out his right-hand revolver before going any closer to the dead Mexicans. Up close, should one of the quartet still be playing possum, a revolver's short length licked the be-jeesus out of the longer range and greater magazine capacity of a rifle.

Neither weapon would have been needed, as the disarming of the *Comancheros* passed without incident. Not one of that evil quartet would ever give trouble or endanger lives and property again. Yet the young Texan did not feel any annoyance at having taken the precautions. The way he saw things, it was well worth taking a few added precautions happen they kept a man alive.

'That's them cleaned,' he remarked, after tossing the last of the *Comancheros'* weapons towards the wagon. 'You'd maybe best stop in the wagon, ma'am, they aren't a pretty sight.'

'They never are,' Calamity answered, putting her carbine's

35

safety catch on and sliding the little gun back into its boot. 'And for Tophet's sake, stop calling me "ma'am".'

'Sure, ma'am,' drawled the young man soothingly.

If there was one thing in the world that riled Calamity more than the rest, it was having a young feller around her age showing off his masculine superiority—not that Calamity would have expressed it in such a manner—and acting all smug and condescending because he wore pants and maybe sported hair on his chest. Well, maybe she might be a mite shy on the hair but she could sure copper his bet on the other score. Unfastening the skirt, she slid it off and, not for the first time, wondered why in hell womenfolk hampered themselves by wearing such garments. Once free of the skirt's encumbrance, she took up her gunbelt and vaulted lightly from the wagon.

'You look a mite disappointed,' she said noticing the way he glanced at her legs.

'Why sure,' the Texan replied. 'When I saw you take off your skirt there, I figured——'

'Well, you was wrong. Let's clean up around here afore the Jones' get back.'

'As you say, ma'am. This isn't your place then?'

'Just passing through, although I did take a few liberties with the fixings,' Calamity answered, her eyes flickering to the window she destroyed in her departure from the cabin. 'And the next time you call me "ma'am" I'll——'

'Ma'am's a good name seeing's we've not been introduced. I figured you was a lady in distress.'

'Boy,' grinned Calamity, although her rescuer could maybe give her a year in age. 'I'm no lady, but I sure as hell was in distress. Fact being I was so in distress that I said, "Calam, gal," I said, "you're sure in distress right now, so where-at's that long, blond, handsome Texan who's going to save your ornery, worthless lady's hide." And dog-my-cats, there you was as large as life and twice as welcome.'

'I talk too much when I want to haul off and fetch up, too,' the Texan told her. 'Like right now.'

For a moment Calamity's temper boiled up hot and wild, quelling the uneasiness in her belly. No matter how often one saw sudden death, the sight never grew any easier on the stomach. Those four Mexicans aimed to rape and kill her, as

36

she well knew, but the thought did little to stop her feeling just a mite sick as she glanced at, then looked away from the gory mess that was the top of Gomez' bullet-shattered head.

However, life must go on. If Calamity sat down and went all woman and hysterical every time she saw a body, she would have spent a good portion of the last three years that way. A freight driver's life was hard and dangerous out West, what with facing the hazards of the elements, Indian attack and the occasional meeting with murderous *Comancheros*, so offered plenty of opportunity for one to see sudden, violent death.

After her mother left her in the care of the nuns at a St. Louis convent, Calamity stayed put until her sixteenth birthday. There being too much of Charlotte Canary's spirit in Calamity for her to take kindly to the discipline of the convent, the girl slipped away on her sixteenth birthday and hid in one of Dobe Killem's wagons as it started its trip West, first working as cook's louse, then learning the mysteries of a team-driver's art. From the men of the outfit Calamity learned much; how to handle and care for a six-horse team, use a long-lashed bull whip as tool and weapon, know more than a little about Indians, and how to defend herself with her bare hands in a rough-house frontier bar-room brawl—a useful accomplishment when dealing with tough dancehall girls who objected to Calamity entering their place of employment. In three years Calamity had seen a fair piece of the West and reached the stage of competence where Dobe Killem allowed her to handle chores alone, knowing he could trust her to come through for him.

'What'll we do with 'em?' she asked, ignoring the unsettled condition of her stomach. 'It'll take a whole heap of digging to plant all four of 'em; and I don't want to do it near the house.'

'We won't have to,' answered the Texan. 'If you've room in your wagon, I'll take them into Austin.'

'You a bounty hunter?' growled Calamity.

Reaching into a hidden pocket behind his gunbelt, the Texan extracted something. He held out his hand, in its palm lay a silver star mounted in a circle. While not a native of the Lone Star State, Calamity still knew and could recognise the badge of the Texas Rangers when she saw it—and she saw one in the palm of her young rescuer's hand.

37

'Ranger, huh?' she asked.

'Yes'm. The name's Danny Fog——'

Calamity slapped the palm of a hand against her thigh and gave an exasperated yelp. Everything slotted into place now, she could see the family resemblance and cursed herself for not spotting it straight off. Of course, there was a mite of difference that could account for her not connecting her rescuer with——

'Damn it to hell!' she snorted. 'I should have seen it. You're Dusty Fog's kid brother.'

Which same was roughly the sort of remark Danny Fog had come to expect to hear when he announced his identity. Danny yielded second to no man in the respect, admiration and affection he bore for his famous brother, the Rio Hondo gun wizard, Dusty Fog. As Danny saw things, a man who had been one of the South's top fighting leaders in the war, became known as a cowhand, ranch segundo and trail boss of the first water, bore a name as a town-taming lawman with few equals, was acclaimed by reliable sources as the fastest gun in Texas, deserved all the credit and fame which came his way. So far Texas had not come under the grip of 'debunkers,' those intellectual young men who, aware of their own complete lack of any qualities of courage or ability, sought to bring everybody down to their level. Dusty Fog enjoyed just fame and acclaim and his brother, Danny, stood first in line to give it.

But it sure riled a mite to be known as 'Dusty Fog's kid brother.' Without boasting of it, Danny knew himself to be intelligent; with his training he considered himself to be a pretty fair lawman; maybe not *real* fast with a Colt—it took him a good second to draw and shoot and in Texas one needed to be able to almost half that time to be considered fast—but a fine shot with a handgun or rifle; capable of reading sign in an efficient manner, and a reckonable fist fighter; these latter qualities stemming from the lessons given by two of Dusty's friends, each an acknowledged master in his field. So he figured he could make a better than fair peace officer, given time to gather experience and reckoned he ought to be able to stand on his own two feet; which was why he joined the Rangers instead of staying on in Rio Hondo County and working as his father's deputy. That way he hoped to gain for himself a separate identity instead of living as 'Dusty Fog's kid brother.'

'You know Dusty, ma'am?' he inquired.

With a remarkable show of tact, Calamity guessed at the cause of the momentary pause which followed her words. So she held down the blistering comment which rose on Danny's repeated use of the word 'ma'am.'

'Met him a couple of times, and the Ysabel Kid—know ole Mark Counter a whole heap better though. Say, didn't they ever mention me?'

'Only gal they ever mentioned that partly might fit your description was a dead-mean, red-haired lump of perversity called Calamity Jane. Only Mark mentioned as how she was a mite fatter'n you and got more freckles.'

'If you're jobbing me——' she warned.

'Me, ma'am?' asked Danny, then a look of horror came to his face. 'Landsakes a-mercy, do you mean to tell me that *you're* Calamity Jane?'

'You did that real smooth,' Calamity sniffed. 'Maybe just a mite over-done, but not bad for a kid.'

A grin flickered on Danny's face and he held out a hand. 'Put her there, Calam. Pleased to know you.'

Taking the offered hand, Calamity shook it and grinned back. 'And boy, was I pleased to hear from you. Say, let's tend to the cleaning up afore we set down to old home week, shall we?'

'Be best, I reckon,' Danny agreed. 'Can we tote 'em in on your wagon?'

'Reckon so. I never took to handling the blister end of a shovel.'

'I'll go bring down my hoss first.'

'Reckon I'll come along with you,' Calamity remarked, throwing a glance at the bodies. 'Feel like stretching my legs a mite.'

'Let's go then,' Danny answered.

He made no comment on the girl's statement, although she figured that her words had not fooled him at all. Side by side they started to walk up the bush dotted slope and Calamity's curiosity got the better of her as she thought of Danny's timely arrival.

'How'd you come to be on hand right when I needed you?' she asked.

'I've been after Choya and his bunch for over a week now.'

'Just one of you?'

'Were three when we started out. Only the *Comancheros* laid for us. Got Buck Lemming, him being the sergeant, first crack and put lead into Sandy Gartree's left wing. I was riding behind the other two and come off lucky. Then when Choya's bunch pulled a Mexican stand-off. I buried Buck, patched up Sandy and sent him back to the Bradded H and took out to tracking those four.'

Which left a considerable amount of the story untold. Danny spoke truly when he said he had been riding behind the other two as they ran into the ambush. What he failed to mention being that he saved Gartree's life by pulling the wounded man to cover under *Comanchero* fire and it had been mainly due to his defence that the four remaining Mexicans—two died before Danny and Gartree's guns—pulled out and ran. In the traditions of the Texas Rangers, Danny attended to his friends and then took out after the *Comancheros* even though the odds be four to one in their favour.

'Sure pleased you did,' Calamity stated. 'Man, there was times when I figured I was due for wings and a harp.'

'*You.* Shucks, only the good die young they do say,' grinned Danny

'One more remark like that out of you and we'll see about it,' she snorted. 'What was you fixing in to do, sneaking down the slope?'

'Take 'em. I'd seen their hosses when they jumped us and recognised those four when I peeked over the top of the rim. Reckoned that Choya and his bunch'd be in the house and aimed to sneak in then take 'em by surprise. Only you come through the window afore I made it. Which same I was lucky, didn't know about that jasper in the backhouse.'

'The Ysabel Kid'd've checked on it afore *he* moved in.'

'Which same I aimed to do,' Danny told her calmly. 'He taught me all he knows about tracking and things.'

'Which same I never saw the Kid show any sign of knowing about—things,' grinned Calamity. 'Though he does know some about tracking.'

'Anyways you stopped me when you came through the window and that jasper came out the backhouse like a coon off a log when he heard the whooping and hollering, and I figured to

40

stay hid until I saw what might be needed. How come you-all was fool enough to get caught, Calam, gal?'

Quickly, her sentences liberally sprinkled with a flow of invective that brought an admiring grin to Danny's lips, Calamity told her story. Nor did his admiration lessen when he heard of the manner in which she prevented the men from recognising her true potential by donning a skirt and acting as the un-suspecting lady of the house. Take it any way a man looked, old Calamity was quite a gal and lived up to the flattering comments Dusty, Mark and the Kid made about her after their return from the first meeting. Not many women would have shown her presence of mind. Fact being, few women, even in the self-reliant West, could have handled things so efficiently or come out of the situation which had faced Calamity as well as she did.

On reaching the top of the slope, Calamity looked to where Danny's horse stood by a large blueberry bush. It came as almost a surprise to see that Danny did not ride a paint like his brother's personal mount. However, the horse looked to be a real fine critter, sixteen hands high and showing good breeding. The horse had a colouration Calamity could never remember seeing before, a light red, almost pinkish roan with a pure white belly.

'What in hell colour do you call that?' she asked.

'A *sabino*,' Danny explained. 'Got him below the line. Mexican cowhands go a whole heap on them for go-to-town hosses and for work.'

'I'll take your word for it,' sniffed Calamity. 'Looks a mite flashy to me. Got me a buckskin with the outfit that'd run his legs down to the shoulders in a straight mile race.'

'Got me a week's furlough to come when I pull in from this lot,' Danny answered, meeting her challenge. 'Happen you can lay hands on your crow-bait, we'll run us a race.'

'You got a deal. Dobe Killem, which same being my boss, told me to wait in Austin for two weeks, grab some work if I could to keep me busy until he brings the rest of the bunch in.'

'So you'll be in for a week with nothing to do,' drawled Danny, taking up his *sabino's* reins. 'Just like me.'

'Must be fate in it someplace.' Calamity answered, eyeing him with interest. 'You got a steady gal?'

'Not steady. Always figgered a young lawman shouldn't get too close or attached until he knows if he's going to make the grade or not.'

'Which same's as good an excuse as any.'

'Sure,' Danny agreed. 'Now let's get down there and tend to those four Mexicans, shall we?'

'I thought you'd never ask,' Calamity answered.

On returning to the cabin, Danny attended to his horse. Then, with Calamity at his side, he returned to the front of the cabin and prepared to start the distasteful task of cleaning up.

'Get their tarps, Calam,' he ordered, 'and bring one of their ropes.'

Normally Calamity might have objected to a new acquaintance, especially a young man, giving her orders. Yet she figured Danny knew what he was doing, and anyways she could always object if she decided he did not. Calamity went to each horse in turn and removed its tarpaulin-wrapped bundle from behind the saddle's cantle. Unrolling the first bundle, she handed the tarp to Danny and, with an express of distaste on his face, he went to work. First spreading the tarp on the ground, Danny pulled Choya's body into the centre of it. Wrapping the body completely inside the tarp, Danny took the rope from Calamity and bound the bundle so the jolting of the wagon would not uncover its grisly contents. Next came a difficult and not too pleasant task, loading the body into the rear of Calamity's wagon.

'I'll lend you a hand,' the girl said her voice just a mite strained.

'*Gracias*, Calam. Take the feet, I'll handle the head.'

Between them, Calamity and Danny lifted first one, then the remainder of the tarpaulin-wrapped shapes into the rear of the girl's wagon, laying them side by side in the space at the back. With that done, the two of them cleaned up, as well as they could, the traces of the fighting. Calamity gathered up the shattered glass while Danny brought shovel-loads of dirt to cover the bloodstains. Finally they stood back and looked over their work.

'I took a bath when I arrived,' the girl remarked. 'Damned if I don't feel all dirty again.'

Danny put a hand to his bristle-covered chin. 'And me. I sure hate to have whiskers growing on me. Say, is there any water inside?'

'I'll boil some for you. Then while you're shaving, I'll go take a bath,' Calamity suggested. 'And then I'll cook us a meal.'

'Sounds like a real good notion,' Danny answered.

Opening his bedroll, Danny dug into his warbag and collected shaving kit. Calamity poured him out some hot water and headed for the swimming hole while he stripped off his shirt to wash and shave. Having been hunting the *Comancheros* alone for the past three days, Danny had not found time to wash and shave, or even take off his clothes. He felt a whole heap better with the growth of whiskers and some of the trail dirt removed from his hide. On Calamity's return, Danny took a change of clothes and headed for the swimming hole. All in all, he both felt and looked a whole heap better on his return. Nor had Calamity wasted her time, but set to and cooked a real good meal for him.

'You cook just like Mark said,' he told Calamity after the meal, having been too hungry during it to waste time in talking. 'Man gets tired of stream water and jerky.'

'Reckon he does,' she agreed then grinned. 'You mean ole Mark said something nice about me?'

'Shucks, Mark always talks real high and respectful about you, Calam.'

'I just bet he does,' smiled the girl.

'There's no chance of making Austin today,' Danny remarked, looking out of the window at the darkening range. 'Happen we start at sun-up, we ought to reach it afore noon tomorrow.'

'That's how I saw it,' agreed Calamity. 'Let's go tend the stock. I reckon we'll leave the four *Comanchero* hosses here to pay for the damage I did to the window.'

Danny gave his assent and they went out to feed, water and bed down the horses. On their return, Calamity lit a lamp while Danny laid his saddle carefully on its side by the wall and unpacked his bedroll.

'It's going to be a mite chilly for whoever sleeps in here,' Calamity said, glancing at the shattered window.

'You take the bedroom then,' replied Danny, courteous to the core as became a Southern gentleman.

43

'Shuckens no. Let's do it fair,' answered Calamity, taking a coin from her pocket and flipping it into the air. 'Heads I have the bedroom, tails you get it. Dang it, Danny, it's tails. We said best of three, didn't we?'

'Why sure,' grinned Danny, taking the coin and flicking it up again. It landed on the table with a metallic clink.

'Three out of five, we said, didn't we?' asked Calamity, looking at the exposed tails side.

Once more the coin sailed into the air. Shooting out a hand, Calamity caught the spinning disc of metal and brought it down to stand on its edge in a crack on the table top.

'Land-sakes a-mercy,' she said innocently. 'It looks like we're due for a stand-off.'

'What'll we do in that case?' asked Danny, just as innocently.

'Didn't Mark teach you nothing about—things?'

'You know, Calam, gal,' Danny drawled, blowing out the lamp. 'He just might have done at that.'

Almost an hour later, just before she went to sleep, Calamity gave a grin. One thing was for sure. Dusty Fog's kid brother could sure act like a man full grown.

CHAPTER FIVE

BREAK UP THAT COW STEALING, DANNY

SID WATCHHORN eased his arm in the sling, glanced at the rider and wagon which entered the compound and then walked back into the office.

'Danny's here, Cap'n,' he said.

'Alone?' asked Murat, seeing his chance of making the Caspar County investigation—and getting away from the tedium of office work—depart.

'Never thought he'd bring any of 'em in alive,' Sid answered. 'Only he's not alone. Got a right pretty lil gal along with him, driving a six-hoss Conestoga.'

Throwing a glance at Sid, the Ranger captain tried to read the tanned, leathery face for a hint that his wounded man made a joke. He saw nothing, which did not entirely surprise him. However, Murat knew handling the ribbons of a *six*-horse Conestoga wagon took skill of a high degree. Coming to his feet, Murat walked from the office and looked in the direction of the approaching party.

'I told you so,' said Sid in doleful delight, 'only you didn't believe lil ole me.'

'Does anybody?' grunted Murat and walked to meet his other Ranger. 'Howdy, Danny. We got a telegraph from Sandy up to Two Trees, said you'd gone on after Choya and his bunch.'

'Huh huh!' Danny answered.

'Catch 'em?'

The words came out more as a statement than a question. No Ranger worth his salt would leave the trail of the men who killed one of his partners and wounded another. Yet Murat could see no sign of the *Comanchero's* horses. Then his eyes went to the wagon's box, studying the various scars on its timber. Two of the bullet holes looked newly made.

'I caught 'em. They're in the back of Calam's wagon.'

Walking by his captain. Sid headed to the rear of the wagon and started to unfasten its canopy's lashings. Calamity jumped down from the box and joined the Ranger at the rear.

'Let me lend you a hand,' she said. 'You look like you need one.'

'Her husband come home early,' answered Sid.

'That's allus the way,' Calamity commiserated.

'How many in there, ma'am?'

'Four, all there was. And happen you don't want the other wing busting quit calling me "ma'am".'

One of the young wranglers dashed up and took charge of Danny's horse. It said much for Danny's trust in the youngster that he allowed the *sabino's* welfare to the boy's hands. However, Danny knew he could rely on the youngster to care properly for the big horse and that he must give his report to his captain as quickly as possible.

'Let's go into the office, Danny,' Murat suggested as the youngster led the *sabino* away.

Following Murat into the office, Danny took a seat at the desk. There was nothing fancy about the room in which the Rangers of Company 'G' handled their paper-work and planned their campaigns against the criminal elements of Texas. Just a desk, its top scarred by spur-decorated boot heels and burned by innumerable cigar and cigarette butts, with a few papers sharing the top with the first edition of the famous 'Bible Two,' the Texas Rangers' list of wanted men that would be brought out each year and read by the sons of the star-in-the-circle far more than they ever studied the original book. Some half-a-dozen chairs stood against the walls, two more at the desk. A safe, its door open and shelves empty, graced one wall, a stove facing it across the room. On either side of the door leading to the cells at the rear of the building were respectively a bulletin board containing wanted dodgers from all over the State, and a rack holding some dozen assorted Winchesters, Spencer carbines and ten-gauge shotguns, all clean and ready for use.

It was not a room conducive to long, leisurely discussion, but a plain, functioning, working-man's premises where business was dealt with speedily and without waste of time.

'Tell me about it,' Murat ordered as they took their seats. He took out the office bottle and poured two drinks, offered the young Ranger a cigar, and settled down to learn how Danny handled things on the hunt for the *Comancheros*.

A feeling of pride came to Danny as he took the drink. It had become a custom in Company 'G' that Murat offered a Ranger who came in from a successful chore a drink before starting business. Usually it would have been the senior man making the report and collecting the drink, but this time—for the first time—Danny found himself receiving Murat's unspoken approbation.

Quickly Danny told Murat all that happened from the time the *Comancheros* ambushed his party. By questions; knowing his men, Murat never expected to learn the one making the report's share of the affair without probing; the captain found out how Danny handled things with his sergeant dead and more experienced colleague wounded. Nodding in approval, he listened to Danny tell how the trailing of the *Comancheros* came to its conclusion at the Jones place. The captain's eyebrows lifted slightly as he learned the identity of the girl on the wagon. It figured, happen a man gave thought to the matter; few other women in the West could handle a six-horse Conestoga wagon.

'Four, and the two you downed when they hit you,' Murat said when Danny came to the end of his report. 'That's the whole damned bunch finished.'

'And it cost us Buck Lemming,' Danny replied. 'He was married, got a family, too, Captain.'

'I know that,' answered Murat. 'It's the way the game goes, Danny.'

'If I'd been up front——'

'Call *that* right off, boy!' the captain snapped. 'Buck rode up front because it was his place as sergeant to be there. Nobody'll blame you for the ambush, and what you've done since sure don't need any apologising for. Well, we can scratch Choya's name out of "Bible Two".'

'Yes, sir. Anything more for me?'

'Yep. I want you to pull out for Caspar, today, if you can.'

'Something up?'

'Cow thieves.'

Danny looked at the commander of Company 'G' and

nodded. A Ranger never knew from one day to the next what new trouble he might find himself tangling in. Fresh off the trail of a band of murderous *Comancheros*, he found himself detailed to ride out the same night to deal with a bunch of cow thieves—even if his captain had not said it in so many words.

'Sounds a mite urgent just for cow thieves,' Danny remarked, knowing such business was mostly handled by the county authorities concerned and did not normally require the State-wide powers of the Rangers.

'It goes deeper than that,' answered Murat and settled down to explain the situation to Danny, including the possibility of far worse trouble than mere cow stealing developing out of the hiring of professional gun hands. Then Murat told Danny the most prime piece of information.

'A woman running it?' Danny growled. 'That doesn't sound possible.'

'Neither does seeing a gal handle the ribbons of a six-horse Conestoga—only we've both just seen *that*. Anyways, she has a perfect set-up to run it. A saloon where cowhands can come and go without attracting any attention; things even a saint* likes enough to make him think about grabbing a couple of un-branded strays, working on them with a running iron and selling them to pay for.'

'That figgers,' agreed Danny. 'Most young cowhands'd take a few chances to get extra liquor, gambling or gals. Only a gal running things makes it just that much harder.'

'It sure does.'

Studying Danny, Murat wondered if the task might be beyond the inexperienced young man's depth. Sure Danny had trailed and downed that bunch of *Comancheros* without calling for help, but that had been a straightforward piece of work. Tangling with the cow thieves and gathering evidence against their leaders, called for courage, brains—which Murat granted Danny possessed—and experience. It was the latter Danny fell short on. Yet he might be a good man for the job. At least he would be the right age for Ella Watson, or whoever controlled the stealing, to regard as a potential cow thief, and he knew enough about cowhand work to act the part without arousing suspicion.

---

* Saint: Cow thief's contemptuous name for a loyal cowhand.

But could Danny swing things up there in Caspar and prevent another range war blowing a further Texas county apart at the seams?

Then Murat remembered Danny's relationship with Dusty Fog. Should Danny find himself in water over the willows up in Caspar County, a word would bring his famous brother riding to his aid. Nor would Dusty ride alone, but bring along his two good and efficient *amigos* Mark Counter and the Ysabel Kid. While none of that illustrious trio had ever belonged to the Rangers, they could handle the trouble in Caspar County with ease.

While rolling a cigarette, Danny watched Murat and guessed at his captain's thoughts. His knowledge did not annoy him as much as it might have done before taking the *Comanchero* gang. Now he had proved himself in his own eyes and one thing he knew for sure. Should he handle the Caspar chore, no matter how difficult the task or how it went, he did not aim to call on Brother Dusty for help. Danny reckoned that if he could not stand on his own two feet by now, he was of no use as a Ranger.

Only having a woman at the back of the business surely made it hellish hard to handle. Danny had decided on the same line of action as that thought out by Murat. Going into Caspar as a drifting cowhand, taking on at a ranch and then letting himself be drawn into the cow stealing, seemed like the quickest way to learn who stood behind the business. Catching the actual thieves would be easy enough that way; but, from what the captain said, they were only dupes. It was the brains behind the stealing Danny wanted. One did not kill a snake by cutting off its rattles, but by stamping on its head. Remove the dupes and the organiser would lie low for a time, then emerge and corrupt another bunch of fool young cowhands, turn them from honest, loyal hands to thieves.

'Reckon you can handle it, Danny?' asked Murat. 'You can go in any way you want. I won't hold you back.'

'I reckon I can,' Danny agreed.

At that moment the office door opened to admit Calamity and Sid.

'We've took the bodies down to the undertaker, Cap'n,' said the Ranger. 'I reckoned you might like to have a jaw with Calamity, so she left her wagon at Smith's store to be unloaded

49

and come back with me.'

'Take a seat, Calamity,' Murat said, rising. 'Could I offer you a drink?'

'Just a teensie-weensie lil three fingers,' she answered, accepting the chair Danny drew up for her. 'Wouldn't say no to one of them fancy cigars, neither.'

With any other woman, the request might have appeared as an affectation. Yet somehow the sight of Calamity seated with a foot raised on the desk, puffing appreciatively at one of Murat's thin, crooked black cigars, looked entirely natural.

'I'd like to thank you officially for helping Danny get the *Comancheros*,' Murat told the girl.

'Shuckens, he helped me more than I helped him. Anyways, to pay me back he promised to show me the sights of Austin City.'

'You done seen me, gal,' Sid remarked. 'Ain't no other sights worth seeing.'

'Leave us not forget Calamity's a visitor to Texas, Sid,' Murat growled. 'Don't make her retch. Anyways, when was this sightseeing to be done?'

'Starting tonight.'

'Only he'll be riding out this evening.'

Calamity's eyes went to Danny, then back and met Murat's. 'Must be something real urgent, Cap'n.'

'Urgent enough,' agreed Murat, studying the girl and remembering all the stories he had heard about her. Maybe some of them were a mite lengthened, but from the way she handled her end of the *Comanchero* business, she had sand to burn and did not spook when the going became rough. Slowly Murat swung his eyes to Danny and read mutual thoughts on the subject of Calamity in the young Ranger's mind. Murat almost gave in, then shook his head. 'No. It just couldn't be done.'

'If I knew what the hell you meant, I'd agree,' Calamity answered.

'I don't see why it couldn't,' Danny put in. 'Calamity's got two weeks at least to hang around Austin afore her boss gets here.'

'Just what are you pair——' Calamity began.

'It'd be too dangerous, Danny.'

'That gal eats danger, Cap'n.'

50

'Hey! What the blue-blistering hell——'

'She might not care for the idea.'

'Why not put it to her, Cap'n?' asked Sid, enjoying watching the expressions on Calamity's face while the conversation went on.

'Hold it! Hold IT!' she suddenly yelled, pounding a hand on the table top. 'Just dig in your tiny Texas feet and let a half-smart lil Northern gal catch up with you.'

'Huh—Oh, hi there, Calam,' Danny drawled. 'Plumb forgot you was here.'

The girl replied in a hide blistering flow of invective which drew admiring grins from the listening men. Throughout the flow Sid listened spell-bound and at its conclusion could barely hold down his applause for a mighty fine demonstration of the ancient and honourable art of cussing.

'How about it, Sid?' asked Murat. 'Will she do?'

'Don't know what for, Cap'n, but it sounds like you want me to say "yes," so being good, loyal and wanting an advance on next month's pay, I'll say it. Yes, I reckon she'll do right well.'

'And me,' Danny agreed.

Clapping a hand to her forehead, Calamity gave a groan. 'My mammy never gave me much advice, but she always told me to stay clear of Texas and Texans. When I first met Mark Counter I figgered she was right. But getting to know you three's changed my mind.'

'Has, huh?' asked Danny sympathetically.

'It sure as hell has!' Calamity yelped. 'Now I *know* she was right.'

'To get serious, Calam,' Murat put in, 'how'd you like to help us?'

'How'd you mean, help you?' she asked suspiciously.

'We've something on that needs a woman's gentle touch.'

'It's nothing to do with some gals getting strangled, is it?'

'No,' answered Murat, sounding a mite startled. 'Why should it be?'

'No reason at all, 'cepting that the last time a lawman said something like that to me, I near on wound up getting choked by a murdering skunk. Enjoyed it so much that I figured I'd like a second go.'

'Happen they get on to you, if you take the chore, you'll

likely get your wanting,' Murat stated and explained his idea to Calamity.

When Murat finished speaking, Calamity looked him over with interested eyes. It appeared that the situation was not as dangerous as she first imagined. No sir, it was even worse. With a rope waiting on their capture, cow thieves tended to be a mite rough should they find a spy in their midst. If she went in to Caspar, she would not have the cover of police escort as she had, until the final night—when, to be fair, she ought not to have gone out—in New Orleans. However, Calamity reckoned she might be able to take good care of herself, especially against another woman; after all no gal had ever licked her yet.

'You'll not be able to go into the saloon dressed like that, Calam,' Danny pointed out.

'Now me, I'd swear every saloon gal dressed this way,' she sniffed.

'We can easy fix the clothes,' Murat went on.

'Yeah,' groaned the girl. 'I figured you might. I can't stay on for long though. Dobe Killem wants me back with the outfit when he pulls out of here.'

'If you haven't got us the proof we need in nine or ten days, you likely won't get it at all,' Murat replied. 'How about it, Calam?'

'You just hired yourself a gal,' she answered, holding out her hand. 'When do we start, Danny?'

'Now slow down a mite, gal,' Murat ordered. 'It's not as easy as all that.'

'Happen I'd thought it would be, I'd never have taken on,' Calamity told him calmly.

Despite her eagerness to try the novel experience of working as a saloon-girl and undercover agent for the Texas Rangers, Calamity knew nothing must be left to chance. She found Murat's preparations remarkably, and comfortingly from her point of view, thorough. Knowing that certain and painful death awaited Calamity if she should be detected as a spy, Murat intended that she should take as few chances as possible. While Danny Fog would also be working in Caspar County, he could not be on hand all the time to protect Calamity. Mostly the girl would have to stand on her own two feet and rely on her brains, courage and ability.

Collecting a trio of horses from the remuda, Calamity, Danny and Murat rode into Austin. During the trip, Murat gave Danny and Calamity instructions. Danny was to take the name Daniel Forgrave, a cowhand who had worked on three different ranches well clear of the Caspar area. Making sure Danny could remember the names of the outfits and their bosses, Murat turned his attention to Calamity. After some discussion they settled on the name Martha Connelly for her and once more Murat gave a list of places where she had worked.

'Remember those four, whatever you do,' Murat warned.

'What if somebody knows them?' she countered.

'That's always a chance, Calam,' admitted the Ranger captain. 'You can always pull out. Fact being, you'd be wise if you did.'

'Never was wise,' she grinned. 'You reckon it's a good thing to use the Golden Slipper here in town, they could right easy telegraph here and ask about me.'

'You'll be all right, even if they do,' Murat promised.

While Calamity trusted Murat's judgment, she figured out one detail that a man would be unlikely to think about. She expected to be taken to some dress shop and fitted with clothing suitable for her pose as a saloon-girl and saw danger in the idea. Then she discovered that Murat had been aware of the problem of dress and knew the answer to it.

Instead of visiting a dress shop, Calamity found herself taken in the rear of the Golden Slipper, one of Austin's better class saloons. Clearly Murat knew his way around the place, for he led his party upstairs to the office of the owner, a big, buxom, jovial woman who greeted him as a friend and lent a sympathetic, understanding ear to the problems facing the Ranger captain.

'Nothing easier, Jules,' she stated after hearing what Murat required. 'You boys go downstairs and have a drink on the house while I fix up Calamity with all she'll need.'

Half an hour later Calamity entered the bar-room, only she looked a whole heap different from the girl who came to town with Danny. Gone were the men's clothing, gunbelt and bull-whip, replaced by a small, dainty and impractical hat, a dress with black and white candy-striped bodice and mauve skirt, some cheap, flashy jewellery and a reticule, such as a saloon-girl would wear when travelling. None of the items were new, but had been selected from clothing left behind by girls who departed into the respectability of married life.

Calamity had figured suspicion might come her way should she show up in Caspar with every item of clothing damned near brand new. However, Murat appeared to have foreseen the danger and countered it by arranging for her to loan a wardrobe suited to the part she was going to play.

'Got all you need, Calamity?' the captain asked as the girl joined him and Danny at their table.

'Just about all,' she replied. 'Got me this outfit, three fancy saloon gal frocks, shoes, stockings and some fancy female dodads you pair don't know the name of, or ought to be ashamed of yourselves if you do. Ain't but one thing more I'd like along with me.'

'And what's that?' asked Danny.

'One of those forty-one calibre Remington belly guns.'

Such an item would not arouse suspicion, or be out of place in a saloon-girl's possession. Many a girl working in a saloon or dancehall carried a Remington Double Derringer, or some other such small, easily concealed firearm, in her reticule, or strapped to her garter.

'There's one in my office and some shells for it,' Murat told the girl. 'I can let you have it as soon as we've bought your stage ticket to Caspar. You'll go on tomorrow's stage and be there in three days.'

'I'll pull out now,' Danny drawled. 'That should see me in town a day ahead of Calamity.'

'Reckon it should,' agreed Murat. 'Break up that cow stealing, Danny.'

'Yes, sir, Captain,' replied Danny soberly. 'I aim to do just that.'

CHAPTER SIX

LOOKS LIKE I GOT HERE TOO LATE

A PAIR of spiralling turkey vultures caught Danny Fog's
eye and caused him to bring his big *sabino* to a halt. The sight
of those black-plumed scavengers hovering in the sky never
struck a western man as being a beautiful sight. When turkey
vultures gathered, they followed death and a corpse, or something near to it, lay below them. Human or animal, it made no
never mind to a hungry turkey vulture. Gliding down from
the skies, the birds tore flesh from bones and leaving only a
picked skeleton behind when they departed.

Two days had passed since Danny rode out of Austin and at
almost noon, he figured he must be on the eastern ranges of
Caspar County, most likely crossing Buck Jerome's Bench J.

'Might be nothing, hoss,' he said, patting the *sabino*'s neck
and glancing at the dun cutting horse borrowed from Sid
Watchhorn to aid his disguise and which now followed the
sabino without fighting the rope connecting to Danny's saddle.
'I reckon we'd best take us a look though.'

Such an action would be in keeping with the character he
must play while in Caspar just as much as when he rode in his
official capacity of Texas Ranger. Any man seeing circling
buzzards—as the non-zoologically-minded Western folk called
Cathartes Aura, the American turkey vulture—would investigate. The attraction might be either an injured man or animal,
or some critter died of a highly infectious disease. In which cases
the knowledge could be useful : in the first to save a life; in the
second, one might prevent a spread of the infection by prompt
action.

From the look of things, the birds circled over a large
cottonwood that spread its branches over the range maybe a
mile from where Danny sat his horse. A touch of his heels

against the *sabino's* flanks started the horse moving and the dun followed it without any fuss. As yet Danny could see nothing of the dead or dying creature which caused the turkey vultures to gather in the sky.

Danny had covered about half a mile when a bunch of pronghorn antelope burst out of a hollow ahead of him. Stopping the *sabino*, he watched the animals speed away, covering the range at a pace only a very good horse could hope to equal. While Danny loved hunting, and lived in an age when game-preservation had never been heard of, he made no attempt to draw his rifle and cut down any of the fleeing antelope. He carried food in his bedroll and would likely be on some ranch's payroll before it ran out. So there did not appear to be any point in killing a pronghorn and he had never seen any sense in shooting some creature just to see it fall.

Led by a buck that carried a pair of horns which would have gladdened any trophy-hunter's heart, the herd held bunched together and went bounding through the bushes at Danny's right, disappearing into a basin. Just as Danny started the *sabino* moving again, he saw the pronghorns bursting wildly through the bushes, scattering in panic as they raced out of the basin once more.

'Now what in hell did that?' he mused and drew his rifle.

Four possible answers sprang to mind: a bunch of wolves denning up among the bushes; a mountain lion that had been cut off from timber country by the coming of daylight and took what cover it could find: a grizzly or black bear hunting berries, but willing to augment its diet by the flesh of a succulent pronghorn; or the presence of hidden men. Predators all, any one of them would cause such panic among the pronghorns should the fast-moving animals come unexpectedly upon it in the bushes when already fleeing from danger.

Danny nudged his *sabino's* ribs and started the horse moving forward. On reaching the edge of the bushes, he halted the horse and slid from the saddle. Not even as steady an animal as the big *sabino* would face the sudden appearance of one of the predators in thick bush and Danny could think of a number of more pleasant ways to die than under the teeth and claws of a startled grizzly after being pitched from the back of a bear-spooked horse. Of course, there might not be a bear in the bushes, but it cost nothing to take precautions.

Leaving the horses standing, the *sabino's* trailing before it in a manner which it had been trained to regard as holding it still as effectively as if being tied, Danny went into the bushes with some caution. He saw nothing to disturb him or explain the panic among the pronghorns. A flock of scarlet-plumed red cardinal birds lifted from among the bushes at his approach, but nothing dangerous or menacing made its appearance. Ahead of him the bushes opened into a clearing at the bottom of the basin. Danny came to a halt and studied the scene before him with worried, calculating eyes.

'Looks like I got here too late,' he thought.

Two bodies lay alongside a dead fire's ashes. Cowhands, Danny concluded from their dress; and of the kind he had ridden from Austin to hunt down if the pair of running irons meant anything. Cautiously he studied the clearing, noting the pair of cow horses which stood tied to the bushes at the far side, then taking in the scene around the fire once more. Moving closer, he looked down at the bodies. One had been shot in the back and must have died without even knowing what hit him. Nor would the second have been given much better chance to defend himself by all appearances. Kneeling by the body, Danny examined the holster and doubted if anything remotely like a fast draw could be made from it. The revolver still lay in the holster, its owner having died before he could draw it.

Cold anger filled Danny as he looked down at the two bodies. Neither cowhand looked to be much gone out of his teens and, ignoring the distortion pain had put on the features, appeared to be normal, pleasant youngsters. These were no hardened criminals, or he missed his guess; only a couple of foolhardy youngsters who acted without thinking. They deserved better than to be shot down like dogs.

Danny was no dreamy-eyed moralist or bigoted intellectual regarding every criminal as a misunderstood victim of society to be molly-coddled and pampered as a warning that crime did not pay. In most cases a man became a criminal because of a disinclination to work and had no intention of changing his ways. As a peace officer and a sensible, thinking man, Danny approved of stiff punishment, up to and including hanging, for habitual criminals. While any form of punishment would be most unlikely to change such a man's ways, it served to deter others from following the criminal's footsteps.

For all his thoughts on the subject, Danny hated to think of the way the two young men died. He promised himself that their killer would pay for the deed.

Throwing aside his feelings, Danny forced himself to think as a lawman and to learn all he could about the happenings of the previous night. Carefully, he studied the ground around him, using the knowledge handed on by that master trailer, the Ysabel Kid. From what he saw, there had been three cow thieves present, all occupied with their illegal business when death struck. The third member of the trio made good his escape, or at least got clear of the fire, for Danny found signs of somebody, possibly the killer, racing a horse across the clearing in the direction taken by the fleeing cow thief.

At that point of the proceedings Danny began to feel puzzled. His examination of the tracks told him that one rider had returned, set free some of the calves and led off three more. Yet the same person did not free the dead men's horses, nor even go near the bodies.

'Sure puzzling,' he mused, turning to leave the clearing and return to his horses. 'From all I've heard, this looks like Gooch's work. He never takes chances and wouldn't give those boys chance to surrender or make a fight. But why would Gooch free half the calves and take the others. And why would he leave the two bodies when they'd fetch a damned sight more bounty than three calves would bring him?'

A possible answer occurred to Danny as he reached the horses. He stood on Bench J, not Forked C land, so it was not the range Gooch had been hired to protect and the bounty hunter did not work for the love of his labour. Of course, it might not be Gooch who killed the cowhands, although everything pointed in that direction. Most men, especially ranchers and honest cowhands, hated a cow thief, but few would go to the extreme of shooting down two in cold blood. No, it appeared the thing Governor Howard and Captain Murat feared had happened. Tired of merely earning his pay, Gooch left the Forked C range to hunt bounty on other property.

Just as Danny swung into the *sabino's* saddle, a distant movement caught the corner of his eye. Turning in the saddle, he looked across the range to where a trio of riders topped a rim and swung their horses in the direction of the circling turkey-vultures.

Taking out his off-side Colt, Danny thumbed three shots into the air. Instantly the trio brought their mounts to a halt, looking in his direction. Sweeping off his hat, Danny waved it over his head and the three men put their spurs to the horses, galloping towards him. Three shots fired into the air had long been accepted as a signal for help, one which would only rarely be overlooked or ignored. The three men might be as interested, as Danny had been, in the circling vultures, but his signal took priority over the sight.

Danny studied the men as they approached. Two of them were cowhands; a leathery man of middle-age, plainly dressed and with a low-hanging Dance Brothers revolver at his side; the second looked around Danny's age, a freckle-faced, red-haired young man, cheery, wearing a flashy bandana and red shirt and belting an Army Colt in a cheap imitation of a contoured, fast-draw holster. From the two cowhands. Danny turned to study the third rider. He sat a good horse with easy grace. Although his clothes looked little different from the other two, there was something about him, an air of authority and command, which said 'boss' to range-wise eyes. A Remington Beals Army revolver hung butt forward at his left side and looked like he could use it. Not that the man bore any of the signs of a swaggering, bullying gunslinger, but merely gave the impression of being mighty competent.

'You got trouble, friend?' asked the third member of the trio.

'Not me,' Danny answered. 'But those two fellers down there—man, have they got trouble?'

'Two?' put in the youngest rider. 'Reckon it's Sammy and Pike, Buck?'

'Best way to find out's to go look,' replied the third man. 'Name's Buck Jerome, friend, this's my range. These gents are my foreman, Ed Lyle and Tommy Fayne, he rides for me.'

'Howdy. I'm Danny Forgrave. Best go down there and take a look though.'

Accompanying the men down the slope. Danny studied their reactions as they looked at the tragic scene in the clearing. He

59

could read little from the two older men's faces, but guessed the scene hit them hard. On the other hand, Tommy Fayne showed shock, his face paled under the tan and his lips drew into tight lines.

'It's Sammy and Pike!' he said in a strangled voice. 'That damned murdering skunk Gooch killed them.'

'Easy, boy,' Jerome said, laying a hand on Tommy's sleeve. 'We don't know for sure it was him who did this.'

'Who else but a stinking murdering bounty hunter'd gun down two kids like Sammy and Pike without giving them a chance?' Tommy answered hotly. 'They weren't neither of 'em good with a gun, and you know it, Buck.'

'Hosses are tied, Buck, that's why they never come back,' Lyle said quietly. 'Happen this feller hadn't found them, they might have laid here for days.'

'Might at that,' admitted the rancher and turned to Danny. 'No offence, but how did you come to find them? You know how it is when you find something like this, questions have to be asked.'

'Sure,' Danny agreed. 'I was headed for those buzzards when I put up a herd of pronghorns and they went down into this hollow. Only they came bursting out like the devil after a yearling. Got me curious to find out what spooked them. I figured it might be either bear, cougar or wolves and that I might be able to pick up a few dollars on its hide. So I came down and found this.'

All the time Danny spoke, he felt the other three's eyes on him taking in every detail of his dress and appearance. Not that he had any need to fear detection on that score. Before leaving Austin, Danny dressed for the part he aimed to play. He retained his hat, boots, gunbelt and saddle, but the rest of his clothing no longer bore the mark of a good tailor. Instead he wore a cheap, gaudy bandana, a blue flannel shirt and faded, washed-out jeans. Not was there anything out of the ordinary in the arrangement. Many young cowhands bought the best they could manage in saddlery, hats and gunbelts, but took what they could afford for the rest of their clothing.

After studying Danny, Jerome and Lyle exchanged glances. Both had reached the same conclusion—and just the one Danny wanted folks to make about him. Although this soft-spoken youngster wore two guns and looked proficient in their use, he had none of the ear-marks of a proddy trigger-fast-and-up-from-Texas kid. A good cowhand, most likely, and probably one with a yen to see new ranges around him.

'If Gooch shot the boys, why'd he leave 'em here?' asked Lyle, voicing one of the problems which had been worrying Danny.

'He knew I wouldn't pay him,' Jerome answered.

'Then why'd he bother shooting?' growled the foreman. 'Gooch didn't give a damn whether the cow thieves stole us blind as long as he got his bounty.'

'He maybe aimed to take the boys back to the Forked C and claim he downed them on Crither's range,' guessed Jerome. 'Cut for sign, Ed, see what you can learn while we start loading the boys. We'll have to take them into town and report this to Farley Simmonds.'

'If he handles this as well as he done the rest of the stealing, we'll sure see some action,' sniffed Lyle and went to obey his boss's orders.

None of the men expected the task of loading the bodies to be pleasant and they were not wrong. While Lyle examined the ground, Danny, Jerome and Tommy wrapped the bodies in their slickers and loaded them, stiff with *rigor mortis* across the two horses' saddles. By the time the task was completed, Lyle had made his examination and came to his boss to report.

'Was another one here,' he remarked, coming up with the same conclusions that Danny had earlier. 'Smallish, not too heavy-built feller I'd say. Took out *pronto* when the shooting started, with somebody after him, both riding fast. Then the small feller come back later, cut free some calves and led the others off.'

'That'd be the ones they'd branded he took,' Jerome guessed.

'Maybe that other feller led Gooch so far he couldn't find his way back to here,' Tommy put in.

'Could be,' admitted the rancher. 'Only I can't think of anybody round here as fits that description, smallish and light built. Can hardly believe that Sammy and Pike were stealing from me, neither. Why Sammy was fixing to get his-self married to one of Ella Watson's gals real soon.'

'Yeah,' Tommy said bitterly. 'Sammy and Pike were my pards. They'd never steal from anybody, boss. Maybe they was

61

trying to stop the cow thieves.'

'Maybe,' grunted Jerome. 'Where'd they go last night, boy?'

'Into town. Sammy wanted to see his gal and Pike went along for the ride. I was fixing to go with them, only one of my mounts was needing tending.'

Danny listened to the conversation without asking any questions or making any comments. Above all else, he must not show too much knowledge of Caspar County affairs. A chance-passing drifter would be unlikely to know much about the situation and showing that he was acquainted with the affairs of the county would cause suspicion. So he kept quiet and listened, which had always been a good way to learn things one wanted to know.

'Let's go into town,' the rancher suggested. 'You'd best come along with us, Danny, the sheriff'll want to see you.'

'Sure,' Danny agreed. 'I was headed that way when I came on this lot.'

'I'd best take the running irons with me, Boss,' Lyle remarked.

'Do that Ed,' answered Jerome. 'Only don't let on that Sammy and Pike were using them. I know their folks and they were good kids.'

The words increased Danny's growing liking for Jerome. Some men would have started ranting about ingrates, or damning the cowhands as stinking, untrustworthy cow thieves and not giving a damn who knew that the youngsters had gone bad. From Jerome, Danny turned his attention to the younger of the hired men. Clearly Tommy was badly shaken by the death of his two friends. But did he possess any guilty knowledge of how they came to die? Maybe the youngster had an idea of the identity of the third cow thief. Or perhaps he was merely thinking that, but for a stroke of luck, it might be him lying by the fire.

Mounting their horses, the men rode out of the clearing, Lyle and Tommy leading the dead cowhands' animals, each toting its stiff bundle. None of them spoke until they came out on to open land. Then the sight of the whirling vultures recalled what brought them together.

'How about those buzzards?' asked Danny.

'They're on our way to Caspar, we'd best check,' Jerome

answered. 'Ed, go scout around and see if you can track down that third jasper. I'll lead Sammy's hoss in for you.'

'Yo!' replied the foreman and gave Danny a calculating glance. 'I'll look around real good.'

Much as he would have liked to accompany Lyle, Danny restrained himself. He guessed that the foreman intended to check on his tracks also, making sure that he was what he pretended to be. Not that Danny blamed Lyle. Under similar circumstances he would have done the same; and Lyle could learn little enough by back-tracking Danny for a few miles.

While riding towards the cottonwood, Danny started to get an uneasy feeling that he could guess what they would find. So he did not feel unduly surprised when, from over two hundred yards distance, he saw a body lying beneath the spreading branches of the cottonwood.

'Another,' Jerome breathed. 'Who the hell this time?'

A few seconds later Tommy supplied the answer. 'It's Bat Gooch. I recognise that hoss of his there.'

At thirty yards Jerome halted the party. 'Hold the hosses here, Tommy. I don't reckon Farley Simmonds'll make much of it, but we'll not muss up the sign in case he wants to come out.'

Leaving their horses, Danny and Jerome walked toward the bounty hunter's body. Both kept their eyes on the ground, studying the sign and reading much the same conclusions from what they saw.

'Can you read sign, Danny?' asked the rancher.

'My pappy was a hunting man. Taught me to know whether a foot pointed forwards or back.'

'Huh huh. Way I see it is that the feller Gooch was chasing got swept off his hoss by a branch. Fell just here and Gooch left his hoss to come over to him. Only the other feller wasn't hurt bad and started to throw lead. How d'you see it?'

'Just about the same,' replied Danny.

However, although he did not intend to mention it, Danny saw more; a whole heap more than the rancher's description of what happened. First thing to strike Danny was the fact that Gooch's gun lay in its holster. No man who knew sic 'em about gun fighting would approach a potentially dangerous enemy without taking the elementary precaution of drawing his gun.

Certainly a man like Gooch would not fail to take so basic a piece of self-preservation. The second significant fact to Danny's mind being the powder burning and blackening around the two bullet wounds in the body. Whoever shot Gooch had been close, real close. As the shooter appeared to have been lying on the ground, Gooch must have been bending; no, that would have put him too high to catch the burning effect of the other's weapon's muzzle blast. Which meant either the other had been allowed to rise, or that Gooch knelt by his killer's side.

Only Gooch would never have allowed the other to rise, or knelt by the fallen cow thief's side, without holding his gun and being sure he could shoot at the first wrong move. Gooch knew gun-fighting and had more sense than take such chances with any man under such circumstances.

And there, Danny figured, he had touched the answer to Gooch's apparent folly. On approaching the fallen cow thief, Gooch would have not only held his gun but would most likely to have sent a bullet into the other just to make good and sure there was no danger to his bounty hunting hide—unless he saw something to make him figure he would not need such precautions.

Something that told him the shape on the ground be a woman, not a man.

Maybe Captain Murat's information about the identity of the brains behind the Caspar County cow stealing had been correct after all!

CHAPTER SEVEN

THE LAWMEN OF CASPAR COUNTY

CASPAR CITY looked little different, nor had any greater right to such a grandiloquent four letters after its name, than a hundred other such towns that existed on the Texas plains for the purpose of supplying the cowhands' needs for fun and the basic necessities of life. It consisted of at most forty wooden, adobe, or a mixture of both, buildings scattered haphazardly along half a mile of wheel-rutted, hoof-churned dirt going by the title of Main Street. However, Caspar bore the supreme mark of solidarity and permanency which so many other towns lacked; a Wells Fargo stage station and telegraph office stood proudly on Main Street between the adobe county sheriff's office building and Ella Watson's Cattle Queen saloon.

To Danny Fog's way of thinking as he studied the town, those silvery telegraph wires contained a menace to his well-being in that they could be used to obtain information about him far more quickly than by using the mail services.

The coming of Danny's party, each man leading a horse bearing a stiff, unnatural, yet easily recognisable burden, brought people from the various business premises along Main Street. Questions were tossed at Jerome, but for the most he ignored them, saving his story to be told to Sheriff Farley Simmonds.

Among others, some half-a-dozen women and a couple of men emerged from the batwing doors of the Cattle Queen, attracting Danny's attention. At least one of the women caught his eye. Even without being told, he knew that black-haired, beautiful woman in the centre of the group to be Ella Watson, female saloonkeeper and maybe the boss of the cow thieves plaguing Caspar County. No ordinary saloon-girl could afford such a stylish, fancy light blue gown; a garment more suited in cut and line to a high-class New Orleans bordello than in the saloon of a small Texas town. The dress did little to hide the fact that its wearer's five-foot-seven figure would be something to see. Cut low in front, it showed off a rich, full bosom, clung tightly to a slender waist, then spread out to eye-catchingly curved hips, although concealing the legs from view. Her face, beautiful yet imperious, carried a look of authority which none of the others showed and set her aside as one above the herd.

'That's Ella Watson, runs the Cattle Queen,' Tommy confirmed, waving his hand to a small buxom, pretty and scared-faced blonde girl who stared in wide-eyed horror at the scene.

'You look like you could use a drink,' Danny replied. 'Soon as we've seen the great siezer, we'll go get one.'

'I can use it,' Tommy stated.

The great siezer, the cowhand's disrespectful name for the county sheriff, was not in his office; having gone along to the Bon Ton Café with his deputy for a meal, according to one of the gathering crowd of onlookers. Throwing a glance at his two hands—he had hired Danny on the way into town—Jerome gave instructions.

'Go get that drink, but keep it to one or two at most. I'll send word if Sheriff Farley wants you.'

Leaving Jerome to take care of the bodies. Danny and Tommy fastened their horses to the sheriff's office hitching rail and then walked back towards the sturdy wooden front of the saloon. The little blonde girl came running from among her fellow workers, making for Tommy.

'What's happened, Tommy?' she gasped. 'Who—what——'

'Easy, Mousey,' Tommy answered gently, taking the girl by the arms. 'Sammy and Pike ran into trouble.'

Danny studied the girl. Wide-eyed horror showed on her pretty, naïve face, She was a fluffy, shapely, if a mite buxom, little thing, wearing a short green dress, black stockings and high-heeled shoes. Maybe not too smart, she looked like she would be happy, merry and good company under normal conditions—and clearly Tommy regarded her as something extra special.

'They were in last night,' the girl said.

'Who with?' growled Tommy.

'Sammy was with Dora, but he left with just Pike,' answered the girl, turning curious eyes in Danny's direction.

66

'Mousey, this's Danny Forgrave,' Tommy introduced, taking the hint. 'He's come to ride for Bench J. Danny, meet Mousey, she's my gal.'

'Howdy, ma'am,' Danny greeted.

'Call me "Mousey",' she told him. 'My real name's Mildred, but I like Mousey better.'

'Then Mousey it is,' Danny replied.

At the same time as he spoke to the girl, Danny became aware that one of the men standing with Ella Watson studied him carefully. The man wore a low-crowned white Stetson shoved back on his head and a scar ran across his skull just over the right ear, the hair growing white along its line and in contrast to the blackness of the rest. Standing around six foot, the man wore a black cutaway jacket, frilly-bosomed shirt under a fancy vest, black string tie and tight-legged white trousers. Instead of a gunbelt, the man had a silk sash around his waist, a pearl-handled Remington 1861 Army revolver thrust into the left side so as to be available to the right hand. Cold, hard eyes in a fairly handsome, swarthy face, took in every detail of Danny's dress, with due emphasis on the way he wore his guns. For a moment the man stared, then whispered something in Ella Watson's ear, bringing her eyes to Danny.

'Let's go get that drink, Danny,' Tommy suggested. 'Come on, Mousey, gal.'

Taking Mousey's arm, Tommy escorted her into the saloon and Danny followed. Inside he studied the place with interest. For a small cow town, the Cattle Queen sure looked mighty elegant. There were tables and chairs around a dance space for use of the customers; chuck-a-luck, faro and blackjack layouts, the usual wheel-of-fortune stood against one wall. A long, fancy bar with a big mirror behind it offered a good selection of drinks and was presided over by a tall, burly man with side-whiskers and bay-rum slicked hair. The bartender nodded to the new arrivals as they came to the bar and laid aside the glass he had been polishing.

'What'll it be?' he asked.

'Beer for me 'n' Mousey,' answered Tommy. 'How's about you, Danny?'

'Same'll do for me, *amigo*,' Danny replied.

'What's all the fuss outside?' the bartender inquired as he

poured the three beers with deft hands.

'We just brought in Sammy Howe, Pike Evans and Gooch,' Tommy explained.

'Whooee!' ejaculated the bartender. 'What happened?'

'How the hell would I know?' snapped Tommy, the tensions of the day putting an edge into his voice.

A dull red flushed into the bartender's cheeks at the words and his hand went under the counter towards his favourite bung-starter; a most handy tool with dealing with cowhands who forgot their menial position in life.

'I thought Gooch maybe——' he began.

'Thinking's bad for a man,' Danny put in quietly. 'Especially when you're talking to a feller who's just lost two good friends.'

Slowly the bartender turned his eyes to Danny's face. Something in the young man's level, grey-eyed stare caused the bartender to remove his hand from the bung-starter. Having a well-developed judgment of human nature, the bartender knew when to sit back and yell 'calf rope,' so he backed water. While he might get by bullying a youngster like Tommy, the bartender reckoned he had best not try any of his games with that tall, blond newcomer.

Then a feeling of relief came to the bartender as he watched the women stream back into his room. At the rear of the group walked Ella Watson and the fancy-dressed hardcase who found Danny so interesting outside. With backing like that, the bardog allowed he might be able to chill the blond Texan's milk. However, he remembered that his boss did not go for rough stuff in the rooms, especially at so early an hour and when dealing with cold-sober and unoffending men.

'Feller seems tolerable took by you, Danny,' Tommy remarked, nodding to the mirror's reflection. 'Ain't hardly took his eyes off you since you come near him.'

'It's not often they get a feller as handsome as me around,' answered Danny, taking up his drink in his right hand, 'Who is he?'

'Name of Ed Wren. They do say he's real fast with his gun. He works here as boss dealer.'

The name did more than ring a bell for Danny, it started a whole danged set of chimes going. In fact, Danny knew more than a little about the gunhand called Ed Wren. Among other things, he knew where the man picked up that bullet scar across the side of his head. A couple of years back Wren had hired out to prevent trail hands taking on to help drive the Rocking H herd to market. Trouble being that the Rocking H's owner was kin to the Hardin, Fog and Blaze clan and so Dusty Fog rode to his kinsman's aid. Dusty had been the first man Wren tried to forcibly dissuade. That white streak across the side of Wren's skull told the attempt had not been successful.*

Not for a moment did Danny believe Wren had forgotten the incident. Which could account for the gunman's interest in him on his arrival. Although taller than his elder brother, Danny's facial resemblance had always been fairly marked. Even now Wren must be trying to decide if this be coincidence or if Danny was either the man who shot him, or kin of the man. Either way, Danny found he had a further piece of trouble he must watch for.

Although Ella Watson did not come to the bar, but stood talking with Wren and casting interested glances at Danny, the other girls swarmed forward, eager to hear the news. Tommy looked them over, apparently seeking for one particular face and not finding it.

'Where's Dora?' he asked. 'I've something to tell her.'

'She's upstairs, taking a bath,' replied a buxom, tough-looking brunette. 'Was that young Sammy you brought in?'

'Yeah,' Tommy replied.

'What happened?' put in another girl excitedly. 'Who shot him?'

Before Tommy could answer, the batwing doors swung open and a tall young man swaggered into the room. Danny studied the newcomer in the bar mirror, not liking what he saw even though the other wore a deputy sheriff's badge. Unless the deputy possessed money of his own, he dressed a whole heap too well and fancy for a junior peace officer in a moderate-sized Texas county and not a rich county at that. From hat to boots, the deputy wore the rig of a cow-country dandy. If the truculent assurance on his sullenly handsome face, the cocky air about him, and the low hanging brace of ivory-handled 1860 Army Colts be anything to go on, he reckoned himself to have something extra special in his presence.

* Told in *Trail Boss* by J. T. Edson.

Crossing the room, the deputy halted behind the two cow-hands and jerked his thumb contemptuously over his shoulder towards the door. A hard expression, or what he fondly imagined to be hard, came to his face as he snapped out an order.

'All right, cownurse. Un—The Sheriff wants you at his office *pronto!*'

Normally Danny would have obeyed a member of the county law and reserved his comments on the other's impolite mode of address until away from the view of the local citizens, so as not to weaken the other's authority and standing in the community; but for once he did not. Aside from his dislike for the manner in which the deputy spoke, Danny had a part to play in Caspar County. He saw a good chance presented for him to establish his character before the woman who might possibly be behind the cow stealing in the county.

'I've not finished my drink yet,' he answered without turning.

Hearing the sniggers of the watching girls, the deputy scowled. He longed to have the kind of reputation which inspired fear, if not respect, in the hearts of all who saw him. So, wishing to grandstand before the girls, he made a mistake. Shooting out his left hand, he caught Danny by the arm and dropped his right hand to the butt of the off-side Colt.

While training as a deputy under his father, Danny was taught never to lay hands on or threaten a man and that he must only place his hand on the butt of his gun when the situation warranted drawing and using the weapon. To Danny's way of thinking other law-enforcement officers should respect the same rule. He did not like the slit-eyed manner in which the deputy studied him, and pegged him as being the kind of hawg-mean show-off who would gun down an unsuspecting man just to be able to claim he had made a kill.

So Danny did not aim to give the deputy a chance. Pivoting around, Danny threw the hand from his sleeve and tossed the remainder of his drink full into the deputy's face. Caught unawares, the deputy took a hurried step to the rear, entangled his spurs and sat down hard on the floor. Although partially winded, the laughter of the watching girls drove the deputy to worse folly.

'Why, you——!' he began and clawed at the right-side Colt

70

once more.

Instantly Danny drew his off-side gun and threw down on the deputy, his thumb cocking back the hammer and forefinger depressing the trigger as the Colt's seven-and-a-half inch barrel slanted down into line on the deputy's body. At the same moment Danny saw Ed Wren move. Give him due, the gunman had speed. The fancy Remington licked out of his sash in around three-quarters of a second—which explained how he came to fail against Dusty who could cut a good quarter of a second off that time. However, Wren could handle a gun faster than Danny and the young Ranger admitted the fact without shame.

'Drop it, cownurse!' Wren ordered.

'Don't see how you can down me without I get to put lead into the deputy at the same time, *hombre*,' Danny answered, making no move to obey the man's order.

Which statement was true enough. Even a head shot could not save the deputy from taking lead; in fact, one would ensure he did get a bullet in him. Danny held his Colt with the hammer drawn back and trigger depressed. No matter where the lead hit, should Wren shoot, the impact would cause Danny's thumb to release the hammer. From then on the gun's mechanical processes would automatically take over, firing the charge in the uppermost chamber of the cylinder and expelling a bullet through the barrel which lined on the deputy's favourite stomach.

Rank fear etched itself on the deputy's face as he remembered that Wren showed considerable interest in becoming a member of the sheriff's staff on his arrival in town. However, Uncle Farley hired only one deputy and could not take on another, even one of Wren's standing. The gunhand now had a remarkably good chance of creating a vacancy in the sheriff's office by shooting the newcomer.

'Just hold everything!' snapped Ella Watson, stepping forward but keeping out of line of fire. 'Ed put up your gun right now.' Not until Wren obeyed her order did she turn her eyes to Danny and continue, 'And you, cowboy, if you know what's good for you. I know Clyde there acted a mite hot-headed and foolish, but he *is* the sheriff's nephew.'

From the woman's tone, Danny could not decide if she gave

warning that the sheriff bore strong family ties and would strenuously object to his nephew going home with a .44 calibre hole in his stomach; or that she merely figured any relation of the sheriff could not help acting foolishly. However, Danny reckoned he had made his point and could rely on the woman to prevent any further need of his Colt. Wren had already returned his gun to the sash, so Danny lowered the Colt's hammer on to a safety notch between two of the cylinder's cap-nipples and spun the gun into its holster. Instantly the deputy let out a snarl and reached towards his off-side Colt. Ella Watson stepped between Danny and the deputy, standing squarely in front of the young Ranger and glaring down at the deputy.

'Now that's enough, Clyde. You asked for what you got and if you want to take in the cowhand under arrest, I'll send for Dean Soskice to act for him.'

Just who the hell Dean Soskice might be Danny did not know; but the name appeared to have a mighty steadying effect on the deputy. With a menacing scowl, the deputy took his hand from his gun and rose to his feet. Once again he jerked his thumb towards the door.

'You're still wanted down at the jail,' he said.

'Why sure,' Danny replied. 'I'll come right now. My drink's gone now, anyways.'

'I'll come with you, Danny,' grinned Tommy, eyeing his new acquaintance with frank admiration. 'The boss said for both of us to go along. See you after we've done, honey.'

'I'll be here,' Mousey promised.

'After you, deputy,' drawled Danny as they reached the door. 'I was raised all polite and proper.'

Still scowling, but with none of the cocky swagger which marked his entrance, the deputy preceded the others from the saloon. Ella Watson watched them go and returned to the gunhand's side.

'Well?' she asked.

'Naw. It's not him. That kid's not better than fair with a gun and Dusty Fog's a whole heap faster. Still he looks a whole heap like Fog, except that he's some smaller and not so hefty built.'

Watching the gunhand reach up and finger the bullet-scar,

72

Ella Watson felt relieved. A man did not soon forget the feller who marked him in such a manner and licked him to the draw—Ella discounted Wren's story that Dusty Fog shot him from behind—and it came as a relief to know the newcomer was not the Rio Hondo gun wizard.

'I hope that fool Simmonds handles things better than his nephew did,' she said. 'I'd like to know more about that cowhand. If he's safe, he's just what we want, brash, looks like he needs money—and not too good with a gun.'

Clyde Bucksteed did not speak to Danny and Tommy as they walked towards the sheriff's office, nor did he follow them as would a deputy taking in a couple of suspects. Instead he walked before them, conscious that most of the folks who saw the procession knew where he should be if bringing the two in and not merely running a message for his uncle. Already the bodies had been taken from the street, but a few folks hung around in the hope of fresh developments, enough to make sure the story of Clyde's failure to control the cowhands be broadcast around the town.

'Who-all's this Dean Soskice?' Danny asked of Tommy.

'A law wrangler. Not a bad jasper though. Talks real fancy and gets us boys out of trouble should we take on too wild and rowdy comes pay day. He sure has old Farley Simmonds buffaloed. Wouldn't be surprised if Dean's not in there right now.'

Knowing the cowhands' usual contempt for law wranglers, Danny looked forward to meeting this Dean Soskice who buffaloed the county sheriff. On entering the sheriff's office, Danny found his wish granted. Not only was the sheriff-buffaloing law wrangler present, but Danny also found himself face to face with the remainder of the Caspar County law.

Simmonds proved to be a florid-featured, sullen-looking man, run to fat and with an air of lassitude about him. For all that he dressed well and looked a whole heap more prosperous than he should. Unlike his range-dressed nephew, Simmonds wore town-style clothing and sported a gunbelt from which he must be able to draw the fancy-looking Prescott Navy revolver in no less than three seconds starting with a hand on its butt.

Although not one to judge by first appearances, Danny decided that he did not care for Caspar County's law-enforce-

73

ment officers. With Simmonds and his nephew running the sheriff's office, Danny could well imagine that the county would be full of cow thieves. In fact, he felt considerably surprised that Caspar County did not serve as a haven for more types of outlaws. From what Danny could see, any help he might require locally would not come from the sheriff's office and he doubted if the secret of his identity would remain a secret for long should he take either Simmonds or the deputy into his confidence.

From Simmonds, Danny turned his attention to the other two occupants of the room. Jerome sat by the sheriff's desk, chewing on the end of a thick black cigar and looking mean as hell. The other man caught Danny's main attention, being the lawyer who buffaloed sheriffs.

Even with the type of man Danny figured the sheriff to be, the young Ranger could hardly believe that he would allow Dean Soskice to bother him. Soskice proved to be a tall, slim young man with long, shaggy brown hair, a pallid, slightly surly face and an air of condescending superiority about him; dressed in an Eastern-style suit, shirt and necktie, none of which showed any signs of lavish attention having been spent on them. As far as Danny could see, Soskice did not wear a gun and in Texas at that period seeing an unarmed man was even rarer than finding one walking the street without his pants. Nothing about the lawyer told Danny how he managed to buffalo Sheriff Simmonds and Danny reckoned it might be worthwhile to try to find out the reason.

'You're the young feller as found the bodies,' Simmonds stated in a ripe, woolly politician's voice, then he turned his eyes to his nephew. 'Say, Clyde, boy, how come you're all wet?'

'He threw beer over me,' Clyde answered sullenly.

'Now why'd he do a thing like that?' asked the sheriff and swivelled his gaze back to Danny. 'You hear me, boy. Why for'd you do that?'

'Feller caught me arm, pulled me around,' Danny answered. 'Next dang thing I knowed, there he was with my beer all down his fancy shirt front.'

Low mutters left Clyde's lips and Soskice moved forward. 'If there's a complaint being sworn out against you, cowboy, I'd advise you to tell the truth,' the lawyer said, his voice that of an

74

educated Northerner.

'You got a complaint against the feller, Clyde?' the sheriff inquired. 'I only told you to fetch him down here for a talk.'

Anger and resentment smouldered in Clyde's eyes as he studied the lawyer's mocking face. However, Clyde recalled other occasions when he had tangled with Soskice on a legal matter and been sadly beaten in verbal exchanges. Soskice knew every aspect of the law as it pertained to working to the advantage of the one Clyde figured on arresting and used that knowledge to build a sizeable following among the cowhands, most of whom had a hefty antipathy towards the peace officers who often interfered with their fun.

'I got no complaint,' Clyde finally muttered, knowing Soskice would worm the cowhand out of trouble should he try to make a complaint stick. 'The cowhand got me all wrong.'

'You'd best tell the sheriff your side of this business, Danny,' Jerome remarked. 'I've told him the way I saw things and he wants to hear what you've got to say about it.'

Just in time Danny prevented himself from delivering the story like a lawman making his report. Instead he told what led up to his discovery of the bodies and left out his own conclusions on the affair.

'Just come on 'em, huh?' grunted Simmonds at last. 'Where'd you come from and why'd you come here?'

'Come up from Austin last and happened by this way looking for work.'

'Been working in Austin?'

'Nope. Just wanted to see what the big city looked like.'

'Where'd you work last?' Clyde asked.

'That's a good question,' drawled Simmonds. 'Only let me ask 'em, Clyde.'

'Sure, Uncle Farley,' was the sullen reply.

'Boy's a mite eager, but he's got a good point,' the sheriff went on. 'Where did you work last?'

'For the Tumbling D, that's Joe Dudley's place down to Ysaleta,' Danny answered, giving one of the places Murat named as references.

'And your name's Danny Forgrave?'

'Allus has been,' Danny answered.

'It's not a summer name then?' Clyde remarked.

When a man did not wish to give his correct name out West, folks rarely pressed the matter. About the closest one came to doubting the speaker's claim was to inquire whether the title given be a summer name, one taken on the spur of the moment and as a temporary measure.

'Summer and winter both, *hombre!*' Danny growled.

'Danny's working for me,' Jerome put in. 'You'll find him around the spread if you're not satisfied with his story. Now what're you fixing to do about this cow stealing, Farley?'

'Doing all I can, Buck. Only the county don't pay me well enough to hire more help.'

'Then send for the Rangers.'

'I wrote a couple of weeks back, but I never heard nothing back,' answered the sheriff.

Which, although he did not intend to mention the fact, Danny knew to be a lie. No request for aid sent by a sheriff was ever passed up by the Rangers and his company had received no letter from Simmonds.

'Well, you'd best do something,' growled Jerome, 'otherwise I'm going to.'

'I thought this business today showed you what happened when folk take the law into their own hands,' remarked Soskice. 'Crither's attempt hasn't been any too successful, has it?'

'I won't be doing it by using a hired killer,' Jerome answered, coming to his feet. 'Let's go, boys.'

After watching Jerome, Danny and Tommy depart, Simmonds gave a grunt. 'Buck sounds a mite peeved. He's no fool either and as tough as they come. I sure hope them cow thieves hold off for a spell.'

'How about that new cowhand?' asked Soskice.

'His story sounded all right to me,' the sheriff replied.

'Why not telegraph Ysaleta and check up on him?' the lawyer suggested. 'And don't look so pained, the county will pay.'

'Yeah, likely it will,' Simmonds admitted. 'Clyde, you go down to the telegraph office and send a message to the sheriff at Ysaleta, ask him what he knows about a feller called Danny Forgrave. The answer might make interesting reading.'

MISS WATSON STUDIES DANNY FORGRAVE

'I DON'T reckon he'll do a damn lot for us,' Jerome growled as he left the sheriff's office with Danny and Tommy. 'Not unless the cow thieves start branding the stuff out on Main Street.'

'Why'd you elect him then?' Danny asked.

'Damned if I know,' the rancher admitted. 'This's a poor county and there were few enough who wanted to take on the office. Being sheriff's a thankless chore and don't pay more than eating money. Reckon Farley looked about the best of a bad bunch at election time. Let's go grab a meal at the Bon Ton, then take a drink afore we ride out to the spread.'

'How about Sammy and Pike?' asked Tommy.

'I'll see about their burying afore we pull out,' Jerome promised.

'I mean what're you fixing in to do about them getting burned down that way, boss,' growled the youngster. 'We ought to see the Forked C bunch and——'

'I'll be seeing Vic Crither,' the rancher promised.

'It was through him that they got made wolf bait!'

'Choke off that talk, boy!' Jerome warned. 'Vic handled things the way he saw them and he sure as hell didn't tell Gooch to prowl our range.'

'He ought to be——!' Tommy began hotly.

'Simmer down, boy,' Jerome said quietly. 'Vic made a mistake in bringing Gooch in, but he never sent that bounty-hunting skunk on to our range, or told him to gun boys down like that.'

'Sammy and Pike were my pards——'

'I know. And they were good boys, too, even if they did go out with running irons by them. But it won't bring them back to start a shooting fuss with the Forked C. All that'll do is get

77

more folks killed. We'll get the same as is happening up in Shelby County and while we're fussing the cow thieves'll steal us blind.'

'You're right in that, boss,' Danny put in. 'I've seen a county that's been torn apart by a range war. The buzzards were the only ones to profit by it.'

Jerome looked at Danny with interest. Knowing cowhands, the rancher had not expected support from that quarter. There was something puzzling about the tall blond stranger. Sure he looked and acted like a drifting cowhand, a wild, irresponsible young cuss no different from thousands of others who followed the longhorn trade. Yet he seemed capable of thought; the question about why Simmonds was elected sheriff proved that; and now he talked sense and peace instead of reaching for a gun and painting for war. It said much for Danny's acting ability that he had so far managed his true nature and play a part well enough to fool so shrewd a man as the rancher.

'Just you listen to Danny, Tommy,' Jerome grunted. 'It's the first time I ever heard a cowhand say anything that made sense—and I've been one. Let's go eat a bite.'

While walking towards the Bon Ton Café, leading their horses, the three men saw a bunch of riders entering town. The newcomers came fast, making a fair racket and all showing signs of being in high spirits.

'Rafter O's coming in,' Tommy remarked. 'Hey, that must be their mean ole bay Joey Jones's leading.'

'What's so special about the bay?' Danny asked, studying the riderless horse led by one of the approaching cowhands. It was a fifteen hand, light washy bay animal with a roman nose, little pin ears crimped at the tips and pig eyes, with the general air of a mean one about it.

'Nobody's ever rode it,' Tommy explained. 'So Rafter O do tell.'

'Never yet been a hoss as couldn't be rode,' Danny stated.

'And never a cowhand as couldn't be throwed,' Jerome countered. 'If you're fixing to take that bay on, don't. I saw it one time at Rafter O. It's a suicide bucker and how it's not killed its fool self, or some danged fool rider, I'll never know.'

With that the rancher led the way to the Bon Ton where they left the horses at the rail and entered the room to sit at a table by the door. Even as they ordered a meal, a group of the Rafter O men entered and came towards the Jerome table. Danny figured the stocky man in the lead to be boss of the outfit and his guess proved to be correct.

'Howdy, Wally,' Jerome greeted.

'Hi, Buck,' replied Wally Stirton. 'How's things?'

'Could be better.'

'They always could. Losing much stock?'

'Lost more than that,' Jerome said, knowing the story would come out sooner or later. 'Gooch cut down Sammy and Pike last night.'

Silence fell on the group of cowhands at the words. While there might be considerable rivalry between the different ranches, most of the hands felt a certain kinship to their fellow workers, especially when one found himself in difficulties. Gooch had never been liked by the free-and-easy cowhands and it might have gone hard for him if he did not already lie dead at the undertaker's shop.

'Where's Gooch at now?' asked one of the Rafter O hands coldly.

'Taking a rest on a slab at Gustavson's,' Jerome answered.

'I figured he'd get around to doing it sooner or later,' grunted the speaker, for Gustavson was the local undertaker.

'Who got him?' Stirton inquired.

'That's what we don't know,' admitted Jerome and told the listening men of his findings on the range.

Knowing cowhands, Jerome figured he had best tell all he knew rather than wait until rumours spread across the range and stirred up bitterness. He did not hide anything, even the fact that his two men had been using running irons when cut down, nor did he excuse Gooch's act on those grounds. Angry mutters rose among the listening men, but all were directed at Gooch and not the bounty hunter's employer.

Danny took advantage of Jerome's speech to study the Rafter O hands. Six in number, they looked like any other bunch of cowhands one might find working on a Texas spread. Three of the six looked to be around Tommy's age and appeared to be badly shaken by what they heard. Danny decided to cultivate the trio in the hope of learning something.

The food came and Danny ate well after a couple of days on

his own fixings. When finished, he returned to the Cattle Queen with Jerome and Tommy, after tending to their horses. Already the hitching rail showed a fair crowd inside and on entering the bar-room Danny saw that business had picked up. Jerome left the younger men to join a group of prosperous-looking citizens gathered at a side table. For a moment Tommy stood looking around, then led Danny to where Mousey sat with the big buxom brunette.

'Hi, honey,' Tommy greeted. 'Where-at's Dora?'

'Upstairs,' Mousey replied. 'She's taking it bad about Sammy.'

'She would be,' Tommy said sympathetically. 'Can I see her?'

Watching the big brunette, Danny thought he saw a smile flicker across her face at the words. Then the expression went as the brunette looked at Tommy and answered. 'I don't reckon so. The doctor's been and gave her something to make her sleep. She's took it bad, even if it don't show. Us girls learn to hide our feelings, don't we, Mousey?'

'I know you do, Maisie,' the little blonde replied.

'Well, unless one of you boys want to buy a gal a drink, I'll get back to work,' the brunette said.

'Call up a waiter, ma'am,' Danny drawled. 'I'll get them in.'

'No beer for me, handsome,' Maisie grinned, nodding to a passing waiter. 'I like it, but it sure don't like my figure.'

'Wine for the ladies,' Danny ordered, with the air of a man who wanted folks to assume he had been around. 'And fetch a bottle of Stump Blaster for us.'

'That's what I like,' grinned Maisie. 'A big spender.'

'Can't think of a better way to get rid of money, Maisie, gal,' Danny replied.

As Danny spoke, he saw Ella Watson passing. The saloon-keeper's eyes came to him and studied him in a calculating manner. From the way she looked, Danny figured he interested her and so aimed to keep on with his role of a reckless young cuss who might be open to offers of making easy money over and above his pay.

'When we've had a drink,' he went on, 'what say we go over and buck the tiger for a whirl.'

'Not me,' Tommy answered. 'Pay day's too far off and I'm saving my money.'

'They're fixing in to get married, settle a lil piece of land and raise kids and cattle, Danny,' Maisie explained with a grin, seeing Ella nod towards Danny.

A red flush crept into Mousey's cheeks and she gasped, 'How you do go on, Maisie.'

'Shucks,' Danny grinned. 'Marriage's real wonderful. Fact being, I don't reckon any family should be without it.'

Maisie laughed with a professional entertainer's heartiness. Having caught her boss's signal and read its meaning correctly, she proceeded to pour out some of the wine brought by the waiter and also to study Danny with careful attention to detail. Before she could reach any conclusions, the Rafter O arrived from the Bon Ton. Halting at the door, the hands looked around the room, their eyes coming to rest on Danny's party. The tallest of the Rafter O group nudged the shortest, nodded in Danny's direction and the whole bunch trouped across the floor, their boss leaving them to join the same group Jerome sat among.

'I tell you, Chuck,' the tallest hand announced in a carrying voice, 'that ole bay's so mean the boss'll never sell it to Bench J.'

'Reckon not, Lanky,' the shortest of the party answered. 'There wouldn't be nobody at Bench J could ride him.'

'I'd bet on that,' grinned Lanky.

'How much and what odds?'

All the Rafter O men looked at Danny as he spoke up. Trying to appear as if they had not meant their words to carry to the Bench J's ears, the Rafter O's exchanged glances.

'Did he mean us?' Lanky asked.

'I sure hope he didn't,' a red-headed youngster called, with a surprising lack of originality, Red, replied.

'Figure he asked us something,' Chuck drawled. 'Only does he mean it?'

Coming to his feet and ignoring Tommy's warning glances, Danny dipped a hand into his pocket.

'Do you Rafter O's talk with your money or only your mouths. I said how much do you bet and what odds do you give that I ride the bay?'

'He wants to bet, Chuck,' Lanky stated soberly.

'Nope,' Danny corrected. 'I want to bet money. He'd be no use to me when I won him.'

Grins came to the Rafter O faces and cowhands took a liking to Danny. The attempt at getting him to ride the bay was in the nature of a try-out, to see if the newcomer had what it took to make a hand. Whenever Rafter O came into town, their boss specialising in horses more than cattle, they brought along a good bucker in the hope of finding somebody game enough—or fool enough—to ride it.

Everybody's attention came to the table, even the gamblers holding up their games, for the Rafter O's reputation in such matters was common knowledge and the crowd eagerly awaited developments. If the blond stranger accepted the challenge, and he appeared to have done so, they ought to see some sport.

'Come on, Rafter O,' Danny continued after a few seconds. 'Make your bet, or set up the drinks.'

'We'll give you two to one and take up to sixty dollars,' Chuck answered after a brief consultation with his friends. 'If you want to go that high.'

'Bet!' Danny said loudly and started walking towards the door. 'I'll get my saddle. Where'd you want me to ride him, in here?'

'Oh, no you don't!' Ella Watson interrupted, coming forward. 'I've an empty corral outside, use that.'

Without giving anybody the chance to request that he showed his money, Danny headed for the door and Tommy followed on his heels with Mousey at his side. They went by the front door, but the rest of the crowd headed out at the rear to form up around the big pole corral.

Danny collected his saddle, stripping off the rope, rifle boot and all other extras ready for what he knew would be a hard, gruelling ride. With that done, he took off his gunbelt and handed it to Tommy.

'You watch that hoss, Danny,' Tommy warned. 'If Rafter O's betting cash money on him, they sure don't aim to lose.'

'Nor me,' grinned Danny. 'Boy, you, me'n' lil Mousey here'll sure have us a time on what we've won.'

Together they walked around the side of the building and towards the corral at the rear. Danny watched Chuck lead up the bay, noting that it appeared to be quiet enough and followed without trouble. Not that he felt surprised for a blindfold covered the horse's eyes, and he knew that even a bad outlaw learned the futility of fighting a rope. The bay did not fight having a saddle put on it, but Danny noted the way its ears flattened down and its muscles quivered. That horse as sure as hell did not intend to be ridden by any man.

Like most Texans, Danny had ridden horses almost as long as he could walk. Following his elder brother's lead, Danny took to riding bad ones and became adept at it before he decided the old saying, 'A bronc buster's a man with a heavy seat and a light head' had a whole lot of truth and so gave up his ambition of becoming a well-known rider of unmanageable horses. However, a man out West often needed to trim the bed-springs out of a horse or two and Danny had never lost the ability to stay afork a snuffy one. He reckoned he ought to be able to handle the bay unless it proved something really exceptional.

With his health, and wealth, at stake, Danny took no chances. He attended to saddling the horse himself. The spectators noted the care he took in the saddling and nodded their approval.

'No you don't,' Danny growled as the horse blew itself out. Bringing up his knee, he rammed it into the animal's ribs and forced a hurried blowing out of the air sucked into the bay's lungs. This reduced the swollen rib-cage to its normal size before the cinches drew tight. If Danny had missed the trick, he would have tightened the cinches on the swollen body and when the bay blew out the air, the saddle was left loose. However, he had seen and countered the move and the saddling went to its completion.

'Are you set to make a start, Danny?' Chuck called, having learned the challenger's name from Maisie.

'Yep,' Danny answered and swung into the saddle. Feeling the bay quiver under him, he knew a hard fight lay ahead. 'Lord,' he thought, 'If I get all stove up, Cap'n Jules'll peel the hide off me.'

Yet Danny did not ride the horse out of sheer bravado or a desire to grandstand. He wanted to further establish his assumed character in Ella Watson's eyes and knew that if he should be injured riding the horse, Murat would understand his motives.

One thing showed right off. Rafter O might stand to lose some money but they played fair. Chuck stood at the horse's head and gripped the end of the blindfold, but he made no move to jerk it from the bay's eyes until Danny had settled down firmly in the saddle.

'Now?' he asked as Danny settled in the leather.

'You watch him, Danny,' Jerome yelled, giving the friendly, if unhelpful advice always handed out to a man about to start riding a bad one. 'He's going to moan with you.'

'He'll need to when I'm through, boss,' Danny yelled back. 'Let her rip, Chuck, boy.'

A quick tug removed the blindfold and Chuck went head first through the corral rails in a flying bound which warned Danny, if he needed more warning, of the bay's danger potential. Instantly the horse came apart and without bogging its head down between its legs as did so many of its kind as a starter to bucking. From standing like a statue, the horse took off in a series of crow hops, bounding up and lighting down on stiff legs in an effort to jolt its rider out of the saddle by the force of impact. Crow hopping was not hard to handle for an experienced rider, but Danny knew he could expect much more.

Suddenly the horse reared high, chinning the moon and waving forelegs in the air. However, Danny possessed that rare sixth sense so vital to a bronc peeler in that he could mostly anticipate the horse's moves and be ready to counter them. Up slid his hands along the reins, gripping just below the connection with the bit. He pulled hard, dragging the horse back to its feet before it could crawfish over on to its back and either throw him or crush him beneath it.

Foiled in its attempt, the bay appeared to go wild with rage. It rocketed across the corral, pitching fence-cornered—leaving the ground in one direction, jack-knifing its hind and forefeet together in mid-air and twisting itself to land at about a forty-five degrees angle to the place it took off. While the horse went high and landed hard, double shuffling to change its gait with every bound, Danny found little difficulty in riding the leaps.

Then it happened. The bay swapped ends, going up facing north and landing with its head aimed at the South Pole. With his rider's instincts Danny knew he was going to be thrown two jumps ahead of the actual happening. Kicking his feet from the stirrup irons, Danny allowed his body to go limp and landed rolling. He saw the bay bounce away from him and Lanky charged into the corral at a gallop, rope swinging ready to throw. On feeling the touch of the rope, the bay quietened down and allowed itself to be led towards the gate.

'Hold it!' Danny called, getting to his feet. 'Bandage him again. I'm not through with him yet.'

'What you doing down there then?' asked Chuck.

'Got off to leave him catch his breath,' replied Danny and walked towards the bay once more.

On mounting, he started to ride the bay again. Three more times Danny hit the dirt for the bay was one smart horse and knew how to ring in changes of style. It rainbowed high with arched back and shaking head; sunfished in leaping crescents that made it appear to be trying to land first one then the other shoulder on the ground while allowing the sun to burn its belly; fought on a dime, or pioneered new ground with each leaping bounce; straight bucked by going high from all four feet and on the way down tossing its hindquarters up again in the manner of the big paint stallion which crippled Danny's uncle, Ole Devil Hardin.* Through all the tricks, except when sent flying. Danny stayed in the saddle and each time down he rose to mount again. To allow a horse the chance of winding up a winner gave it bad ideas; it happened to the bay often enough to turn the animal into an outlaw.

'Give it up while you're ahead, *amigo*,' Chuck yelled as Danny rose from the fourth throwing.

'Hell yes!' agreed Lanky. 'You'll likely get hurt bad if you don't. He'll go to fighting blind if you keep riding him. We'll call the bets off if you like.'

'I *don't* like,' Danny replied. 'Seeing's how I aim to win your money. Set on that bandage again. He don't know who's boss.'

'Now me,' grunted Lanky, giving Danny an admiring glance, 'I'd say he knows right well who's boss. It's *you* that don't.'

'Likely,' grinned Danny and headed towards the bay once more.

Standing by the fence, Ella Watson watched Danny mount the bay again. A keen student of human nature, she found Danny interesting and a young man with certain possibilities— if he was what she expected. Her eyes went to Jerome who stood at her side.

'That's a real game boy,' she remarked. 'He's new here

* Told in *The Fastest Gun in Texas* by J. T. Edson.

85

though, isn't he?'

'Just today rode in,' replied the rancher. 'It was him found Sammy and Pike. I took him on to ride for Bench J.'

Further conversation ended as the bay, given its head, started to buck. A fresh danger had entered the fight, just as Lanky predicted. In addition to the normal risks attendant to riding a bad horse, the bay panicked and began to buck blind; not watching where it went as long as it shook the hated man-thing from its back. Desperately Danny fought to keep the bay's head up; always of prime importance when taking a bad one. However, he had been shaken badly by the throws and felt himself tiring. Night was coming and soon he would not be able to see enough to continue riding. Yet he could see no way of ending the bay's fight.

Twice he just managed to swing the bay clear of the corral rails and prevented a collision. Still bucking blind, the horse charged across the corral, headed for the other side of the enclosure. Only this time Danny felt too exhausted to argue the matter.

'Go ahead, you blasted fool critter!' he growled. 'Run in head on and bust your fool neck happen that's how you want it. Only I'm not fixing to go with you.'

Yells of warning rang out. Hurriedly those onlookers lining the section of rail towards which the bay rushed leapt backwards. Jerome gave a low curse and opened his mouth to yell for the doctor. Everybody watched Danny being carried straight at the rails and expected to see horse and rider pile head-first into the stout timber.

At the last moment Danny swung his right leg forward, up and over the saddle horn, thrusting himself clear. Even as he lit down, he heard the crash of the bay's collision with the corral rails. Only the give of the rails saved the horse from a serious injury and even so the bay rocked backwards, staggering and winded by the impact. Danny whirled and ran back, going into the saddle, catching up the reins and applying his spurs. Weakly the bay responded with a few mild pussy-back jumps, arching its back like a hound-scared cat and bouncing up into the air about a third of the height previously managed. Then the horse halted, Danny raked its sides again and brought off another short spell of fighting. The next time Danny used his spurs, the bay stood with heaving flanks and hanging head. Even without the excited and delighted whoops of the crowd who came crowding into the corral, Danny knew he had won. With heaving chest, he slid from the bay's saddle and leaned against the animal's sweat-lathered side.

'Are you all right, Danny?' Tommy asked, reaching the blond Ranger first.

'I—I've—felt better,' admitted Danny, then grinned as Lanky thrust through the excited crowd and held out a fistful of money. 'Fact being, I feel better right now. Thanks, Lanky. Loser walks the hoss, don't he?'

'Yep,' Lanky agreed and shot out a hand to grab a suddenly-departing Chuck by the collar. 'Which same you reckoned you'd do it.'

'Hell, everybody knows I'm a liar,' answered Chuck and reached for the bay's reins. 'You wait, I'll get me a ladder, rest it again you, climb up and beat in your knee-caps.'

'Go ahead, Chuck,' Ella smiled. 'I'll save you an extra big drink. The rest of you, first one's on the house.'

Which same started a rush for the saloon. Jerome came over to ask if Danny felt all right and, finding his new hand to be a mite tuckered out but in one piece, slipped a ten-dollar bill into a grimy hand and remarked he had won fifty off the owner of the Rafter O, then joined his party and returned to the bar.

'Go on in, Mousey, Tommy,' Ella smiled as everybody else streamed away. 'I want to congratulate the winner.' After the little blonde and Tommy left, Ella turned to Danny. 'You rode well, I never thought you'd get back the last time.'

'I had to, ma'am,' Danny replied.

'Why?'

'I didn't have any money to pay off with if I lost the bets.'

Watching the blond youngster headed for the bar, Ella Watson smiled. Her guess had been correct. A young man that keen to lay hands on money had possibilities and might make a good recruit for her illegal side interests.

CHAPTER NINE

ELLA WATSON HIRES MARTHA CONNELLY

CALAMITY JANE hated riding any kind of vehicle unless she held the ribbons and controlled the team. So she did not enjoy her trip to Caspar City and felt relieved when the driver drew rein before the depot at her destination. Luckily the stagecoach had not been one of the main runs, or she might easily have found the driver to be an acquaintance who could let slip her identity and wind her up in an early grave.

Throwing open the stage's door, the agent gallantly offered his hand to help Calamity alight, ogling the exposed ankle and lower calf with frank interest.

'Tuck 'em in, friend,' Calamity ordered as she swung herself on to the sidewalk and looked around.

'Huh?' the man grunted.

'Your eyes, they're bugged out a mite. Come down to the Cattle Queen tonight and look all you want, I'll be paid for it then.'

Flushing a little, the depot agent jerked around and yelled for the driver to drop down the gal's bags. There were no other passengers to alight at Caspar and Calamity took her two bags, carrying them along the street towards the batwing doors of the Cattle Queen.

'Calam, gal,' she mused. 'Just keep remembering you're Martha, call me Marty, Connelly. You learned a lot that last night in Austin, don't forget it or you'll be a long time dead.'

One thing Calamity had early learned was to face up to the truth. It would do her no good to pretend danger did not lay waiting for her on this chore. To do so might make her careless. So she intended to remember the danger and in doing so would be more likely to recall all the details drummed into her during the evening and morning before she left Austin to start her task.

Sucking in a breath, Calamity pushed open the batwing doors and entered the Cattle Queen's bar-room. It was the first time she had ever entered a saloon as a potential employee and she found the feeling novel. The time being shortly after noon, only a few customers sat at the tables or stood by the bar. Looking around, Calamity found only one girl to be present. That one sure looked a tough handful. She had red hair, stood Calamity's size and weighed at least twenty pounds heavier. From the way the red-head's dress fitted her, and the firm muscles apparent in her arms and legs, Calamity figured she would be as strong as they came; the kind of girl Calamity sought to tangle with when employed at her normal trade.

'Looking for somebody?' asked the buxom red-head.

'The boss. That you?'

'Me? Nope. The name's Phyl. I work here. Come on up, I'll take you to the boss. What's your name?'

'Marty Connelly. I'm looking for work.'

'Didn't take you for a circuit-riding gal-preacher,' Phyl sniffed. 'Come on, we'll see Miss Ella.'

Following the other woman, and holding down a temptation to plant a kick on the plump butt end so alluringly offered for such treatment, Calamity crossed the room and climbed the stairs. They walked along a passage and Phyl knocked on one of the doors.

'Gal to see you, boss,' she said, looking in.

'Show her in, Phyl,' replied a female voice.

On entering the room, Calamity took her first look at the woman who might be the leader of Caspar County cow thieves. All in all, Calamity felt a mite disappointed, for Ella had not long been out of bed and wore a dressing-gown which prevented the other girl from gaining any impression of how the saloon-keeper might stack up in a ruckus.

'So you're looking for work,' Ella said. 'Where were you last?'

'At the Golden Slipper in Austin.'

'Why did you quit?'

'That's my business.'

Hardly had the words left Calamity's mouth when she felt a hand clamp on her wrist and her arm was twisted behind and up her back in a practised move. Phyl was strong and real capable; Calamity gave her that as the twisted arm sent a wave of pain shooting through her. Holding down her first instinct, Calamity let out a yelp of pain. She figured showing her considerable knowledge of self-defence might make Ella suspicious and anyway if she tangled with Phyl, win or lose she would not be in any shape to get on with the chore which brought her to Caspar. So, instead of stamping her heel down hard on Phyl's toe then giving the buxom girl an elbow where it would do most good, Calamity stood still and croaked to be released.

'When Miss Ella asks a question,' Phyl answered, still holding the trapped arm, 'she expects an answer.'

Pain almost made Calamity forget her act, but she fought down her desires and whined, 'Leggo my arm! I quit 'cause I didn't like it there.'

'Why not?' Ella asked.

'T—too much law.'

The grip on Calamity's arm relaxed and she brought the limb in front of her to rub the aching wrist. Looking sullen—and promising herself that she would hand-scalp that fat, over-stuffed, loud-mouthed, hawg-stupid, cat-house cull before she left Caspar—Calamity awaited the next development.

'Are you in trouble with the law?' Ella inquired.

'Me?' yelped Calamity, trying to sound just right. 'Naw! Why should I be?'

'You mean they couldn't prove anything?'

'Yes—no,' Calamity answered. 'I—I got tired of Austin.'

'Then why come here?' Ella asked.

'This's as far as I'd money to go.'

While speaking, Calamity watched Ella and gained the impression that the other might be a real tough gal in her own right and not entirely dependent on Phyl to protect her interests.

For her part, Ella studied Calamity with equal interest. Shorter hair than the usual fashion, a tan to the skin that make-up on the face could not hide, hands roughened by hard work; all the signs of a girl who had spent some time in the female section of the State Penitentiary. A hard cuss, too, or Ella missed her guess. Maybe Phyl had come off easier than she deserved in twisting the newcomer's arm. A telegraph message to the Golden Slipper would clear up the matter of why the girl left Austin. If, as Ella suspected, the town marshal saw the girl on her way for reasons of unproven dishonesty, well, the Cattle Queen had use for such talents.

'What's your name?' Ella said.

'Marty Connelly.'

'All right, Marty. I'll take you on. And get this, I run a quiet house. You don't start lifting wallets, or finding a partner to run a badger game—and don't try looking innocent with me—unless I give the word. There's a small place out back, half-a-dozen rooms in it. If you want to sleep with any of the customers, you go there and do it through me and I get all you make. I'll give you your cut out of it. Those are the terms. Take them or leave them.'

Wishing she knew more about the working conditions of saloon girls, Calamity did not reply for a moment. She hung her head and stared down at the floor, trying to decide what would be the best answer. Then she made her decision. Ella could not suspect her and be trying to lay a trap. Maybe the conditions might be a mite harsh but probably the saloon keeper figured a girl without money would be forced to accept them.

'All right, Miss Ella,' she said. 'I'll take on.'

'I figured you would,' Ella answered mockingly and Calamity knew her guess must be right. 'What rooms have we vacant, Phyl?'

'Only Mousey's,' Phyl replied. 'I'll put her there.'

'Huh huh,' Ella grunted and nodded her head. It might be as well to keep the new girl in ignorance of the saloon's other business for a time and Mousey knew less than any of the other girls about what went on outside work hours. 'See Marty steeled in, Phyl.'

'Sure, boss. Come on, Marty.'

In the passage, Phyl grinned at Calamity. 'You'll find Miss Ella a damned good boss to work for, as long as you play straight by her. If you don't, me 'n' Maisie, she's the other boss gal'll tend your needings and, kid, that's painful.'

At that moment the tall, slim, untidy shape of Dean Soskice appeared at the stairhead. The young lawyer slouched along the passage by the two girls, glancing at Calamity in passing and walked towards Ella's room, entering without knocking.

'Who's he?' asked Calamity.

91

'The boss's lawyer,' Phyl grunted. 'So you just keep good and real respectful around him, Marty gal.'

'Like that, huh?' grinned Calamity with a knowing wink.

'Just like that. Now me, I'd prefer more muscle on mine.'

'And me.'

'Well, come on. I'll show you where you bed down. The kid you'll be with's all right and not in your class. There'll be a meal downstairs in about an hour.'

Ella Watson looked up from her work as Soskice entered, although she knew that only one person in town would have thought to enter her private quarters without showing the courtesy of knocking first.

'Who was the girl with Phyl?' asked the lawyer.

'A new one. She came in on the stage. Got run out of Austin by the law, and has been in the State Penitentiary or I miss my guess. Anyway, I'll have a message sent to the Golden Slipper asking about her.'

'Do you always hire jailbirds, Ella?'

'They're the safest kind. Naïve fools like Mousey are all right for attracting certain kinds of cowhand, but you daren't let her kind know you're doing anything illegal. You can't rely on, or trust, kids like Mousey, but you can trust a dishonest dame as long as she doesn't know too much and has something to lose.'

'You should know,' sniffed Soskice, sinking into a chair. 'Why'd you chance going out with those two cowhands who were killed?'

'They had a small bunch of unbranded stuff but were scared by Gooch. So I went along to show them how safe it was. Only it wasn't. Gooch found us.'

'There's nothing to tie you in with them, is there?'

'Not a thing. Don't worry, you're in no danger. Only the two cowhands knew I was going with them. I met them after we closed and wore men's clothing. Nobody would have recognised me, even if they'd seen me. Why didn't you come here before?'

'I—I was busy all yesterday,' answered the lawyer.

'What were you doing?' asked Ella bitterly. 'Packing ready to run if I was proved to be involved and caught?'

A dull red flush crept into the lawyer's cheeks and sullen

anger etched itself on his face. However, he held his comments and thoughts back. Much as he hated to admit the fact, even to himself, he needed Ella Watson's aid to carry out his plans much more than she needed him for hers. Without Ella, he could get nowhere for the cowhands regarded him with amused contempt, ignoring the fact that he bore the results of an Eastern college education and felt he ought to be honoured and respected for it.

'It wasn't that,' he said. 'You know we have to be careful. What do you make of the man who found the bodies?'

'Danny Forgrave? He's a cowhand, likes money and isn't too worried how he gets it,' Ella answered and told about the bets Danny made the previous evening.

'Sounds a likely one for you then,' remarked the lawyer. 'Is he good with his guns?'

'Not better than fair. Either Wren or Stocker could take him.'

'You haven't heard from the packing plant about the next shipment they'll want, have you?'

'Not yet, but I ought to some time this week. We've a fair bunch held at the hideout, all wearing Stocker's brand,' she replied then looked in a calculating manner at Soskice. 'What're you getting out of this, Dean?'

'Huh?' grunted the lawyer.

'I'm in it for money. Not because I hate the big ranchers for working and building something my old man didn't have the guts, intelligence or ability to make. I pay the cowhands to steal, to take all the chances, then get the money back off them in the saloon. It's all clear profit for me. What do you get out of it?'

For some reason Ella knew her question would not be answered. Soskice looked around the room, down at the floor, anywhere but at her and when he spoke, the words had nothing to do with her question.

'The ranchers are getting riled about the stealing. Maybe they'll call in outside help.'

'Not another bounty hunter, after what happened to Sammy and Pike,' Ella assured him. 'And only the county sheriff can call in the Rangers. I don't reckon Farley Simmonds would chance that.'

93

'I don't know about that. He moved fast enough to send to Ysaleta and get word about that cowhand. I saw him on the way here. It seems that Forgrave pulled out of Ysaleta a few steps ahead of being told to go.'

'I thought so. That boy'll be useful to us if I can get to him, and *that* won't be hard. But you didn't answer my question, Dean.'

'Maybe I do it so I can be close to you.'

While Ella doubted if Soskice ever did anything for anybody unless he saw a very good profit motive coming his way, she did not mention the thought. For all his faults, Soskice could sure make love and she reckoned that she might as well get something out of their association.

'All right,' she said. 'I'll go tell Phyl to send a telegraph message to the Golden Slipper in Austin and find out about Marty Connelly. Go wait in the bedroom and when I'm through we'll see how close we can get.'

Not knowing that her *bona fides* were to be checked, Calamity set about making herself comfortable. She took a liking to her room-mate from the start and found the feeling mutual. Having only just left her bed—the previous night's celebrations lasted very late—Mousey wore only her nightdress; but she bustled around showing Calamity where to unpack and chattering away like she had not talked for weeks and looked for a chance to do so.

Although the girls' room was anything but grandiose—it consisted of a couple of small beds, a dressing table, washstand and a small cupboard for storing the bulk of their clothes—Mousey appeared to be highly satisfied.

'I never had anything like this before,' she told Calamity, clearing her belongings out of two of the dressing-table's drawers. 'Always lived in a shack. Six of us kids shared one room, it had a dirt floor and we used to pass down clothes one from the next. Boy, this is living here.'

'Yeah,' Calamity answered. 'Where's a gal take a bath?'

'Down the street at Ling Sing's Chinese Laundry. He runs a bath-house at the back. I'll come with you, but let's grab a meal first.'

All in all, Calamity found Mousey to be quite a talker. By the time they reached the small staff dining-room, Calamity knew

94

all about Tommy and the little blonde's intentions in that direction. It seemed that while Mousey enjoyed the glamour of being a saloon-girl, she still appeared to be quite willing to return to a small cabin with a dirt floor—provided Tommy went with her.

'The other girls laugh at me when I talk about it,' Mousey said wistfully. 'But I know Tommy will marry me as soon as we've saved enough money to buy in on a little place of our own.'

On entering the dining-room, Calamity began to see the reason for Mousey's almost pathetic eagerness to be friends. All the other half-dozen girls seated around the table appeared to be either older, or at least more suited to the life of a saloon-girl. Brassy, hard-faced, none of them would be the sort of friend an innocent kid like Mousey wanted and most likely her attempts at making friends met with constant rebuffs.

More than any of the others, one girl took Calamity's attention. There was trouble, or Calamity had never seen it. The girl was a blonde, slightly taller and heavier than Calamity, shapely, beautiful; and knowing it she had an air of arrogant truculence about her.

For the rest, they looked like the kind of girls one expected to find in a saloon. Maybe a mite younger and better-looking than one figured on in a small town such as Caspar, but run-of-the-mill. Even the buxom brunette who sat at the head of the table and smoked a cigarette, she would be one of the boss girls and, while looking tough and capable, did not strike Calamity as being out of the ordinary.

'How do you feel, Dora?' Mousey asked sympathetically, going to the blonde.

'Great, how else?'

'But I thought——' the little blonde gasped.

'God! You're dumb!' the bigger girl spat out.

'She's not alone in that,' snapped the buxom brunette. 'If your brains were gunpowder and went off they wouldn't stir your hair.'

An angry glint came into Dora's eyes, but she knew better than give lip to Maisie. So she turned her spleen on somebody else. Her eyes went to Calamity who still stood at the door, taking in the red-head's travel-stained clothing and lack of make-up.

'Who're you?' she asked.

'This's Marty Connelly,' Mousey introduced, sounding puzzled. Dora did not act like a girl grieving for a dead lover. If it had been Tommy who—here Mousey stopped herself with a shudder—well, she wouldn't act like Dora did at such a time.

Smarting under Maisie's rebuke, Dora watched Calamity walk towards the table decided to establish her superiority over the newcomer. Which only went to prove that she had no right to call anybody else dumb.

'Is the boss hiring tramps now?' she sniffed and a couple of her particular friends giggled.

Calamity looked Dora up and down with cold eyes. While she had refrained from handing Phyl her needings upstairs, Calamity figured there must come a time when meekness stopped; and that time had arrived right then. If she allowed Dora to push her around, her subsequent social position would be under the blonde; which Calamity reckoned might be mighty undesirable.

'Looking at you,' Calamity said calmly, 'I'd say the boss started hiring *old* tramps some time back.'

'My my!' Dora purred, twisting around in her chair. 'Aren't you cute?'

With that the blonde hurled forward and lashed around her right hand in a savage slap calculated to knock its receiver halfway across the room and reduce her to wailing submission. Only to achieve its object the slap had to land on the other girl first.

Throwing up her left hand, Calamity deflected the slap before it reached her. Before Dora recovered balance or realised just how wrong things were going, Calamity drove a clenched fist into the blonde's belly. The blow took Dora completely un-unawares, sinking in deep and driving waves of agony through her. Croaking with pain, Dora folded over and caught Calamity's other fist as it whipped up. Dora came erect, a trickle of blood running from her cut lip, and caught a round-house smash from Calamity's right hand. The fist crashed into the blonde's cheek just under her eye and sent her sprawling backwards to land with a thud on her butt by the table.

'All right, you alley-cats!' Maisie yelled, throwing back her chair and coming to her feet. 'Simmer down. If you want to fight, save it until tonight and do it in the bar for the paying customers.'

'I'll take her any time!' Calamity hissed, crouching with crooked fingers as she had seen so many belligerent girls stand at such a moment.

'How about you, Dora?' asked Maisie, knowing the entertainment value of a good hair-yanking brawl between two of the girls.

Dora did not answer, but sat on the floor trying to nurse her swelling, pain-filled eye, soothe her puffing-up lip and hold her aching, nausea-filled stomach, sobbing loudly all the time. Never a popular girl, Dora received little sympathy from her fellow-workers.

Looking down at the blonde, one of the other girls gave a laugh and said, 'I don't think Dora feels like tangling with Marty.'

Walking to Dora's side, Maisie bent down and pulled the blonde's hand from the eye, looking at the discolouration forming.

'Whooee!' said Maisie with a grin. 'That'll be a beauty soon. Anyways, it'll keep you out of the way for a few days. Which's a good thing, the way you're acting. You'd queer the boss's game going on like you are when you're supposed to have lost your own true love. Now shut your yap, or I'll turn Marty loose on you again.'

Knowing that Maisie meant every word she said, Dora stifled her sobs. She dragged herself to her feet and limped slowly from the room. Looking around the table, Calamity did not figure she would have trouble with any of the other girls.

Now all she had to do was start learning the proof of the saloonkeeper's part in the Caspar County cow stealing.

CHAPTER TEN

BRING ME HIS WALLET

ALTHOUGH Calamity wondered how Ella Watson would take the news of her actions, no complaints came down from the boss's office. Over the meal Calamity became acquainted with the other girls. She let it be known that she left Austin at the town marshal's request, but none of the other girls pressed her too deeply about her past. Having seen how Calamity handled Dora, a tough girl in her own right, the rest figured that the red-head might resent too close questioning and had a real convincing argument for anybody who tried. One thing Calamity made sure the others knew, how Mousey stood with her. Always a generous and good-hearted girl, Calamity had decided to take Mousey under her wing and intended to give the friendship the little blonde craved but found missing among the other saloon workers.

After eating, Calamity waited until Mousey dressed and then they left the Cattle Queen. While walking along Main Street towards the Chinese laundry's bath-house, Calamity listened to Mousey's chatter and kept her eyes peeled for some sign of Danny Fog, but saw nothing of him. However, Mousey, telling of the discovery of Gooch and the cowhands' bodies, let Calamity know that Danny had arrived and appeared to be well involved in the business which brought them both to Caspar County.

Even without formal training, Calamity used the best technique for a peace officer involved in such a task; she let the others do most of the talking. With Mousey that proved all too easy. Starved for friendship and loving to talk, she prattled on and gave Calamity some insight into the doings of the area.

'That Dora!' Mousey sniffed indignantly. 'She was in love with Sammy, yet she doesn't even look as if she cares about him being killed.'

Calamity doubted, from the little she had seen of Dora, if the girl really loved a forty-dollars-a-month cowhand. However, Mousey's words gave Calamity an idea of how Ella Watson ensnared the young cowhands into her cow-stealing organisation. Women were far outnumbered by the men out West and the local young cowboys would easily become infatuated by a saloon-girl. After that, the rest would be easy.

'She's a mean cuss all right,' Calamity admitted. 'Does she pick on you?'

'A little. If I could fight like you do she wouldn't.'

'You're danged tooting she wouldn't,' grinned Calamity and felt at Mousey's nearest arm. 'Say, you're a strong kid. She'd be like a bladder of lard against you if you stayed clear of her and used your fists instead of going to hair-yanking. I'll teach you how, if you like.'

Thinking of all the mean tricks Dora had played on her, Mousey gave a delighted nod. 'Boy, that'd be great, Marty. Where'd you learn to fight?'

'Here and there. Hey, isn't this the place we want?'

On their return from the bath-house and while waiting for the evening trade to arrive. Calamity began to teach Mousey a few basic tricks of rough-house self-defence in their room. From the way the little blonde learned her lessons, Calamity could almost feel sorry for Dora and next time she tried her bullying.

When Calamity and Mousey reported to the bar-room to start work, Dora was nowhere in sight, being confined to her room with an eye that resembled a Blue Point Oyster peeking out of its shell. So Mousey did not find opportunity to put her lessons into practice.

Calamity found the feeling of wearing a saloon-girl's garish and revealing clothing and being in a bar as a worker a novel sensation. Not that she did much work at first. Until shortly after eight o'clock only a few townsmen used the bar and they showed little interest in the girls, having wives at home who took exception to the male members of the family becoming too friendly with female employees of the saloon.

Shortly after eight a few cowhands began to drift in and the place livened. The girls left their tables and mingled with the new arrivals. Laughter rang out, a couple of the games commenced operation and the pianist started playing his instrument. A couple of the customers came to where Calamity and Mousey stood by the bar.

'Hey, Mousey, gal,' greeted the taller customer, a cheerful young cowhand sporting an early attempt at a moustache, 'Where-at's Tommy?'

'He's not in tonight,' Mousey replied.

'Then how's about you and your *amigo* having a drink with me 'n' Brother Eddie?'

'That's what we're here for,' Calamity told him. 'The name's Marty.'

'This's Stan and Eddie,' Mousey introduced. 'They work for the Box Twelve.'

'Sure do,' Eddie, a shorter, slightly younger version of Stan, agreed. 'Say, what'll you gals have to drink?'

'It'll have to be beer until I've seen Miss Ella,' Stan warned.

'My mammy always told me never to look a gift-beer in the froth,' replied Calamity.

'Lord, ain't she a pistol?' whooped Eddie. 'I'll buy 'em until you get your money off Miss Ella.'

A frown creased Stan's face as he glared at his brother. 'You hold your voice down, you hear me, boy?'

'I hear you,' Eddie answered, dropping his voice. 'Hell, these gals are all right, Stan.'

'Sure we are,' agreed Calamity. 'First thing a gal learns working in a saloon is to mind her own business.'

Apparently the words mollified Stan for he started to grin again. 'Sure, Marty. Only folks might get the wrong idea if they heard Eddie.'

'He's only young yet, not like two old mossyhorns like us,' Calamity answered. 'Say, do we have to stand with our tongues hanging out?'

'Huh?' grunted Stan, then started to grin and turned to the bar. 'Four beers Izzy, the ladies're getting thirsty. Say Mousey, where-at's the boss lady?'

'Upstairs, I think,' Mousey replied.

'Just have to wait a spell then. Here, Marty, take hold and drink her down.'

The beers came and the cowhands drew up their chairs, sitting with Calamity and Mousey at a table. While drinking,

Mousey and the cowhands discussed local affairs. Calamity noticed that any attempt to bring up the subject of cow stealing was met with an immediate change of subject by the cowhands. Not that she kept asking questions, but Mousey seemed to be interested as might be expected from one who had been some time in Caspar County. While Stan and Eddy cursed the departed Gooch for a cowardly, murdering skunk, neither appeared eager to discuss why he might have shot down the two Bench J cowhands. Showing surprising tact, Mousey changed the subject and told of Danny's defeat of the Rafter O's bay. A grin played on Calamity's lips as she listened; it appeared that Danny Fog had been making something of a name for himself since his arrival.

'Let's go have a dance,' Eddie suggested.

'Sure, let's,' Mousey agreed.

Already several couples were whirling around on the open space left for dancing. Calamity, Mousey and the two cowhands joined the fun and it was well that Calamity had always been light on her feet for cowhands did not often make graceful partners. However, Calamity had long been used to keeping her toes clear of her partner's feet when dancing and found little difficulty in avoiding Stan's boots as they danced in something like time to the music.

Calamity saw the two buxom girls who acted as Ella's lieutenants standing by the bar and watching her. For a moment she wondered if they might be seeing through her disguise. If she had heard their conversation, she would not have worried.

'That Marty doesn't dance too well,' Maisie remarked.

There was a considerable rivalry between Phyl and Maisie and the red-head took the comment to be an adverse criticism of her as she took Calamity to see Ella and had her hired.

'Maybe she's out of practice,' she answered. '*You* should know they don't go much for dancing classes at the State Penitentiary.'

Before Maisie could think up a suitable reply, Phyl walked away. The matter dropped for neither girl felt sufficiently confident in her chances of winning to risk a physical clash that would establish who was boss.

'Hey, Phyl,' called Stan, leading Calamity from the dance floor. 'Where-at's Miss Ella?'

'She's still up in her room, but she ought to be down soon,' Phyl answered. 'You wanting to see her real bad?'

'Bad enough. We, me'n' Eddie's going with the boss to take a herd to Fort Williams and'll be away for a month. I wanted to see if—well, she'll know.'

'I'll go up and see her,' Phyl promised.

On reaching Ella's door, Phyl knocked and waited.

'Who is it?' Ella's voice called.

'Phyl. It's important.'

The door opened and Phyl entered to find Ella standing naked except for a pair of men's levis trousers. This did not surprise the red-head for she knew that her boss had not been in the room all afternoon.

'What's wrong?' Ella asked. 'I've only just got back from the hideout.'

'It's Stan, that kid from the Box Twelve. He's down there and wanting to see you. Only he's pulling out with a herd and won't be back for a month.'

Ella frowned as she went to her bed and removed the pants. Knowing why Stan wished to see her, she did not care for the last piece of Phyl's information. The cowhand had delivered ten stolen yearlings to Ella's men and awaited payment, but she knew that if he rode out with the money her place would never profit by it.

'Who's he with?' she asked, standing clad in her black drawers and reaching for her stockings.

'His kid brother.'

'I mean of our girls.'

'Mousey——'

'She's no good for what I want,' Ella interrupted.

'That new gal, Marty's, with them. Her and Mousey's got real friendly.'

'Marty, huh? This might be a chance to find out just what she's like.'

'Hey, that reminds me, boss,' Phyl put in. 'You had an answer to that telegraph to Austin. Marty *was* put on the stage by the town clown, for lifting a drunken dude's wallet.'

'I thought as much,' Ella stated, drawing on her stockings. 'Go down and tell Stan I'll be in soon, and after I've paid him off, you can let me have a word with Marty.'

Half an hour later Ella strolled downstairs dressed in her usual work-day style and showing no sign of having sneaked out of town that afternoon, taken a long ride and not long returned from visiting the hiding place of the stolen cattle.

'Did that feller see you-all, Miss Ella?' Stan asked eagerly as she came up.

'Sure, Stan,' Ella answered and held out the envelope she carried. 'Say, what's in this?'

'Poker winnings, ma'am.'

Like the rest of the cowhands who became involved in the cow stealing, Stan believed that Ella merely acted as an innocent go-between for the hard-case Stocker who took the cattle from them. Taking the envelope, Stan opened it and extracted the money. He slipped four of the ten-dollar bills into his wallet and turned to the bar.

'You've been lucky,' Ella remarked, watching him thrust the wallet into his hip pocket.

'Sure have, ma'am,' Stan agreed with a grin. 'This'll sure buy us a time when we get to Fort Williams.'

'So you're deserting us, Stan,' Ella smiled.

'Shucks, it'll only be for a spell. Say, ma'am, can I buy you a drink?'

'I'll take a brandy, Stan, thank you.'

'One brandy, two glasses of whisky, something for the gals and one for you, Izzy,' ordered the cowhand. 'Say, when's old Pedlar Jacobs coming up here again?'

'Don't know, Stan,' replied the bartender. 'He comes and goes. What's up?'

'Got him a real fancy white-handled Army Colt last time he was in. I figured I might buy it. Is he a friend of your'n?'

'Not especially,' grunted the bartender and moved away to attend to another customer. One thing Izzy did not wish to discuss was his association with Jake Jacobs, particularly before his boss.

'Drink up and have another, gals,' Stan told them, ignoring the departing Izzy. 'I'm just going out back.'

As Eddie elected to go along with his brother, Ella had her chance to talk with Calamity. First Ella sent Mousey off with a message for Phyl, then turned to her latest employee.

'When Stan rides off, I want you to bring me his wallet,' the saloon-keeper ordered. 'And don't try to look shocked or innocent. I heard from Austin and know why you left town.'

'Oh!' said Calamity flatly, not quite sure how she ought to react.

'You don't need to worry about that here, either. As long as you only do it when I tell you. Go to it and lift his leather for me.'

'Yes'm,' said Calamity.

Yet she felt worried by the assignment even though it presented her with a chance to gain Ella Watson's confidence. Calamity remembered Murat's warning that she must not become a party to any crime by actual participation. Even without the warning Calamity would have shrunk from stealing and did not want the young cowhand believing she was a thief.

At that moment Stan and his brother returned and Ella drifted away. The two young cowhands behaved in a more steady manner than Calamity would have expected, knowing how most of their kind acted when in the money. Although Stan and Eddie bucked down to enjoying themselves, they did not go beyond the ten dollars the elder brother retained for his payment. Of course, ten dollars could get a couple of cowhands reasonably drunk, even when buying drinks for various friends.

'Ten o'clock, time we was riding, Brother Eddie,' Stan remarked after bringing Calamity from the dance floor.

'Sure thing, big brother,' grinned Eddie. 'See you around Mousey.'

'Now me,' Stan stated, his arm around Calamity's waist, 'I've got more good sense than to pick up with a gal who's got a feller. You-all coming to see me on my way, Marty, gal?'

'I sure wouldn't miss it for the world,' replied Calamity.

Arm in arm, she and Stan left the room, with Eddie following on their heels. Outside the youngster left his elder brother on the sidewalk while he went to collect the horses. Slipping his arm around Calamity's waist, Stan looked down at her.

'Do I get a kiss afore I leave?' he asked.

'Not out here. Let's go into the alley.'

'We're on our way, Marty, gal.'

On reaching the shelter of the alley, Calamity turned to face the young cowhand. Like she figured, he might be trying to sprout a moustache and act all big and grown-up, but Stan lacked practical experience in such matters. In her time Calamity had been made love to by some prominent gentlemen, the kind of fellers who could near on curl a girl's hair just by taking her in their arms. Stan did not come into that class by a good country mile.

After fumbling for a moment, he got to slipping his arms around her and brought his face to her own. Calamity slid her arms between his and around his body then burrowed her face to his, kissing him. And when Calamity set her mind to it, she could kiss better than most gals with far greater advantages in more formal education. One thing was for sure, when Calamity started in to kissing him, Stan could have been jabbed by a sharp-rowelled spur and never noticed the pain.

While kissing, Calamity lowered one hand and slid the wallet from Stan's hip pocket. The very ease with which she removed it made Calamity decide to change her plans. On leaving the saloon she had merely intended to give Stan a slight return for a mildly enjoyable evening and then return to Ella Watson with the story that the cowhand did not give her a chance to lift his leather. Finding how easy the removal was, Calamity changed her original plan.

Just before she could put her plan into operation, Stan pulled his head away from her. Calamity found herself in an embarrassing position, standing with the cowhand's wallet in her right hand. Of course, he could not see the hand, but at any moment he might miss his wallet. So, like any good general, Calamity decided the best defence would be to attack.

'Whooee!' she gasped. 'You sure kiss up a storm. When a gal's been kissed by you, she sure knows she's been kissed.'

Which same coincided with what Stan had always suspected. 'Want another?' he inquired.

'What do you think?'

Once again Calamity kissed the cowhand. His arms gripped her tightly, but she managed to extract the money from the wallet. Still holding Stan's attention, she slid the money into his pocket and retained the wallet.

'Stan! Hey, Stan!' Eddie yelled, riding into sight on the street and leading a second horse. 'Let's go.'

Releasing Calamity, Stan stepped back. Just in time Calamity slipped her right hand behind her back so he could not see the wallet it held. Stan looked at the girl and grinned.

'Dang it, Marty,' he said. 'I've got to go now. Say, will you be here when I get back?'

'Sure will,' she agreed.

Turning, Stan headed for his horse and went afork in a flying mount. A wild cowhand yell left his lips and he put the pet-makers to his horse's flanks. With a few more whooping yells, the brothers galloped out of town. Calamity watched them go, a grin on her face. Quickly she slipped the wallet into the front of her dress and walked back to the saloon.

'Did you get it?' Ella asked as Calamity walked over to her.

'Sure. Where'd you want me to give it to you?'

'In the office. Come one.'

Following the saloonkeeper, and with Maisie and Phyl on her heels, Calamity went into Ella's office; a small room with a desk, a couple of chairs and a safe, and used for general saloon business. Taking out the wallet, Calamity handed it to Ella, wondering what would come next.

'What's this?' Ella snapped as she opened the wallet and stared at its denuded interior. 'It's empty!'

'Empty!' said Calamity, Phyl and Maisie; Calamity in well simulated surprise, Phyl in a startled tone, and Maisie with a mocking glance at the red-headed boss girl.

'All right, Marty!' Ella hissed. 'Strip off!'

'Huh!' Calamity gasped.

'Come on, you know what the boss means!' Maisie snapped, delighted to have scored on Phyl, for the red-head was the one who took the new girl to see Ella.

'All right, don't get mean!' Calamity yelped. 'So search me! How was I to know it was empty? I couldn't look in it with him watching, and I'd be crazy to try lifting the cash then bringing an empty wallet.'

'She's got a good point there, boss,' Phyl put in.

'Or maybe she's just smart,' sniffed Maisie. 'Peel off, girlie, or I'll do it the hard way.'

Normally such a threat would have been met eagerly by Calamity, but she held down her desire to jump the buxom brunette and hand her a licking. Giving a shrug, Calamity peeled off the dress and stood clad in a combined chemise and drawers outfit, stockings and shoes—and with the Remington

Double Derringer, borrowed from Captain Murat, in a garter holster. Calamity had hoped to keep her armament hidden from the other saloon-girl's eyes but knew her secret was out. All three women looked at the gun, yet none seemed concerned by it.

'You don't need *that* here,' Ella remarked, nodding to the Derringer.

'I wouldn't reckon you'd have any virtue to defend,' Maisie went on, giving Calamity's dress a thorough search. 'I'll do that.'

The last came as Phyl started to examine the rest of Calamity's clothing as it was removed. An angry red flush crept to Phyl's face at the words.

'Don't you trust me?' she hissed and made no attempt to put down the garments she held.

'Check the Derringer's got nothing but bullets in it, Maisie,' Ella interrupted. 'Phyl, go ahead with the underwear.'

While she encouraged the rivalry between her two boss girls, Ella had no intention of allowing them to decide once and for all who had the higher social standing by means of a fight. Knowing that hell had no fury like an annoyed or humiliated woman, Ella preferred to let them simmer than have one embittered by defeat and maybe looking for revenge by talking of the saloon's other business to interested parties.

'Nothing,' Ella said after the check. 'No hard feelings, Marty, but you know how it is.'

'Sure, boss. I'm sorry I didn't do better. Why'd you think he had something in his wallet?'

'Just a hunch. It looks like he either changed places, or let Eddie hold the money when they went out back. Young Stan's smarter than I thought. Go back out front and do some work, Marty.'

After Calamity left the office, Maisie scowled at Phyl and asked, 'Do you reckon she could have hid the money outside before she came in?'

'And bring in the empty wallet?' scoffed Phyl. 'She'd need to be real dumb to even think about it. Anyway, we heard those cowhands ride by just before she came in. Stan must have changed the money while he was outside, like the boss said.'

'Sure. I think Marty'll work out right for us,' Ella stated.

'Let's get out and see if there's anything happening.'

'We lost some money,' Maisie pointed out.

'*I* lost some,' Ella corrected. 'Don't worry, we'll get it back later.'

Out in the bar-room Calamity joined Mousey and found the little girl bubbling with curiosity about the reason for the visit to Ella's office.

'It wasn't much,' Calamity answered. 'The boss just wanted to know if I'd settled in all right.'

'Oh! I thought you might have been in trouble. Did you see Stan and Eddie off?'

'Yep,' Calamity smiled. 'I reckon I did.' Then a thought struck her. 'Say, when do I get to meet this Tommy of yours?'

'He'll maybe come in tomorrow,' Mousey replied. 'Hey, if he brings Danny Forgrave in, maybe you and him can make up a foursome with us. You'll like Danny, he's a real nice boy.'

Thinking of the night in the Jones cabin beyond Austin, Calamity smiled. 'I reckon I might at that.'

She figured Danny would take the opportunity to come to town with Tommy and that ought to give them a chance to get together and discuss what they each had learned so far.

CHAPTER ELEVEN

MISS CANARY INVOLVES MR. FOG

DANNY FOG could not truthfully admit to making any progress
in the few days spent on the Caspar County ranges. Even with
his findings of the first day, he might have been no more than
an ordinary drifting cowboy who stopped off at the Bench J for
work, for he knew little more about the cow stealing than when
he arrived.

Clearly Ed Lyle regarded Danny as being all right when the
foreman returned from tracking the remaining cow thief, then
back-trailing Danny to establish that the young man had told
the truth about coming from Austin City way. The foreman
could find no sign that Danny had come from any other
direction and so was prepared to treat him as he would any
other hand. As to the other matter, Lyle told Danny that the
cow thief's tracks disappeared on to the Rock Pile, a large,
barren rocky area on the edge of the county and over which
following tracks was impossible.

During the next few days Danny rode the ranges and performed the routine work of a cowhand. His skilled use of the
borrowed cutting-horse when working cattle lulled any remaining suspicions the foreman might have held, for a cutting-horse
was a specialist animal and the fact that Danny possessed one
tended to make his pose as a drifting cowhand more acceptable.
Mostly Danny worked with Tommy and from the youngster
learned much about the affairs of the county. Tommy told
Danny how, soon after the stealing became noticeable, Turk
Stocker had the other ranchers search his spread on the Rock
Pile but they found only his runty, poorly-fed stock on it. So they
concluded that the cow thieves ran their stolen animals on to
the Rock Pile to make tracking impossible, then could go in any
direction to wherever they sold their loot. While Tommy ad-

mitted he did not care for Soskice, he said the lawyer had his uses when the sheriff picked up one of the boys. Simmonds appeared to be regarded as a harmless nuisance hired by the town to keep cowhand horse-play in bounds. Of Sammy and Pike's behaviour before their deaths, Tommy said little. It appeared that Sammy found his 'love' for Dora came real expensive, far more so than a cowhand could afford and that Pike, like the good friend he was, did what he could to further his *amigo's* romance. Only small things came out of Danny's talks with Tommy, yet they helped him build up a better picture of the situation in Caspar County.

When the story of how Danny stood up to the deputy and Ed Wren made the rounds, and of how he rode the Rafter O's bay reached the ears of the other hands, he found himself regarded as being quite a feller. The feeling pleased him, for this time he had made the grade without anybody thinking of him as Dusty Fog's kid brother and treating him to second-hand respect on that relationship.

However, when Saturday arrived, little had been done to either prevent the cow stealing or find the folks behind it. No further losses had been discovered and none of the crew went out at night to do the necessary riding needed to locate brand and deliver the stolen animals.

'Are you coming into town tonight, Danny?' Tommy asked as they rode towards the Bench J's main buildings on Saturday afternoon.

'Reckon so. I've some money just itching to be spent. Are you fixing to see your gal tonight?'

'Sure am. Why don't you get one?'

'Me? Way I see it, Tommy, *amigo*, ain't but the one thing worse'n getting left afoot, and that's tying in with a good woman.'

'*Compadre,*' Tommy replied soberly, 'you'll never know how wrong you are until you've tried it.'

'Tell you then,' grinned Danny. 'Happen I find a real nice gal. I'll think about trying it.'

After a meal in the cookshack, the two young men joined the other hands at washing, shaving and generally preparing for a trip to town. Such an occasion called for one's better clothing and the use of one's go-to-town horse; this latter being selected for its good appearance rather than any ability for working purposes. Once prepared, the hands mounted their horses ready for the ten-mile ride to town.

A fair crowd had already gathered in the Cattle Queen when the Bench J crew arrived. Jerome left his hands to attend to a few pieces of business around town, and some of the crew went to deal with personal affairs, but Danny and Tommy headed for the saloon.

'Hey, Maisie!' Tommy called as he entered and looked around the bar-room. 'Where-at's my gal?'

'Not down yet,' Maisie replied. 'Set a spell, she'll be along.'

'Go grab a table, Tommy,' Danny suggested. 'I'll fetch in the drinks.'

While waiting for Mousey to make her appearance, Danny and Tommy sat at a table and drank beer. Danny looked around for some sign of Calamity, yet she did not appear to be present. Pointing out various people in the room, Tommy named them for Danny's benefit. At last the youngster nodded to a pair of men sitting at a table between them and the stairs leading to the saloon's private quarters.

'That's Turk Stocker and his foreman, Dutchy Schatz,' Tommy remarked. 'How the hell they manage to make that spread up on the Rock pile pay, I can't figure.'

Danny glanced at the men. Both appeared to be tall, Stocker slim and with a whisker-stubbled face, Schatz heavier built, with close-cropped hair and a scarred face that looked tough and mean. Each man wore a gun in a contoured holster and dressed a little more prosperously than might be expected for the boss and sole hand of a run-down ranch in a most unsuitable area. From the little Danny had seen of the Rock Pile, it would prove mighty useless for profitable cattle-raising and be unlikely to provide more than a bare living for its owner. Of course, Stocker could have a side-interest such as hiding wanted outlaws to account for his wealth. Danny decided a visit to the Stocker spread might be worthwhile before his identity as a Ranger became known.

Even as Danny made his decision, he saw Mousey and another girl enter the room. Only when he took a second and longer look did Danny recognise Calamity and he decided his fears that she might have been recognised were groundless.

Following the direction of Danny's gaze, Tommy grinned broadly.

'Hey, Mousey's done got company. Look's a right nice gal, too.'

'Sure does,' Danny agreed.

However, before the girls could arrive at the two cowhands' table, they had to pass where Stocker and Schatz sat. After eyeing the girls up and down, Schatz shot out a hand and caught Mousey by the arm.

'Hi, there, Mousey, gal,' he greeted in a harsh, guttural voice. 'Sit down and have a drink.'

'I've already got one ordered,' Mousey replied, trying to pull her hand free.

'What, beer with some fool kid?' growled Schatz. 'You can do better than that, little gal.'

'You let me go!' Mousey yelped.

Tommy's chair went flying backwards as he came to his feet and shot across the room. At the bar Ella caught questioning glances from her two bouncers and Ed Wren but shook her head. Things were a mite slow and Ella knew that nothing livened up a Saturday evening better than a fight, provided it did not get out of hand and she doubted if one between the burly Schatz and young Tommy would go too far.

'Get your cotton-picking hands offen her, Schatz!' Tommy yelled as he rushed forward.

While Tommy did not lack guts, he showed a considerable amount of poor judgment in his method of attack. Schatz thrust himself to his feet, still holding Mousey with his left hand. Even before Tommy could land a blow, the burly man's big fist shot out. Running in added force to a powerful blow and Tommy went down like a pole-axed steer.

'Tommy!' Mousey screeched and landed a kick on Schatz's shin with enough force to make him howl and release her. 'Tommy!' she repeated and dropped to her knees at the youngster's side.

'Why you little whore!' Schatz snarled and started to move forward. 'I'll——!'

'Get your lousy, buffalo-mange stinking, gut-turning self away from her, lard-guts!' Calamity spat out. Lacking her whip, she reached for the neck of the nearest bottle as a means of defence.

Before Calamity could lay hands on the weapon, Schatz turned and caught her by the arm. 'I likes a gal with spunk,' he told her.

'You like licking kids, too,' a cold voice cut in.

Slowly Schatz turned, pulling Calamity around after him. In that he might have counted himself lucky, for Calamity had just been preparing to drive up her knee into his lower regions hard enough to chill down his milk for a spell. However, she refrained as she saw the speaker and hoped that Danny had learned fighting in the same school as his elder brother; because if he had, mister, that unwashed, square-headed, bristle-haired, no-account hard-case was sure as hell due for a real Texas-size shock.

'My, the cowhands are sure snuffy tonight,' said Schatz and shoved Calamity away from him, then launched a blow straight at Danny's head.

Only this time he struck at a different proposition to his previous challenger. Danny might not be much older than Tommy, but bore the advantage of training at the hands of masters of the art of rough-house brawling.

Up came Danny's left hand, but he did not clench his fist. With the open palm he slapped Schatz's driving-out right arm in a snappy motion which deflected it away from him. Instantly Danny ducked under the deflected punch and took a short step forward with his left foot so as to halt slightly behind Schatz's back. At the same time Danny brought up his right arm, across Schatz's body to grip the burly man's shirt at the right shoulder. Pushing hard on to the shoulder with his hand, Danny hooked his right leg behind Schatz's left calf and thrust with it. The moves took Schatz by surprise. He gave a startled yell as his feet left the floor and he went over to land on his back.

Calamity gave a sigh of relief. It appeared that Danny had learned fighting at the same source as did his illustrious elder brother. From the expression on Schatz's face as he came up from the floor, Calamity figured Danny was likely to need all the learning he could lay hands on.

Watching Danny's fists come up, Schatz charged at the blond Ranger with big hands raised to grab. Only he fell into the trap Danny laid for him. Danny did not figure to try using his fists against the bigger man—not until after setting Schatz up for them.

Suddenly and unexpectedly Danny raised his left leg and drove it out to land a stamping kick on the other's kneecap, bringing Schatz's rush to a sudden halt. Even as agony knifed through Schatz and he bent to clutch at the injured knee, Danny threw a right-hand punch. It landed hard and with precision on the side of Schatz's jaw and the big man crashed to the floor again. Spitting out curses and blood, Schatz jerked the Colt from his holster but did not get a chance to use it. Danny leapt forward and stamped down with his left foot. A cowhand's boots carried high heels designed to spoke into the ground and hold firm while roping cattle or horses on foot. Human flesh being less hard, it did not stand up well to the impact of a boot heel smashing down upon it. Schatz let out a screech of pain, lost his hold on the Colt and jerked up into a sitting position. Like a flash, Danny kicked up with his other leg. The boot toe caught Schatz under the jaw, snapping back his head and slamming him down again. This time he did not look like he would be getting up to make more trouble.

'Hold it, Stocker!' a voice boomed.

Hearing the order, and the accompanying click as a gun came to full cock, Stocker froze. He had only half rose and his haid still gripped the butt of his gun, but a glance at the main doors of the saloon told him the futility of going further. Holding his Remington ready for use, Jerome stood just inside the doors and Lyle leaned a shoulder against the door jamb at his boss's side.

'Who cut you in, Jerome?' Stocker growled.

'Danny there rides for me,' answered Jerome. 'What happened?'

'I'd say that Schatz just got round to picking the wrong feller,' Lyle remarked calmly, looking to where Danny stood over the burly hard-case.

Ella Watson knew better than allow such a situation to develop too far. So she thrust herself from the bar and walked across the room, taking care not to come into the line of fire.

'All right, boys,' she said. 'The fun's over.' Her eyes went to Stocker and she went on, 'I've told you before about Schatz abusing the boys.'

'Looks like he picked on one as didn't take to being abused,' Lyle drawled and walked to where Mousey helped Tommy to rise. 'You all right, boy?'

'Just about,' Tommy answered and felt his jaw. 'Where's he at?'

'Sleeping. Got his-self all tuckered out,' grinned the foreman.

Seeing that nothing more of interest would come from the situation, the occupants of the room resumed their interrupted pleasures. Jerome watched Ella's bouncers haul Schatz from the room, then he turned to Ella and asked what started the fuss.

'It wasn't Danny here's fault,' she replied, 'Schatz started to rough-handle Mousey and Tommy, then Danny cut in. That boy's some fighter. Dirty, but good.'

'Always reckoned it's better to fight dirty and win, than fair and get all licked, ma'am,' Danny put in and turned to Calamity. 'Say, how's about taking a drink with me, Red?'

'Right with you and the name's Marty, not Red,' she replied.

Watching the two walk away, Ella decided that an efficient young man like Danny Forgrave ought to be a valuable asset to her organisation. Of late there had been a considerable amount of independence building at Stocker's end and she guessed that the rancher might be figuring he could run the business without her aid. Wren could take Stocker, but lacked the experience in cattle matters to handle the holding of the stolen stock. Given the right kind of bait, say plenty of money, that blond Texas cowhand might make an ideal replacement should Stocker go too far.

For a time Calamity and Danny celebrated in typical cowhand-saloon-girl style, helped by Mousey and Tommy. They had a few drinks, tried the gambling games with Tommy winning a few dollars, danced and generally enjoyed themselves. Ella watched it all, noting the way 'Marty' persuaded Danny to spend more and more on her. The girl had the right idea and it seemed that Danny was struck on her. This showed in the way he blocked any other customer's request that the girl danced or joined him. So Ella watched and waited for a chance to speak with her latest employee away from the crowd.

Ella's chance came when Calamity and Mousey left the room to go out back. On their return, the girls found their boss waiting in the rear passage behind the bar-room. Telling

Mousey to go on in, Ella kept Calamity with her.

'You're handling that cowhand real well, Marty,' she said as Mousey went through the door to the bar-room.

'Shucks, that's no problem. He reckons I'm the only gal in the world and wants to prove it.'

'Keep him going. I want him broke, but eager to come back for more.'

'Sure, boss. Say, he wants to go to the cabin with me for the night.'

'Take him up on it and sting him for ten bucks. If you can get any more than that off him, it's yours.'

'Yes, ma'am,' Calamity said eagerly and turned to go.

Shooting out a hand, Ella caught Calamity's arm and stopped her. 'Don't act stupid, Marty. No rolling him or anything like that. I want him coming back here all hot and eager for another session. Understand?'

'Yes, ma'am. I understand.'

While Mousey did not go to the cabin with the customers herself, she had a fair idea of what went on in it. She wished that Marty would not go, but made no objections when her new friend left with Danny. Sighing, the little girl looked at Tommy and wondered whether she ought to make an exception in his case, then decided against it as they could not afford the money Miss Ella insisted was paid for the loan of a room.

'We're going to have to play this straight, Calam,' Danny remarked as he entered the dimly-lit cabin and located the room allocated to them.

'Reckon we are,' she agreed with a grin. 'I wonder how much can be heard in the other rooms?'

'I don't know, but let's hold our voices down.'

Calamity stripped off her dress and sat on the edge of the bed to peel the stockings from her legs. There was not much room in the section allocated to them and the window had heavy drapes covering it. Danny blew out the lamp and blackness descended on the room.

'How's it going, Calam?' he asked, holding his voice down.

'Fair. I don't figure they know me or think I'm anything but what I say I am. And I know how they get the cowhands involved. Fact being, I'm supposed to be involving you right now.'

'That figures. Young Sammy was caught like it. He was one of the pair Gooch gunned down.'

'I know,' Calamity grunted. 'Had words with his grieving sweetie, only she wasn't grieving until after I got through with her.'

'Know anything more?'

'Not much. Ella's in this real deep, likely behind it. She slips out of the saloon at nights, and sometimes in daylight, dressed in man's clothes and goes off some place.'

'Does huh?' said Danny.

His interest sounded plain in his voice and Calamity tried to see him in the blackness of the room. 'What's that mean?'

Quickly Danny explained his findings when he located the bodies of the two cowhands, then of the circumstances surrounding Gooch's death. He mentioned the fact that the bounty hunter's gun had been in its holster; and also about the third cow thief, the one who escaped death at Gooch's hands.

'What do you reckon about that?' he asked.

'Same as you,' Calamity replied. 'Gooch wouldn't've gone up to any man with his gun still in leather, but he might to a woman. I could say she done good for the world if it was her who downed Gooch.'

'Maybe,' Danny drawled. 'Only don't let that stop you finding out all you can. The sooner we nail this business shut the happier I'll feel. Tempers are a mite high about Sammy and Pike. Comes pay day and the Forked C getting to town at the same time as the Bench J, there might be trouble. The boys are sore enough to start it. Say, do you see much of that lawyer?'

'He comes around visiting with the boss. I don't know how he figures in the game though. Reminds me of somebody, only I can't put my finger on it.'

'Looks and sounds like one of them radical Republicans who used to run with Carpetbag Davis' bunch,' Danny remarked.

'You hit it!' Calamity whooped.

The next instant Danny's hand clamped over her mouth. 'Hold it down, hot head!' he growled.

'Sorry, I forgot,' she whispered when he moved his hand. 'That Soskice acts and talks like that cuss who was strangling the gals early this year in New Orleans. He was one of Henry George's bunch, them Socialists or whatever they call themselves and Soskice carries the same brand.'

'Then why's he down here?' Danny mused. 'They hate the guts of us Southern folks and I can't see one of 'em coming down here to live unless he'd good reason. We bust up the best reason when we run Carpetbag Davis' bunch of scum out.'

'I'll watch him, see what I can learn. Say, how do we play this lot between you and me?'

'Just how Ella Watson wants it. I've been trying to make her think I'm a young hard-case with a yen for money and who isn't too particular how he gets it.'

'You've done it,' Calamity told him. 'I've got to lead you on, get you all broke and eager for more of me. Then she'll move in, or I miss my guess.'

'Then that's how we'll play it,' drawled Danny.

'What're we going to do right now?' inquired Calamity, sliding into the bed.

For a moment Danny did not reply, then he said, 'Well, I *have* paid my ten bucks.'

'Danged if I ever afore got paid for *that*,' remarked Calamity.

Half an hour passed before either spoke again.

'Say, Calam,' came Danny's voice.

'Yeah?'

'How in hell do I mark down that ten dollars on my expenses?'

CHAPTER TWELVE

I WANT TO STEAL SOME OF YOUR CATTLE

By Tuesday Danny figured he had set things up to the point where Ella Watson would make him an offer. He spent the night with Calamity on Saturday and took the girl along with Mousey and Tommy on a picnic the following afternoon. Monday evening found him in town again, watched by a worried Mousey as he spent money on Calamity and the red-head urged him to extravagance. All in all, Danny gave a good impersonation of a lovesick young cowhand making a big play for a money-hungry saloon-girl.

Ella Watson walked across the room on Tuesday evening and looked down at Danny as he sat moodily staring into a glass of beer. Knowing the signs, she came to a halt and smiled at him.

'Hi there,' she greeted. 'You look like a man with worries.'

'Reckon I am, ma'am,' he replied. 'Where-at's Marty?'

'She'll be down soon. How serious are you about her?'

'Mighty serious, ma'am. She's a real nice gal.'

'But expensive. A girl like Marty is used to living high on the hog, Danny.'

'Yes'm.'

'Short of money, are you?' asked Ella sympathetically.

'Not short, ma'am. Flat busted.'

'The trouble is that Marty likes money spent on her,' the saloonkeeper went on, glancing to where Stocker sat by the door. 'That's the way we women are. She loves you, of course, but a girl has to live.'

'Reckon so, ma'am. Trouble being, a cowhand's pay don't go far.'

'I know. Well, I've work to do. If you want another drink, Danny, tell Izzy to let you have what you feel like and pay me back when you've some money.'

'Gee, that's swell of you, ma'am,' Danny answered. 'I don't know how to thank you.'

'Just keep Marty happy is all you need do,' she smiled and walked away.

Although Ella did not go near Stocker, Danny saw her nod to the man and then walk into her office. A few seconds later Stocker rose and slouched out of the main doors. For half an hour nothing more happened. Danny crossed to the bar and gave the bartender Ella's message, then asked for another bottle of beer. He took his seat again, sipping the beer and idly smoking.

The batwing doors opened and Danny saw Stocker and Soskice enter. Crossing the room, they halted at his table.

'Mind if we join you?' Soskice asked.

'Feel free,' Danny replied, glancing first at the lawyer then looking hard in Stocker's direction. 'But I thought——'

'Hell, I had to stand by Dutchy,' Stocker interrupted. 'He rides for me and comes cheap. Mind, I admit he's a mean cuss when he's likkered.'

'Sure!' Danny grunted.

'Liked the way you handled him, though. Have a drink to show there's no hard feelings.'

'Couldn't buy you one back,' Danny warned.

'Don't expect it. I know having a gal keeps a young feller short of cash.'

'It sure as hell does,' agreed Danny, wondering why the lawyer sat in on the deal and waiting to find out.

Both men bought Danny a couple of drinks without bringing up anything more than casual conversation. So Danny decided to put out a couple of feelers and see if he could stir anything up.

'You fellers being so friendly and neighbourly, it sure riles me that I got to wait to pay day afore I can repay you.'

'Reckon you'd like to earn a mite more, afore then?' Stocker asked.

'I sure as hell would.'

'Look, boy,' the rancher said, dropping his voice. 'I got crowded up on the Rock Pile because the big ranchers took all the good land. A fair number of my cattle stray down there. I'd pay well for any you found and brought back.'

'How'd I know which was yours?' asked Danny.

'If they'd got the Bradded S brand on 'em, they'd be mine.'

'Shucks, I've not seen any Bradded S stuff on our range,' Danny groaned.

'How about unbranded stuff?' the rancher inquired.

'You mean unbranded Bench J stock?'

'Under the law, Danny,' Soskice put in, 'an unbranded animal is property of the man who lays his brand on it.'

'Is that the legal law?' asked Danny, wide-eyed and eager.

'It sure is,' agreed the rancher. 'Hell, I bet all the ranchers have branded dozens of mine. You'll only be helping me get my own back. It'd be justice and I'd pay you five dollars a head.'

'I'll just bet you would,' Danny drawled, a crafty glint coming into his eyes. 'I risk a rope for five dollars a head, when you'll likely sell them for thirty. Mister, I may be——'

'Hold your voice down!' Soskice hissed. 'You want money——'

'Not bad enough to risk a hemp bandana for that price.'

'You risked it when you rode the Rafter O's bay,' Soskice pointed out, silencing Stocker's angry growls with a wave of his hand.

'Sure, but for a damned sight more than you're offering,' Danny answered. 'I'll sell at ten dollars a head, no less.'

'Ten doll——!' began Stocker.

'All grown beef. Got me twenty head located right now, not a brand on 'em and ready for picking.'

Suspicion glinted in Stocker's eyes. 'How the hell——'

'Shucks,' drawled Danny. 'Word's got around about the cow stealing up here. Why'd you reckon I come. I figured sooner or later I'd tie in with the right folks. Where'd you want 'em bringing?'

Stocker and Soskice looked at each other, then a grin creased the rancher's face. 'You're a smart cuss,' he told Danny. 'Brand 'em someplace and deliver 'em to Bowie Rock. Do you know it?'

'That one with a top shaped like the clipped point of a bowie knife, down by where the Talbot River flows off the Rock Pile?' asked Danny.

'That's the one. I'll be there from midnight until three in the morning tomorrow night. You deliver the cattle and collect your money in town.'

'Can't say I like that idea.'

'It's the way we do it,' Stocker growled.

'And it's better that way, Danny,' the lawyer put in. 'Safer too. If anybody sees you, you claim you found the cattle straying. They can search you and Turk and not find any money on you, so they can't prove you aimed to sell them to him. And if your boss catches you coming in late and wants to know where you've been, he'll not find you with more cash in your pockets than you should have.'

'You fellers look like you've got it all worked out,' Danny said admiringly.

'We sure have,' agreed the rancher. 'Do you want in?'

'Deal me in,' drawled Danny, glancing to where Mousey and Calamity entered. 'I'll see you-all tomorrow night.'

'What do you think?' Soskice asked as Danny rose and walked to meet the two girls.

'He's a slicker young cuss than I reckoned,' answered the rancher.

'Too slick, maybe,' said the lawyer. 'Of course, the ones who think they're the smartest always fall for a girl. Watch him, Turk, and if he makes a wrong move, kill him.'

'Dutchy'd like the chance to do that,' the rancher replied.

Danny managed to get Calamity alone long enough to tell her of his progress, then he left the saloon, collected his *sabino* and rode back to the ranch. On his arrival, he put up the horse and walked across to the main house.

'Like to see you, boss,' he said when Jerome answered his knock on the front door. 'Can you take a walk down to the corral with me?'

One look at Danny's face told the rancher that something serious was afoot. So, without asking any questions, Jerome stepped out of his house and walked towards the corral at Danny's side. Jerome did not know what to expect. It could be that the youngster had found some serious disease among the stock and wanted his boss to hear of it in privacy. There might be any of a dozen other reasons for the request. Never would Jerome have guessed the real reason for Danny's visit; and when he heard, he could hardly believe his ears.

'I want to steal some of your cattle,' Danny remarked casually.

While noted for his skill as a poker player, Jerome could not help coming to a halt and staring at Danny.

'Reckon you'd best take that again—slow, Danny.'

Reaching into the concealed pocket built into his gunbelt, Danny extracted his badge and held it so Jerome could see the star in the circle. 'I'm a Ranger in Captain Murat's company and was sent up here to bust up the cow stealing.'

'Well, I swan!' swore the rancher. 'You sure as hell had me fooled.'

'And a few other folks—I hope,' drawled Danny and went on to tell the rancher of his activities, including the offer he received. 'I want proof enough to take the whole danged bunch into court, boss.'

'Then we'll jump 'em when they take the cattle,' Jerome suggested.

'It wouldn't do any good. They'll just claim they know nothing and it's two men's word against mine. I figure to learn where they hide the stock, who they sell to and bring in the whole danged bunch.'

'We'll play it your way. Say, can I let Ed in on this?'

'Sure,' Danny confirmed. 'I'll need help to handle the stuff, too.'

'Don't reckon me or Ed'd do for that,' grinned the rancher.

'Or me. Can't see them being dumb enough to buy a rancher or his *segundo* becoming cow thieves. I'll take young Tommy.'

'Tommy?'

'Sure. He's got a good head and he's steady enough where Mousey's not involved. If you've still got those two running irons we found by Sammy and Pike, I could use them, too.'

'I'll see to it,' Jerome promised. 'And anything else you may need.'

The rancher proved to be as good as his word. Next morning Danny, Tommy and Lyle rode out on what appeared to be an ordinary routine ranch chore, except that the two younger members of the party each carried a running iron hidden under his saddle-skirts.

During the ride Tommy listened with awe and admiration as Danny told what he knew about the cow stealing. Although Tommy had a cowhand's disrespect for local law enforcement officers, he regarded the Texas Rangers as being something real special and his admiration for Danny grew rather than lessened on learning the other belonged to that famous body of men. Eagerly Tommy agreed to help Danny and listened carefully to his instructions.

Being older, Lyle hid his feelings and merely remarked that he had figured all along that there was more to Danny than met the eye. With his knowledge of the range, Lyle took the others to where groups of cattle grazed. Scanning the animals, Danny's party picked out and cut any unbranded grown beef they saw, hazing it ahead of them until they drove twenty head before their horses.

'We'd best play this the right way,' Danny remarked. 'Let's use that hollow where the boys were killed to do the branding.'

'Sure,' the foreman agreed. 'I sure as hell never figured I'd be using a running iron on the boss's cattle.'

'Or me,' Danny admitted. 'Say, Ed, I've been kicking a fool notion around in my head. Let's make sure we can identify our stock by running a small Bench J where it won't show, say under the animal's belly.'

'You've got a right smart notion,' the foreman grunted.

Once down in the hollow where two men died, the three cowhands set to work and branded the stock. While Tommy held the cattle, Danny cut out each animal in turn and led it to where Lyle kept a fire burning and the running irons heated to a glowing cherry-red. Showing his riding and roping skill, Danny put the captured animal down. Lyle hawg-tied it and then burned a prominent Bradded S on the animal's left hip and traced a smaller Bench J under the belly where it would escape notice unless specifically searched for. In range terms, a brand was 'something that won't wash off,' so the cattle carried a mark of legal ownership as well as the cow thieves insignia.

The hidden brand, known as a 'sleeper' became a standard weapon in the war against cow thieves in Texas and more than one light-fingered, wide-looped gent met his just deserts through Danny Fog's 'fool notion.'

Hard work and skilled handling saw all twenty head branded before darkness fell. With the preparations made, Danny and Tommy left Lyle to carry out the next part of their business; meeting Stocker and selling their 'stolen' cattle.

'Good luck,' the foreman said as they parted.

'We'll likely need it,' Danny answered with a grin.

Turning his horse, Lyle headed back in the direction of the ranch to report to his boss that all had worked out satisfactorily so far. Danny and Tommy moved the cattle a couple of miles from the hollow which held such painful associations for the animals, then halted to wait out the time until midnight.

'Do we take 'em tonight?' asked Tommy as they mounted their horses ready to make for the rendezvous.

'Nope. Not unless we have to. I want them all, from top to bottom, not just Stocker and his bunch.'

'All?'

'There's more than just Stocker involved,' Danny told him. 'All we do is ride up, deliver the stuff and pull out. Then I'm going to trail Stocker to where he hides it. Once we know that, we can move.'

'You're the boss,' grunted Tommy.

Shortly after midnight the two young men drove their twenty head of cattle towards the rock shaped like the clipped point of a bowie knife.

'Just act natural, Tommy, boy,' Danny warned in a low voice.

'I'm as nervous as a hound-scared cat,' the youngster groaned back.

'That's how you should be,' Danny replied with a grin. 'This's the first time you've ever done any cow stealing. Can't expect you to act easy on it. Just follow my lead though—and don't spook.'

As they drew closer to Bowie Rock, the two young men saw a pair of shapes ride into view from a clump of scrub oaks at one side of the outcrop. Coming closer, the shapes turned into a recognisable Stocker and his bulky foreman, Schatz. The burly man's right arm looked unnaturally white but Danny realised this to be caused by a bandage around the place where his heel stamped into flesh.

'Hold it!' Stocker growled suspiciously. 'There's two of you.'

'Needed two to handle the branding,' Danny replied. 'Anyways, there's two of you, too.'

'Who's the other one?'

'Tommy Fayne.'

Hearing Danny's reply, Schatz growled something inaudible

but Stocker spoke to cover the sound.

'Allus figured you for a "saint," Tommy.'

'Reckoned I'd never get enough money saved to marry Mousey by sticking to cowhand's pay,' Tommy replied.

Relief hit Danny as he heard Tommy's response. While the youngster's voice sounded a mite strained and odd, it held nothing to make the other men suspicious. If they noticed the difference, they would put it down to his nervousness at becoming a cow thief. More than that, the youngster had given the one reason which might turn a loyal cowhand into a cow thief; Stocker had seen at least two other hands go the same way.

Everything appeared to be going the right way, Danny decided—then Schatz, still smarting under his defeat at Danny's hands, damned nigh blew the whole thing into the air. A nasty snigger left the big hard-case at Tommy's words.

'So you're fixing to marry that——' Schatz began.

'Call him off, Turk!' Danny interrupted before the other could finish his insulting words. 'If he doesn't stop, I'll muzzle him. And you watch the cattle, Tommy, we don't want to lose 'em now.'

The low-spoken warning prevented Tommy spoiling the business at hand. Like Danny knew, the youngster tended to get a mite hot-headed where Mousey was concerned. Normally Danny would have regarded the loyalty to a feller's gal as being praiseworthy and expect one to defend his sweetheart's honour; but he did not want Tommy tangling with Schatz until after they had finished their business.

Stocker also appeared to desire peace. Being a businessman, if one engaged in an illegal business, Stocker had an eye on his profit and loss account. While he would be paying Danny double the price given to the more naïve local hands, Stocker figured the young cowboy would be worth it. Even in the darkness he could form some idea of the quality of the stock Danny brought for sale. The cattle appeared to be two to three-year-old animals, ideal for marketing and most likely Danny Forgrave knew where more of them could be gathered. So Stocker did not want trouble.

'Go get the lantern, Dutchy,' he ordered. 'And leave Tommy be, we don't want any fuss. No offence meant, Tommy.'

'None took, neither,' Danny answered for his young friend. 'You sounded a mite edgy when we rode up, Turk.'

'So'd you be in my place. It don't do to take chances.'

'Sure admire to be working with a careful man,' Danny drawled. 'We've only brought twenty head this time.'

'Mind if I look 'em over?' asked the rancher.

'Feel free,' replied Danny.

Clearly Stocker had the cow stealing business well organised. On his return from the clump of trees Schatz carried a bull's-eye lantern and directed its light on the 'stolen' stock. While a longhorn was dangerous to a man afoot, one could approach the animal while riding a horse without any great risk. Closing on the twenty head, Stocker examined their running iron brands in the light of the lantern. Watching the two men, Danny felt tension mounting on him but held it in check. His right hand rested on the butt of his off-side Colt, for if Stocker discovered the sleeper brands under the cattle's bellies Danny reckoned he would need a gun in a hell of a hurry. Across at the far side of the small bunch of cattle, Tommy felt sweat trickle down his face. The youngster twisted restlessly in his saddle and looked towards Danny; but his nervousness attracted no attention for Stocker and Schatz had become used to such a reaction from the cowhands they dealt with when handing over the stolen stock.

After checking each animal in turn, Stocker nodded and Schatz closed the front of the lantern. The rancher rode to where Danny sat his *sabino* and nodded in approval.

'They'll do, Danny. We can use more stuff like this, and I'll keep paying you ten dollars a head—only don't mention it to anybody else.'

'You figure a fair profit for yourself, Turk,' Danny replied.

'Hell, they don't cost you anything. And I've overheads to meet out of my end,' the rancher objected.

'Likely. Want Tommy and me to lend .you a hand to move them?'

'Nope. You'd best not be out too late, you don't want to get Buck Jerome all suspicious.'

Danny had not expected finding the hideout for the stolen stock to be so easy and was not wrong, however, a man always liked to try to smooth his path if he could. So he went on with something he must not forget to ask.

'How'll I let you know when I've some more for sale?'

'Go to the Cattle Queen. If I'm not there, leave word with Miss Ella. Say you've found some of my strays and want to deliver 'em. She'll pass the word to me and I'll meet you here at around midnight the following night.'

'Mighty obliging lady, Miss Ella.'

'Sure,' the rancher agreed, then went on just a shade too quickly. 'She don't know a thing about what I'm doing. When you go in ask her for the envelope the man left and she'll give it to you. You'll find the money for this lot in it. Only don't mention any names.'

'I won't,' Danny promised. 'See you, Turk.'

Turning, Danny rode to where Tommy sat waiting for him at the rear of the bunch of cattle. Just as he reached the youngster, Danny heard the drumming of hooves. Somebody was riding through the night, coming in their direction at a fair speed. One thing Danny knew for sure. The newcomer would not be bringing news of joy and good cheer for him and his young friend.

'Coming from town,' Tommy said in a low voice, showing again how clear-headed he could be.

'Get set for trouble,' Danny replied, swinging his horse to face the suddenly alert and suspicious Stocker and Schatz.

'Stocker!' yelled the fast-riding shape as it drew closer. 'Danny Forgrave's a Ranger. Get him!'

CHAPTER THIRTEEN

HOLD HER UNTIL I GET BACK

BUSINESS was slack in the Cattle Queen. Only Wally Stirton, boss of the Rafter O, a few of his hands and a handful of townsmen used the bar-room. Calamity Jane and Mousey sat at a table clear of the men, idly talking and waiting for customers to arrive. Phyl crossed the room and came to a halt by the two girls.

'Aren't your fellers coming in tonight?' she asked.

'Don't look like it,' Calamity replied. 'It's gone nine now and no sign of them. They'd've been in afore this if they was coming.'

'Things are always quiet on Wednesdays,' Mousey went on.

At that moment the batwing doors opened and a man entered, halting just inside to look around. Yet he did not have the watchful caution of a hard-case gun fighter who might find enemies inside and wanted his eyes to grow accustomed to the bar's lights after coming from the darkness. Glancing at the door, Calamity stiffened slightly; recognising Jake Jacobs, the pedlar who sold information to peace officers. For a moment Jacobs stood at the door, then he walked forward in the direction of Phyl and the other two girls. Calamity felt Jacobs's eyes studying her with more than normal care. Maybe he recognised her, although she doubted it. As far as she knew, the pedlar left Austin before she arrived, but he might remember her from some other town. Calamity decided she must find out what brought the man to Caspar.

'Where's the boss, Phyl?' Jacobs asked, giving Calamity another long, searching look then turning to the buxom redhead.

'Up to her office. You want to see her about something important?'

'She'll think so.'

Phyl studied the man for a long moment. Knowing that Ella was preparing to ride out and visit Stocker, Phyl did not wish to disturb her boss. However, Phyl knew that Jacobs often brought news of importance and so decided to take him upstairs.

'Let's go see her then,' Phyl said. 'Only she'll for sure blister your hide if it's not important.'

Watching Phyl and Jacobs make for the stairs, Calamity decided she must try to learn what brought the pedlar to town. A couple of the cowhands drifted over and asked Calamity and Mousey to join them. Rising, Calamity told Mousey to go ahead and she would sit in once she had been upstairs to collect a handkerchief.

By the time Calamity reached the head of the stairs she found that Phyl and the pedlar were just entering Ella's room. Calamity waited until the door closed, then walked over and halted by it. Glancing along the passage, she could see no sign of life. However, she wished she knew where Maisie might be as the big brunette had not been in the bar-room. Calamity did not wish to be caught eavesdropping at Ella's door, especially by Maisie for the brunette disliked her due to her friendship with Phyl. Seeing no sign of Maisie or any of the other girls, Calamity placed her ear close to the door and listened to the muffled, but audible conversation inside. She only heard a few words before deciding it had been a good idea to come up and take a chance to discover Jacobs's business.

In the room Ella Watson sat behind the table and looked at Jacobs with cold, speculative eyes. For his part, Jacobs stared back with frank interest. On his arrival, Ella had been about to change into the clothes she wore when riding the range on visits to the stolen stock's hiding place. At such a time Ella wore men's clothing with only a pair of drawers beneath the shirt, levis, boots and jacket out of sight and pulled on her robe. While this covered her naked torso, it gave more than a hint of her state of undress underneath.

'This's private, Miss Ella,' Jacobs said, glancing at Phyl.

'Likely,' the saloonkeeper replied. 'Spit it out, Jake, and put your eyes back in, it won't do you any good.'

'I got something to tell you,' the pedlar told her, jerking his eyes away from the valley between her breasts.

'I didn't think you'd just dropped in to pass the time of day.'

'Just come up from Austin way,' Jacobs went on, not put out by her apparent lack of interest.

'So?' asked Ella calmly, although she did not feel calm inside. The nearest company of Texas Rangers had their base in Austin as she well knew.

'So I heard something as might interest the right folks up here.'

'I'm busy and tired, Jake. Come to the point, or let's miss you?'

'I'm a poor man, Miss Ella,' the pedlar whined. 'Not like these cow thieves up this ways.'

'Let's have it!' Ella spat out, opening the table drawer and taking out a five-dollar bill. 'Damned if I know why I'm bothering, but if you've something interesting you can have the five.'

'I hear tell Cap'n Murat's sent a feller up here to bust the cow thieves.'

'Why should that interest me?' Ella asked, trying to keep her voice normal although her throat felt dry and her body cold.

'No reason—'Cepting that if this feller does it, you'll lose a fair few good customers.'

'Hey——!' Phyl began.

'I see,' Ella interrupted.

Only with an effort could she hold her voice even and Phyl's obvious agitation drew a warning scowl from Ella. Annoyance at the red-head's reactions stiffened Ella and enabled her to hide her true feelings. Clearly the pedlar knew something. In some way he must have learned that she ran the cow-stealing organisation. Yet he could not know, unless—at that moment Ella remembered a remark passed a few days before, about her bartender's friendship with Jacobs. Izzy must have sold her out, either accidentally or deliberately. Well, that matter could wait until later. More important right now was to discover the identity of the man sent by Captain Murat. Ella did not underestimate the Texas Rangers. The trouble with a Ranger was that he wore no uniform and kept his badge concealed. There had been one new arrival in the area who claimed to have come from down Austin way, she recalled.

'All right,' she said. 'Supposing I give a damn for my

customers. Who is this Ranger?'

'Like I said, ma'am——' Jacobs started to say.

'I know,' Ella cut in, 'you're a poor man. Here's twenty dollars. Who is he, Jake?'

There she had the pedlar, but he did not intend to mention the point. While Jacobs had gathered a vague rumour that a Ranger left town headed for Caspar County, he could not learn which member of Company 'G' was assigned to the task. However, Jacobs could put two and two together so as to come up with a reasonable answer.

'One of them fellers brought in Choya's bunch of *Commancheros* a few days back. Only he's not in town any more, left near on as soon as he come in. I figure he's the one.'

'And his name?' asked Ella.

'Danny Fog. He's Dusty Fog's kid brother.'

This time Ella could not hold down her startled gasp. Danny Fog—Danny Forgrave—it must be true. Ed Wren claimed that Forgrave reminded him of the Rio Hondo gun wizard. So he would if he was Dusty Fog's younger brother.

'What does he look like?' she snapped.

'Tall, blond, youngish, not bad looking. Rode a big *sabino* stallion last time I saw him.'

'Forgrave!' Ella and Phyl said at the same moment.

Even as they spoke the door of the room flew open.

Calamity had just figured that she must find some way of warning Danny of his danger when she found she had troubles of her own. So interested in the conversation had she been, that she forgot to stay alert. Maisie stepped from her room, took in the sight and crept stealthily along the passage towards the listening Calamity. Instead of hearing the gentle pad of bare feet, Calamity missed the sound. The first knowledge she had of Maisie's presence being when one hand gripped the scruff of her neck and another jerked her arm up behind her back.

Dropping the hand from Calamity's neck, Maisie twisted on Ella's door handle and pushed open the door. Before Calamity could make a move to prevent it, she was shoved into the room.

'What's all this, Maisie?' Ella asked.

'I just caught her listening at the door, boss.'

Pain in her trapped arm, and a natural aversion to being pushed around, caused Calamity to take action. Lifting her foot, she stamped the heel down hard on Maisie's foot. The big brunette let out a screech of pain and released Calamity's arm, then started to hop on her other leg, clutching at the injured toes. Before Calamity could turn and take the matter further, Phyl leapt forward and pushed her against the wall. Even as Calamity tensed to throw herself into the attack, Ella rose, jerking open the table's drawer and bringing out the Remington Double Derringer which took Gooch's life.

'Now just hold it right there!' the saloonkeeper ordered. 'Phyl, take her gun. Keep back, Maisie.'

The latter warning came as the brunette prepared to hurl herself at Calamity and take reprisals for the vicious stamp on her foot. Knowing her boss's temper, Maisie halted and watched, scowling and muttering to herself, as Calamity stood still and allowed Phyl to pull up her skirt and remove the Derringer from its garter holster.

'She's a liar, boss!' Calamity yelped, getting her defence in before the attack began. 'I'd only just come up here.'

'She was listening, boss!' Maisie screeched.

'All right! Shut it, both of you!' Ella spat out. Her fingers drummed on the table top, then she frowned as she remembered that Calamity came to town from Austin. 'How many Rangers did Murat send, Jake?'

'One. That Danny Fog like I told you,' the man replied, staring at Calamity once more. 'Say, I seen that gal afore somewheres.'

'In the Golden Slipper at Austin, you skinny goat!' Calamity snapped. 'You come up here to tell the boss how I got throwed out of town. I knew you'd got me marked down from the minute you come into the bar downstairs.'

'Hell, you saw the way he looked at me right from when he come in, Phyl,' Calamity said, turning to the red-head.

'He sure did, boss,' Phyl agreed and glared at Maisie as the girl gave a disbelieving sniff.

'How about it, Jake?' Ella inquired.

'Sure I looked at her. Thought I'd seen her around someplace. Only I don't reckon it was in Austin.'

'Where'd it be?' asked Maisie, going back to rubbing her aching foot.

'Sure it was Austin, you danged fool!' howled Calamity. 'You come here to tell the boss that I'd been run out of town. I've heard about you.'

'What've you heard, Marty?' purred Ella, watching the Jewish pedlar's face rather than studying Calamity's expression.

'That he'd sell his own mother if he thought the price was right,' Calamity replied. 'Hell, I saw him talking to Cap'n Murat down a back street in Austin a couple of days before——'

'That's a damned lie!' Jacobs screeched, and no other word could describe the sound.

'Just stay right where you are, Jake!' Ella ordered, swinging the Derringer in the pedlar's direction.

'Hell, Miss Ella,' whined the pedlar nervously. 'Murat only stopped me to ask about a gun I'd tried to get for him.'

The pedlar did not make his words sound very convincing and Ella's suspicions deepened. If 'Marty' told the truth, Jacobs would just have reached Austin after his visit to Caspar City. So he might have been selling information which brought Danny Fog to Caspar.

'All right, Jake,' Ella said. 'I believe you. You'd better get going and let me talk with Marty here.'

Turning, Jacobs hurried from the room. His one desire was to collect his wagon and put as many miles as possible between himself and Caspar City, for Ella's words had not fooled him at all.

'You letting him go, boss?' Maisie asked after Jacobs left.

'Go get Wren,' replied Ella, which answered the question after a fashion. When Maisie left the room, Ella turned her eyes to Calamity. 'I'm not sure about you, Marty. Hold her until I get back, Phyl.'

'Sure, boss,' Phyl replied. 'Come on, Marty, we'll wait in my room.'

'Wait,' Ella ordered, rising and removing her robe. 'You saw a lot of Danny Forgrave, Marty. Do you think he might be a Ranger?'

Calamity's first instinct was to scoff at the idea, then she decided not to appear certain. She figured Danny could take care of himself, and had her own escape to think about.

'Seemed a mite slicker than most cowhands,' she admitted. 'Only I thought he was just more crooked than most.'

134

Which just about coincided with Ella's judgment of Danny's character. The saloonkeeper drew on the man's shirt, taken from its hiding place and slipped into a pair of levis pants. Watching Ella, Calamity remembered what Danny told her about Gooch's death. Calamity studied the bare flesh under the shirt as Ella fastened its buttons and formed her own conclusions.

A knock sounded on the door as Ella finished buttoning the levis. She called 'Come in!' looking at Phyl and Calamity as Wren entered followed by Maisie. 'Take Marty to your room, Phyl,' Ella went on.

'I'll go with her,' Maisie growled.

Anger etched a scowl on Phyl's face, but she did not argue. Phyl and Maisie escorted Calamity to their room, leaving Ella to give orders to the cold-eyed hired killer.

Although she hid the fact, Calamity felt worried. Danny Fog's life hung in the balance and somehow she must try to escape then warn him that his secret had been sold out. Yet before she could do anything, Calamity must escape from the two buxom, powerful boss-girls. For once in her life Calamity knew fighting was not the answer. She might be able to take one or the other girl, but not both at once; and even against one of them, skilled bar-room brawlers that they were, she would be in no condition to make a hard ride straight after the fight.

The boss-girls shared a room slightly bigger, but not much better equipped than the type used by the ordinary female workers. On entering, Maisie leaned her back against the door and stood scowling at Calamity. None of them spoke for almost ten minutes. Calamity sat on the edge of Phyl's bed and the red-headed boss-girl crossed the room to look out of the window.

'Girlie,' Maisie finally said, 'I sure as hell hope you don't come up with the right answers.'

'Why?' asked Calamity. 'So it'll put Phyl in bad with the boss.'

Turning from the window, after seeing Wren and Ella leave by the side door. Phyl scowled across the room at Maisie. Suspicion glowed in the red-head's eyes and she said:

'You may have something there, Marty.'

'Sure I have, Phyl,' Calamity answered, taking her chance with both hands. 'You've seen how she's always trying to put you in the wrong.'

'I don't reckon I'm going to wait until the boss gets back!' Maisie hissed and thrust herself away from the wall.

Before Maisie could reach Calamity, Phyl blocked her path 'You'll leave her be, fatso. She's——'

Drawing back her arm, Maisie swung it, hand knotted into a fist, against the side of Phyl's cheek. The blow landed hard, sending the buxom red-head staggering. Maisie knew she had started something she must finish with Phyl before attempting to handle Calamity. So the brunette hurled herself at Phyl and walked into a punch between the eyes which stopped her in her tracks. The long pent-up hatred burst like a wrecked dam wall and the two buxom women tore into each other with flying fists, grabbing fingers, kicking feet, oblivious of everything except for their dislike of the other and desire to injure her as badly as possible.

While Calamity would have liked to stay through the fight and enjoy what looked like being a hell of a brawl, she knew time would not permit her to do so. Letting the two women become fully engrossed in their hair-yanking brawl, Calamity headed for the door and left the room. She ran along the passage and into her own quarters, closing its door behind her. Even while running along the passage, Calamity had been stripping off the cheap jewellery. In the room, she jerked off her dress and kicked aside her shoes. Opening the cupboard door, Calamity lifted out the grip in which she brought her spare saloon-girl clothing.

Before Calamity left Austin, a saddler worked all night to fit a false bottom into the grip. Reaching into the apparently empty grip, Calamity pulled up the cover of the false bottom and lifted out her normal clothing. The loss of her Derringer did not worry her, for her gunbelt, Navy Colt and bull whip all lay in the hidden cavity and Calamity had managed to keep the gun clean even while working in the saloon.

Outside Calamity's room voices sounded. She could guess what had happened. Hearing the sounds of the fight between Phyl and Maisie, the other girls were coming up to investigate. Moving fast, Calamity drew on her shirt, then pulled the levis pants on over her stockings. Her kepi and moccasins came next, then she slung on the gunbelt and when she thrust the bull whip into her waistband, she felt at ease for the first time since accepting this chore.

Most of the girls stood in the passage outside Phyl and Maisie's room and from the sounds beyond the door there had been little easing of the fight. One of the chattering, excited girls happened to glance in Calamity's direction, then gave a yell which brought every eye to the transformed red-head. None of the girls made a move, but Dora scowled and opened her mouth.

'The name's Calamity Jane, gals,' Calamity announced before Dora could say a word. 'I'm working with the Rangers to bust up this cow stealing and I've no fuss with any of you.'

Most of the girls had nothing to lose by the wrecking of the cow stealing organisation and anyway that bull whip looked a damned sight too dangerous for them to start arguing. However, Dora still hated Calamity for the humiliation handed out on the red-head's arrival. Now she saw a chance to take her revenge.

'Get he——!' she began.

Once more Dora was interrupted. Mousey did not know for sure what was happening, or why her friend Marty dressed in men's clothes and claimed to be Calamity Jane. All the little blonde knew was that she now had a good chance to tangle with Dora and put Calamity's self-defence lessons into use. Catching Dora by the arm, Mousey turned her and brought across a punch which staggered the bigger blonde back across the passage.

'Why you——' Dora hissed.

Down went Mousey's head and she charged, ramming Dora full in the middle of the body. In her childhood, Mousey lived hard and still had strong little muscles. These, backed by the lessons Calamity gave her, enabled her to tangle with Dora and make the bigger girl believe a bobcat had jumped her.

'Sic her, Mousey!' Calamity whooped. 'And use your fists like I taught you.'

The other girls let Calamity depart unhindered. Unlike Mousey, Dora had never been popular, so the girls saw no reason to halt what shaped up to be a good fight; especially as Mousey appeared to be getting the best of it.

Wally Stirton, boss of the Rafter O, his men and the other

customers gathered at the foot of the stairs, listening to the screeches, yells and other sounds of female brawling which drifted down. Then the men stared as Calamity came into sight and ran down the stairs towards them.

'What the hell?' Stirton growled. 'Hey Marty——'

'Get your boys on their hosses and lend me a mount, Wally,' Calamity interrupted. 'We've a chance to bust up the cow stealing.'

Give him his due, Stirton threw off his surprise and got moving without wasting time or asking fool questions. He and his men headed for the door on Calamity's heels and the girl told him her true identity, also of Danny's danger.

'Lanky's out back with one of the gals,' Stirton drawled as they left the saloon. 'Take his dun, Mar—Calamity.'

At that moment the sheriff and his deputy came running along the street. Calamity did not give them time to start asking questions, but pointed to the saloon and yelled, 'There's a fight upstairs, Sheriff!'

Then she and the Rafter O men hit their saddles. Before the sheriff could ask any of the questions which boiled up inside him, the entire bunch went racing out of town. In the lead Calamity told Stirton to head for Bowie Rock. She rode as never before. Knowing it to be a race against time—with Danny Fog and Tommy Fayne's lives hanging in the balance.

CHAPTER FOURTEEN

IT WON'T WORK THIS TIME, ELLA

DANNY FOG and Tommy Fayne had one advantage over Stocker and Schatz when Ella Watson screamed out her warning. The two young men knew they were fakes and both expected trouble as soon as they heard the rapidly approaching horse coming from the direction of town.

Even though Danny could not figure out how Ella discovered his secret, he wasted no time in idle speculation. Already he held a Colt in his right hand for he had never professed to be real fast with a gun and knew he could not match Stocker in a straight draw-and-shoot fracas. Even as the rancher heard the words, let out a startled curse and grabbed for his gun, Danny went into action.

'Yeeah!' Danny yelled and fired a shot into the air.

Never the most stable and easily handled of animals, even less so when newly branded and being held against their will during the night hours, the longhorns needed little encouragement to spook and take to running. All twenty head heard the yell and crash of the shot, then they went to running—straight at Stocker and Schatz. While a longhorn could be handled, under normal conditions, safely enough from the back of a horse, that did not apply right then. Both rancher and segundo took one look at the wild-eyed, charging animals and jumped their horses clear of the rush of scared longhorns.

Cattle streamed by Stocker as he threw two shots at Danny. Shooting from the back of a horse had never been noted as an aid to accuracy, especially when using instinctive alignment, so the bullets missed the Ranger. Danny fired in return— only he took the extra split-second to raise his Colt shoulder high and use the sights, and his *sabino* stood like a statue under him. Flame licked from the barrel of Danny's Colt and the muzzle-blast blinded him for an instant. When his vision cleared, Danny saw Stocker pitching down from his saddle. Even as he saw Stocker fall, Danny heard the crackle of shots to his right.

Tommy had drawn his Colt even as Danny started the cattle running. Often Tommy day-dreamed about becoming involved in a gun fight and now he found himself tangled in a real shooting match. Buck-ague sent rippling shivers of excitement through the youngster and his hand shook at he threw up the Colt. Guns roared and Tommy heard a flat 'splat!' sound which he failed to recognise as the cry of a close-passing bullet for he had never heard one before. He saw the bulky shape of Schatz charging at him and shooting as he came. Only the fact that Schatz handled his gun with his left hand saved Tommy from death. Three times the burly man fired, his lead coming closer with each successive explosion.

Pure instinct guided Tommy's hand. He lined his Colt, feeling his horse fiddle-footing nervously under him and guessing the movement helped to save his life. Tommy never remembered firing his Colt. All he knew was that the gun roared and bucked against his palm. Next moment Schatz tilted backwards, sending a bullet into the air, and went down from his horse, landing under the feet of Tommy's mount and letting the gun fall from his hand.

Tossing his leg over the *sabino's* saddlehorn, Danny dropped to the ground and moved towards Stocker. The rancher had come to his knees, but saw Danny approaching and noted the gun the Ranger held. Remembering the lawman's rule for dealing with such a situation, Stocker released his injured right shoulder and raised his left hand hurriedly into the air.

'Don't shoot, Ranger!' he yelled. 'I'm done. Hold your fire.'

The rancher appeared to be making more noise than one would expect; or so Danny decided. With every instinct alert and working full-time, Danny soon discovered the cause of the noise. Dark shapes moved out of the clump of scrub oaks from which Stocker and Schatz had emerged. Even as Danny saw the shapes, guns bellowed from them and muzzle-blasts flared in the darkness—but not aimed in his direction.

'Hit the ground, Tommy!' Danny yelled, throwing two shots at the shapes and changing his position as he fired.

Showing remarkable presence of mind considering it to be his first involvement in a corpse-and-cartridge affair, Tommy left his saddle and lit down on the ground. Although his horse spooked, it did not go far with the reins trailing but came to a halt a couple of hundred yards away. Crouching behind a black mound, Tommy raised his Colt. Then he realised that the hump hiding him was in reality Schatz's body. The man lay without a move.

'If you shoot, Tommy,' Danny called, rolling over as he spoke and sending another shot at the approaching men, 'move straight after it.'

Before Tommy could profit by Danny's advice, they heard more hooves thudding from the direction of Caspar City. So did their attackers. Coming to a halt, the Stocker men read danger in the approaching riders, for they knew one set of hooves could not make so much noise.

'Get out of here!' yelled a voice.

Not that the speaker needed to give any warning. Even before he yelled out his sage advice, the others had turned and started to run back in the direction from which they came. In his excitement Tommy thumbed off two shots, but failed to make a hit.

Stocker saw his hired help take a Mexican stand-off and painfully dragged himself on to his hands and knees after flattening down to allow his men to shoot without fear of hitting him. Holding his bullet-busted shoulder with his left hand, the rancher prepared to make a dash for safety.

'Hold it right there, Stocker!' Danny barked, coming to his feet and lining the Army Colt. 'I won't tell you twice!'

Knowing that nobody would blame a Texas Ranger for shooting down a cow thief, and not being sure whether Danny would carry out the threat or not Stocker came to a halt. Crashes and the snorting grunts of disturbed horses told the rancher that his men were going fast and that he had no hope of escape.

'All right,' he said. 'I'm done.'

'Danny!' yelled a voice from the approaching party. 'It's the Rafter O!'

'Come ahead,' Danny replied.

Bringing his horse to a halt, Stirton pointed off to where the fleeing Stocker hands could be heard. 'Want for us to take after them?'

'Nope. They'll not be back,' Danny answered. 'How'd you get here just at the right time?'

'That gal Marty told us you was a Ranger and likely to need help. Say, she reckons she's Calamity Jane.'

'Don't you going tell nobody now,' grinned Danny. 'But she is Calamity Jane.' He looked around then went on, 'Say where is she now?'

'Took off after one of the bunch who cut away across the range. Sent us on in to help you.'

'Stay on here and tend to Stocker, Wally. I'll go look for her.'

'Is Stocker in on this stealing?' growled the rancher, looking at the suddenly scared, wounded man.

'Up to his dirty li'l neck,' replied Danny.

'Then we'll hold him for you,' Stirton promised.

Something in the rancher's voice brought Danny to a halt as he started to turn away from Stirton.

'I want him alive when I get back,' Danny warned. 'You hear me?'

'Danged if you aint' a spoilsport,' grunted Stirton. 'He'll be alive and kicking when you come back.'

Turning, Danny walked to the waiting *sabino* and swung into the saddle. He looked to where a couple of the Rafter O hands stood over Schatz's body, one of them holding the bull's-eye lantern and directing its beam downwards. Tommy stood to one side and even in the feeble light Danny could see the pallor of the youngster's usually tanned cheeks.

'He's done,' said the hand with the lantern. 'Hit straight between his two eyes. Who got him, Tommy?'

'Let's ride, Tommy,' Danny put in before the youngster could answer.

Tommy raised no argument. One of the Rafter O hands had collected his horse and he swung into the saddle.

'I'll tend to things here, Ranger,' Stirton called. 'Need any of my boys?'

'Reckon me and Tommy ought to be enough,' Danny replied. 'Fix Stocker's wing and put out some guards in case his boys come back to try and pry him free.'

For a time Danny and Tommy rode in silence. Danny looked

sideways at Tommy and guessed how the youngster must feel.

'It's never easy, killing a man, Tommy,' he said.

'It sure ain't,' agreed Tommy. 'I felt like fetching up, only I didn't want Rafter O to see me do it.'

'There's no shame in it. Only remember this. It was him or you. He sure as hell aimed to kill you and you'd every right to stop him any way you could.'

'Yeah,' answered Tommy and gave a shuddering sigh. Then he threw off the feeling of nausea. 'Say, how do we find Calamity?'

'Just ride on for a spell, then stop and listen some.'

Following Danny's plan, they rode on for about half a mile before halting their horses and sitting in silence. Only the ordinary night noises came to their ears and after a few seconds Danny started his *sabino* moving again.

'Which's the shortest way back to town, Tommy?' he asked.

'Over that ways,' Tommy answered, pointing to the right.

Swinging their horses in the desired direction, the two young men continued their ride. Ten minutes passed and Danny brought his *sabino* to a halt again. This time he heard something, so did Tommy.

'What the hell?' Tommy asked, listening to the screams, squeals and scuffling noises that came faintly to their ears.

'Reckon ole Calam done caught up with Ella Watson and just couldn't resist temptation,' Danny replied. 'Let's go take a look.'

When Ella Watson saw the approaching Rafter O hands even though she did not recognise them as such, as she knew her reign as boss of the Caspar County cow thieves had come to an end. From the number of shots and the shouted conversation between Danny Forgrave—or Fog, whichever it might be—and Stocker, she figured that the attempt at killing the Ranger had failed. So she decided to pull out, make a fast ride to town, empty her safe and be well clear of Caspar before the posse could return with news of Stocker's capture.

A yell from the posse told Ella she had been seen and one of the riders spun out of the group to give chase. Ella urged her horse to a gallop, yet she doubted if the animal could outrun her pursuer's mount. Hearing the yell Stirton let to warn Danny of his coming, Ella knew she did not have a chance in a race. The Rafter O specialised in breeding good horses, while her own mount had been selected more for its gentle qualities and steadiness rather than speed.

After half a mile of riding Ella swung her mount in the direction of the distant town and safety. Although still ahead of her pursuer, she figured it would not be long before they came together. Yet she did not wish to kill the one following. With Gooch it had been different. Then she fled before a wanton murderous bounty hunter and her life would have been forfeit if she fell into his hands. So she decided to use her trick merely to draw her pursuer in close. Then she would take his horse, leaving him afoot and unable to interfere, ride relay with it and her mount, make better time to town and have a longer start on the posse.

Having made her decision, Ella unbottoned the shirt and pulled it open to expose her naked breasts. With bait like that any cowhand would walk straight into her trap and fall easy prey to her.

Twisting around in her saddle, Ella glanced back at the other rider. At the distance separating them she could not distinguish the other, or recognise him. It was not Danny For—Fog, of that she felt sure. However, he might prove too smart to fall for her trick. Probably the rider was one of Stirton's younger hands trying to make a name for himself. If so, he ought to be easy to handle.

Ella's horse slid down a gentle slope and as it reached the open ground at the bottom she reined it in. Before the pursuer came into view, Ella slid out of her saddle, dropping to the ground and lying flat on her back. She tossed the hat aside with her left hand, allowing her hair to hang over her face. With the right she took out her Derringer and held it concealed. From above came the sound of the other horse, then the noise ended and she knew the rider had halted. She figured he could not see enough yet, but would come in closer.

For a few seconds nothing happened. Ella lay still, hardly daring to breathe in case she scared the other rider into shooting in panic. A faint scuffling sound came to her ears as the other started to come down the slope. Any second now he ought to come close en——

'It won't work this time, Ella, gal,' said a voice.

Shock ripped into Ella at the words, for she saw the failure of her plan. No man addressed her, but the voice sounded mighty like that of the girl she knew as Marty Connelly. Somehow, Ella could not think how, the girl must have escaped from the Cattle Queen, gathered a posse and ridden to Danny's aid. Cold fury gripped Ella and she tensed to roll over with a roaring Derringer in her hand. Even as the thought came to her, Ella heard the low click of a Colt coming to full cock.

'Don't try it, gal!' the voice went on in cold warning tones. 'A stingy gun like that Derringer's no good at over fifteen foot and I'm more than that away.'

'What'd you want?' Ella asked, debating whether to chance rolling suddenly and throwing a shot at the other girl.

'Throw the gun well clear of you,' came the reply.

'Go to hell!'

'In good time, I reckon. Only this's the last time I'll ask you to throw that stingy gun away.'

Ella could tell from the tone of Calamity's voice that argument, or trying to roll over and shoot, would do no good. Being a smart girl, Ella knew when to call the game quits. Carefully she lifted her right hand, then tossed the Derringer a fair distance away across the level floor at the foot of the slope. Then she sat up slowly and shoved her hair back before turning to look at her captor. One glance told Ella the other girl spoke truly in the matter of relative gun ranges. From the casually competent manner the red-head held the Navy Colt, she knew how to handle it and could likely have put a bullet into Ella had the saloonkeeper made a wrong move.

Standing up the slope, Calamity watched the Derringer sail away into the darkness. On her arrival at the head of the slope Calamity had left her borrowed horse standing with trailing reins, hung her whip around the saddlehorn and moved in ready to hand Ella a shock.

'Who are you?' Ella asked, coming to her feet.

'The name's Martha Jane Canary——'

'Mar—Calamity Jane?'

'I've been called worse,' Calamity admitted. 'Let's ride back to Bowie Rock and meet Danny Fog.'

'If he's still alive,' answered Ella.

145

'I figure he will be. That boy's real smart.'

'How'd you get away from Maisie and Phyl?'

'They got to fussing with each other after you left.'

'I should have figured that,' Ella sniffed. 'Say, you and I can't come to some arrangement, can we?'

'Sure. You just arrange for yourself to get on that hoss and we'll head back to Bowie Rock.'

'You've nothing on me,' Ella remarked as she walked slowly towards Calamity.

'Maybe. Only I figure somebody'll start to talk once we begin the round-up and haul them down to the pokey.'

Knowing some of her confederates, Ella did not doubt Calamity's words. So she decided to try another line of reasoning, one which might appeal to a young woman like Calamity Jane.

'What have I done that's so wrong?' asked Ella. 'All I did was buy a few head of cattle from the cowhands——'

'Don't say you didn't know they'd been stolen,' Calamity interrupted.

'Had they? They weren't branded——'

Once more Calamity cut in. 'Most of them come from branded herds, and you knew it all along.'

'All right, so I knew it. I gave the cowhands a few bucks. Hell, the ranchers would lose more to the weather or stock-killing critters in a year than I took.'

'Losing's one thing. Having 'em stolen's another.'

'So who got hurt?' asked Ella.

'How about Sammy and Pike from the Bench J?'

'You can't blame me for that!' Ella gasped, for her conscience troubled her more than she cared to admit over the death of the two young cowhands. 'I only happened to be along that night. They always used that same place to brand the stuff. Even if I hadn't been along, Gooch'd've found them.'

'And how about Gooch?' said Calamity quietly.

'If you *are* Calamity Jane, you've been around long enough to know what Gooch was. He aimed to rape me before he killed me—Hey, how did you know that I killed Gooch?'

'That was easy. Jake Jacobs told Cap'n Murat you was running the cow stealing. Both me and Danny figured you must have killed Gooch. Gooch might have been as bad mean as a

146

man could be, but he'd a damned sight more sense than walk up to a *man* with his gun in leather. So it figured that a woman killed him and you seemed most likely to be the one. When I saw you coming in wearing those men's duds, I knew how you got Gooch in close and stopped him being suspicious.'

'And you blame me for killing Gooch?'

'Nope. For turning decent kids into thieves. Get going.'

'Nobody made them steal,' Ella pointed out as she walked by Calamity.

'Nope. Only your gals got them so they didn't know which way to turn.'

Slowly Ella walked up the slope with Calamity following. Suddenly the saloonkeeper appeared to slip. Ella's feet shot behind her, striking Calamity's legs and tangling with them. Letting out a yell, Calamity went over backwards and lost her gun as she fell. Even as Calamity rolled down the slope, Ella stopped herself sliding after the red-head and grabbed up the fallen Navy colt. Coming to her feet, Ella lined the gun down at Calamity.

'It looks like we don't need any arrangemènt now, Marty,' Ella said.

'Reckon not?' replied Calamity. 'There's no percussion caps on the nipples.'

'We'll see about that,' Ella answered and squeezed the trigger.

Instead of the crack of exploding powder, a dull click came to Ella's ears as the Colt's hammer fell on a bare cap-nipple. Fury gripped Ella as she thought of how she had been tricked into tossing aside her fully-loaded Derringer—which used rimfire bullets and did not need separate percussion caps to ignite the powder charge.

Calamity had not made the move intentionally. While she had stored the Colt with powder and a lead ball in each of the cylinder's chambers, Calamity knew too much about guns to leave percussion caps on the nipples when the weapon was not in regular use. In her rush to get out and try to save Danny, she clean forgot to put the caps in place and did not remember this basic—and vitally necessary—precaution until just before she caught up with Ella. Then it had been too late, so Calamity made a damned good bluff.

Giving a squeal of rage, Ella charged down the slope. She swung up the Colt and launched a blow aimed at Calamity's head. Bringing up her hands, Calamity caught Ella's wrist as it brought the Colt down. Pivoting, Calamity heaved on the trapped arm and her pull, aided by Ella's forward momentum, sent the saloonkeeper staggering by her. Ella lost her hold of the Colt and went sprawling face down on the ground. Rolling over, she spat out a curse and sat up, glaring at the advancing Calamity.

'Give it up,' Calamity ordered. 'Or do you want to wrassle it out?'

Seeing that she could not escape unless she got by Calamity, Ella prepared to take action. Quickly Ella hooked her left foot behind Calamity's right ankle, rammed her right boot against the red-head's knee, pulled with the left, hoved with the right, and brought Calamity down on her back. Then Ella reared up and flung herself on to Calamity.

From the moment Ella landed, Calamity knew, as she figured on their first meeting, that the saloonkeeper could take care of herself in any girl's kind of tangle.

Calamity's kepi went flying as two hands dug deep into her hair and damned near tore out a pile of red curls by their roots. Pure instinct guided Calamity's response. Even as she screeched in pain, her own hands hooked strong fingers into Ella's black hair and Calamity braced herself, heaving up then rolling Ella from her. Swiftly Calamity twisted on to the top of Ella, trying to bang the black head against the ground. Not that Calamity stayed on top for long. Over and over the two girls rolled and thrashed. Neither showed any kind of skill, or gave a thought to anything more scientific than clawing hair, swinging wild slaps and punches or biting at first.

Nor did the situation improve for almost three minutes. Then, how it happened neither girl could say, they found themselves on their feet. Ella stood behind Calamity, arms locked around the red-head and pinning Calamity's own arms to her sides. Just what advantage Ella aimed to take from the situation is hard to say. She retained her hold and crushed on the red-head, but could do little more. Gasping in fury more than pain, Calamity lashed backwards, her heels landing on Ella's shins hard enough to make the other girl yelp and loosen her hold a little. Then, Calamity clasped her hands together, forcing outwards against Ella's grip with her elbows and sucking in a deep breath. Suddenly Calamity exhaled and felt the encircling arms relax their grip. Before Ella could tighten again, Calamity twisted slightly and rammed back with her elbow, driving it into the other girl's stomach.

Giving a croaking gasp, Ella lost her hold and stumbled back. Jumping in to attack again, Calamity discovered that the other girl was far from beaten. Ella's left hand shot out, driving the fist full into Calamity's face, then the right whipped across to connect with the other girl's jaw. Staggering, Calamity caught her balance just in time to meet Ella's rush.

For over ten minutes the girls put up a hell of a fight. They used fists, elbows, feet, knees, punching, slapping, kicking, pushing and shoving. Twice they rolled over Calamity's Colt without giving it a glance or thought. However, Calamity slowly gained the upper hand. Her normal working life offered greater advantages in the matter of staying fit and strong than did Ella's career in the saloon.

Gasping in exhaustion, her shirt torn open and minus one sleeve, Calamity landed a punch which sent the sobbing, exhausted Ella sprawling to the ground. Calamity stumbled forward. Through the mists which roared around her, Calamity heard horses approaching. She came to a halt and started to look at the newcomers. That look nearly cost her the fight. Ella had come to her feet, swaying and barely able to stand. Yet she still swung a wild punch that ought to have flattened Calamity; only it missed the red-head by a good two inches. Once more Calamity's instincts came to her aid. Ignoring the two men who rode towards her, she turned and lashed out with all she had. In missing, Ella staggered forward and walked full into the punch Calamity threw. It clocked like two rocks cracking together as they fell down a cliff, Ella shot sideways, landing face down and lying still. Weakly Calamity followed the saloonkeeper up and dropped to her knees by the still shape.

'Ease off, Calam!' Danny yelled, leaping from his horse and running to where Calamity rolled the unconscious Ella over. 'She's done!'

'Know something?' Calamity gasped. 'I'm not much better myself.'

Five minutes later Calamity recovered enough to tell Danny what had happened. Ella sat moaning on the ground to one side and Calamity looked at Danny with a wry grin as he said:

'I'd swear you let her jump you and get your gun just so you could fight.'

'Shucks,' grinned Calamity. 'Can't a gal have any fun at all?'

CHAPTER FIFTEEN

CLEAN UP IN CASPAR COUNTY

AT nine o'clock on Thursday morning, Danny Fog stood before the desk in the Caspar County Sheriff's office and looked at Simmonds. The young Ranger had not shaved and looked tired after a night without sleep. Once Calamity patched up her own and Ella's injuries, Danny took them back to Bowie Rock. There he found Stocker to be in a most co-operative mood and from the rancher learned all he needed to know to make sure he could smash the cow stealing in Caspar County for ever. Once Danny knew everything, he left Stirton's party to bring in the prisoners and rode ahead. In Caspar City he visited the sheriff's office to offer the local law enforcement officers the chance of winding up the affair.

'And that's how it was, Sheriff,' Danny said, finishing his explanation of why he came to Caspar County and what he had achieved. 'Ella Watson suckered the cowhands into stealing for her. Then she took the money paid to them back out of their pockets in the saloon. Stocker got all eager to help and talked up a storm.'

'Where'd he hide the stolen stuff?' asked Deputy Clyde Bucksteed, an attentive listener to the Ranger's story. 'I was out with the ranchers when they went over the Bradded S range and we never saw hide nor hair of any stolen cattle.'

'You just didn't know where to look,' Danny explained. 'There's a hidden valley, got good water and decent grazing in it. You can only get in through a tunnel at the back of a cave the ranchers probably never bothered to search. They'd figure the cattle couldn't be inside, I reckon, so they missed finding the hideout.'

'How'd they get rid of the stolen stuff?' inquired the sheriff, showing interest for the first time.

'The agent at the Kaddo Reservation bought it from them. Got it at cheaper than the market price.'

'You should have told me you was a Ranger,' Simmonds complained. 'Sounds like you didn't trust me.'

'Figured I'd work better alone,' Danny replied. 'There's only one thing left to do now.'

'What's that?' grunted Simmonds.

'Go to the Cattle Queen and pick up Soskice and Ed Wren.'

A look of worry came to the sheriff's face. 'I don't figure this's any of my fuss, Ranger. You come here without asking, played things as they suited you. Don't rightly see that I should tangle with a feller like Ed Wren just to please you.'

'Won't come, huh?' asked Danny.

'Can't see my way to doing it,' Simmonds replied.

'Then I'll take them alone.'

Turning, Danny walked towards the office's front door. Clyde Bucksteed watched the Ranger and an admiring look came to his face. Slowly Clyde lifted his left hand to touch the badge he wore. In that moment Clyde Bucksteed changed from an office-filler, holding down his position because of his relationship with the sheriff, and became a man.

'I'm with you, Ranger,' he said and followed Danny from the room.

Just as they stepped from the office, a man came racing his horse towards them. Seeing how excited the newcomer appeared to be, the two young lawmen halted and waited to see what caused the man's haste.

'I just found that pedlar, Jacobs. He's lying out there 'bout a mile from town. Somebody shot him in the back. From the look of his wagon, feller who done it was after his money.'

'How about it, Ranger?' Clyde asked.

'Let's go see Wren first. We might save ourselves some work,' Danny answered. 'Jacobs sold me out to Ella Watson, but he'd sold her to Cap'n Murat first and I reckon she sent Wren after him.'

'Best go see him then,' said the deputy.

'Sure had,' Danny agreed. 'Let's go.'

Before they had taken three steps along the street, both saw the batwing doors of the saloon open. Wren, Soskice and one of the bouncers walked out, all wearing guns. While Soskice remained standing on the sidewalk. Wren and the bouncer stepped out, moving across the street.

'What're you wanting, Forgrave?' Soskice called.

'You and Wren. We caught Stocker last night and he told us everything.'

'So now you plan to arrest me,' the lawyer went on.

'That's about the size of it,' Danny said, not breaking his stride.

'How about it, Mr. Wren?' asked the lawyer, a sneer playing on his lips.

'He'll have to pass me first,' Wren replied.

'My brother managed it easy enough that time in Granite City,' Danny said quietly, watching Wren's face and leaving the handling of the bouncer to Clyde.

For an instant the confident sneer left Wren's face and he stared at the tall, blond young Ranger.

'Your brother?' croaked Wren and Danny detected a worried note in the hired killer's voice.

'My brother, Wren. My name's Danny Fog.'

In that moment the scene came back before Wren's eyes. He was standing with the two men who hired him, looking at the Rocking H wagon and three cowhands who flanked it. The small, blond man on the big paint stallion did most of the talking for the other side, winding up by saying, 'Start the wagon, cookie.'

'They's in the way, Cap'n,' replied the cook reaching for the reins.

'Happen they'll move,' Dusty Fog replied.

Well, the two fellers who hired Wren *had* moved, but the gunman could not without losing face. Instead he grabbed for his gun, meaning to down the small man. Only Dusty Fog did not look small any more. Suddenly he seemed to be the tallest of them all; and never had Wren seen such speed at drawing a gun. The Rio Hondo gun wizard's left hand flickered across his body and fetched out the Army Colt from his right holster even before Wren could clear his Remington. Wren remembered the sudden shock hitting him, the stunning knowledge that his speed failed to bring him through. Flame licked from Dusty Fog's gun and Wren's world dissolved first into red agony, then sank into black nothingness. When Wren recovered, he found he

153

had lost a job and gained a bullet scar across the side of his head.

Now Dusty Fog's brother came towards Wren. Cold fear gripped the man, driving out the smug superiority which formed a gunfighting hard-case's best defence. Faced by Wren's look of expectancy and complete assurance that the gunman expected to be the one on his feet at the end of the affair, most men felt scared, unsure of themselves, hesitant and marked down as victims. Only this time Wren could not adopt the attitude as he studied the resemblance between the Fog brothers.

Uncertainty filled Wren. Maybe Danny Fog was not as fast as his brother. If so Wren ought to have a chance. If Danny Fog should be fast—Wren did not wish to think of the possibility. Yet Danny had not looked fast that first day. Of course, Fog would not have shown his true speed, knowing it might excite interest he wished to avoid in the performance of his Ranger chore. The thoughts ran through Wren's head as Danny and the deputy came closer, by the end of the saloon and halted not thirty feet away.

'Throw down your gun, Wren!' Danny ordered.

'Like hell!'

Letting the words out in a screech rather than a defiant snarl, Wren went for his gun. He beat Danny to the shot, but in his present nervous state the bullet missed the Ranger by inches. On the heels of Wren's shot, Danny got his right hand Colt out and working. Twice Danny fired, cocking the Colt on its recoil and slamming the two .44 bullets into Wren's chest. Danny shot the only way he dared under the circumstances, to kill. Knowing Wren to be faster, Danny did not dare give the man a chance to correct his aim. Caught by the bullets, Wren reeled backwards. His gun fell from his hand as he crumpled to the ground.

Clyde Bucksteed had practised fast drawing and shooting and now the training saved his life. Drawing, the deputy slammed a bullet into the bouncer an instant before the other threw down on him. Spinning around, the bouncer hit the hitching rail and hung on it yelling he was done.

Before leaving the saloon, Wren had sent the other bouncer through the side door to cover him. Coming down the alley between the saloon and the Wells Fargo office, the man stepped on to the street behind Danny and the deputy and brought up his gun. A rifle cracked further down the street and the bouncer—he had been the second of the hired guns reported by Jacobs to Murat—keeled over, a bullet in his head. Whirling to meet what might be a fresh menace, Danny and Clyde saw Simmonds standing outside his office, a smoking rifle in his hands.

'Watch Soskice!' yelled the sheriff, ambling forward.

Although he wore a gun, Soskice did not stand and fight. Instead he turned and flung himself back through the batwing doors, meaning to make his escape by the rear of the building. No sooner had the lawyer entered than a thud sounded and he shot out again, reeling backwards across the sidewalk and crashing to the ground at Danny's feet.

Blowing on his knuckles, Izzy walked out of the building and looked down at the fallen lawyer. Having seen the way things went in the street, Izzy decided a change of sides might be to his advantage. So he prevented the lawyer's escape in an effort to prove his sterling regard for law and order.

His head spinning from the unexpected blow. Soskice looked up at the three lawmen as they gathered around him. Licking his lips nervously, he forced himself to his feet. Suddenly he no longer felt smug and superior to those humble, dull-witted fools who became peace officers because they lacked intelligence to do anything better with their lives.

'I—I want to help you!' Soskice whined. 'I'll tell you enough to convict Ella Watson. It was her who sent Wren to kill that old pedlar.'

Danny gave a look of disgust as he turned to the sheriff. At least Ella Watson had refused to say anything either to avoid the blame or shift it on to somebody else.

'Take him to the jail, will you, Sheriff?' Danny said. 'Hey what made you change you mind and cut in like that?'

'Got to figuring what Maw'd say if anything happened to Clyde and reckoned I didn't want it, her doting on the boy way she does. 'Sides, I might not be the best lawman in the world, but I reckoned the folks paid me for more than I'd been giving 'em. Let's go, Mr. Soskice, unless you know some law's says I can't take you down to the pokey.'

Clearly Soskice could not think up a single law to avoid his arrest, for he went along with the sheriff in silence. Danny watched Clyde start some of the onlookers on cleaning up the street, then turned to the bartender.

'Is Mousey all right?' Danny asked.

'Got her a black eye and a few scratches and bruises, but nothing worse,' Izzy replied. 'She licked Dora good though, Phyl and Maisie stove each other up bad but the doctor tended to them. I wasn't in on anything, Ranger.'

'I just bet you weren't,' Danny said dryly. 'Why'd Soskice and Wren stay on instead of running?'

'Miss Ella's got all the money in her safe and they hoped she'd get back to give them travelling money. Is there anything I can do?'

'Sure, go back in there and hold the place until we come and see you.'

Leaving Izzy to take care of the saloon, Danny walked along to the sheriff's office. There he and Simmonds interviewed the scared Soskice. At first the lawyer tried to lay all the blame on Ella Watson, but found he failed in his attempt to shift the blame.

'Us folks down in Texas might not be so full of high-minded ideas as fellers like you,' Danny drawled. 'So I'd surely hate to see what folks around here do to you when they hear that you've sold out your partner and tried to rail-road a *woman* to save your hide.'

'They'll start reaching for a rope and looking for a tree,' the sheriff went on.

Nor did Soskice doubt Simmonds's words. 'Y—you'll protect me!' he whined, yet his tones lacked conviction. 'It's your duty to protect me!'

'After the way you've belittled and mean-mouthed me all these months?' the sheriff replied. 'You've dripped contempt over us lawmen all the time you've been here. So we'll be as useless as you reckon we are. If folks come a lynching, me 'n' Clyde'll be long gone out of town.'

'You—you won't let it happen, Ranger!' Soskice squeaked, turning to Danny.

'My work's done here,' Danny answered. 'I'll be riding real soon.'

Raw fear glowed in Soskice's eyes. 'W—would you protect me

if I told you what brought me here? It's important to the peace of Texas.'

'Try telling us,' Danny said.

With the words pouring out in a flood, Soskice told all and laid bare a vicious scheme to wreck the flimsy peace of the Lone Star State. He belonged to Henry George's Socialist Party and was one of a group of college-educated intellectuals who wished to see Reconstruction continued until the Southerners they hated were smashed and the ex-slaves ruled the South. So some of their number came to Texas with the intention of stirring up so much trouble that the Federal Government brought back the old Reconstruction régime. In his fear for his life, Soskice named his friends and mentioned how the Sutton-Taylor feud and the Shelby County war had come about through the machinations of the intellectual bigots.

'Another range war going would have done it,' Soskice finished, after telling how he helped Ella organise the cow stealing. 'Not that I wanted things to go as far as that.'

'Got to talking to Vic Crither the other day,' drawled the sheriff. 'He said as how it was you as first put the idea of hiring Gooch in his head.'

'That's a lie!' yelped Soskice. 'You can't prove it!'

'We'll try, *hombre*, we'll surely try,' warned Danny. 'Reckon you figured a killer like Gooch'd stir up fuss between the ranchers, especially if he downed the wrong men. It could have worked.'

'It would have, if you hadn't happened along, Ranger,' the sheriff put in. 'I'm sure pleased I wrote for help.'

And it proved later that Simmonds told the truth. He had written to Murat, but the letter went astray and did not arrive until days after Danny left for Caspar County. Nor was Simmonds as dishonest as Danny imagined. The sheriff's prosperity came from having sold his business, not from accepting bribes.

A telegraph message fetched in a judge and the heads of the Caspar County cow thieves were brought up for trial. Despite the killing of Gooch and Jacobs, Ella Watson received only five years in the penitentiary. Stocker did not intend to be alone in his punishment and so incriminated Soskice that they each drew ten years and might have counted themselves lucky to receive fifteen years each. Rangers swooped on the other members of Soskice's political gang and drove them out of Texas before they could make any more trouble.

'Well, that's the end of it, Calam, gal,' Danny said as he and the girl rode side by side out of Caspar County. 'It's a pity we couldn't stay on for Tommy and Mousey's wedding. At least the folks raised a collection that'll give them a good start, for Tommy's part in ending the cow stealing.'

'Sure,' agreed Calamity. 'There's times I wonder what it'd be like to marry and settle down.'

'Why not try it and see?'

'I'd never marry anybody who'd be fool enough to marry a gal like me,' grinned Calamity. 'Look at all the fun I'd miss. Say, I feel a mite sorry for Ella Watson. She was a dead game gal, even if her tracks ran crooked. And she gave me a danged good whirl. Wonder if she learned her lesson?'

Years later word reached Calamity of another cow stealing gang operating in Wyoming and following the Caspar County methods of using saloon-girls to ensnare the cowhands into the stealing. Then came news that the irate ranchers had caught and hung the man and woman involved. People called her Cattle Kate; but Calamity knew better, reckoning that Ella Watson had failed to change her ways and so met a cow thief's end.

THE END

J. T. EDSON OMNIBUS VOLUME 1

Of all the characters created by J. T. Edson, Dusty Fog –
that small, softly spoken hero who strikes when least
expected – is surely the most famous, the most popular.

Here, for the first time, are three Dusty Fog stories in one
volume. *You're in Command Now, Mr Fog: Kill Dusty Fog!:
The Devil Gun* all deal with Dusty Fog's exploits during the
Civil War.

0 552 13602 6

RAPIDO CLINT STRIKES BACK

BY J. T. EDSON

Nobody noticed the little Texan till the trouble began . . .

It was a typical country-house party, though perhaps a touch
more decorous than most – perhaps even a tiny bit dull. Then
suddenly all hell broke loose. The host was found murdered
and the house was bristling with hard men whose methods of
extracting information were anything but polite.

But nobody bothered about Rapido. And Rapido kept pretty
much to himself. In fact the slow-moving, slow-talking
Texan seemed remarkably ill-named. That is until danger
threatened, and the quiet man, transformed into a deadly
fighting machine, treated the English to a showdown worthy
of *Gunfight at the OK Corral*.

0 552 13623 9

J.T. EDSON TITLES AVAILABLE
FROM CORGI BOOKS

THE PRICES SHOWN BELOW WERE CORRECT AT THE TIME OF GOING
TO PRESS. HOWEVER TRANSWORLD PUBLISHERS RESERVE THE
RIGHT TO SHOW NEW RETAIL PRICES ON COVERS WHICH MAY DIFFER
FROM THOSE PREVIOUSLY ADVERTISED IN THE TEXT OR ELSEWHERE.

☐	13602 6	**EDSON OMNIBUS VOLUME 1**	£3.99
☐	13603 4	**EDSON OMNIBUS VOLUME 2**	£3.99
☐	13604 2	**EDSON OMNIBUS VOLUME 3**	£3.99
☐	13605 0	**EDSON OMNIBUS VOLUME 4**	£3.99
☐	13606 9	**EDSON OMNIBUS VOLUME 5**	£3.99
☐	13607 7	**EDSON OMNIBUS VOLUME 6**	£3.99
☐	13609 3	**EDSON OMNIBUS VOLUME 8**	£3.99
☐	13541 0	**MARK COUNTER'S KIN**	£2.50
☐	13341 8	**J.T.'S LADIES RIDE AGAIN**	£2.50
☐	13623 9	**RAPIDO CLINT STRIKES BACK**	£2.99

All Corgi/Bantam books are available at your bookshops or newsagents, or can be
ordered from the following address:

Corgi/Bantam Books,
Cash Sales Department,
P.O. Box 11, Falmouth, Cornwall TR10 9EN

Please send a cheque or postal order, (no currency) and allow 80p for postage and
packing for the first book plus 20p for each additional book ordered up to a
maximum charge of £2.00 in UK.

B.F.P.O. customers please allow 80p for the first book and 20p for each additional
book.

Overseas customers, including Eire, please allow £1.50 for postage and packing
for the first book, £1.00 for the second, and 30p for each subsequent title ordered.

NAME (Block Letters) ....

ADDRESS ....

....